A Girl's Best Friend

But that night, resplendent in swirling chiffon in three shades of pink; shocking, pastel and rose, diamonds at her throat and in her ears, her figure once more slender, nobody would have said other than that Olivia Gaylord Randolph Bancroft was fully in control; of herself, her household, this fabulous party. She was the perfect hostess, making the perfect apology for her husband's absence with just the right small moue of the mouth and a shrug of the shoulders that said: 'Oh Billy ... we all know Billy, don't we ... nothing must come before business ...' If people knew otherwise they looked away before the implacable challenge in her eyes. Nothing was said, then or later, in her presence, about the fact that she was married to a tom cat of prodigious appetite. So she gracefully made the speech that Billy was to have delivered. There was nothing more he could do to her now that she could not withstand, for she had suffered enough humiliation and grief to inure her to anything. She thought.

Vera Cowie has written eight previous novels, including *Face Value, Secrets* and *A Double Life*, which is also available as a Mandarin paperback. She is a ... e and lives in Bishop Stortfor ...

VERA COWIE

A GIRL'S
BEST FRIEND

Mandarin

A Mandarin Paperback
A GIRL'S BEST FRIEND

First published in Great Britain 1993
by William Heinemann Ltd
This edition published 1994
by Mandarin Paperbacks
an imprint of Reed Consumer Books Ltd
Michelin House, 81 Fulham Road, London SW3 6RB
and Auckland, Melbourne, Singapore and Toronto

Reprinted 1994

Copyright © Vera Cowie 1993
The author has asserted her moral rights

A CIP catalogue record for this title
is available from the British Library
ISBN 0 7493 1087 1

Printed and bound in Great Britain
by Cox & Wyman Ltd, Reading, Berks

1

Among the mourners were three Rockefellers, two Vander-bilts, a Mellon, a Whitney, a sprinkling of the Supreme Court, a goodly few senators, several august members of the House of Lords, and a prominent member of Margaret Thatcher's government, but the majority were women; the many friends of the deceased. The small church of Saint John was standing room only, since it had been built, in 1714, as the family church of the Randolphs. It stood only some three hundred yards from the big house, built at the same time, both of them separated from the Rappahannock River by a fringe of trees and a stretch of lawns which, Billy Bancroft was wont to say, were as good as anything back home. By which he meant England but which those who had known-him-when found amusing, since grass had been – was still – hard to come by in Whitechapel, where he had been born.

'Heavens, but it's hot,' one woman murmured to her neighbour. 'The scent from those flowers is overpower-ing.'

They were all-white; Livy had specified the colour in the

detailed instructions she had left concerning her funeral. The flowers were arranged, French fashion, *en masse* in Randolph crystal; masses of dogwood, iris, narcissi, shaggy-headed daisies with great golden eyes, roses, carnations, lilac; every bloom from the great hothouses of King's Gift, so-named because the land had been given to John Randolph by Charles II, after the former had procured for His Majesty a particularly fetching Maid of Honour whose virtue had not been easily captured. This particular truth had long been obscured by the Randolphs and replaced by the legend that John Randolph had saved the King's life during an attempted assassination. During Livy's tenure as Mrs John Peyton Randolph VI, she had always referred to the Founder as 'Randy Randolph' and made no bones about the origin of the Randolph fortune. For all her breeding and good taste she had always been very down to earth.

'I shall miss her,' the first woman sniffed emotionally. 'I keep expecting her to swish in any minute and capture every eye, like always.'

'She was unique,' agreed her companion, but without the little pang of jealousy she usually felt whenever she said or heard those words. Now that Livy was gone, there actually was a chance for her to make her own mark; one that had been invisible under Livy's bright light. 'Poor Diana is terribly upset,' she went on, glancing sympathetically across the church to where Livy's youngest daughter was sobbing uncontrollably, her face buried in one of the several handkerchiefs her husband had thought to provide from his own top drawer. The other children – his, hers and theirs – were stone-faced and erect, like their father, who stood at the end of the pew nearest to his wife's coffin; a coffin made of

English oak, for Livy had died in England, where she had lived since marrying Billy Bancroft some twenty-five years before.

'Diana always was the emotional one. Ros, now there's a different kettle of fish. A Randolph, through and through. That's probably why she and her stepfather never got on. Ros is like her grandmother. Remember old Dolly Randolph? Hewn from the living rock. I remember her at poor Johnny's funeral. Her only son dead at thirty-four and there wasn't so much as a flicker, whereas poor Livy was devastated ...'

The church rustled as the congregation stood for the first hymn.

'Of course! You have to remember that Livy *adored* her first husband ...'

Forty-five minutes later, the huge drawing room of King's Gift stood open to the porticoed terrace and lawns. White-gloved men-servants circulated with silver trays of Livy's favourite champagne: Krug's *Blanc de Blancs, Clos du Mesnil*, as the mourners ate an al fresco buffet luncheon. Round tables were laid with white damask on which stood great bowls of Chinese porcelain filled with peaches, cherries and strawberries, all, like the flowers that had filled the church, from the gardens and hothouses of King's Gift. There were chafing-dishes of fried chicken – southern style – and saffron rice, quails' eggs and tarragon mayonnaise, a choice of various crisp salads, and one of the vast tortes of which Livy had been so fond; this one of coffee and cognac, flown over from Fauchon. It was all, Livy's friend Abby Singleton said, on an envious sigh, quite, quite perfect, like everything Livy

3

had *ever* done. 'Was there ever anyone quite like her?' she asked rhetorically.

Out on the lawns: 'Poor Bill,' said one of his long-time friends to another. '*Now* what is he going to do? Livy ran all his interference for all of their married life.'

They both looked to where the Man-of-Distinction clone that was Billy Bancroft, – first Baron Bancroft these past three years – stood with immense dignity accepting the condolences of those who had been closest for longest to his wife, and whom she had wanted to be present at her last appearance, even if it was in spirit rather than flesh.

'Remarkable woman,' said the other man, like Billy a member of the House of Lords. 'I never saw her with so much as a hair out of place. Always looked as if she'd just been lifted out of tissue paper. My wife says that takes simply enormous effort and organisation.'

'That was Livy. The perfectionist of perfectionists. But then ...' a shrug, 'she was married to Mr Perfection himself.'

'But this is her first husband's family seat, isn't it?'

The American looked across the lawns at the house, its red brick faded now to a rosy pink, its white pediment and windows providing a trim contrast.'Yes,' he smiled conspiratorially. 'Apparently she always intended to be buried here. I gather Billy was furious.'

Everyone knew about the mausoleum he had had built for himself and his wife: he intended to spend his death in the same sort of state as he had spent his life. This decision of Livy's to spend eternity lying next to her first husband was an act of defiance wholly surprising in a woman who had never been known to raise so much as her voice.

4

On the other side of the lawn, two schoolfriends of Livy were discussing the Bancroft children. Lulu de Fries told Abby Singleton that she had seen Diana disappear upstairs with her husband the moment they got back here, and later he had come back down alone, leaving his wife 'resting.' 'Sobbing her heart out, more like,' she murmured. 'Diana simply adored her mother ...'

'Well, if you measure adoration by imitation I suppose she did.'

'That was the trouble,' Lulu said. 'Livy Bancroft was beyond imitation, but it never stopped Diana from trying ...'

'Something Rosalind does not need to do. When I saw her come into the church I felt quite a *frisson*.'

'Yes. Ros is the image of her mother.'

'Out of her hippy garb, she is. I gather that phase is over.'

'I should hope so. Ros is thirty-four years old!'

Abby winced as the age of Livy's eldest reminded her of her own true age, carefully amended these many years. Seeing this Lulu trod spitefully on the sensitive spot. 'After all, the fact that she did not look it in no way alters the fact that Livy Bancroft was fifty-four years old when she died, or that we were all at school together ...'

The two women looked round for Livy's two sisters; spotted Delia talking to the British ambassador and the Duke of Roehampton, from whom Billy had just bought – for a very great price – his last Gainsborough; while Toni was sharing a tete-a-tete with Lord Ancrum, with whom, current gossip had it, she was more than friends. Looking further round the gathering Lulu found Toni's husband where she had known he would be; talking to the prettiest and youngest

5

woman present. Thank God, she thought on a relieved sigh. Some things *never* change.

Brooks Hamilton finally managed to have a private word with Billy. 'Are you all right?' Married to Diana, Brooks admired his father-in-law inordinately, and was concerned because he thought Billy looked pale and to be tiring rapidly. Not surprising since he was fifteen years older than his wife.

'Yes, I'm fine,' Billy said, without the brusque impatience he would have used to anyone else, even one of his own children, since he did not approve of such intimate questions. Your health was your own business. More than one of his wife's friends was of the opinion that if Livy had been able to make hers more of a concern to him, the cancer that eventually killed her might have been caught in time.

'They'll be making a move soon,' Brooks said, hopefully. 'Then you are coming back to the Farm with us. A few weeks R&R is what you need. These past months must have been hell.'

'I've known better,' Billy admitted, 'but I don't want to hibernate, you know. That's not my style. And I've got to get back to the book ...'

Billy was writing (through a ghostwriter) his auto-biography, which had been half-done when his wife entered her final illness. As always, his pragmatism asserted itself. When one thing was over and done with you got on with the next.

Looking over the beautifully landscaped peninsula, a member of what her husband had always disparagingly referred to as 'one of Livy's arty gang' observed to another: 'Seeing all

6

this I can't help thinking that Livy gave up a hell of a lot for Billy Bancroft.'

'What else is new? It was what he expected, after all.'

'Did you ever know Johnny Randolph?'

'Before my time, but I'm told he was as handsome as he was rich, and he was *very* rich.' Pause. 'But he hadn't a brain in his head.'

'One thing you cannot say about Billy.'

'Is there anything that cannot be said about Billy Bancroft?'

'If there is I'm not aware of it.'

'I've never been able to understand how that man has always been able to have any woman he wanted.'

'Money and power,' the prompt answer came with its accompanying shrug. 'Both prime aphrodisiacs.'

'Plus the fact that he just happens to be hung like a horse.'

'A fact to which every woman here except his relatives could testify.'

'Don't be so quick to dismiss the relatives.'

Inquisitive interest flared. 'So it *is* true about him and Toni von Anhalt?'

'Except she wasn't Toni von Anhalt then. She was married to that asshole Junior Standish, which makes her taking up with Billy much more understandable.'

'Do you think Livy knew?'

'I doubt it; but if she did, she would never admit to it. You know Livy … loyalty was a quality she prized. Which is my cue to have yet another glass of this glorious champagne, something else to which she was loyal all her life. You realise that from now on, it will seldom come our way again …'

*

'They don't look like Billy, do they?'

'Who, dear?'

'His sons. Rupert and Jeremy.'

'Oh, them. No ... not really. I believe they take after their mother, Billy's first wife.'

'Just who *was* she exactly?'

'Nobody. Nothing. As was Billy at that time. But he was already looking for his Livy.' A contemptuously knowing smile appeared.

'Can you imagine what and where he would be now if he had not found her? She *made* Billy Bancroft.'

'Socially, you mean?'

'Of course! Any fool can make money and Billy is nobody's fool. But to marry Olivia Gaylord Randolph! Now that takes *chutzpah*.'

'I often wondered what she saw in him. I mean, after Johnny Randolph ...'

'Johnny was sweet, but he never matured. I always thought he and Livy were children playing at being grown-up. They were so young when they married, but at least Livy developed. I doubt if Johnny ever would have. He had it all too easy. A name, money, this fabulous house and plantation, but really he was never more than a very sweet boy. And I mean boy. It never ceased to amaze me that he fathered Ros and Johnny. He never seemed to me to have any idea what the proper procedure was.' A pause. 'But with Dolly Randolph for a mother ... *She* was anything but pleased when Livy took up with Billy Bancroft and he, if you ask me, never had any childhood at all!'

'But he did make Livy *Lady* Bancroft, and she did get to sit Margaret Thatcher on her right many times!'

8

'All the same, I shall never understand what possessed her to marry Billy Bancroft. Never!'

Rosalind Randolph saw her sister Diana, pale but finally composed, come out onto the terrace and went over to her. 'Are you sure you are up to this?' she asked, knowing well her half-sister's friable emotional state.

Diana produced the smile she had practised for years until she got it just right. The smile her mother had used when she was dismissing pretensions. 'Of course I am. I can't leave it *all* to you, can I? That wouldn't be fair.' The innocence was artless but laid over spite and her voice was brittle, her eyes unnaturally bright. Diana was finely balanced on the edge of hysteria and swaying dangerously.

Searching the crowd, Ros managed to catch Brooks Hamilton's eye and beckoned him over with a nod. He frowned – he was still talking to his father-in-law – but Ros stared at him quellingly until she saw him murmur something to Billy before making his way towards them.

When he saw his wife he frowned. 'Is this wise?' he asked her. Diana ignored him as her eyes feverishly searched the throng.

'I'll make my own decision about that,' she dismissed. 'Go and work the crowd, Brooks. There must be some first-class business opportunities out there this afternoon,' she turned to him. 'And we both know how important business is to you, don't we, darling?' The sweetness made Ros's teeth hurt, but since she knew her half-sister was trying her best to cope with her own agony, she said nothing. Besides, it was none of her business if Diana and her husband were at outs again.

Diana finally saw several faces she knew, smiled in their direction, and head up, shoulders back, began to make her way towards them. Her husband stared after her, a scowl on his well-chiselled features. Then he turned to his sister-in-law. 'She's terribly upset,' he said, as if in explanation.

'We all are,' Ros reminded.

'Yes, but Diana was *very* close to her mother,' he reminded in turn, wielding his own knife. They were old adversaries. Ros held his gaze levelly and he was the first to break the connection, turning to look out over the gardens.

As Ros followed his gaze she stared disbelievingly for a moment before saying politely: 'If you will excuse me, Brooks, I must go and welcome some late arrivals.' She left him to make her way purposefully in the direction of a woman who had just stepped onto the lawn and was in the act of helping herself to a glass of champagne.

'Bitch,' Brooks Hamilton muttered after her. He had never liked Rosalind Randolph, being of the opinion that his sister-in-law was far too clever for her own good – and knew it. The one flaw in the marble statue Brooks Hamilton had mentally erected to Billy was that, for some unaccountable reason, Billy Bancroft was wary of his step-daughter.

'How did you get in here?' Ros demanded of the blonde woman. 'This particular occasion is by invitation only and I did not send *you* one.'

The woman regarded her insolently, 'You won't speak to me like that when I am Lady Bancroft.'

Ros goggled at her. 'When you are *what*!'

'Hasn't Billy told you yet?'

10

'The time is long gone since I believed anything *he* ever told me.'

'You can believe this. I am going to marry him. After a decent period of mourning, of course,' she tacked on hastily.

Ros laughed. 'Since when did you ever do anything decent? I want you off this lawn, off these grounds and away from here in the next sixty seconds or else I shall have you publicly and shamefully escorted from them. This is the day we buried my mother, your paramour's wife, and I won't allow you to sully her memory with your presence. Now get out!' Ros's voice was not raised, but every word was a blow.

The woman bridled but put down her glass, drew her black mink jacket – totally uncalled for since it was not cold – about her, and hastily donning a pair of sunglasses, retreated somewhat hurriedly down the paved path that disappeared into a stand of oaks which gave onto the main drive.

Ros turned to stare at her step-father, the centre of a group of women – as usual, she thought, curling a mental lip. As though he felt the molten heat of it he raised his head, searched for and met her eyes. She saw his face blank out, as it always did when confronted by something unpleasant, but it was he who turned away first.

Ros made her way to the nearest man-servant, where she picked up a crystal flute of champagne and drained it at a gulp.

'Steady on, kid,' a voice said from behind her. 'That's potent stuff and not to be treated like a can of coke!'

Ros turned to see her Aunt Toni – Antonia Gaylord Lancaster Standish von Anhalt – her mother's younger sister, grinning at her, but the grin faded to be replaced by concern.

'What is it, Ros? You look like you've lost a fortune and found a dime!'

'I have just been told something so absolutely outrageous – so tacky beyond belief that I still can't quite believe it!' Ros told her Aunt what she had heard.

Toni von Anhalt's carefully tightened jaw dropped momentarily, then she put back her head and guffawed her famous laugh. 'Snap!' she crowed.

Ros's own mouth dropped open. 'What …?'

'Not five minutes ago I heard that same statement from Sissy Bainbridge.'

'Sissy Bainbridge!' It exploded from Ros's mouth like a missile.

'I kid you not. You know she and Billy have been having a thing off and on for years.'

'Yes, but –'

'But me no buts. She was deadly serious – and that doesn't come easy to Sissy, believe me.'

'My God, I don't know which is worst …'

'I do! The bleach job, of course! At least Sissy is One of Us … Now then, don't get on that high horse of yours, you know very well what I mean; more to the point, so does Billy. After Livy, do you think he would ever lower himself to that blonde's level?'

Ros said nothing, but the expression on her face did.

'All right, so Billy can't get any lower as far as you are concerned, but really, Ros, Billy distributes promises to women like corsages used to be given when I was a girl. They are meant as a tribute, no more.'

'I don't give a damn about how many women he proposes to; it's his timing! We have only just buried my mother, his wife!'

12

Toni levelled a look. 'Sweetie, Billy's a compulsive; a poor randy old goat who can't help it; it's a natural reflex. Don't you just hope and pray he gets stuck with somebody who won't stand his womanising and give him hell if he strays? Now that would appeal to my sense of justice!'

Meeting her irrepressible aunt's twinkling sea-green eyes, Ros had to laugh.

'That's better. Just remember your mother knew what Billy was and chose to look the other way.'

'It isn't your way.'

'No, but Livy loathed "making a fuss," you know that.'

'Know what?' a deep voice asked, and they both turned to the eldest Gaylord sister, Cordelia – Delia – Winslow, who had come up behind them.

Unlike her sisters Delia had gone grey at forty, and now her hair was pure silver. Livy had been untouched by grey thanks to her own special dye, while Toni's blondness had been preserved for many years. Delia was sixty-three, Toni was fifty-nine; both looked not a day over forty – well, forty-five. Both wore black superbly, but neither had ever been in the same league as their sister.

'About Livy never making a fuss,' Toni answered.

'Livy needed everything to run smoothly', Delia agreed, her mind running back over the years. 'Even as a child she could not cope with upsets.'

'Talking about upsets ...' Toni told her sister about the two women and their shared announcement.

'Of course,' Delia, unmoved, lifted one eloquent shoulder. 'I've heard exactly the same thing from Marguerite Barnard and I would not be surprised if there were half a dozen more.'

13

'But to say so at my mother's *funeral*!' Ros said in a low, angry voice.

'Billy is a catch, my dear niece,' Toni said pragmatically.

'Well I think it's horrible! He can marry whoever he likes but I'm not having his women broadcasting their so-called triumph. Not her, anyway! Now, if you will excuse me, I have guests to attend to …'

Looking after her: 'If only Livy had had one tenth of Ros's strength,' Toni sighed.

'At times like these, Ros reminds me of our mother,' Delia mused.

'God, now *she* was tough.'

'Tough on us because she wanted so much for us … especially Livy. You know how she absolutely doted on Livy.'

'So did Pa. His white swan, he used to call her, remember?' There was no jealousy in Delia's voice.

Ros was making sure the caterers cleared away properly; that all the china and glasses matched the totals that had been provided to them; that the damask tablecloths – handstitched and irreplaceable – were put to one side where the Randolph laundress would wash them by hand; that the Chinese porcelain was not carelessly put in the dishwasher.

'Just like mother,' Diana said, leaning against the door of the vast kitchens, hung with copper pans and smelling of fresh tarragon. 'Why couldn't I have been the organised one … you never gave a damn for mother's perfectionism yet look at you now … "Have you done this? Are you sure you've done that? Let me check the other." You *have* changed.'

'I hope so,' Ros answered, ignoring the sarcasm. 'You are supposed to, as you mature, I believe.'

'Meaning I haven't?'

Ros straightened from counting silver. 'Diana ... let's not carry on where we left off. If you want me to believe you have at long last really grown up then let me see some sign of it!'

Diana had an empty glass in one hand, now she brought up the other to reveal the bottle of champagne she was clutching before proceeding to fill the glass. 'How about if I get drunk? And on champagne ... Mother's tipple, as Daddy calls it.'

'Mother liked champagne but she never got drunk.'

'Mother never did lots of things ... especially the ones you thought she should have done.' Diana swigged at her champagne. 'She wouldn't have invited that cheap blonde, for instance. The one I saw you talking to. Somebody from your California commune?'

'She was an uninvited guest – unless she came at your father's suggestion.'

Diana bridled. 'Always *my* father! He's yours too, you know; has been ever since the day he married your mother!'

Ros was rolling the heavy Georgian silver cutlery in green baize and tying it into bundles before placing them in their own specially made Rosewood box which would in turn go into the silver safe. Pausing in her task she looked up at her half-sister. 'Never,' she said quietly, but in such a way as to make Diana go scarlet.

'Hi!' a voice said into the twanging silence. 'Have I interrupted yet another meeting of the Sister sorority?'

Ros looked up to see Diana's brother David leaning – as

15

only he knew how – against the door jamb. Her smile was warm. David had the charm Diana lacked, as well as the looks. He was also much more likeable. And by both sexes. Just like his mother.

'So where is the rest of our Happy Family?'

'Johnny is on the phone talking to Sally –'

'Any developments yet?'

'Not as far as I know.' John Randolph Jr's wife was expecting twins at any moment, which was why she had not attended the funeral.

'The other set of twins is huddled together somewhere, no doubt also on their portable telephones checking that all is well with Daddy's billions, while the Lord' – Ros's name for Billy since he received his barony – 'is somewhere outside communing with nature and his chief acolyte.'

'I could use a cup of Celestine's coffee – all that champagne. Is there any?'

'Go and ask her. She's in the linen room.'

David turned to go, then turned back as if reminded of something. 'Who was the man with the diamond in his ear?'

'His name is Julio Hernandez and he's an artist. Mother had been going to his studio for lessons before she became too ill to make the trip to Bayswater.'

'Oh...' David went to look for Celestine.

'That's another thing!' Diana said aggrievedly. 'Since when did mother ever have an interest in being a painter?'

'All her life,' Ros answered.

'She never told me.'

Ros shrugged, in a way that had Diana flushing again. 'I'm going to look for Daddy and Brooks,' she announced haughtily, spoiling it all by stumbling drunkenly as she went through the doorway. She put out a hand to steady herself and in doing so dropped her glass. 'Oops!' she said unguiltily. 'There goes another Randolph heirloom, but then this place is full of them, isn't it? Daddy says it's always the insecure ones who keep parading their heritage in front of everybody.'

'He should know,' Ros murmured.

'I would have thought there were more than enough Lords and Ladies here this afternoon to please even the high and mighty Randolphs! And they were all Daddy's friends.'

'Were they?' Ros asked.

'Well, it was a fine turnout, you can't deny that! Lords and Ladies and senators and congressmen and Uncle Tom Cobley and all ...' Diana gulped more champagne. She seemed desperate to get blindingly drunk but could not manage to get beyond a certain point. She had a glaze on but it was thin, and repeated applications only kept sliding off. 'I've never particularly cared for this place, but then *I'm* not a Randolph; I'm a Bancroft, as was made only too plain when your dear grandmother was alive. You were the Randolphs, you and Johnny, so you got preferential treatment. She only suffered me and David, but Mummy brought us so she had no choice but to put up with us.'

'She was an old lady and set in her ways.'

'So, it seems, was Mummy. Why else would she want to be buried here, with her first husband? It's almost as though she wanted to wipe out her years with Daddy.'

'Perhaps she did,' Ros said.

Feeling her half-sister's glare Ros raised her eyes to meet it, and Diana once again felt the old familiar jealous rush of rage to the head. *It was not fair*! Why should Ros, who had always fought so bitterly with their mother, be the one to look like her, talk like her, be possessed of the same slender elegance? Why, oh why, had fate determined she should look like her father? She hated being an insipid blonde, and having to watch her weight – very much a Bancroft trait – and she hated being short. She always wore heels, just as her father wore specially built-up shoes because if he didn't, his wife would have towered over him. Yet there was Ros, who had the height and the looks and that indefinable something which Diana, who had tried – God, how she had tried – could never achieve. As her husband was constantly reminding her. Bastard! she thought hatefully, draining her glass. He was probably off somewhere licking ass, as usual.

Ros went back to counting silverware. Diana had come out of her grief-stricken anguish only to go straight into her 'why doesn't anybody love me' routine. Once a spoiled brat, always a spoiled brat, Ros thought, but if Diana drank the rest of that bottle there would be trouble for sure.

Just then, Johnny came back in. 'No change,' he said. 'A few twinges but they don't develop. I think it's time I got going. I want to get back to Boston tonight. I promised Sally I'd be there and if I'm not she'll give me hell. Besides, how many men get to see the birth of two babies!'

Ros's smile was full of affection. Like his father, this Johnny was an amiable, sweet-natured airhead, but he had a strong-minded proper Bostonian wife who ran things. As his father had liked fast cars, so his son was crazy about boats, for which he had a natural, God-given aptitude, and he was in the process of designing and building what he was sure would be *the* yacht to bring back the America's Cup. It was costing him a fortune, but since Dolly Randolph had made him her principal heir, he could have afforded to build one every time the competition came round. And his wife had money too.

'How are you getting back?' Ros asked.

'Billy's helicopter is on the pad and he's got a company plane at Norfolk.'

He came across to hug and kiss his sister, who said: 'You'll call as soon as you've any news?'

'You bet. You staying here?'

'For tonight, anyway.'

'If I'm not a father by morning I'm dead!' Johnny winced as he realised what he'd said. 'Sorry ...' he mumbled.

Used to his unthinking verbal blunders, Ros shook her head before saying: 'Mother's spirit is very much alive in this place.'

Johnny nodded but looked uneasy. Ros was too deep, too intense, too clever for him; always had been. Polly, his wife, said that was why Ros had never married. No man would be able to cope with her.

Billy was down at the spot on the bluff known as Sunset Point, because from there you could see the molten glow of the sun put out by the wine-dark expanse of the sea. His son-in-law Brooks Hamilton was in attendance. He was always in attendance.

Billy was feeling melancholic, a slight amelioration from his choleric disposition of the last week or so. Now that the worst was over, he felt a need for soothing scenery. King's Gift, he had to admit, provided it in large measure. It had been a good funeral, something else he had to admit. Livy knew how to do this sort of thing. The small church crowded and the guest list as illustrious as they came. He thought he

19

had carried it off very well. There had been talk, of course, but he had simply ignored it. As far as he was concerned, said his attitude, this was what his wife had wanted, and, as everyone knew, what Livy Bancroft wanted her husband provided.

He thought again what it was going to be like without her there to arrange everything for him, and found the prospect dismaying. Like having to deal with the distribution of Livy's estate. He had been furious when he discovered she had made her will without recourse to either his advice or his opinion. Livy had left her Randolph money to her Randolph children and he supposed that was fair enough; he wasn't leaving them any of his, but she had distributed her furniture, her paintings, her crystal, her china to those friends she thought would appreciate them, leaving a precise list as to who got what, with its value listed for probate purposes. She had arranged trust funds for Diana and David; divided jewellery between Diana and her daughters-in-law, for Billy's twin sons were also married with children. Ros had not been left any jewellery since she never wore it. Livy's furs, including the fabulous floor length Russian sable he had given her last Christmas, she had left to be auctioned for the cancer charities. She had also left a sum to provide fresh flowers to be placed daily on the grave where she lay with her first husband.

That, Billy thought for the thousandth time, was what still rankled. That Livy should have been so unshakeable in her determination to be buried as a Randolph rather than a Bancroft. When everyone knew Livy had deferred to her husband all their married life. It made him look all kinds of a fool.

Billy stood up so quickly that Brooks almost fell off the seat.

'What is it?' he asked.

'I'm cold. Let's go back to the house.'

2

Judged critically, by the classical standards of beauty, she was far from perfect. Her lips were too thin and her mouth too wide; her nose too long and with a flared tip, her jaw far too much. But she had perfectly set, slightly elongated eyes as black as jet, set in a skin that looked as though lit from within, a cloud of gloss-silk black hair and a long, graceful neck.

Her posture – instilled by her mother – was perfect, her bones long. Her legs began at the armpit. Taken as a whole, these disparate elements came together as a work of art. She had a light, clear voice which could be either meltingly soft or ringingly crisp, but nobody ever heard it raised. Her charm was legendary. As was her chic. She stood five feet nine inches tall in her stockinged feet and she was a perfect size eight. She did not need to diet; food held little interest for her, but she drank several potfuls of sinfully black coffee every day. And when she was alone she chain-smoked.

She was born in Philadelphia on a late September afternoon in 1936, the youngest of three sisters. Her father was Henry Charlton Gaylord, the last male of a family which had established itself in that city in 1736, but whose fortunes had declined to the point where all that was left was the original house on Walnut Street, to which his mother clung fiercely and to which he brought his bride, Millicent Stebbings, who took one look at the decaying elegance and proceeded to take things in hand. Under her direction – for Henry, though a brilliant lawyer, lacked application – the family fortunes took a distinct turn for the better. By the time the first Gaylord daughter was born Henry was the associate partner in a small but thriving law firm. By the time the second daughter came along he was junior partner, and by the time Olivia, the third and last daughter and his heart's darling, completed the family he was the senior partner.

Henry was forty-five when America entered the war, added to which he had a congenital heart-murmur. His wife saw to it that he made his war effort elsewhere, and by the time Olivia was eleven, her father was a Judge of the Pennsylvania Supreme Court, where he finally found his niche and began to carve a name for himself on the piece of marble quarried by his wife.

Millicent was tireless in her dedication to her husband's welfare and the progress of her daughters. Driven by her own poverty-stricken childhood (something she was careful to obscure completely along with her real name – Marya Steblinskaya) on an Ohio farm, she was socially ambitious to the *Nth* degree, and determined to obtain for her girls the very best husbands; her interpretation of best being a man who was socially prominent and wealthy enough to maintain his status in perfect condition.

All the girls were good-looking; Cordelia in a handsome, distinguished way – a true Gaylord, her paternal grandmother used to proclaim proudly, with dark hair and eyes;

23

Antonia was blonde, like her mother, but her stunning sexuality was entirely her own. Olivia was something else again. Once through adolescence – anything but awkward in her case – Millicent knew she had the classic pearl beyond price, and her ambition soared like the new rocket planes making the headlines. She instilled perfectionism into them from the word go, and as they held her in awe – their emotions were reserved for their father, who bought them forbidden Hershey bars, took them for sodas and let them play hop, skip and jump in the street, all activities proscribed by their mother – they accepted her word as gospel. Their father sometimes acted as the buffer between them and their mother's insatiable social ambition. 'One day,' he would comfort after a particularly stringent lecture, 'you will come to understand that everything she does is for your own good.' After all, he reflected wryly, it had worked for him.

A quiet, contemplative man, Henry Gaylord was nevertheless devoted to the strong-minded woman who ran his life. He was subject to occasional uncontrollable bouts of black depression; at those times his wife protected him, ran things so that nobody had any idea. To the world *he* was the master of his household. When asked about anything Millicent would always say: 'We must consult the Judge,' deferring to him in a way that made them marvel that such a quiet, courteous man could control such a Valkyrie of a woman. And as the family prospered so Millicent came into her own. She was always elegantly dressed; she set a good table and entertained superbly, though she was known to be an exacting mistress to her servants. She was just as exacting when it came to teaching her daughters.

At the age of seven Livy knew how a table should be set;

how to match linen to china to cutlery to the flower decorations; how the appearance of food was equally as important as its taste. She knew how to leave her father to himself when he was in one of his black depressions, but she also knew what to do when he started to come out of it, how to run for his velvet slippers and an ashtray – he smoked three packs a day – and present him with his crisply ironed copy of the Philadelphia *Daily Record*.

Millicent firmly believed that it was every husband's right to expect perfection and every wife's duty to provide it. He was the breadwinner, after all; it was thanks to his efforts and the money he made that they enjoyed such creature comforts as they had. She left untold her own efforts, without which Henry would still be toiling as a lowly paid drudge in a Center City law firm.

She had a quick temper but never displayed it in the presence of her husband. 'A man who has been working hard all day needs to come home to a tranquil house, a loving smile, a tender word. That is what being a wife means,' she taught her daughters. From the time they could understand what she was talking about she prepared them for the only destiny they would know: to marry well. Very well. *Very well indeed*. Millicent intended to place her daughters at the very top of the social tree.

Cordelia obliged first. In 1949 she managed to snare Edward Winslow, the only son and heir of the inordinately rich Winslow family. Old New York and not only on the pinnacle but owning the mountain.

Four years later, Toni landed Hugh Lancaster, maybe not *quite* as rich but every bit as social – perhaps even more so since he was descended from one of Washington's Generals.

Millicent fairly gave off sparks as she presided at not one but two hideously expensive, very High Society weddings. It also meant that when Olivia made her début she could be presented by one or other of her sisters at a glittering affair in New York.

From the elegant Winslow house on Upper Fifth Avenue, Olivia entered Society with a bang, literally, because in the vast gardens which at that time – 1954 – still existed at the back of the house, hundreds of fireworks were set off to the delighted oohs and aahs of some four hundred guests enjoying a brief respite from dancing to Lester Lanin or listening to Eddie Duchin.

'Aren't they pretty!' Livy enthused, clapping her hands as a starburst of crimson and gold exploded overhead.

'Not as pretty as you!' declared her companion gallantly. Livy turned to smile at him. He really was too handsome, she thought glowingly. So clean-cut he was positively chiselled. A Virginia blueblood, with a lineage like some middle European princeling, his family lived in a house described in *Great Houses of America* as "the quintessential Tidewater mansion". Her mother had pronounced him perfect.

John Peyton Randolph VI had first met Livy at her sister Toni's dinner party in her honour the previous week, and was instantly smitten. But Olivia Gaylord was not what Dolly Randolph wanted for her adored only son. While she approved of *who* and *what* she was, even being prepared to overlook the fact that Olivia had no money of her own (though she had two sisters with more than enough), she was unable to overlook Millicent Gaylord. Meeting that lady made it painfully clear to Dolly why she was so enthusiastically promoting the match. She had done a sight better than any mother with three daughters had any right to expect. Already she had married two of them into two of America's oldest families; Dolly Randolph had no intention of letting the woman sandblast her way into a third, even though Olivia Gaylord was undoubtedly the *belle* of her season; enjoying to the full the parties, the dances, the new clothes, the weekends in the country.

Millicent Gaylord had prepared her youngest daughter very carefully for her coming out. Above all, she had taught her how to deal with men. Olivia could rest her chin on one cupped hand, fix her glorious eyes on the particular one talking to her at the time and concentrate her attention in such a raptly absorbed way as to convince him he was the most attractive man in her life – ever. And Johnny Randolph, the most eligible bachelor of the year, had eyes for no one else.

Much later that night, after they had finally bid farewell to the last guests, Livy was in her bedroom brushing her hair free of its styling when her sister Toni knocked, then put her head round the door before asking: 'Decent? Can I come in?'

'I'm always decent,' retorted Livy, throwing a teasing glance in the mirror at her sister's semi-transparent negligee. 'More than I can say for you.'

'Well, you and Johnny Randolph were turning all heads tonight.' Toni settled down on one corner of the cherry-wood four-poster. 'When are you going to put him out of his misery?'

'He was most certainly not miserable tonight! Far from it!'

'Do I take it that he asked you to marry him yet again, then?'

'He does it every time we meet.'

'Why don't you say yes?' Toni lit a filter cigarette. 'Mother is positively champing at the bit.'

'I know.'

'So why aren't you putting *her* out her misery, then? I thought Johnny had made an impression on you?'

'I like him, I like him a lot, but I'm only eighteen years old. I want to live some, have fun, before I settle down.'

'You can be married and still have fun, you know.'

Again Livy looked at her sister through the mirror. 'Like you do?'

Toni shrugged, not one whit put out. 'There are – accommodations to be reached.'

Livy shook her head decidedly. 'I don't want that. I want what Mummy and Daddy have.'

Drawing deeply on her cigarette Toni eyed her sister from under her long (false) eyelashes. To each her own, she thought. Mother has left her imprint on you in a way that has you marked for life, much more than she ever did with Delia and me. You just don't have any idea that the portrait of married life mother painted was not drawn from reality. And far be it from me to enlighten you as to the truth about *that*. Johnny Randolph is an Only Son. It took his parents five tries and four Junior Misses before they managed to get him. His mother can afford to look a hell of sight higher than you so don't count your chickens. You might just turn out to have been sitting on golf balls.

The door opened again and this time it was Delia. 'I thought I'd find you here,' she smiled. 'Just like the old days.'

28

'I was the one who asked the questions then,' Livy remembered. She swung round on her quilted stool and leaned across to hug her eldest sister. 'Thanks a million for a marvellous party. I had an absolutely splendiferous time!'

'That's one of Daddy's pet words,' Delia said, smiling broadly. 'I only wish he could have been here to see his beautiful swan; he would have been so proud of you. Trust the Court to be sitting on the horns of a dilemma ...'

'Never mind, mother was more than proud enough for both of them,' Toni said, in such a way as to have her eldest sister slide a speculative glance in her direction. Toni was far from malleable. Toni was tough, self-willed, and should the occasion call for it, aggressive. She and Delia were closer to each other in age than they were to Livy, and both had always been protective of their younger sister, but in the occasional squabble Delia had always been the peacemaker. Her nature was that of her father; clever and calmly reasonable. When Toni had profoundly horrified her mother by becoming the mistress of the man she later married, Delia had been the go-between in the rift that developed. Once Toni became an honest woman all was forgiven, though Millicent, whilst loyally proclaiming her affection for her second daughter's husband, never forgave him for making her his mistress before he made her his wife.

Stubbing out her cigarette, Toni rose to go. 'There'll be another two dozen roses in the morning, you mark my words,' she said to Livy. 'Take my advice. Don't keep him hanging on. Not only roses droop, you know.'

As Toni swept out, Livy looked at Delia who shrugged and admitted: 'Yes, he's done it again.'

'Who this time?'

'Some long-stemmed show-girl.'

'But why? Toni is always exquisitely dressed, and men find her attractive – why does Hugh feel the need to cat around?'

'He can't help it. Some men can't.'

'Well I think it's *awful*!' Livy was emphatic. That will *never* happen to me, her tone said. *My* marriage with be different.

It was back down the aisle of the Randolph family church, one year later, that Mr & Mrs John Peyton Randolph VI came to pose for *Vogue*, for which magazine Livy had 'worked' until she left to prepare for her marriage. It had been given the exclusive rights to the coverage of her wedding, and Livy smiled from the cover of its next issue, in Christian Dior pure white silk organza and the Randolph Chantilly lace veil surmounted by a wreath of tiny white roses.

Her only attendants were her eldest nephew, Edward Gaylord Winslow, who solemnly bore the ring on a white silk cushion, and her eldest niece, Camilla Lancaster, who carried Livy's ten foot train.

The wedding was one of the biggest events of the social season of 1955, and after a six-week honeymoon in Europe, the newlyweds returned to set up home on the Upper East Side in a house that was part of a large parcel of real estate owned by the Randolphs. Then, while Johnny spent a few hours each morning at the Randolph family bank – a man had to have *something* to do, his mother said, and they could cover for him there – before going to the Racquet and Tennis Club every afternoon, Livy scoured the antique shops for pieces to complement the fine French furniture bestowed on them by Mrs Randolph. She had an eye for the right *bibelot*; small boxes of Battersea enamel, vermeil and porcelain candlesticks, Chelsea figures and Waterford crystal chandeliers.

The Randolphs perfectly suited the life of an upper-class, Upper East Side, upper-income-bracket couple in the late 50s. They entertained frequently; their invitations were much sought after, and their circle of friends was large and fashionable.

Even though still very young, Livy was already beginning to create her own legend; she now had money and could afford to buy the best, but she had something money could never buy: style. When, in the course of a dinner party, she removed one of her large baroque pearl earrings because it was pinching, the next night most of the women at a different dinner likewise wore only one earring. When she got a piece of grit in her eye while passing a building site on her way to the hairdressers and had to wear an eyepatch, she had it made in black silk embroidered with seed pearls and diamante; that too became the 'in' fashion accessory. Her mother had always served afternoon tea; so did Livy, thus instituting another new fashion. She and Johnny were rarely alone; Johnny was gregarious and loved entertaining, so it was a rare night which found them with nothing to do and nowhere to go. Life was, as Johnny put it enthusiastically, 'fun.'

Exactly one year after her wedding she had her first child, a daughter she named Rosalind, following her father's love of Shakespeare in naming his own offspring. She was four months pregnant with her second child when her father suffered the stroke that killed him.

Livy mourned her father deeply; his death was the first real upset of her so-far cloudless life. She grew listless, spent hours just sitting in her father's rocking chair – for which she had asked – rocking and staring out of the window. Worried, Johnny took her on a six-week cruise around the world, cosseted her, tended to her. His mother had made it clear it was his duty: his wife was expecting what might very well turn out to be the son who would carry forward the Randolph dynasty. But when they came back with Livy still remote and distant it was her own mother who said briskly: 'Livy needs something to do. While you were away I found just the place in the country you have been looking for, but it needs doing up. Just the thing for Livy. That will take her mind off her brooding.'

It was on Long Island's north shore; an area of old money, old families, old social graces, the twelve-room gatehouse of an enormous estate with a vast sixty-room mansion which the present owner – rumoured to be a Greek shipping millionaire – never visited. Though Mrs Randolph thought they should have looked to Virginia rather than Long Island, she had to admit that having a house to create gave Livy a new lease of life. She was soon busy choosing fabrics, matching paints, deciding on pictures, arranging furniture. She stopped looking haunted, began to smile again, as well as to gain instead of lose weight, and her obstetrician told her approvingly: 'That's more like it!'

John Peyton Randolph Junior was christened with great style and pomp in the family church at King's Gift in Virginia, and Mrs Randolph presented Livy with the family diamonds, always given to the newest bride once she had done her duty and produced the son and heir.

The family – Johnny, Livy, Rosalind and The Heir – had their portrait painted by a fashionable artist, which Livy hung in the drawing room of Illyria, which is what she called their weekend retreat, and their lives proceeded tranquilly and uneventfully until their tenth wedding anniversary.

Johnny liked fast cars, and so Livy's present was the latest and fastest E-type Jaguar, painted dark green, the Randolph colour. He was ecstatic, had to take it out there and then. Livy went to work in the garden, on her knees planting daffodils, for having created the house she was now creating a garden. The children were not there; they had gone to stay with Cordelia, on the Winslow estate some fifteen miles away, so that Livy and Johnny could celebrate their anniversary alone together. Livy was half-way down the first border when Ito, the Japanese man-servant who had looked after Johnny when he was single, came hurrying across the lawn to tell her that two policeman were asking to see her.

'Why?' asked Livy.

'Don't say. Ask for you.'

Livy glanced up at the sky. 'I want to get this border done before it rains … ask them to come out here, Ito.' She sat back as they approached, looking up at them from under her wide-brimmed straw hat. One look at their faces and she was on her feet. 'What is it? What has happened?'

'An accident, ma'am.'

'Oh, my God… Johnny!'

'He's not dead, ma'am – but he's pretty badly injured.'

Pale but steady: 'Take me to him,' she said.

He was all but smashed to pieces, his injuries multiple, internal as well as external, since the Jaguar, after striking a tree, had bounced off it before somersaulting its way down a steep slope, finally coming to rest upside down, crumpled as if by the remorseless strength of a giant hand. Kindly but inexorably the doctors told Livy that her laughing, boyish husband was beyond any kind of medical help. It was only a matter of time.

That time was short. Only forty minutes after Livy arrived he died as he had lived, quietly and without fuss, relinquishing life with the good manners that were as much a part of him as his sunny smile. It was Livy who went to pieces, screaming wildly and refusing to accept this callously casual blow which had smashed her life as surely as it had destroyed her husband's. For the first time in her life and to everyone's astonishment, she abandoned her tight control of her emotions and howled like a mortally wounded animal, refusing to accept that Johnny was gone. Over and over again she screamed the one word: 'No! No! No! No!' until they managed to subdue and sedate her, from which state she emerged as a zombie, moving and speaking with all the life of a robot under remote control.

A Randolph funeral had its own pattern and Johnny's mother was well practised in setting things in motion. Despite her own grief, she was sensitive enough to her daughter-in-law's anguished state of mind to suggest to Livy's mother that perhaps it would be best if Livy did not attend; that such an absence had been customary until the First World War, when three male Randolphs, including Johnny's grandfather, had been killed in France and the women of the family had insisted on attending their funerals to honour them.

Millicent reacted with indignant dismay. Her daughter

would be at her husband's funeral if she had to be carried there, she proclaimed. It was unthinkable that the chief mourner should not attend. To that end she set out to prod, chivy and ignite some spark of response from the rubber-doll her daughter had become. 'You must be there,' she nagged remorselessly, 'you are the chief mourner. You cannot allow Dolly Randolph to take the limelight – which she would love, of course. When people talk of Mrs John Randolph it is you they mean, not her. What would people say if she was there and you were not? Imagine the gossip.' Millicent's campaign was pitiless. 'They would ask questions, wonder if the marriage had been as happy as it was supposed to be. You owe it to your position to be there, at the forefront of everything. Have I not brought you up *always* to remember the absolute importance of outward appearances? Especially when one is a public figure, as you are. I did not bring you up to go to pieces at the first sign of trouble. Now come along, pull yourself together. You have a fitting for your blacks at ten-thirty. What a mercy that Frenchman is a personal friend as well as your couturier ...'

Long conditioned to obeying her mother in all things, Livy did so now. But she took to going into the nursery at night, sitting by her children's beds, weeping uncontrollably until Ros, who did not sleep as deeply as her untroubled brother and was herself in a state of friable emotions, awoke and tried to comfort her.

Ros had always been close to her father; her first memory was of him tossing her into the air, she screaming with delight. Livy had never played rough and tumble with her children; she did not like her clothes or hair being mussed, so Ros was bewildered when a woman who sounded like

35

her mother but looked nothing like her, untidy and un-made up, her face blotched, eyes sore with weeping, bent down by her bed, put her face against hers and wept as if her heart would break.

'Don't cry, Mummy,' Ros told her staunchly, forcing back her own tears, knowing instinctively her mother needed her, even if it was for the very first time. 'You still have me and Johnny. We will always be here with you. We will be three instead of four, that's all, but we will be a family again, you'll see ... We will look after you ... don't cry ... please don't cry ...'

At the funeral Livy did not cry. She was white-faced but perfectly composed, thanks to an injection from a doctor Millicent knew who specialised in preparing distraught celebrities for public consumption. When Toni found out what her mother had done, and being the one daughter who was not afraid of her, she gave her a tongue-lashing which reduced even Millicent to affronted silence. But she was still able to appreciate the effect her daughter's simple elegance had on the mourners and the watching public. Livy's plain black coat had been cut by the hand of a master, and with it she wore a small tricorne of shiny black straw from which a fine mist of veiling shadowed but did not obscure her face. She held the hands of her two children as they followed the coffin, her daughter as controlled as she was, her son unable to hide his tears, and throughout the service and the internment bore herself 'like the Great Lady she is,' as Millicent complacently heard one mourner comment admiringly to another.

After the funeral, Livy retreated to Illyria, where she saw nobody, coping with bereavement in her own way by working long hours in her garden. She and her sisters had never been allowed to sit with idle hands, and the kind of rest the doctors prescribed for her – doing absolutely nothing – would have driven her mad. She was no reader, except for gossip columns and fashion magazines, so she would have had nothing to do but think, and Livy was no thinker either. To be alone with one's thoughts was something beyond her comprehension. Besides, she could think just as well while she worked; better, in fact, for then she filled her mind with plans and pictures of what her garden would eventually look like. Besides, her most intense feeling was anger, and she could dig and uproot as violently as she liked in order to express it. For this was not how it was supposed to have been. She should have had years of happy married life ahead of her. Instead, here she was, a widow at twenty-nine. What had gone wrong? She had been a good wife, followed her mother's precepts to the letter, been to Johnny everything he had wanted.

And they had been happy. Loved each other. Enjoyed their lives. All she had done was buy him a car she had seen him admiring in a magazine, heard him talk about in the most enthusiastic of terms. He had been thrilled with it; hugged her in delight when she took off the blindfold she had made him wear until she led him by the hand out of the house and down the steps to the drive, where the E–type awaited. And it was not as though he was not used to fast cars. Fate had slipped them a mickey finn, and for the life of her she could not think *why*.

True, the world had changed. The sixties were so very different from the fifties, when she had married Johnny in that glorious Dior gown, now carefully packed away in tissue and sprigs of lavender in a big box in the attic. They had obeyed the strictures of their time and not slept together before their wedding night. Livy had been taught that Nice Girls Didn't and Johnny was a gentleman who would not expect her to anyway. Besides, at that time there had been a whole thrilling *mystique* about The Wedding Night; it was a ritual you ignored at your peril. Nowadays, it seemed that people fell into bed as casually as pouring a drink. Everything was supposed to be 'loose'. New people had emerged whose sole *raison d'etre* was making money. Flashy, selfish people. Pop stars. Dolly birds. She neither liked or approved. If she and Johnny had joined them, become part of this 'new' society, then perhaps she could understand fate turning on them, though such a reproof did strike her as unwontedly severe. But they hadn't. They had gone on as they had always gone on, in spite of the new jargon, the talk about 'anti-heroes' and 'boutiques' and 'discos.'. They had not lowered their standards. Why, then, why had things turned out the way they did? What had they done wrong? Livy wondered, digging her trowel deep into the already dug-over earth, planting a carefully designed carpet of multi-coloured spring flowers: daffodil, hyacinth, primula, crocus, bluebell, tulip and snowdrop.

At night she lay in the double bed – her mother had advised against singles – listening to the chirp of the crickets and the distant sound of a car and missing Johnny. Not so much his conversation, Johnny had not been a talker, but his presence in the big French bed. He had been such a neat sleeper; Livy was the one who sprawled and tossed around. They each had a lamp angled so as not to disturb the one who was not using theirs, and sometimes she had leafed through *Vogue* or *Harpers*, occasionally showing him a picture of a dress and saying: 'What do you think?' and he'd put his head on one side, purse his lips and say either: 'Yes; that's definitely you, Livy,' or 'Mmmmmm … a bit much, don't you think?' Johnny had had an English nanny and his talk was peppered with English expressions. Like when he would be reading a motor magazine, showing Livy a picture of some car or other and saying besottedly: 'Isn't that the absolute end?' He'd even had something of an English accent.

She had the children, of course, but they had their own nanny, also English, and she was such a stickler for routine. For the first time in the ten years she had been married, time dragged. Ten minutes seemed longer than those ten years. Where had they gone?

Now, as she read the papers and magazines she had ordered for Johnny and not had the heart to cancel since they were a link she was loathe to sever, she realised that all sorts of things had been going on around her; enormous upheavals, protests, war, peace, liberation, (not the least that of women) movements. Livy's life had centred around her family. She had filled her head with looking after two homes and Johnny and their children: with dancing lessons, riding lessons and visits to the paediatrician. There had been long discussions as to which school was the best; whether John Jr needed braces now or was it too soon? And there had been their vivid and crowded social life; cocktails, dinners, showings, first nights, charity bashes; Livy's thrice–weekly lunches with the 'girls' and the more intimate ones with her sisters, as well as regular visits to Philadelphia to see one grandmother, and vacations in Virginia with the other. Now, Livy was that shuddering thing: an extra woman, or would be when she entered society again.

'Which,' said her sister Toni practically, one afternoon, 'you will have to do sooner rather than later. You have been hibernating far too long. Time to come back into the real world.'

'This is my real world,' Livy said, indicating with a sweep of her arm the green lawns, the lovingly created dells, the lake, the trees, the flowers.

'It will be if you continue to hide away in it.'

'I'm not hiding. I just don't feel like leaving it.'

'Scared?'

'No, not sufficiently interested.'

'What you need is a man who is interested in you – once you are over your mourning, of course,' Toni tacked on as she saw her sister's expression.

'Nobody will *ever* measure up to Johnny.'

'Was he that big, then?' her sister marvelled innocently, before laughing at Livy's grimace of distaste. Privately, Toni had always thought Johnny Randolph a charming adolescent; not a real man. His wife, though, obviously held a different opinion. But truly, they had been babes in the woods, Toni thought. Kindred spirits. Friends rather than lovers. Livy had never seemed that interested in sex, while Toni had wondered, before he married her sister, if Johnny was not a neuter. But they had produced two children so obviously they had known what it was for.

So it can't be the sex she is missing, Toni thought now, as she observed her sister's cameo face. In fact, I don't think Livy knows what it is *really* for. What she needs is the right man to teach her.

40

Toni herself, after divorcing her first husband for his infidelity whilst concealing her own, thus acquiring a very handsome settlement, had married a second time even more profitably and had got more fun out of her second marriage in two years than she had out of her first in ten.

That was what Livy needed. Fun. She needed to meet new people. She and Johnny had not moved beyond the circles in which they would meet their own kind. Toni, on the other hand, had friends all over the place and on all levels of society. That was what Livy needed. A shake-up. The world was changing, and at a sometimes alarming rate. Nowadays, anything went – just so long as you had the money to pay for it. Toni did, so she availed herself of everything that was on offer. All she had to do was persuade Livy to relax her stance a little. She was still – just – under thirty, and as elegantly beautiful as they came. What a waste if all that tremendous chic was left to wither away unseen. And she's got plenty of money. Johnny left her wonderfully well provided for.

Some new clothes, a trip perhaps, and who knows what might happen? I must think about this, she decided, as her chauffeur drove her back to New York. There has to be a way to prise her loose. For Livy could be infuriatingly stubborn. Fortunately, not two days later the perfect event did present itself. Cordelia's husband was appointed United States Ambassador to the Court of St. James, and would be leaving to present his credentials within the next couple of weeks.

'Yes, of course you must bring Livy to London,' Delia agreed when Toni put it to her. 'She needs to get out of herself, meet some nice people. Ward is a tremendous

41

Anglophile, you know, ever since Oxford, and he knows just about everybody. I'll cull his list for the most eligible – and presentable, of course – prospects. We both know how particular Livy is. Let us get settled in at the embassy and then I'll arrange some cocktail parties and dinners.'

'I have to persuade her to make the trip first, then see if mother will come up from Philadelphia to take charge of the children.'

'Try and stop her,' Delia said dryly.

Toni began her campaign by asking Livy to come and help her choose a wardrobe for a European trip she was planning. 'You have such perfect taste,' she said truthfully. 'I really would appreciate your advice and suggestions.'

Since Livy adored clothes, she agreed, and for the first time in months drove into New York, where she stayed with her sister in Sutton Place and went with her to Toni's favourite designer. Unlike her two sisters, but like their mother, Toni was quite short, and she did not have their long bones covered by the minimum of flesh. Toni was pouter-pigeon shaped, with a bosom that had played a large part in her sexual conquests, and a rear that had brought a greedy light to many a male eye. High fashion such as Livy wore was not for her since such clothes did not hang right on her 'tits and ass' as she called them (but not in the presence of her mother).

Toni had cunningly arranged for other designs – what she called 'haute Livy' to be brought to her, whereupon she would say regretfully: 'Not for me, alas. My sister can wear this sort of thing perfectly, but I can't.' And she would say casually: 'Right up your street, Livy. Try it on, see how it looks …' And as always, it would look stunning.

42

'Mrs Randolph can wear anything,' the fitter would murmur, admiring not only Livy's long, narrow elegance but the way she wore the clothes, rather than the other way round.

Livy could even improve on an original design; setting a neckline ever so slightly to one side, for instance, changing the look to something even more chic. She would take a belt, tie it a certain way, and the change would be subtle but – invariably – for the better, or she would leave a button undone and add an indefinable something. She was the first woman anyone knew to wear a navy blue shirt with jade green pants; a pink silk blouse with a nubbly red wool suit.

Her shoes – 9AA – were always immaculate, as were her handbags and gloves. She rarely wore hats – her hair was always perfectly coiffed – but if she did they were devastatingly chic and almost impossible for any other woman to wear as well. She could take a string of furs and throw them about her throat and shoulders in a way that was impossible to copy, try though many women might, and when she had a grey flannel pants suit made, which she wore with a white, polo-necked cashmere sweater, she started yet another fashion.

Now, the fitting room became her stage as she tried on, discarded, amended, changed, substituted. The designer himself had the good sense to see that what was being done to his clothes enhanced his basic design and allowed Livy to adapt them to her own, inimitable style. Now and then she would add something to a dress that was a stroke of genius. Like the column of white crepe with a diagonal plunging neckline to which she pinned, at its base, a circle of rose petals made entirely out of rubies. 'Darling, you have got to come with me on this trip and show off these clothes,' Toni said, as though the idea had just occurred to her.

'I don't think I should be seen in bright colours just yet ...' Livy demurred.

'For heaven's sake, it is 1966 not 1866!' Toni exclaimed.'Do I detect a touch of Old Virginia?'

'It is only three months.'

'Three and a half – four by the time we start the trip. Even Royalty doesn't wear black *that* long!'

But Livy was stubborn, and mindful of her mother-in-law, so the clothes she chose were either black, white or black and white. Her version of half mourning. And they caused a sensation.

They sailed on the *United States* and their first stop was Paris, where more clothes were bought and Livy was escorted by several very eligible Frenchmen, causing much gnashing of envious teeth. From there they went to Rome, and from Rome to the Riviera, where Livy was assiduously courted by a handsome but impoverished Hungarian Count who made her giggle and paid her poetic compliments. She found it balm to the soul to be pursued by men once again; she had forgotten what it was like. It was fun to sit and smoke and giggle with Toni and compare notes, to have Toni agree that no one met so far was worth more than a brief flirtation. 'Perhaps when we get to London ...' was her verdict.

Livy arrived there feeling pleasantly exhausted yet exhilarated by her success. She had thought it would be different as 'the extra woman', the one without a man of her own. She had heard talk about such females, usually from women who suspected their own husbands of being objects of long-range planning on the part of a particular, former 'old and close friend', now regarded as a dangerous enemy because she was single, on the loose and on the hunt. So far, Livy had not met up with even the slightest sign of hostility, but when she remarked on it casually to Toni, her sister levelled a thoughtful look and said: 'This is Europe, sweetie. They do things differently here. Wait until you begin to re-circulate back home …'

But Livy learned the truth long before then.

It was at a grand party at Winfield House. Livy had been enjoying herself immensely, dancing, gossiping, quaffing champagne, when her eyes, roving the room, were caught by a couple standing on the sidelines, eyes only for each other. They were young, a good ten years younger than Livy and Johnny, but something about them, the way they stood close together, the way their eyes met and clung, the secret smile they shared, reminded Livy of herself and her dead husband so much that it pierced her heart like a lance. A wave of melancholy swept away her gaiety and the old suffocating sense of despair she thought she had conquered rose before her like the spectre at the feast. She knew that if someone asked her what was the matter she would burst into tears, and as always, her mother's precepts dictated her actions. Putting down her champagne glass she began to slide away, melting inconspicuously to the edge of her group in the artfully aimless way Millicent Gaylord had taught her years before, away from the party and up the stairs to the one place where she knew she could be alone; her sister Cordelia's sumptuous bathroom with its own adjoining dressing room. It was never used by guests. There, she could give way to her desolation. But as she turned the heavily ornate door-handle, ready to throw herself down on Cordelia's leather-covered massage table and sob her heart out, she realised that though the dressing room was dark, there was someone in it.

'Who's there?' a woman's voice cried out, startled and filled with panic.

'I'm so sorry,' Livy answered quickly, instantly retreating, 'I had no idea –'

'Oh, it's you,' the voice said, and before Livy could shut the door the light went on and she saw who it was she had disturbed.

'Sally?' she blurted incredulously, shocked at the sight of a woman she knew only because she was a long-time friend of her sister Cordelia: they had gone to Miss Porter's together, but Livy had never seen her in such a state. Sally Remington was known in their world as one of its most exquisite inhabitants; always elegantly dressed, superbly coiffed and dazzlingly bejewelled. The same age as Cordelia she normally looked ten years younger, but tonight she was a dishevelled wreck. She had obviously been crying; her eyes were chopped liver, her incredibly pearly skin blotched and puffy, her normally immaculate blonde hair a haystack through which she had been dragged backwards. Livy was so shocked she almost showed it.

'Come in and shut that damned door,' hissed Sally frantically. 'And lock it. I don't want anyone else seeing me in this state.'

'I'm sorry,' Livy said, appalled and embarrassed. 'I was not expecting –'

'Me to be here? Did you have the same idea? To be alone in order to confront the wreckage of your life? We were – are – both in the same boat, aren't we? Both single women again; you a widow, me a divorcee.'

46

Stung by the comparison, which she thought unjust, for Sally had chosen to divorce Steven Remington, Livy said stiffly: 'If you are so upset about the divorce why did you go through with it? I had no say in what happened to *my* husband.'

'Upset about that two-timing snake? Don't be ridiculous! I don't give a damn about him. It's *my* life which upsets me! This solitary – existence. I put up with Steve's philandering for years until I couldn't *not* do something about it. Not after he was all over the columns with that cheap tramp! He made me look a fool – but God, I was an even bigger one to kick him out because of it.' She began to sob again. 'I don't like not being Mrs Steven Remington. Too late I now see that I'd always taken it for granted ... being Somebody. First of all Sarah de Witt then Sally Remington. Now I'm just another divorcee; on the loose and ripe for the picking. Just another lone woman in an already glutted market.' Sally smeared her fists across her eyes. 'Then there's the matter of one's pride; of keeping up those all important appearances – not letting people know how desperate you are; of working hard to make them think you are leading a rich, full life, accepting charity jobs they would not have dared to offer Mrs Steven Remington, but not daring to turn them down in case you don't get asked again. I had no idea it would be like this; that I – Sally de Witt Remington – would be expected to pay –' a loathing-filled sneer twisted the full-lipped mouth – 'you know the kind of payment I mean – for a crummy dinner or an evening at the theatre. Along with the attitude that I am lucky to be given the chance in the first place! And your friends' husbands think you are both ready and willing because you must also be desperate. Why,

47

even Ward –' Sally bit off the rest of the sentence then sat upright and asked: 'Pass me that box of tissues, will you?'

Livy reached for them, handed them over, once again masking her shock at what Sally had almost revealed. Ward! Stuffy, conservative, pompous Ward had propositioned Sally! Head reeling, Livy felt punch-drunk. All she had wanted was to be alone …

'Thanks.' Sally wiped her eyes and blotted her face, threw away the tissue, reached for another and blew her nose soundly. 'God, what a wreck,' she winced, eyeing her bedraggled self in the wall of mirrors above the dressing table, until her gaze met Livy's. 'Don't stay a widow for long,' she advised intensely. 'Fortunately, you are only thirty. Time is on your side. I shall be forty next birthday – and you don't tell *that* to a soul – which makes it that much harder for me.' She fixed Livy with a manic stare. 'Find yourself another husband, don't go down my road. It goes nowhere. What is it – six months? Make it no more than another six. People are sympathetic now to the young, tragic widow, they don't expect you to be dangerous – yet; still in mourning, and all that, but in a year – you watch; you'll find yourself juggling engagements round blank pages in your diary; pretending you are in demand when you've got nothing, absolutely *nothing* planned. Yes – even you!' she insisted in the face of Livy's obvious doubt. 'You will find that just keeping yourself in circulation will take enormous effort; the *plotting*, the *scheming* to get yourself invited to places where you were first on their list before, and as for entertaining on your own … God … that's a nightmare.'

Sally shuddered, shook her head in dire warning. 'Take me as your object lesson. Marriage is all you know too. If I'd had a career, as women are beginning to nowadays, I'd have something to turn to, but we were both brought up to regard marriage as the be all and end all. Neither of us knows anything but how to be a wife. So what do I do now? Who wants a forty-year-old reject?'

There was a long, heavy silence, during which Sally got up and went into the shower. Over the hiss of the water Livy sat on, numb and incredulous. What she had just heard had indeed been an eye opener and hers were still wide with shock. It had never occurred to her that a woman as rich, as beautiful and as socially prominent as Sally Remington would find life any different as a single woman than she had as a married one, but her cry of despair had revealed things which in her inexperienced naïvity Livy had not even suspected.

The thought of not going out to dinners and parties, of not constantly entertaining in her own house, of not always having places to go and people to see, of not being able to pick and choose from her dozens of invitations, not buying lots of pretty clothes to wear to them, not receiving admiring compliments from envious friends … all this shocked and alarmed her. She needed those things. They were the fabric of her life! All right, so I'm frivolous, she admitted defiantly, but these things are important to me. Like Sally, I am a social animal and *not* meant to live alone. It is not in my nature. And then, making a second truthful admission and realising it with almost happy relief: I am one of those women who is *meant* to be married!

The shower door opened and Sally came out, wrapped in a towel and bringing the fragrance of Cordelia's *Fleur des Alpes* shower gel. Before Livy's fascinated eyes she sat down at the dressing table, switched on the bank of lights, leaned forward and said briskly: 'Time for a restoration job, I think ...' as if their conversation had never happened.

Livy had gone up to Cordelia's room feeling sorry for herself, ready to have a good cry, because she felt fate had been unkind. Now she saw that unless she pulled herself together there were far worse things in store. Johnny was gone for ever; so was the life she had led with him. Playing the grieving widow would get her nowhere – except keeping Sally Remington company. And that was the last thing she wanted. No ... the past was over and done with. What she had to do now was decide what kind of a future she wanted and then go out and find the man who could give it to her. And that, she thought confidently, would not be difficult. Not for Olivia Gaylord Randolph...

3

'What on earth were you talking about for so long with Billy
Bancroft?' Toni Standish asked her sister one night a few
weeks later. They had just come back from a dinner party at
which he had also been a guest and, afterwards, he and Livy
had sat together on a sofa holding what was obviously a
tête-à-tête.

'Nothing in particular,' Livy yawned. 'just – you know –
anything and everything.'

Toni eyed her sister. There was a creamy self-satisfaction
about her that spoke of hidden things.

'Actually, he was reminding me of the first time we met,
about six years ago, in New York,' Livy admitted, dimples
showing.

'That's Billy, all right. He never forgets a face – especially
one as lovely as yours.'

Livy regarded her sister, wide-eyed. 'He remembered
yours, too,' she observed innocently.

'I should hope so. I've known Billy for quite a while,'
Toni's own smile was equally innocent.

Livy was stripping off her jewellery – emeralds and

diamonds – dropping it into a pile her maid would lock away. 'What does he do, exactly?' she asked casually.

'Make money. Lots and lots and lots of money.'

'I know, but how?'

'Billy is not particular about the means so long as his ends meet, and by now I should think he is able to wrap them several times around Hyde Park.'

'Is he a crook?'

'Not the kind the police are familiar with, but he has a reputation for being very fast on the deal.' Toni bent an interested eye on her sister. 'Do I detect an interest on your part?'

'I am – curious?' allowed Livy. 'He is not like the men I usually meet.'

'Of course he isn't. They were born. Billy Bancroft is self-created.'

'And on the make?'

Surprised at her sister's unusual shrewdness, Toni replied: 'He always has an eye – both eyes – out for the main chance, but he is very well respected in the City and the Queen knighted him a year or so ago.' Toni let ten seconds tick by. 'You know there is a Lady Bancroft?'

'Yes. He told me she is a permanent invalid. Something went wrong after the birth of their twin sons; some kind of post-natal depression that got worse instead of better. She has been in a nursing home for years.'

'So that's why nobody ever sees her ...' Raising her eyebrows: 'You did have a cosy little chat,' Toni observed narrowly.

'He is very easy to talk to.'

'So will you be talking to him again?' Not that Toni

thought for a moment her sister would ever take Billy Bancroft seriously. A self-made, married, Jewish entrepreneur was the last man to interest Olivia Randolph.

'Oh, I am sure we shall be seeing him around,' Livy said vaguely.

Which they did. He seemed to pop up everywhere, and though he gave Toni no cause to believe he was pursuing her sister — what was the point? He was married and Livy was not looking to be any man's mistress — he did seem always to end up sitting next to Livy at dinner or partnering her in one way or another. All Livy ever said was a wide-eyed: 'He is amusing, he makes me laugh, and he knows absolutely *everybody* ...'

And Billy Bancroft already knew everything there was to know about the widowed Mrs John Peyton Randolph VI. He did a great deal of lucrative business in the United States, which entailed his spending at least four months of every year there, and the men with whom he did business invited him to functions where he met people from Livy's world. He had first met her at a reception at the United Nations. Johnny was alive then, and Billy had at once dismissed him as a blue-blooded bonehead, but the marriage, he was told, was solid, added to which Livy was then only twenty-four and he still a relative newcomer to the Manhattan smart set. When he met her again in London six years later, she was a widow and he was Sir William Bancroft, now courted by those same circles on both sides of the Atlantic where once he had been received with a certain condescension. He was known to have the ear of certain Very Highly Placed people in the British government and to be headed for Higher

Things; not the least a seat in the House of Lords. It did not do to remember the fact that he had once been Billy Banciewicz of the Whitechapel Road whose first million was made by some astute dealing in war surplus. People who incurred his wrath had a habit of incurring disaster of one kind or another. It was better to incur his pleasure. Which was what Livy did.

Watching her down the cricket-pitch length of the dinner table at Winfield House, Billy had thought she made every other woman there look second-rate. That night she wore a wide, sweeping skirt of heavy satin, the colour of perfectly beaten egg-whites, under a plain black crêpe-jersey top, which skimmed perfect shoulders and left her forearms bare but for twin inch-wide bracelets of delicate flowers made up of diamonds and pearls. Matching flowers were in her ears, and her short dark hair was crisply brushed up and away from her face. She moved with the grace of a swan, and her voice was soft, her smile warm. She was everything Billy had ever promised himself. No man with any common sense would allow such a rare piece of perfection to get away. And Billy had never lacked for sense, common or otherwise. So he was circumspect, deferential, made his mark with invisible ink. But he knew it was there. More important, so did she.

All that summer they swirled around each other as they met at dinners, cocktails, receptions, balls and the hallowed haunts of the London Season. At Ascot, Livy was a guest in Billy's box; his influence procured her an invitation to one of the Queen's garden parties at Buckingham Palace, and when the Queen, recognising him, smiled and stopped to speak, Livy's name was murmured by an attentive aide and she made her curtsy.

But Billy was far too clever to make her the focus of gossip. All the time he was meeting Livy here, there and everywhere, giving her the benefit of his financial expertise and advising her how best to handle the income from the trust fund Johnny had left her, he was also conducting a long-standing affair with the fourth and much younger (what would decades later be called 'pleasure wife') of a much married media tycoon. It was common knowledge that Joyce Eastman would like nothing better than to become Lady Bancroft, and that she was becoming increasingly impatient with Billy's disinclination to comply with her wishes. People watched greedily as Joyce smouldered while Livy glowed; nodded wisely when Livy took every advantage of being new in town and the invitations such newness brought.

Joyce made it far too obvious, they said. Olivia Randolph took nothing for granted, and her attitude to Billy was in no way marked by any hint of special treatment. He was one of many, no more. And thank God it is not less, Livy thought, one morning, opening the pile of envelopes on her breakfast tray and seeing with relief that almost all were invitations. There was as yet no hint of the cold-shoulder Sally Remington had described, but she was always on the look-out, for at the first sign it meant she had to take steps – and in the right direction.

Her mother, apprised by the detailed letters of a helpful friend also spending the summer in London, of the fact that her daughter was seeing a lot of a man who was not only fifteen years older than she was but married to boot – and to an invalid wife, at once put pen to paper to express her reservations. He might be 'Sir' William Bancroft, but he had been born Banciewicz; no more than a nobody who had made himself somebody and become inordinately rich in the process. Millicent Gaylord thoroughly approved of a man hauling himself up by his bootstraps, but she could not approve of such a man being allowed to enter the Inner Circle around Mrs John Peyton Randolph VI. Especially since this particular Somebody was a Jew. Very definitely Not one of Us.

Livy read her mother's letter then put it carefully away. She had her plan made. Either it would work or it would not. If it didn't – well then, she would take her mother's advice. In the meantime, she was enjoying the attentions of a man who knew to a nicety how to pay them.

Johnny had been from her world; predictable, not at all exciting, but steady and utterly trustworthy, the sort of man whose word was his bond. Billy Bancroft was totally unpredictable – she never knew what to expect from one meeting to the next – exciting unto breathlessness, reliable only insofar as you could rely on him to do the unexpected, and she was not sure she trusted him except where money was concerned. Billy took money too seriously to treat it with anything other than respect.

He had not been brought up – as she understood the meaning of the word – at all. He had worked since he was fourteen years old. He had never gone to college. His father had been a Whitechapel tailor whose father left Poland before the beginning of yet another Jewish pogrom. Yet there was nothing he could not talk about, with both fluency and a seemingly deep knowledge of the subject.

He knew about precious stones, for instance. Livy wanted to create a pearl necklace to her own design, so Billy took her to a small dingy office in a seedy building in Hatton

Garden, where an old man wearing a yarmulke opened a black velvet bag and poured into her cupped hands perfect pearls as milky and glowing as solidified moonbeams. Used to sitting in a chair in her own drawing room while someone from Harry Winston or Bulgari displayed their wares on velvet cushions, Livy found it all so utterly different as to be disturbingly stimulating. As was the time he took her to Petticoat Lane one Sunday morning, where he talked to the stallholders in a language she did not understand, who all paid her fulsome compliments in heavily accented English, kissing their fingers at her. It was flatteringly exciting, but even more impressive was the way they treated Billy. Like a King.

Livy was a woman of the world: her world. Billy was a man of many worlds, most of which he bestrode like a colossus. She had never met anyone like him in her life.

Which knowledge, promptly sent to her mother, caused that lady to have such severe heart palpitations that she was hospitalised. Within twenty-four hours Livy was at her bedside in Philadelphia. Millicent made a rapid recovery once she had Livy on her side of the Atlantic while Sir William remained on his. She was even more relieved when Livy took up with an old flame; a diplomat back in America after years of foreign postings. He had been deeply in love with Livy the year she made her début, and for a while had been one of her most constant swains, but Johnny Randolph had pushed him out of the picture. When Livy became Mrs Randolph the young diplomat was on his way to Delhi, since when he had spent time in Tokyo, Brussels, Madrid and Buenos Aires. Now a First Secretary he was home on extended leave, and still unmarried, only too happy to take up where he had left off. He and Livy became an item, but Livy turned down his immediate offer of marriage.

'It is not quite a year,' she demurred, 'not to mention those that have elapsed since we last saw each other. Let's get to know one another again ... Court me, Larry. I feel the need to be courted. We were so young then ... Now I'm a widow and you are a seasoned diplomat.' Her dimples appeared as she tilted her head to one side, eyes as bright as those of some brightly plumaged bird, smile demurely teasing. 'Practise some of that diplomacy on me, why don't you?'

Which he did, to the extent that soon they were a frequently reported couple whom people confidently expected to announce their engagement once Livy's year of mourning was over.

But while the mature Laurence Styles was a vast improvement on the immature one, he was not what Livy wanted. He was nice but he stirred no feelings, held no mystery as Billy Bancroft had done, mysteries she was eager to solve even as she found she had qualms as to the solutions. She was not 'in love' with Billy as she had been with Johnny, but she found he fascinated her. After Johnny's simplicity Billy was as complicated as a good Swiss watch; one which kept its own time. After knowing him for three months she had not even begun to comprehend the convolutions of his character, but she was convinced that with time and patience, understanding would be very rewarding.

She was also aware that his 'mongrel' background held the appeal of strangeness. Johnny had come with a certified pedigree from which she knew to expect predictable behaviour. Billy was bred only in the most basic understanding of the word, but that meant an exciting unpredictability. At

58

times there was a harshness about him which made her shiver, but pleasurably, like a rough towel on sensitised skin. There were also times when he frightened her. Like when he lost his temper. Not with her; never with her, but with some luckless person who had transgressed by acting without permission. *Nobody* made decisions for Billy. But Livy had found that when she leaned on him he stood firm. On the other hand, he could not be pushed. The thing to do, she decided, was lead in a certain direction to see if he would follow.

It took a month. He turned up one evening as she was dressing to go out to dinner with Larry Styles, and when she sent down a message to that effect, determined to squeeze every advantage she could while she could, taking her leisurely time about creating the perfect impression, he patiently waited for her. When at last she came down, her peony-red chiffon floating around her, diamonds sparkling, smile sweet but cool, showing him that she was as aware of her worth as he was and not to be regarded as his creature, he was not one whit abashed. He merely looked at her in a way that had her skin pricking before asking, in the amused voice of one who knows the answer before the question is posed: 'Where do you want to be married? Here or in London?'

'It won't do, Toni, it just won't do,' Millicent Gaylord said agitatedly. 'Oh, he's presentable enough, and heaven knows he is rich enough, but who is he? What is he? And what has he done with the invalid wife? How come he is suddenly free to make Livy Lady Bancroft and, more to the point, why, oh why, is she so eager to let him?'

59

'He got a divorce,' Toni said for the umpteenth time.

'How? When? Where? Nobody in London knows a thing. I know because I asked them to find out. If he got divorced it must have been in some hole in the corner place nobody knows about.'

'If it was good enough for Wallis Simpson ...'

'Exactly,' Millicent pounced. 'That was all very carefully arranged too, by power and influence, and I don't care what *she* said her mother *did*, Alice Warfield did keep a boarding house.' Sounding distressed: 'I only wish I could keep Livy from making this terrible mistake.'

'You are exaggerating, as usual,' Toni pointed out on a sigh.

'Oh, no I am not. I am an excellent judge of character and in my opinion Livy has no idea of the true nature of this Sir William Bancroft. What are his sons like?' Millicent changed tack without announcing the fact, as she was wont to do.

'I've never met them. They are both up at Oxford, so they must have brains. At a good college – Balliol, so Ward tells me.'

'Well, I suppose that is something ... but eighteen-year-old twins! Livy is only thirty, for heaven's sake. Far too young to be a stepmother. And what do they think about all this? How do we know they either approve or like the idea of their father abandoning their mother to marry again?'

I doubt if they have been consulted, Toni thought to herself. Billy never consults anyone but himself. Millicent squirmed in her squabbed chair. 'I don't know what has come over Livy. It is not as though she *needs* to marry again.

She has more than enough money, and as Mrs John Peyton Randolph she has a position in Society. It is only a year since poor Johnny was killed ...'

'True, but he is dead while Livy is alive. She is also young, attractive and fit for nothing except what you brought her – all of us – up to be; the wife of a rich, powerful, socially prominent man. Livy has not only done it once, she is about to do it again, and even more successfully. Livy is bent and determined to become Lady Bancroft,' Toni advised her mother, 'so why don't you just let it happen? Don't waste your breath on trying to stop this marriage; concentrate instead on what you will wear to it ...'

But to her sister, Toni said: 'You know mother is in a tizz about you marrying Billy and, to be quite honest, I have wondered about it once or twice myself. He is no Johnny Randolph, you know. This is not a boy you are marrying. This is a man. A very demanding man. Are you sure you'll be able to handle him?'

Livy's smile was sardonic. 'Wasn't I trained to handle men? To pander to them, flatter them, make them think it is always *their* idea?'

'That's what I mean. As far as Billy is concerned it always *is* his idea. Billy tends to put what he wants first – and last and always.'

'I know what I am doing,' Livy said uncompromisingly.

'Fine, but *why* are you doing it?'

'You divorced one man to marry another. There was no hiatus in your married state. I've been on my own for a year now, and if I had my druthers, then I'd rather be married. Okay?'

'But why Billy? Larry Styles is crazy about you. Why not him?'

'I don't fancy being just another embassy wife.' Livy turned to face her sister. 'Billy can give me the world,' she said simply, 'not just a small corner of it. As his wife I'll have everything I want.'

'Just so long as he has everything *he* wants,' Toni reminded. 'And Billy is a man who wants – expects – a very great deal.'

'I am prepared to be the kind of wife he wants.'

'You've discussed it, then?'

'Of course.'

'But you are not in love with him.' When Livy did not reply. 'Are you?'

'No,' Livy admitted, chin up. 'But he fascinates me, he's very – complex. Life will never be dull around him. And I find him attractive in a – an earthy way. He is so – well, almost exotic! To be honest, there is so much *more* to him than Johnny …'

'Of course. Billy is a mature male in a way Johnny never was. I think Billy was mature by the time his voice broke …' Toni hesitated. 'Just … be careful. Billy is not always aware of the pressure he exerts. And all he does when something breaks is replace it.'

'He has never exerted the least pressure on me,' Livy told her sister truthfully. Her dimples appeared. 'I am the one who seems to do that …' A faint pink enveloped the dimples. 'He is very – masculine.'

Once Livy had agreed to marry Billy she had also allowed him other privileges hitherto forbidden. Like making love to her. It was a revelation. At last she understood what Toni had meant when she complained bitterly about how useless her first husband was in bed. Sex with Billy was vintage champagne which made your head buzz and your legs weak. With Johnny it had been lemonade. And you *never* got drunk on that ...

It emboldened her to ask something which had her curiosity at fever pitch: what had decided him to obtain his freedom and how he had done it.

When he answered, it was in such a way as to make it plain that he would answer this time, but that the subject was not for discussion in the future. 'I always had the key,' he told her, 'but it was not until I met you that I felt the need to use it.'

And with that, she had to be content. And she was. Fate had been kind. Her plan had worked. But then, she had heeded Sally Remington's advice. Not for Olivia Randolph the humiliation of being caught sobbing her heart out in somebody else's bathroom; of being the tag-end 'extra woman'; propositioned by men who had hitherto treated her with humble respect, since she had no man to protect her. She would be Lady Bancroft. She would have position, several beautiful houses, a blank cheque for entertaining, another for clothes. Billy would give her the full, rich life she needed, a prominent position from which she could shine, while she would bring him the social cachet of being married to Olivia Gaylord Randolph.

It was, she thought, a very equitable arrangement.

Millicent Gaylord sat and watched her daughter being fitted for her wedding dress: a narrow column of champagne-coloured silk-jersey with crushed drapery of a deeper colour crossed over the breasts, and the long, tight sleeves Livy loved because they showed off her narrow wrists and long, elegant hands.

'I think a little more here … see … below the shoulder,' Livy was saying to the fitter, scrutinising herself in the triple mirrors of the fitting room. 'Look …' She bent her arm towards her and the fitter nodded, snapped his scissors and the sleeve came free of the dress before being re-set so that this time when Livy raised her arm there was no pull and the whole bodice sat differently.

When it comes to choosing clothes Livy's judgement is unerring, Millicent thought. When it comes to men …

It was not that Billy had done anything untoward. On the contrary he had not set himself out to charm, to flatter, to woo. His attitude was that of a man who knew his own worth, but at the same time was well aware of the prize he was getting. Even Millicent had to admit that the ring he had chosen for Livy was not only in the best possible taste but a stone of rare quality. Not a diamond, not an emerald but a cabochon *padparadschah* or pink sapphire of a glorious deep apricot colour. It was so unusual that it quickly became a talking point, especially when Billy presented Livy with a matching necklace of the same stones interspersed with flawless pearls.

Oh, Billy had taste, all right, but where had he got it from? That sort of thing took generations to acquire. While Billy did not hide the fact that his father had been a Whitechapel tailor, he did not trumpet the fact either. Millicent was certain that he would rather the fact had not been brought to light at all, but then, she was also of the opinion that Billy Bancroft hid a great many other things, and it was what they were that worried her.

64

She had met his sons, at last. They had been present at the reception she had held to mark the engagement. Not identical twins but twins nevertheless, and obviously so. Polite, well-mannered boys of nineteen who spoke when spoken to and minded their father at all times. Toni had at once labelled them Tweedledum and Tweedledee, shortened to Dum and Dee. Rupert and Jeremy, Millicent thought on a snort. Upper-class English names if ever she heard one. Which meant that Billy had planned his social ascent years before. As he plans everything, she thought uneasily. Nothing left to chance. Not with that one. Livy probably fits the specification he had drawn up – and down to the smallest detail. Yes, she thought. Cold. And hard. And ruthless. For a brief moment her flesh crisped. What, she thought as fear suddenly ripped through her, is my Livy getting into here?

'Yes ... that's better,' Livy was saying, critically studying herself in the mirrors that gave her an all-round view of herself. She was extricated from the dress which was reverently carried away to be finished, and stood in her lace-encrusted slip waiting for what would be her going-away suit to be fitted. It had a soft, standing collar, fiendishly difficult to drape properly, and Livy watched critically as the little man who always supervised her fittings ripped away stitches at one edge and proceeded to re-shape the muslin interlining so that when the collar was pinned once more it sat on the jacket with perfect precision. 'Perfect,' smiled Livy. 'Simply perfect.'

The skirt came next, to be altered at the waist and the length (always critical when it came to balancing it with a jacket) adjusted to that point exactly below Livy's knee – she had not and never would take her skirts above that point even though she had legs well worth showing – which had her saying: 'Yes … that's it,' turning so that the intricate triple pleating at the back which allowed for ease of movement, rippled seductively.

'That is the most *gorgeous* colour,' one of the assistant fitters said, of the soft but intense Parma violet of the suit, which was lined with lilac silk. 'And doesn't it suit you, Mrs Randolph.'

'Thank you,' Livy smiled, pleased.

They finished off the rest of the fitting; three evening dresses, another suit, this time in light navy, one of Livy's favourite colours, and worn with a red, white and blue striped chiffon blouse which tied in a pussy-cat bow at the neck.

'What's next?' Millicent asked, as they went out on to Fifth Avenue.

'The lingerie I ordered at Countess Czceska's … you don't have to come if you've had enough.'

'Well, if you don't mind, unless we can go and have a nice sit down at Rumplemeyers …'

'I haven't time, Mother. I'm on a tight schedule.'

'Whose schedule?' grumbled Millicent.

'I'm meeting Billy at six and I want everything done by then. You know how he hates being kept waiting.'

'A man in love should not mind waiting,' her mother observed tartly.

'Billy likes things to run smoothly, that's all.'

'And what happens when they don't? What will he do? Stand you in the corner?'

Livy laughed. 'Don't be silly, Mother.'

66

But Millicent did not feel she was being silly. Livy was not seeing clearly, blinded as she was by the dazzle of being Lady Bancroft. Millicent had tried to draw her out of the light and show her how things looked in shadow, but Livy saw only what she wanted to see.

'It's because he is so much older than me, isn't it?' Livy attacked directly. 'Because I am only thirty and he is forty-five, with sons of nineteen. But I have no trouble with Rupert and Jeremy; and Billy gets on marvellously with Rosalind and John Jr.'

'John may but Rosalind does not like Billy and it is no use pretending she does.'

On a dismissive shrug: 'Rosalind was always daddy's girl,' Livy said. 'But it will be more than a year since Johnny died by the time I marry Billy and I can't mourn for ever, not even to suit Rosalind.' Angrily, for she was always on the defensive for Billy where her mother was concerned: 'It's because he's Jewish, isn't it? You are prejudiced. You don't approve of me abandoning my Randolph status to become the second wife of a man who has no status at all in your eyes!'

'I will not deny that I have reservations – '

'Yes, in a WASPs-only hotel!' Despairingly, because she wanted her second marriage to be as warmly welcomed as her first: 'We are being married in a civil ceremony, in your cottage next to Delia's vast pile, *and* by a Judge who sat on the Supreme Court with Daddy! What more do you want?'

'I want you to be happy,' said her mother. Then in the stubborn voice of conviction: 'And I don't think you will be with him.'

Livy drew a deep breath: Now! she thought. She had

never gone against her mother's will before. But this time there was too much at stake: her future life, for instance. 'You don't know what you are talking about,' she said coldly, and turning on her heel she headed for the huge black Rolls Billy had insisted she use for going about New York. The chauffeur was stationed by its open rear door and in a moment he had shut it on her, before getting back into the driver's seat and drawing away from the kerb, leaving her mother standing.

Livy did not look back. She knew that if she did and saw her mother ostensibly abandoned, she would be lost. It was one thing to defy, it was another to win *any* argument with Millicent Gaylord.

'What am I going to do with her, Toni?' she asked her sister despairingly that evening, as Billy and Junior Standish discussed the merits of the Rolls Royce versus the Bentley on the other side of the coffee table. 'She has set her mind against Billy and nothing I can do or say will make her change it.'

'But that's mother all over. Her opinions are rarely changed once formed.'

'I thought she'd be so pleased with another wedding to organise, and to have me off the shelf again,' Livy said. 'It must be because he's Jewish, yet I would never have said Mother was prejudiced. Daddy had a host of Jewish friends.'

'Billy is also English. You will be living a long way away.'

'Billy spends a lot of time over here. We'll be back and forth all the time.'

'She'll come round eventually,' Toni said. 'You'll see.'

But to her sister Cordelia she said: 'Do you think Livy will be happy with Billy?'

'Of course. She is in seventh heaven. Billy denies her nothing. If ever I saw a man in love it is Billy Bancroft. He positively *dotes* on her.'

'Well, she is giving him something he has craved all his life.'

Puzzled, for though Cordelia was intelligent she had not her sister's insight: 'What do you mean?' she asked.

'Haven't you noticed anything about Billy?'

'Like what?'

'His ambition.'

'Everyone knows about *that*!'

'I mean his social ambition. Haven't you noticed that all the people Billy knows over here; the people he sees, entertains, who entertain him, are all white, Anglo-Saxon protestants? There's not a Jew among them – well ... one. David Solomons, but Billy does a lot of business with him so the friendship is probably a calculated one.'

'Well, really!' Cordelia exclaimed in disapproving tones. 'I thought you of all people were Billy's champion. You knew him first, after all, and were the one who introduced him to Ward ...'

'Exactly,' Toni said.

Frowning: 'You mean – that was what he wanted you to do?'

'Among other things.'

'Well!' Cordelia said again, uncomfortably, before veering away from that particular no-woman's-land. 'Mind you, he has been very helpful to Ward. One thing I will say for Billy is that he never forgets his friends.'

'Not the ones who matter, anyway.' Toni's smile was of the kind that would cut glass.

'I thought you liked him,' Cordelia said in dismay. Toni had always appeared to have a very free and easy friendship with Billy Bancroft. She had been the one to bring him into their circle, and he had been very agreeable, anything but pushy. Billy also had contacts that were worth their weight in pure platinum, and his advice was of the kind you could rely on. He was also the absolute in discretion. Once Billy knew a thing it sank without trace. Cordelia thought that Livy was extremely fortunate to be marrying such a paragon.

The wedding took place on a balmy August evening in the twelve-roomed 'cottage' on the Winslow Estate which Edward Winslow had presented as a gift to his mother-in-law some years before. Livy's dress was a triumph and on her dark hair she wore a wreath of apricot-coloured roses to match her engagement ring. Her wedding ring was a double plait of gold which, Billy said, had belonged to his Polish great-grandmother.

The reception was held out on the lawns, though there were not that many people present; only the respective families and their children and a handful of their closest friends. The atmosphere was relaxed, almost informal, though Billy was formally dressed in a dark grey suit. He seemed unable to take his eyes off his bride, who glowed in her champagne coloured dress. They fed each other pieces of the wedding cake, and posed for photographs taken by Livy's friend Richard Avedon.

Millicent, resplendent in flowered silk and a straw hat trimmed with matching silk flowers, looked thoroughly pleased, no matter what she felt. But her ten-year-old grand-daughter Rosalind, who stuck close to her maternal grandmother (her paternal grandmother had declined to put in an appearance, offering her failing health as an excuse: a blatant lie since Dolly Randolph had the constitution of a pampered ox), did not bother to hide her dislike of the proceedings, though her brother John had no reservations and enjoyed himself thoroughly with his Winslow and Lancaster cousins.

The newlyweds left in a shower of rose-petals to drive to New York, where they would spend their wedding night at the Plaza before leaving on the *United States* for a honeymoon to be spent in Europe, some of it in the Mediterranean on the yacht of Aristotle Onassis, who was a good friend of Billy's.

By the end of 1968 they were established in London in a large house in Chester Square. Livy was decorating it to her taste, which meant gutting it from top to bottom and starting from the bare walls up. It cost a fortune, but Billy gave her a blank cheque. He himself was making money hand over fist, diversifying his holdings and expanding an investment portfolio which was tended diligently by the senior partner and specialist staff of a firm of stockbrokers who did nothing else.

Billy was also cock-a-hoop because his wife was pregnant. Only the Queen's obstetrician was good enough for Lady Bancroft, for Billy proved to be a nervous expectant father. He planned for a daughter; never referred to the expected offspring as anything else but 'her' and when Livy, after a Caesarean ordered by her obstetrician since the baby was big and she was narrow, gave birth to an eight-and-a-half-pound girl, he was, as she observed amusedly: 'Like a dog with two tails.'

'Never mind that,' Billy grinned proudly, 'I did all right with the one I've got, didn't I?'

Once Livy would have blushed, but she knew better now. She was also relieved that Billy had got what he wanted. She already had experience of what he was like when he didn't. So she watched him hanging besottedly over the hand-made, be-frilled and be-ribboned cot of his daughter and thanked her lucky stars.

She also let him have his way over his daughter's name. She would have liked to continue her father's tradition and name the child Beatrice, but Billy said: 'Beatrice Bancroft! God, no! It sounds like some silent movie star. Her name is Diana ... Diana Frances.'

When, years later, another girl born in the sixties and given the same names became the Princess of Wales, Billy smiled and shrugged. 'Told you,' was all he said.

As it was he made a big production of the christening, which was performed by a bishop in a fashionable church with much pomp and circumstance, the baby wearing a White House original of pure white silk organza and Brussels lace, carried by her Norland nanny and slumbering peacefully throughout the proceedings. Her godparents were Edward and Cordelia Winslow, Lord Benwell, a recently ennobled publishing tycoon, Lady Margaret Devenish, a new friend of Livy's who was an Extra-Lady-in-in-Waiting to Her Majesty the Queen, and the Earl and Countess of Morpeth, with whom Billy was negotiating to buy Morpeth House in St. James, since the Earl, who had recently inherited, was having to stump up several million pounds in death duties.

'Every little helps,' he told his unforthcoming wife. 'Not only times have changed, so has society. One has got to be on good terms with people like Billy Bancroft these days, because they are the only ones with enough money to keep it going.'

His wife's aristocratic nostrils flared. 'At least he has a presentable wife, even if she is American.'

The christening was duly photographed and written up for *Tatler*.

'Told you,' Toni Standish murmured to herself, as she read it later. 'Not a Star of David to be seen ...' But she sent the magazine to her mother who, having become a martyr to arthritis, had been advised not to undertake the long journey.

Millicent read it with a glow of pleasure so intense it eased her pain no end. Obviously she had been wrong about her son–in–law. In the photograph, Livy's smile was radiant; she looked *happy*. Being Lady Bancroft evidently agreed with her. What more, she thought luxuriously, could any mother ask?

Millicent's pre–wedding doubts however had proved to be founded on fact. Livy may have looked happy, but it was not how she felt, and had her mother not been 3,000 miles away but able to look at her daughter in the flesh, she would have seen the first signs of strain. Being Lady Bancroft was no sinecure, and more than once Livy had cause to be grateful to her mother's intensive training, honed by the practice received during her tenure as Mrs John Peyton Randolph. Even then she found that in Billy Bancroft she had met her master.

He was obsessive about quality. He expected his needs not only to be met but anticipated. He was a martinet when it came to timekeeping. He expected his whims to be catered for, and his mercurial changes of mood and decision to be accepted without question. Above all, he expected his wife to be perfectly presented at all times, even first thing in the morning.

Not for Livy the peignoir or dressing gown, no matter how exquisite or beautifully tailored. In Billy's households, everyone was present and dressed for eight o'clock and breakfast was a meal as perfectly cooked and elegantly presented as any dinner. And Billy liked an English breakfast. Bacon, scrambled eggs – and Livy went through a plethora of cooks until she found the one who could match Billy's specifications for them – one perfectly grilled tomato, mushrooms fried in unsalted butter, and a slice of granary bread likewise fried, but this time in olive oil. The oil had to be Italian, from a certain grove which, to ensure a steady supply, he bought. He drank Jamaican Blue Mountain coffee, and owned a small plantation on the island which supplied nobody but him. You were well in with Billy if he presented you with a bag of his very own coffee beans. He drank his first cup black, and he liked big cups, so Livy always used the Spode Blue Italian china for breakfast. His second cup he drank with the top of the milk from a freshly opened bottle of Channel Islands milk from Jersey cows: again, the dairy supplied him specially. Livy would sit at her place at the table, and although for years her breakfast had been no more than a cup of sinfully black coffee, she now usually played with a croissant, silently, because while Billy expected her to join him at breakfast he did not talk to her. He read his *Times* instead. Only when he had eaten his breakfast and Livy had poured, milked and sweetened (one half-teaspoonful exactly of molasses sugar) his second cup of coffee, did he talk. Which was usually to issue instructions. As to what he would be doing that day and where; about what he would like for dinner should there be a dinner party that night – and there usually was. Billy entertained lavishly, though he was difficult to reach at other times. Few people had his private telephone number, and once he had left the house for the day his time was his own and only a dire emergency would excuse his being disturbed by a domestic concern.

While Livy had always considered herself, as did everyone else, to have excellent taste in clothes, she soon learned that she had also to match up to her husband's exacting standards.

She bought her wardrobe in Paris. Even though Livy had enough money of her own to be able to afford the very best, Billy gave her a dress allowance. He did not like her using what he termed 'her Randolph money' now she was his wife. He was the provider; he suggested she invest the millions Johnny had left her in trust for Rosalind and Johnny. Livy took his advice but for a small fund – about quarter of a million dollars annually – which she called her 'mad money'; to be spent on frivolities and trifles or whatever her fancy lighted on. Billy knew nothing of this, and she was careful to attribute anything she bought with it and he commented favourably on, as being bought with his money.

Livy ran the various Bancroft households, always subject to Billy's final and absolute authority. By the time she was pregnant with their second child, they had four: Morpeth House in St. James, Winslow House on 5th Avenue at 85th Street which Billy had bought from his brother-in-law once Ward and Delia had decided that it was far too big for just themselves now that their children had left home; Wychwood, an Elizabethan manor house deep in the Cotswolds on the Oxfordshire/Gloucestershire border, and the single-storey villa which Billy had had designed specially for him, set on a cliff overlooking the Caribbean on a small private island – which he also owned – about three sea miles from Nassau, in the Bahamas. Livy had it decorated in shades of blue and white, a cool contrast to the vivid intensity of the sea, with rattan couches complete with deep cushions on which guests could stretch out on the shaded veranda which ran right round the house. To receive an invitation to Clifftops was to be honoured; only the closest and most intimate of friends and relatives got invited there. And always in the winter, to escape the rigours of the New York or London weather.

Early in 1970 Livy brought her mother down, hoping the sunshine would be good for her increasingly painful arthritis. Millicent had not been well for some time, so Billy sent his private plane for her, and she was winched aboard it in her motorised wheelchair, but Livy was alarmed when she saw how much her mother had aged. Millicent had lost a great deal of weight; she was drawn and her skin seemed to be tinged with grey. A natural stoic, she was not one to always be running to the doctor, but Livy called her own in New York and asked him to come down and see just what was wrong.

'Such a fuss over nothing,' Millicent grumbled. 'I am getting on, that's all it is. I am seventy-two years old, and aches and pains are to be expected at my time of life.'

But Livy's doctor, after a preliminary examination, said he would like certain tests done, so Millicent was flown to Miami where, after several days of tests and a biopsy, it was ascertained that she had an ineradicable cancer of the stomach and at the most, three months to live.

Livy's fourth pregnancy was a bad one. She had never had

a trouble-free one but she had always before been able to give herself up to the ministrations of other people and let herself be cosseted, wrapped in the softest and purest of cotton wool, spending a good deal of her time in bed.

Her mother's condition came as a terrible shock to her, and brought with it a constant nausea and faintness. At first Billy was immensely supportive; he brought her little surprise gifts, turned her room into a bower of flowers, engaged a nurse to look after her. But Livy did not want this; she wanted the strength to be with her mother for the last months of her life.

'Sweetheart, this is ridiculous,' he told her, in that oh-so-reasonable tone of voice she read as a warning amber light. 'You are not well enough. The best thing is to let your mother go into hospital ... I'll arrange for a suite in the Harkness – '

'My mother will not die among strangers,' Livy said, tight-lipped. 'She will die among her family.'

'Then let her go to Delia or Toni ... you are pregnant and in no state to cope with a dying woman.'

'She wants to stay here, with me.'

'Your mother has more commonsense than to inflict herself on you at a time like this. She needs proper care and attention and quite frankly, a good hospital is the right place to find it, not a house on an island in the Caribbean.'

'When the time comes I will get her into the right hospital. Until then, she stays where she wants to stay – which is with me!'

Livy was distraught, otherwise she would have seen the look which came over Billy's face, recognised the shrug, the edge to his voice when he said: 'As you wish.' That it was not his wish he made plain by leaving the island next day in the plane that had been sent to bring Livy's sisters.

'A prior business engagement I simply cannot get out of,' he told them smoothly.

'Of course,' Cordelia nodded understandingly. She was used to that with her own husband, but Toni thought: Considering you had, according to Livy, made sure you had a whole series of blank pages in your diary before you even left London, where has this one come from?

Livy answered her question when Toni went in to see her, shocked at how drawn her sister looked, even though she was her usual elegant self in a wonderful Japanese kimono of brilliantly coloured silk, with her hair – which she found she could not bear to have anyone fiddling with – bound up Caribbean style in an equally brilliant silk square. Her face was exquisitely made up but underneath the maquillage her face was that of a woman struggling to come to terms with something unpleasant.

'Has Billy gone?' she asked, after greeting her sisters.

'Yes,' Cordelia said. 'Such a pity, but I know how it is … I've lost count of the times when I've had something arranged and Ward had to beg off because something came up. Especially since he's been Ambassador …'

But Toni was monitoring her sister's face closely and saw the flicker in the shadowed eyes, noted the tenseness of the mouth as she asked: 'Have you seen mother?'

'She's resting. Later, her nurse said.'

Livy nodded. 'She is spending more and more of her time asleep. I'm glad.'

'And you. How are you, darling?'

'I've been better … I can't seem to stop being sick no

matter what I do.' An appealing shrug and a small moue that said, 'You know how it is.' 'Billy hates it … he hates any sort of illness. His instant reaction is to have you taken to hospital but you can't very well do that with a pregnancy; not for nine whole months … Poor darling, he just can't cope with my being ill … it upsets him so.'

Upsets his schedule, more like, Toni thought. And since when was pregnancy an illness anyway? It's mother. He doesn't want to be around her. She's the one he wanted to be taken away to hospital, out of sight and – where he is concerned anyway – out of mind. I'll bet we don't see him again until the funeral.

'I'm glad you are here.' Livy said tremulously. 'Family is all I want right now. No other visitors… not while I feel so low …'

'Of course, darling. We'll keep everyone away.' So they won't remark on Billy's absence.

But once Toni saw her mother, she understood why Billy had fled the field. Her mother had been marked by death. In the three weeks since Toni had last seen her she had deteriorated alarmingly. Her dark eyes, so like Livy's, were huge and sunken, and the hand she held out to her daughter was skeletal in its lack of flesh, curiously fragile in spite of the big bones. She must have lost forty pounds! Toni thought, appalled. And when she spoke her strong vibrant voice was no more than a whisper. 'All … together … now,' she said, making an effort to smile.

Two days later she began to have difficulty in breathing, in spite of the oxygen that was administered; a plane came to take her to hospital in Miami, and she died there, quietly, in her deeply sedated sleep, during the early hours of the following morning. Her three daughters and two of her sons-in-law were with her. Billy arrived next day, after the body had been taken to the mortuary, visibly upset and tender with concern for his wife, who looked at him but did not seem to see him.

But at the funeral she was all that he could have wished. Her black coat, cut so as to conceal her pregnancy, now in its fourth month, was heartbreaking in its simple elegance, as was her small hat with its half-veil. And although the funeral was private, somehow or other – and though Livy never mentioned it she knew exactly how – a photographer from one of the glossies managed to capture several shots of Lady Bancroft, leaning on her husband's arm as they walked back to their car after the committal.

After that, Livy went back to England and into seclusion for the rest of her pregnancy. David Gaylord Bancroft was born, again by Caesarian, in a London nursing home after complications due to eclampsia. He was tiny, with breathing problems, for something had indeed gone wrong early on, and he had not been receiving enough nourishment. He was placed in an incubator and it was three months before Livy was allowed to take him home. And not because the doctors counselled her not to. It was because Billy did not want a sickly baby disrupting his routine.

4

Livy took a long time to recover from David's birth, and she was advised not to undertake any further pregnancies. She was content to accept the advice. She was not one of those women who looked on pregnancy as a gift from God. Hers had invariably been something to be endured. Always a fragile creature, she knew she lost her swan-like elegance so long as her body was grotesquely swollen, though she always wore exquisite drifts of caftans to disguise the fact, and spent most of her time on a chaise-longue with a light coverlet over her, to further disguise what Billy considered, she had painfully come to realise, her ugliness. During her pregnancies, from the moment they were confirmed he never touched her, forcing her to face the fact that with a sex drive like his he had to be satisfying it elsewhere. The jewels he showered on her after the birth of his son and daughter were, she knew, not so much for giving *them* to him, as for giving back herself – the long, slender, breathtakingly elegant self he wanted. It had not taken many months of marriage to him to understand why.

Billy was a narcissist. Whatever was done – by him or by

anyone else – had to reflect favourably on him, and if it did not, his displeasure could be extreme. He demanded that his life run on oiled wheels, but he did not expect to be the one to see that it did. That was Livy's job. And she was – had to be – very good at it. It was the main reason he had married her, and because Livy was both proud and had high standards herself, and was a little afraid of Billy, it was more than her life was worth to be found wanting – even if it meant neglecting the children.

Not that Livy would have seen it as neglect. The warmth and almost cosiness of her own childhood and marriage to Johnny were long gone and presumably forgotten. As long as her children looked presentable, behaved properly, and kept out of Billy's way when he was not in the mood, however many governesses and nannies it took to ensure this Livy felt she was fulfilling her obligations as their mother.

Billy was a distant father; emotionally and physically. In all their houses he insisted that the children had their own wing, and as soon as the two Randolphs were old enough they were sent away to school – in America, since Dolly Randolph was still alive and as always a powerful influence where anything Randolph was concerned. Billy did not mind; he never minded anything which emanated from somebody as High-WASPish as Dolly Randolph.

His own sons from his first marriage were ciphers who moved only to their father's jerk on their strings; after coming down from Oxford they took up jobs in one of his companies; one in the capacity of an accountant the other managerial. They had their own homes and both were married by the time they were twenty-five; quietly and without any publicity. Billy's wedding present to each was a house, fully furnished down to the last coffee spoon, and bought and paid for (excepting the token mortgage for tax purposes.) Livy wondered at the time what the wives thought about such arbitrary selection of their homes, but as nothing was ever said – in her presence anyway – she could only assume that they were happy to accept the dictates of the Benevolent Autocrat, as Rosalind had nicknamed him.

Livy had always held the impression that the twins were terrified of their father; that his wrath was something they would do anything to avoid. It was not until she came up against it herself for the first time that she understood why.

Livy had created in all their houses, as Billy had known she would, the perfect setting, and in the first years of their marriage he used to come home early from the office to find her waiting for him, freshly bathed and perfumed and dressed in such a way as to make his eyes kindle. She would have the drinks tray ready, and pour him a glass of his favourite single malt, no water, no ice, and he would sit in the chair opposite hers, sipping it while he told her about his day, or as much as he wanted her to know.

Livy loved those pre-dinner tête-à-têtes; her mother had told her how important they were, and she had thought Billy loved them too. But in the months after her mother's death, the last months of her pregnancy with David, as her delicate body became heavy and clumsy, Billy ceased to arrive home at around six. It became seven, sometimes eight; often he did not arrive home at all and an impersonal message would be telephoned by Miss Penworthy, his long-time personal secretary, to say that Sir William had been unavoidably detained.

Then one night, after he had promised to be home on time (she had made a point of asking him to) he had come home even earlier than expected. The slam of the door ought to have warned her, but she was distracted and when Billy did not come into her sitting room as usual, she went looking for him. She found him in his dressing room, in the act of changing to go out again, his valet busy inserting into a dress shirt the black pearl studs that had been her Christmas present to him.

'Billy ...' She began instinctively to protest.

'Now what?' His barely contained rage was a further warning which in her fretful state she failed to recognise, or the way Billy jerked his head at his valet who silently left.

'I thought you were coming home to spend some time with me. Now here you are going out yet again. I hardly ever see you any more. You are up and out of the house early and never come back until late ...' Fraught nerves and hours of lonely brooding took her close to the verge of the tears which came so easily lately.

'For Christ's sake!' Billy snarled, before turning a face on her which had her clutching at the door jamb. 'What the hell is there to come back for, tell me that? You looking like death, for ever clutching a handkerchief to your lips and needing to be heaved out of your chair? What the hell would a man want to come home to that for?'

Livy recoiled, while from her throat came a cry the like of which she had not believed she was capable. Turning, she stumbled blindly away from him, running as best as her lumbering bulk would allow but inevitably catching her foot in her caftan and stumbling. Only Billy's hand – for he had followed her – saved her from sprawling her length. His grip was powerful as he raised her upright and the look on his face was anxious, but she read it now with fully open eyes, which perceived that his concern was not for her but for the child she carried.

She said nothing. She could not, her heart was in her throat at her narrow escape and the enormity of what she had just discovered.

'Look,' Billy said abruptly, 'perhaps its best we keep out of each other's way until all this is over, eh? You know you can have whatever you want, whoever you want ... the place is full of servants, or why not ask one of your sisters to come and stay for a while. Once it is all over then things can get back to normal, hmmm?' She saw his eyes surreptitiously go to his watch. 'This is not man's work,' he attempted humour, 'my work was done back at the very beginning. The rest is up to you. All I can do is see that you get whatever you need to cope with it, and you know that means *anything*.' His dark brown eyes held a glow she now, with her brand new eyes, recognised as the one which appeared when he was striving for a show of sincerity.

'Except you,' Livy said.

The glow was switched off. 'You haven't heard a word I've said, have you?' he accused with a scowl.

'Oh, yes I have. That's the trouble ...' Drawing herself up to her full height, which was just that much taller than him, she said distantly, in full Olivia Gaylord Randolph mode: 'You have no need to concern yourself – even the little you are willing to show. I shall not trouble you again,' before turning her back on him and proceeding to sail, a top-heavy galleon, down the corridor back to her own suite. Once there, she shut the door behind her before sliding down it in a welter of tears, where she was rescued by her anxious maid, who put her to bed and then called her sister.

Once David was born, the old Billy, fulsome, expansive, proud and as fatherly as she could have wished, instantly replaced the coldly distant, don't-bother-me one. He showered her with presents, just as he had after Diana's birth; extolled her virtues as a mother to anyone within earshot, hung over his son's cot as if he did not already have twin sons who were now adults. This volte-face was accomplished without so much as a break in step; it was as though he was transmogrified by the words: 'You have a fine son, Sir William.'

Once Livy was up and about again he insisted that she clothe her newly regained elegance of body in an entirely new wardrobe. He despatched her to Paris with her sister Toni and gave her *carte-blanche* to spend until she dropped. When she came back he insisted she put on a fashion parade for him, and liking one dress in particular, a Balmain of turquoise pure silk-satin, he conferred with Bulgari who designed a necklace, bracelet and matching earrings in turquoise and pearls interspersed with diamonds. She wore them to the first big dinner they held six weeks after her return to Society.

Life was back in its smooth, well-oiled groove and Billy was once more his attentive self to the Livy he demanded her to be; the one capable of silencing a crowded room merely by appearing in the doorway; or who could come down the stairs in a soft susurrus of black silk, interspersed with the soft tinkling of bells which she had had sewn in the ruffles of her skirt. The one whose picture appeared at least once a week in one or more of the glossies. The woman all other women copied and desperately tried to emulate. He was triumphantly proud to be the husband of this woman. But something had hardened in Livy, had died even: an imperceptible cooling and distancing visible to no one, not even most of the time to Billy himself. The lessons of the previous months had been hard, but as always the obedient pupil, she had learned them well. Livy knew that she could expect no support from Billy and she must never again put herself in the position of needing any.

Too late, she thought, to admit that when I married Billy I did not wish to look beneath the surface, see the man he really was. I have never been one for probing beneath the surfaces. Too many nasty things live there.

Now she realised that Billy had known this when he was courting her. Instead of her playing him, teasing him with Larry, he had manipulated her. By the time he asked her to marry him she was beginning to worry that he might not. So, the other Livy said on a shrug, that's the way it is, and that is the way it always will be. Either you take Billy as he is, or you don't take him at all.

No! NO! I am not going back to *that*. Look at Sally Remington now, living with the twenty-six-year-old drummer of a pop group! She shuddered. Being married to Billy was no picnic but living Sally's kind of life was far, far worse. 'Poor Sally,' was how people referred to her now.

Is that what you want? To be 'poor Livy'?

No! A thousand times, *no*! Anything but that!

Then stop whining. Make an 'accommodation'. Isn't that what Toni says life is all about? All right, so it is a first, since up until now you have always expected life to make its accommodation with you, but make it you must. Or else …

Johnny did. I see that now. Whatever I wanted … That was his motto. And I blithely thought that naturally he wanted the same things. If he didn't he was too well brought up to say so. Billy is neither well brought up nor afraid to say so. He calls the shots this time around.

On a sigh: truth to tell, Olivia, you are right out of ammunition …

Things between them continued on an even keel for a while; Billy's mood was sunny and Livy's reputation was in the ascendant. Until she discovered him in the midst of an affair with a twenty year old.

It was her sister Cordelia's twentieth wedding anniversary, and Toni and Livy had planned a surprise party to be held in Morpeth House, which was big enough to hold all the people they wished to invite. Billy had amiably agreed to whatever Livy had in mind – his mood of late had been unexpectedly benign.

Until on the Friday afternoon. While Livy was in the midst of her detailed preparations, she was summoned to the telephone. It was Billy.

Removing one of her large, shell-shaped gold and coral earrings before putting the receiver to her ear: 'Have you forgotten to tell me something?' Livy asked. It was a trick of Billy to make last minute amendments, and it infuriated her, since she was always organised down to the last detail.

'As a matter of fact I have; something I arranged some time ago for tonight. You'll have to go ahead without me.'

'But everything has been arranged with you as part of it!' Livy was outraged. She had spent weeks on this dinner party and the reception to follow. She had made every arrangement to his taste and now he was leaving her high and dry to do the whole thing herself.

'It is supposed to be a party hosted by Antonia and Olivia Gaylord and their husbands for Cordelia Gaylord and her husband on the occasion of their twentieth wedding anniversary!' seethed Livy. 'How is it going to look if you are not there? And it plays havoc with my table plan!'

'Oh, you can fix that. You've done it before.'

'So why can't you be here, then? What is more important than this party?'

'A business arrangement – one I made some time ago. People I just have to see.'

'They can't be that important if you forgot about them!' Livy's by now well-tuned ear had caught the oh-so-brief hesitation before his answer; the one which signalled that it was a lie. It was a habit of Billy's she was by now familiar with. He had no idea he did it and she was not about to enlighten him. She had few enough advantages as it was.

'Who are they? Do I know them?' she demanded.

'I don't think you've met them … Harry Dennison and his wife Lucy and her sister … Carol, I think her name is. Harry is a big man in computers and the market for them is about to take off. I want to get in on the ground floor.'

As well as his wife's sister's bed, Livy thought, icy with rage, seeing all, understanding all. The casual 'Carol, I think her name is' had given the game away. Billy was a master at prevarication but when he was on a sexual hunt, a peculiar timbre roughened his voice when he had to say the name of

89

the object of his pursuit. It had sounded when he'd spoken the name 'Carol'.

'So, these ... Dennisons ... are more important than your own family? I seem to remember you thought it was a wonderful idea to celebrate a marriage as happy as Cordelia's, and you are always so admiring of Ward – '

'I'll try and join you later in the evening at the reception – if I can. Why do you have to argue about every goddamned thing?' His voice had taken on a note of cold anger Livy recognised.

But: 'Why do I always have to do the changing?' she demanded angrily, hurting.

'Because I say so,' was the answer, followed by a clunk and the burr of a broken connection. Livy stared at it disbelievingly. 'Bastard,' she whispered. 'Son-of-a-bitching bastard!'

So he was having an affair again. Until now she had refused to recognise the signs, which had become so humiliatingly familiar during her pregnancies: the sudden affability which could just as suddenly turn vicious, the overly casual manner, the secretive telephone conversations behind closed doors, the glassy stares. It was not jealousy she felt – she knew she had not one tenth of Billy's sexual voraciousness; since the babies her desire for sex, never strong at the best of times, had all but gone – it was resentment that he should think her such a fool as not to suspect.

But that night, resplendant in swirling chiffon in three shades of pink; shocking, pastel and rose, diamonds at her throat and in her ears, her figure once more slender, nobody would have said other than that Olivia Gaylord Randolph Bancroft was fully in control; of herself, her household, this fabulous party. She was the perfect hostess, making the perfect apology for her husband's absence with just the right small moue of the mouth and a shrug of the shoulders that said: 'Oh, Billy … we all know Billy, don't we … nothing must come before business …' If people knew otherwise they looked away before the implacable challenge in her eyes. Nothing was said, then or later, in her presence, about the fact that she was married to a tom cat of prodigious appetite. So she gracefully made the speech that Billy was to have delivered. There was nothing more he could do to her now that she could not withstand, for she had suffered enough humiliation and grief to inure her to anything. She thought.

There was worse to come.

It began with a crumpled scrap of paper found in the pocket of one of Billy's suits which she was sending to a Nearly New Shop in Sloane Street. All his suits were made by Huntsman and she considered them far too good for Oxfam. But this particular suit was not one she remembered ever having seen before. It was off the peg, for one thing, and when she looked at the label she saw it bore the familiar St. Michael label of Marks & Spencer.

Livy yielded to no one in her admiration of a chain-store she considered – as did just about everyone else – to be the best in the world, but Sir William Bancroft never bought his suits there. Added to which it was black. Billy never wore black. Except to funerals. And even then it was never a true black but a grey so dark as to appear black.

She checked the other three suits he had told her to dispose of. At any one time he never had more than a dozen in his wardrobe; when he acquired new ones he always made room for them by discarding an equal number. The other three to be disposed of now had all been made in Savile Row.

What was an off-the-peg suit doing in his wardrobe? When – if ever – had he worn it? Not in his wife's presence, that was for sure. He was as particular about his clothes as he was about everything else. The Billy she knew would not be seen dead in chain-store tailoring, no matter how excellent. So what was he doing with this one? Even the cut was different. The cloth was of excellent quality but it was one of many; not a one-off.

She picked up the crumpled piece of paper, smoothed it out, saw it was a receipt. The letter-heading was that of a private nursing home in the north of Scotland. It said that payment had been received in full concerning the late Yetta Feldman, and it was dated 1967. The year she had become Lady Bancroft.

Yetta! Livy's flesh crisped.

According to Toni (for Billy had never spoken to his second wife of his first other than as 'my wife') that was the name of the first Mrs Bancroft. But Feldman? Livy had never heard that name before. Perhaps it had been her maiden name, and she had reverted after their divorce.

About which Livy knew nothing, except that it had all been settled in the month Billy had spent in England prior to their engagement. When she had ventured to question him about his first marriage he had said only that it had been a mistake; made when he was too young to realise its consequences. The way he said it made it clear she was never to mention it again. For a while she had wondered if she might do better if she casually asked the twins, but once she got to know them she realised that they were much too

92

circumspect to say anything to their father's second wife about his first.

She had occasionally (very occasionally considering they were Billy's sons) dined in their houses, where there were no framed photographs of their mother, only their father, and then always at one or other of his public triumphs. Outside Buckingham Palace in morning dress, displaying his KCB; showing the Queen round one of his many industrial developments, which she had just opened; visiting the new studios of the independent television company in which he held the major shareholding (and a licence to print money) as well as the honorary title of Chairman; making a speech before the members of the CBI, and so on. And when Livy had been shown their personal photograph albums they were full of pictures of themselves; at school – Rugby, or university – Oxford; being married, or on holiday with their own children. There was not one picture of the first Mrs Bancroft. It was as though she had never existed.

Livy possessed a stack of her own thick, leather-bound photograph albums giving a pictorial record of Billy's second marriage. From the wedding itself through the christenings of their children, birthday parties, Christmas celebrations – Billy insisted that no family occasion should go unrecorded. Obviously, he had nothing to be ashamed about where his second wife was concerned. Which made her wonder what had been so unmentionable about his first. Why had all trace of her been totally obliterated? Had she been *that* awful?

Livy came back from her thoughts to find herself still holding the crumpled piece of paper. It seemed to her to be a pointer, presented to her for a reason, like following it up; finding out about Yetta Feldman, what she had been like, this woman who had been Billy's first wife. Livy had been so eager to marry Billy that she had accepted his every word as to the dissolution of his first marriage as gospel truth, telling herself that it had not been a real marriage anyway. How could it be with a wife who spent all her time in hospitals and private nursing homes? It was only now, after living with him, that she knew how truth, like everything else, was subject to his own particular interpretation.

But how to find out? If 'the late Yetta Feldman' had indeed been the first Lady Bancroft, how had she died, and where? There had to be ways of finding out; the trouble was that just about all of them were proscribed for somebody as well-known as Olivia Bancroft.

Her first thought was to employ a private detective, until she realised that she would be giving him ammunition for future blackmail. As Caesar's wife she could not afford the luxury of paying someone else to do her dirty work. Especially if what was discovered turned out to be unsavoury or in some way injurious to Billy's reputation. The consequences – for herself as well as Billy – had her shuddering.

But she could not bring herself to put a match to the piece of paper – the only safe way to get rid of it. It was important, she knew it. It was the key to unlock a part of Billy's life about which she, or anyone else who knew him now, knew nothing. And then she remembered Petticoat Lane. That one time Billy had taken her down there; introduced her to people whose names she no longer remembered since she had neither seen or heard of them again, but who had, it seemed, all known him a long time. Especially that little man with the dress shop ... Small, plump, effusive ... Jacob! Yes, that was it. Jacob. But Jacob what? That was gone. But she remembered his shop; all the dresses hung up outside, everyone of them a glitter with rhinestones and paillettes. She could find him again, she felt sure. But she had to have a good excuse – a very good excuse – for looking him up after all this time. And she had to do it without Billy knowing.

It was not until a few days later, opening her mail one morning, when she drew out a square of engraved cardboard inviting Sir William and Lady Bancroft to a charity fancy dress ball, that she had the excuse she needed.

A week later Billy left on a business trip for Australia and the Far East. He would be away ten days. Now! Livy thought.

On the Sunday morning she left the house ostensibly to go to Winfield House to see her sister Cordelia, having put on the kind of clothes she never normally wore. Jeans, a white silk shirt and a navy-blue blazer. She also donned a pair of big black sunglasses and hid her hair under a Hermès silk scarf wrapped tight around her head and throat. But even then she was a figure of rapier-sharp elegance; one who would instinctively draw a second, lingering glance. She could not help it. It was innate in her; as natural as breathing. Finally, she took one of the Bancroft staff cars – a little Rénault 5 – and after checking the route in her copy of the London AZ street atlas, drove herself to Liverpool Street before walking the rest of the way.

The Lane was crowded at half past eleven on a Sunday morning, and the shop she remembered – Siegal's – yes! that had been his name ... Jacob Siegal ... was packed. She looked around and recognised him at the back of the shop, trying to convince an overweight blonde that the red dress she had squeezed into was just right for her. Livy pushed her way towards him, until she was close enough to listen to him extolling the virtues of his merchandise as she pretended to examine a black suit with extravagantly embroidered lapels.

The blonde didn't have a hope; Jacob made his sale, and having done so turned to Livy, still seemingly torn for choice. 'Now then ... a lady like you, with a figure like yours ... that suit is a godsend. It will fit you like the proverbial glove. Here, go and try it on ... see if you won't find it impossible to take off again!'

'Actually, it is not a suit I am looking for, Mr Siegal,' Livy said.

He looked at her sharply. 'You know me? How come I can't return the compliment?'

'We met once – briefly, a few years ago.' Livy took a deep breath and plunged. 'I was with Billy Banciewicz.'

'Billy! The great Sir William as he is now? You know him?'

'Yes.'

'He sent you to me?'

'In a way.'

'Billy always knew quality. Nothing but the best. All his life nothing but the very best. I've seen his wife – the present one, that is. Billy always could pick 'em.'

'Thank you,' Livy said.

Jacob Siegal looked sharply at her and then as she took off the dark glasses opened his mouth to recognise her vocally only to have Livy lay her finger to her own on a quick shake of the head. 'I am not supposed to be here,' she said very quietly. 'It is a surprise for my husband.'

Quickly she explained about the masquerade, showed the

invitation, her idea to go as someone who would really surprise her husband: someone from his past, perhaps. With the right dress, a wig, whatever additional props might be needed. It was to be a complete surprise.

'Surprise! It will shock him speechless,' Jacob said. Then in a different voice. 'Billy does not have anything to do with his past now. When he brought you here it was the first time in five years I had laid these eyes on him. Billy Banciewicz is now Sir William Bancroft and what has one to do with the other any more?'

Livy looked disconcerted. 'You think it would not be a good idea?' she probed, sounding disappointed.

Jacob shrugged. 'Who can tell how Sir William thinks – except that for sure it is as Sir William. You ask me how Billy Banciewicz thinks I can tell you; him I knew since his father sewed bespoke suits for a living; him I toasted at his first wedding.' Jacob's head wagged. 'To poor Yetta, God rest her soul. Such a sweet girl. Such a tragedy.'

'You knew her too?' Livy led where she hoped he would follow.

'Everybody knew Yetta Feldman. Her father owned most of the shops around here; I rented my first from him more than thirty years ago. She used to collect his rents. Such a pretty little thing, but delicate. Like a butterfly. Never the same after the twins were born.'

'Billy told me she was an invalid.'

Jacob lifted one shoulder in a shrug that spoke volumes, all with preface, index and comprehensive bibliography. 'Billy was too much for her. She got left behind.' He slid Livy a knowing look. 'And you know what people do when they feel they have been left behind.'

Livy said nothing; she could think of a dozen things. What she wanted to know was what Yetta Feldman had done.

'They find comfort somewhere else ...' Livy noted the *somewhere* rather than *someone*.

She must have looked puzzled because Jacob nodded and said: 'I thought as much. Billy was never one to advertise his failures. Yetta drank. Her solace was alcohol. And once she lost her sons –' Jacob shrugged. 'Naturally Billy wanted to give them the best; see they did not have to fight and struggle as he had. Yetta could never understand that, but Billy insisted they be given the choice. Their mother or him. No way could they have both, for by then Billy was on his way and nothing was going to stop him.' A sigh. 'Who can blame the boys for going with their father to his new world?'

'Their mother,' Livy said to herself. Jacob's eyes met hers then he spread his hands in the age-old gesture of, 'So what else is new?'

'Thank you for telling me,' Livy said, finally. 'I think you are right. My idea was not a good one. But I did not know ...'

'Why should you? You are Lady Bancroft. Yetta was Mrs Banciewicz.'

'Were you at her funeral?'

'No. She died in Scotland. She was in some private home there, you know the kind. We wouldn't have known at all except Billy had to tell Yetta's father, who was far too ill by then to attend the funeral. Billy saw to everything. Not six months later old Mr Feldman himself was dead. Heart. He'd been on digitalis for years.'

Livy felt her arm patted briskly. 'It is over. And Billy was never one for regrets. Believe me. Besides, he has you now. You are what he always wanted. Why else do you think he brought you down here? A place – a life – he had left behind a long time ago? It was to show us how far he had gone, the kind of wife he had now. Always he liked to wear his achievements where they could be seen.'

And hide his failures, Livy thought. Like an alcoholic wife. He did not divorce Yetta before he followed me to New York; he buried her.

Why? she pondered as she walked slowly back to her car. Why go through the charade of pretending to get a divorce? And then it hit her so hard that she stopped dead. Because she killed herself! Yetta Feldman committed suicide! She had lost everything that meant anything to her: her husband and her sons. What then had she to live for? *That's* why he told me he was divorced, not a widower. He wanted that can of worms left unopened. An alcoholic wife who killed herself would not look good in the newly created Family History of Sir William Bancroft.

Bemused and blinded by her flash of insight, Livy resumed her walk. She was instinctively certain she was right. Yetta had been hidden in a private nursing home hundreds of miles out of the way in the empty bleakness of northern Scotland. Under her maiden name. When she had died, it had all been handled very discreetly, Billy possessing the money and the power to see that there was absolutely no publicity. Nobody who might recognise him at her funeral. Probably nobody there *but* him. In a chain-store suit. Bought for the occasion then thrust to the back of a closet out of sight and out of mind until something brought it to light again when it was consigned for disposal.

Livy felt very cold suddenly. She had come to know Billy was ruthless, but this … this chilled her to the bone. He had figured it all out beautifully. All the pieces in place. Except for one. That overlooked receipt. Shoved deep down into the jacket pocket of a suit he would never wear again. Poor, forgotten Yetta. Why had Billy married her in the first place? The answer flashed onto the screen of her mind instantly. Money. What else? Her father had owned property. Jacob Siegal had been one of his tenants. Billy must have married her for her dowry. Jewish brides still had dowries, didn't they? It was no doubt hers which gave him his kick-start. Once he was off and running he did not need her any more.

Livy wanted to laugh; knew she dared not because it might lead to something far worse. Oh, Yetta Banciewicz had been an invalid all right. *Invalid* in every sense of the word.

What a cruel fate. And one she was determined would never be hers. Livy had learned many things since the first heady days as Lady Bancroft. And the most important – which if she had listened to Toni and her mother at the time would not have come as such a rude shock later – was that, as Olivia Gaylord Randolph, she gave Billy credence socially on both sides of the Atlantic; in her more honest moments she admitted that it was why he had married her.

You do have value, she told herself emphatically as she drove along the Embankment, great value. Hang on to that. And act accordingly. You may need Billy – for let's be honest here, another marriage does not appeal; God forbid you should end up like Sally Remington – but Billy needs you even more. The thought of losing his Winslow and Standish connections is not to be entertained for a second! No more 'my brother-in-law, Ward Winslow' or 'my brother-in-law the American Ambassador'. And what would Billy do if I deprived him of his seat at Ward's farewell luncheon party at Buckingham Palace? He would kill, that's what. You have a trump card, Livy. Don't play it; just flourish it at him every now and then. Show him a little tit for tat. If he wants the very best then give it to him, but make him pay for it. In the only way he knows how ...

Billy returned from Australia to find his wife waiting for him, smiling, elegant as only she knew how.

'Good trip, darling?' she asked, offering her cheek.

'I got what I wanted,' Billy said. 'I'm also starved. I have a distinct fancy for oysters. A dozen Colchester oysters and a pint of black velvet ...'

'Of course, darling,' Livy agreed serenely, consigning her planned dinner, – already being prepared – to oblivion. As Billy went upstairs to shower and change, Livy picked up the house telephone and pressed a button. A few minutes later the door to her sitting room opened. 'Ah, James,' she said. 'A little task for you ...'

She had found him in Harrods Food Hall, as she was pondering over the merits of rival brands of Earl Grey.

'That one,' a voice had said, with the absolute authority of One Who Knows. 'There really is no other.'

Livy had turned to face a tall, elegant Englishman in a well-cut suit that had once cost a great deal of money, many years ago, over a shirt that only upper-class Englishmen knew how to wear; wide red stripes and a stiff white collar. His trilby was that of the racing fraternity and his shoes were glacé-shiny. He had a long, narrow, ineffably well-bred face and the bored, clipped-vowel voice of the English aristocracy.

'Thank you,' Livy said. 'It is not for me. I am a coffee drinker but it is intended as a gift for someone who is something of a connoisseur.'

'Then quite definitely that one. It has not been mucked about with by adding jasmine or other appalling florals.' He smiled; his eyes, as blue as the stripes on the Union Jack, smiled too. 'Take my word for it,' he said.

'Oh, I do.' Livy knew authority when she met it.

'My family imported tea for Queen Anne; my great-great-grandfather Leigh spent most of his life in China.'

'I was there last year with my husband; he was part of a trade delegation. I'm Olivia Bancroft.'

'I know,' he said. 'My name is James Luttrell-Leigh.' They shook hands.

'If you know me, should I know you?' Livy hazarded. She met so many people, but surely she would not have forgotten this man.

'We did meet once, briefly, but some years ago, before I went abroad this last time. You were living in Chester Square.'

Livy nodded, smiling at him, liking what she saw. He was about her own age, give or take a few years, and he still had the tan of hot climes. 'Where have you been – out of England, I mean?' she asked.

'Africa.'

'More tea?'

'No. Coffee.'

'Ah, now that I know about.'

102

'Then may I invite you to partake of a cup?' Livy liked the humour that lurked behind the cultured voice. Something told her that here was a kindred soul. 'I should be delighted,' she answered truthfully.

Upstairs, in the pink-tableclothed restaurant, she discovered more about him. His family was ancient but no longer rich, their once vast land-holding now sold off to pay a disastrous series of death duties, their highly profitable tea warehouses long confiscated by the Chinese government when the Communists took over. But he was extremely well connected, and to most of the families in *Debrett*. After Eton and Oxford there was the army – the Household Cavalry – but three years of that had been enough, added to which it was more than he could really afford, so after resigning his commission he had taken what jobs had come his way. He had travelled extensively, done just about everything. Before Africa he had been in India – jute; in Hong Kong – a bank; in Brazil – beef; in Australia – sheep.

They discovered they knew the same people; that James' eldest sister was married to a Montfort, who were English cousins of Ward Winslow; that James knew people in New York, Philadelphia and Boston whom Livy knew. He was home from Kenya after a three-year contract and, for the nonce, relatively flush. 'Nothing to spend one's money on in Kenya now; not like the old Happy Valley days.'

He held Livy rapt, with sparkling eyes and caught breath, as he related gossipy tales of the life his father's younger brother – the then black sheep of the family – had led there in the decade between 1930 and 1940 before it all came to an end under the double blow of the war and the murder of the Earl of Erroll.

103

Livy was so taken with him that she invited him to lunch next day, and since he had seemed to be something of a gourmet – he was as knowledgeable about food as he was about everything else – she ordered with care. She had an idea in mind which, the more she thought about it, the more she liked. If Billy didn't ... well, too bad. Just turn over your trump card, she reminded herself.

When she put it to James over the salmon-trout *en gelee* he did not hesitate. 'What a splendid idea,' he agreed. 'I was hoping to find something that would let me stay in England for a while. One can become surfeited on expatriates.'

'You would not find it – demeaning, in any way?'

'To be P.A. to the wife of Sir William Bancroft? Good heavens, no! Anyway, I cannot afford such "niceties." One has to live, after all, and I have no doubt that being part of the Bancroft ménage will be interesting, to say the least. Not many people lead lives of such positively sybaritic luxury in this day and age. The only comparison I can make is with the Mountbattens before the war. Edwina was a good friend of my mother's.'

Livy filed that away for future use should Billy prove difficult, but went on to make clear just who James would be working for. 'You would be assisting me rather than my husband. He has his own P.A. – two, in fact. I need your exclusive services to make my own job running things that much easier. You obviously know your way around and where to get just about anything.'

'I do know an awful lot of people,' James admitted modestly. 'One does get to know them, you know, at school and university and suchlike. Then there are one's relations ... I seem to have a plethora of them.' He helped himself to more salmon and nodded to the butler's offer of a second glass of Montrachet.

When they were alone again: 'My husband is a very demanding man,' Livy admitted candidly. 'He expects whatever he orders without fumbling or excuses. If there is absolutely no hope of fulfilling his wishes then so be it; there are some things beyond even me, but it is my job to see that there are very few such lapses. I think you could be of enormous help – in steering me in the proper directions, answering questions, giving me information, making suggestions. You would have your own quarters – bedroom, sitting room and bathroom, and I would provide you with a car. And a commensurate salary, of course.'

'How commensurate?'

Livy named a figure, at which he raised his eyebrows. 'Commensurate indeed,' he murmured. His mischievous smile danced. 'When would you like me to move in?'

He had done so that very night, arriving by cab with two battered but still beautiful Asprey leather trunks, a set of golf clubs in the same condition – 'belonged to my father' – and an ancient portable typewriter. 'Do a bit of writing in my spare time.'

He approved of his 'suite', on the first floor above that of the Bancrofts, and by the time he had bestowed what he called his 'bits and pieces' which included, Livy noted, several family photographs framed in heavy silver, a lot of books, and a collection of native art from each and every country he had worked in, he looked as though he had been there for years. After his first week it seemed as though he had. He was invaluable. He knew where to find anything and everything; he was attentive, capable, a mine of information on the most esoteric things and best of all, he made Livy laugh. The day before Billy was due back, her sister Toni dropped in on her way to Paris, took one look at James, rounded her eyes, pursed her lips and said: 'Well, well, you sly puss ... *Where* did you find *him*?'

'He found me. In the Food Hall at Harrods.'

'I know they can supply *anything*, but this is going some even for them! Put me out of my misery, for God's sake. Tell me all!'

'Nothing to tell ... I thought it was about time I had a right hand, that's all. Somebody to share some of the load I've been carrying alone. Billy has assistants by the dozen, so I did not see why I should not have one.'

'Of course,' Toni agreed, in such a way as to have her sister saying calmly: 'And you can take that look off your face. James is a homosexual.'

Toni's face changed.

'He made it perfectly clear from the start. No false pretences, he said.' In a lower voice: 'I think that is the real reason he has been abroad these past twelve years.'

Toni laughed. 'Hasn't he heard that in England, homo-sexual acts between consenting adults have been legal since 1967? It's not often the English get the march on us, but I have to say that in this one respect back home we are still in the dark ages.' Toni sighed. '*What* a waste. He is the kind of Englishman one reads about but meets so seldom. A dying breed. You have not forgotten how Billy feels about queers?'

'James is not a queer. That word brings to mind all sorts of horridly effeminate little men like your friend Truman Capote. James is not attracted to women sexually, that's all. He says it starts at school ... evidently all English public

106

schools are hotbeds of homosexuality. And Billy will suffer a queer if he is of the right kind. Look at Tom Driberg, he is notorious yet he and Billy are thick as thieves. James happens to be the real McCoy. His elder brother is the sixteenth Viscount Chelm, but I rather think James is the black sheep of his family.'

'He can be pink with purple stripes as far as Billy's concerned if he is *that* well-connected. Have you told him?'

'No.'

'Hang on to your hat when you do.'

Now, as James came in, Livy said: 'Oysters, James. One dozen. Sir William has a fancy for them.' Her shrug said it all. 'Fortunately, they are still in season – just, but pay whatever you have to.'

James bowed. 'Sir William shall have his oysters, my lady,' he told her gravely, in the manner of a long-standing upper servant.

Livy's mouth twitched but she said only: 'As soon as possible, if you please.'

Another bow. 'Of course.'

That was what was so wonderful about James, Livy thought on a giggle as the door closed behind him. He was totally unflappable. And he had a list of telephone numbers worth its weight in gold. She had no doubt that if Billy had ordered an elephant steak James would have known the best shop to supply it. Best of all he did it with a graven-image deference to which Livy played up shamelessly, but every now and then it would become too much and they would both collapse with laughter. James was a *find*, Livy realised happily. And there was no way she was ever going to lose him. His unfailing cheerfulness and dry wit had revived her sagging spirits and already defused her self-pity, though meeting him had increased her resolve. With James she could giggle over choice bits of gossip, for that was something else he possessed in great quantities, and relax in a letting-go way she had never found possible even with Toni, formerly her only confidante, although she still kept one cupboard locked: the one that contained the truth about her marriage. Always reticent about her private affairs, Livy found it difficult to open up to anyone, no matter how sympathetic and understanding, though in James she knew she had found her kindred spirit. It remained to be seen, though, what Billy's reaction would be.

When he came downstairs, it was obvious he was not going out again because he was wearing the dark-red silk jacket and matching velvet slippers, embroidered with his initials, Livy had bought him for his birthday.

'Come and talk to me,' he said to Livy, as he went into the small dining room – Morpeth House had two; one for family dinners, seating a dozen, one for dinner parties, seating a hundred.

Livy did as she was told.

The oysters were waiting, on their bed of ice, the black velvet in the act of being poured into a silver tankard by James.

'Hello!' said Billy, raising his eyebrows. 'Who are you?'

'This is James, darling, James Luttrell-Leigh,' Livy said. 'My new personal assistant.'

'I trust everything is to your liking, Sir William,' James said suavely. 'They are the very best, Colchester oysters. The champagne is Krug, the stout Guinness, of course. I find these particular two to be the best combination.'

He placed the tankard in front of Billy, who drank deeply, pursed his lips as he dabbed froth from them, then said: 'Good ... very good.'

James smiled and then looked enquiringly at Livy. 'If there is nothing else, my lady ... ?'

'Nothing, thank you, James,' Livy said, deadpan.

Billy began on his first oyster. 'You have something to tell me,' he enquired.

'I thought it was time I had some help,' Livy returned calmly. 'You have more than enough, I have had none up until now. And he is extremely well connected and very knowledgeable.'

Billy paused in the act of consuming another oyster. 'How much are you paying him?'

Livy quoted the figure.

Billy nodded.

Livy released a silent breath. That meant Billy was not displeased.

'What's a man like him doing as your personal assistant?'

'I suspect he finds it amusing,' she replied with a shrug. 'He is sufficiently secure in both himself and his background not to find anything – demeaning – in it. And he really is a find, darling. I honestly don't know how I have managed so long without him.' She sat back, smoothed the skirt of her 'at-home' dress; a pure silk shirtwaister the colour of newly opened magnolias which suited her fine skin, dark hair and magnificent eyes. 'He will be invaluable if I have to go anywhere and you are not here to take me; just think of the *frisson* that will cause. I mean, how many women employ a Viscount's brother as their personal assistant.'

She could see that Billy's ceaselessly working mind was

109

already calculating the permutations, adding up the total and finding it satisfactory. 'He is related to half of *Debrett*, not to mention *Burke's*,' Livy went on, just in case Billy was not already staggering under the heavy load of James' perfection. 'It was absolutely providential I should have been in Harrods that morning.' Billy looked at her. He was smiling, and not just his mouth. His brown eyes were surmising. 'Yes. Wasn't it,' he said.

With delight and an uplifting of the heart Livy saw over the next few days how quickly James took the measure of the master of Morpeth House. There was no need for her to warn him that Billy was not to be relied upon; that what he enthusiastically promised one moment could be blankly and coldly denied the next, or that the smouldering threat of displeasure had a very low flash-point. James soon realised that the repeated snap of Billy's fingers meant the DANGER switch had been thrown, but what made Livy abjectly grateful was the skilful way in which he deflected that danger away from her.

Within a week she knew she had found the friend she so desperately needed; but life with Billy had made her cautious so she made herself wait. There had to be not even the slightest doubt, but she would have had to be blind not to see that James was highly appreciative of his new lifestyle. What she wanted him to appreciate also, was that keeping it entailed keeping her happy. Once she was sure he fully understood that, then she would take him into her confidence.

For once Livy had read it right; James Luttrell-Leigh knew he had landed on his feet the minute he decided to chance his arm and speak to Olivia Bancroft that morning in Harrods

110

Food Hall. It would seem that at long last, the fates have decided to relent, he had thought that first night, relaxing in a Turkish-sized bath filled with bubbles redolent of Floris *Lime*.

He had not had an easy time of it since leaving the army, which had been a stupid mistake on his part in one direction – that young trooper had been around the block several times – but a godsend on the other, since his mess bills were beyond a joke and his brother had flatly refused to give him any more money. So he had become an exile, taking a succession of boring jobs that just about kept the wolf from the door but did not allow for buying a gun to shoot it.

Until now. He had fallen into a bed of clover. Billy Bancroft was another name for Croesus. Like those of Jimmy Goldsmith and Robert Maxwell. Why, only on the plane coming back from Nairobi he'd read that Sir William Bancroft had sold his £50,000 stake in Bradbury Properties (made back in 1953) for £50 million in 1973! Anybody who could make that sort of profit was to be respected. What was unexpected was that he was also charming. Taller than James had surmised, and with an expensively maintained tan enhanced by the still thick silver hair. There were few lines on a face full of character that had held a quizzical smile when James had been introduced. No doubt about it; he had charisma all right. Then he mentioned that he knew James' sister; that his brother-in-law, Ward Winslow – the American Ambassador – was related to the Montforts – distantly, of course, since the Winslows had been in America for a couple of centuries, but it was there for all to see on the family tree Billy had had done by some genealogical expert.

'It's a hobby of mine, family trees,' he'd told James.

'The only gardening you ever do, isn't it, darling?' his wife had asked, lightly teasing.

Despite the lightness of tone James had caught the cutting edge to her voice. It confirmed his initial impression that this was a couple whose respective pieces did not fit into the puzzle picture entitled: The Bancroft Marriage. There is always a price to pay, he'd mused cynically. I get five-star room and board plus a damned good salary, but my employer is a woman living on nerves and valium, while her husband is a man who, past experience tells me, should not be given the benefit of even the slightest doubt. Tread carefully where he is concerned, James my boy. In fact, around Sir William Bancroft it would seem best to go on tiptoes, having previously relocated one's eyes to the back of one's head.

Something his wife had obviously neglected to do.

What in God's name is a work of art like her doing married to a sod like him? James puzzled. If ever I saw a woman repenting at leisure it is Livy Bancroft. Under those superlatively elegant clothes I'll bet there is a pair of very sore knees …

Ah, well, he thought smugly, preparing to retire to his pocketed-springs bed, the good thing about it all is that when she starts looking for a hand to hold, the nearest one will be mine.

Just as long as I never forget whose hand operates the till …

Some six weeks later he was called upon to remember his initial impressions when Livy, having decided he could be

112

trusted not only to do what she wanted, but keep his mouth shut about it afterwards, summoned him to her sitting room. There she told him about Yetta Feldman, showed him the forgotten receipt from the Scottish nursing home, then confided her uneasy suspicions regarding the death of her husband's first wife.

'You have to find out the truth,' he sympathised at once, 'for your own future peace of mind if for no other reason. And since it is not possible for you to undertake the kind of enquiries necessary, *I* take it that *you* have taken me into your confidence in order that I may do so?' He held Livy's large dark eyes with a penetrating stare of his own, and in that one, long exchange of understanding, allegiances were sworn and sides were taken.

'Would you?' Livy asked in a low, vibrant voice.

'I am at your service in this and all other things. What is it you wish me to do?'

He saw the change which came over the lovely face; the staggering relief she felt, the courage his words had given her, the resolve they bolstered. 'Sir William leaves for Rio the day after tomorrow. He will be away ten days ...'

James caught the ball and ran with it. 'I have a favourite aunt in Argyll. My father's sister Maud. I have not seen her in an age; high time I paid her a visit.'

'An excellent idea,' agreed Livy. 'You could go up on the night Pullman.'

He was gone three days. On the morning of the fourth he returned bearing a twelve-pound salmon and several jars of wild heather honey. 'Aunt Maud makes it herself ... Keeps the bees in hives in her paddock. Talks to them, believe it

113

or not. Pushing eighty and still does the Gay Gordons at Hogmanay.'

When they were ensconced in Livy's sitting room, a poem of silk-hung walls in palest pistachio and furnished entirely in Louis XVI, he said: 'I have something for you,' and laid down on the marquetry top of the little table where the coffee tray was laid, a photostat. Livy picked it up. It was of a death certificate. For one Yetta Feldman aged forty-five. The cause of death was given as alcoholic poisoning. 'Caused by the ingestion of almost a bottle of a very good single malt,' James said, 'though from where is not known. She drank it like it was lemonade, passed out and died without regaining consciousness. She was cremated. There is nothing in the crematorium Book of Remembrance, nothing anywhere except the death certificate and the memory of the people who run the nursing home where she was a patient. She was an alcoholic with a death wish. They were surprised she did not manage it sooner. Her next of kin was her "brother-in-law," a Mr Banciewicz, who had been paying her bills.'

He held Livy's intent gaze. Finally: 'Thank you,' Livy said.

James nodded. He picked up the certificate, folded it like a spill, held out the silver box of cigarettes to Livy, took one himself then put the spill to the flames of the bright fire burning in the Adam grate. When it was burning well he lit their cigarettes with it, before throwing it into the fire. Within seconds it was black, curling ash. With a steady hand Livy poured them both a cup of coffee, adding cream and sugar to his. Then she sat back: 'Tell me about Scotland,' she said.

★

That night, she took out the receipt from the concealed pocket in her alligator address book and burned that too. No names, no packdrill, as the British said. Livy sipped the brandy she had poured. Although the fire she had ordered to be lit was burning brightly, she felt chilled to the bone.

5

In July 1973 Rosalind Randolph returned from school in the
United States to spend part of the summer holidays at
Wychwood, the lovely Elizabethan manor house in the
Cotswolds that was her favourite of all the Bancroft residences. She had already spent a month at King's Gift with her
Randolph grandmother, with whom she had a very close
and loving relationship. Dolly Randolph could be very *grande
dame* but never with her grandchildren, especially Johnny.
His sweetness and good nature were that of her adored son.
Rosalind was a different matter. Dolly was seventy-five, not
so active as she had been, but with every mental faculty in
perfect working order, and though she would never have
admitted it she looked forward to the battles she had with
her grand-daughter. When she admonished: 'Well-brought
up girls do not do such things,' should Rosalind want to do
something of which her grandmother did not approve,
such as wearing jeans, she would ask challengingly: 'Why
not?' When her grandmother proceeded to expound she
would rationally and ruthlessly demolish every argument, in
much the same way as her grandfather had handed down a

judgment from the Bench. But Rosalind loved King's Gift, and being in the throes of a passionate love affair with horses, was only too happy to spend most of her time riding. It was because she would not be far from them – or King's Gift – that she had agreed when her grandmother suggested she go to Foxcroft; her mother had wanted her to go to a school in England. Dolly's will had also prevailed in sending John Jr. to Lawrenceville, which his father had also attended.

'I shall be sorry to see you go, child,' Dolly said to her grand-daughter, as she watched her preparing to depart. Her son's children were much nearer her heart than those of her four daughters. Their children seemed insipid, somehow; without Johnny's sincerity or easy charm, and totally lacking Rosalind's spirit. That she had bullied her daughters into the shadows they became or that they in turn counselled extreme caution to their own children never occurred to her.

'Needs must,' Rosalind answered practically.

'Whose needs? Not yours, surely.'

'Mummy expects me at Wychwood for the rest of the summer. Why don't you come with me for a visit? You'd like it there. It's a lovely old house; filled with history and tradition.'

'But no longer belonging to the family who built it.' Dolly Randolph shook her head. 'That will *never* happen here. No strangers will ever buy King's Gift. I have seen to that.' Her nostrils flared. 'Far too much new money is taking over. People like your stepfather. Nobodies from nowhere who have the knack of making money but nothing else.'

'Well, I'm glad he bought Wychwood. It needed a lot of restoration and I will say that he did not stint in bringing it back to what it was originally.'

'In the hope that it might bring him closer to his goal. I'll not spend time I cannot afford to waste in the company of that mountebank. I will never understand why your mother married him. Never!'

Nor, as the Jumbo took her across the Atlantic, would Rosalind. When her mother had told her she was getting married again, and to Billy Bancroft, Rosalind had been incredulous. 'But you can't!' she'd blurted, at the age of ten not yet in control of her unruly tongue.

'I was not aware I needed your permission,' Livy had said, icily.

'But – not *him*!' Rosalind had protested.

'And why not him?'

'Because you were married to Daddy! How you could marry *anybody* after Daddy? Besides, this man is old.'

'There are only fifteen years between us,' Livy defended.

'It might as well be fifty! And he doesn't like children.'

'You know nothing about what Sir William likes!' Two spots of colour had hoisted themselves to her mother's cheeks. Truth to tell, Livy had always been somewhat intimidated by her daughter's brainpower. She had been reading and writing with ease by the time she was four. Johnny had been admiring but never awed. 'She's a Randolph all right,' he used to chuckle.

Yes, Livy had thought. Mostly your mother. But she had also seen more than a trace of her own.

Johnny was never any trouble. Rosalind argued about *everything*. And she had been far too close to that last governess. Taking a child to listen to the speeches at the UN! Not to mention letting her read books that Livy herself had not been permitted to read at sixteen! When Dolly Randolph had urged Foxcroft Livy had been glad to acquiesce. Having her eldest daughter a long distance away at boarding-school was – well, to be honest, it was a relief. Livy wrote a weekly letter at first, but that soon became a weekly long-distance call, which became shorter and shorter.

Well, Livy consoled herself, she has her grandmother not far away; and she has always been closer to her than she ever has to me. Which for some unaccountable reason she both resented yet found a relief.

Diana was so much easier, thank God. Diana's plump little face always lit up when her mother visited the nursery, while David was a cherub. Both were Bancrofts rather than Gaylords. Diana already strove for her mother's approval, showing her the drawings she had done – usually of a stick-figure hung with jewels – saying: 'Look, Mummy … it's you …' While David, with the confidence of one who knew he would never lack for female approval, merely held up his face to be kissed. They were always happy to see their father on his infrequent encounters with them, he could usually be relied on to produce a present. There was no sense of strain as there was with Rosalind, though Johnny, his father's happy-go-lucky image, was always greeted affectionately by his stepfather.

It was Johnny whom Rosalind found waiting for her at Heathrow. 'Oh, thank God!' Ros exclaimed, throwing her arms around him. 'I was dreading Hanks and the funereal Rolls!'

'He's driving Pops today. There's some big shindig in town. Ma's with him.'

'On duty?' Ros enquired, lemon-drop sweet, as they went to get the car. 'Dressed to the nines, not a hair out of place and playing Lady Bancroft to the hilt?'

'Look, you know how things are,' her brother reminded. 'Why do you persist in kicking against them? All you'll get are bruises.'

'I see why you don't,' Ros said, raising her eyebrows as Johnny stopped by a bright-red, brand-new BMW. 'And what did you do to earn this pretty thing? You're not old enough to drive it, yet.'

'I was sixteen back in May, remember?'

'That's still not old enough to get a licence over here.'

'I know. That's why I've brought Jeff with me. He *is* old enough.'

A lanky, carrot-topped preppy uncoiled himself from the driver's seat. 'Hi, Ros,' he grinned.

'I thought you two were in Cap Ferrat.'

'My old lady took off in the Niarchos yacht so I came back with Johnny.'

Jeffrey de Santos was the only son of a woman who had inherited two hundred million dollars from her father, married another two hundred, and since remarried and divorced a further three times. Jeff was a nice boy, brought up by servants, but miraculously unscathed by the experience. He adored Livy and was genuinely respectful of Billy, who encouraged the friendship. Marina de Santos came from a long line of Stuyvesants, Van Renselaers, Schermerhorns and Schuylers while her first husband's family had helped settle California when it belonged to the Hidalgos. Just the sort of boy the stepson of Sir William Bancroft should have for a best friend.

'Won't you be bored?' Ros wanted to know. 'I wouldn't have thought the depths of Oxfordshire to be your favourite stamping ground.'

'It's better than droning around the Mediterranean with a lot of old fogies. Besides, there's always a houseful at Wychwood and lots to do.'

'True … Billy would not go there otherwise. Who have we got this year?' Ros asked, getting into the back seat as her luggage was loaded.

'Oh, the usual,' Johnny answered indifferently, then, offhand: 'But Mom's got a new personal assistant.'

'A *what?*'

'Somebody to assist her – you know, running things for Pops.'

'He is not *my* father,' Ros denied sharply.

Jeff groaned inwardly: Jesus! It's Pavlov's dog with her and Billy, before making an attempt to deflect her: 'Wait until you've had as many stepfathers as me,' he advised. 'Then you can complain.'

'One is too many for me, thank you,' Ros snapped, causing her brother to protest:

'You never change your mind do you? Once you get a down on somebody that's it! They are never allowed to get up again. Pops has never been anything but a good father to me, step or not! He bought me this car as a birthday present because he knew I'd set my heart on one! And he lets me drive it around the estate just so long as I promised not to take it out on the roads. He's good to Ma and I don't notice you lacking for anything! The world is made up of a hell of a lot of other people besides the God–Almighty Randolphs, you know!'

Ros surveyed him scornfully. 'Idiot! *I'm* not the one who thinks that to be a Randolph is the be–all and end–all! It's your dear old Pops! Do you think he would give you the time of day if you were Bernie Schwantz? Don't you understand yet that he is your stepfather precisely because our mother *was* a Randolph when he married her? For God's sake, Johnny, don't you ever use your brain — what there is of it, of course!'

'I see what goes on around me,' he maintained stubbornly, 'and it's not what you see, that's for sure. You won't ever see Pops except through those prejudicial glasses of yours. If you would only take them off for one minute you might see a very different man ...'

'You can paint a leopard fifty times over and it will still keep its spots!'

'You never wanted Ma to marry again, that's why you don't like him! You'd rather see Ma living alone but for us; devoting her life to her children and deserving charities, right? Well I prefer her as she is now; with a loving husband and two more loving children. Ma has a full life, not the empty one you'd rather she lived, and don't think she doesn't know it either!'

Ros was about to turn and rend, but Jeff, used to these sibling set-tos, stepped between them. 'Hey, come on you guys ... you haven't seen each other since Christmas and you were fighting then, as I recall. Give it a rest, okay? I have enough to concentrate on what with driving on the wrong side of the road.'

Ros was too pleased to see them both to be angry for long. 'You know, you are right,' she admitted on a grin and after a moment's thought. 'We were fighting last time we saw each other.' She leaned over the front seat. 'Pax?' she asked, holding up her right hand, little finger crooked. Johnny hooked it with his left and they gave a mock handshake. 'Pax.'

It was how their first English nanny used to make them end their quarrels, frequent even then.

'Till the next time,' Ros said dulcetly. Her brother laughed. Peace was restored.

'So, tell me, what is Mummy doing with a personal assistant,' Ros asked, her curiosity aroused. 'Like why on earth should she need one. The ratio of servants in any Bancroft establishment is always two to one.'

'This one's a doozy! Right out of P.G. Woodhouse.'

'Oh my God! Not a Bertie Wooster!'

'No …' Jeff put in. 'More an aristocratic Jeeves.'

'You're kidding!'

'Wait and see, then.'

'Put your foot down, Jeff,' Ros instructed. 'I can't wait!'

Although the host and hostess were away for the day, their guests were taking full advantage of the comforts provided. The hundred-foot pool Billy had had built where there had been a series of lily ponds was in use, its paved surround strewn with steamer chairs on which people soaked up the sun or chatted over drinks. There was a match in progress on the tennis court, also laid by Billy, and another on the croquet lawn.

'Good God! How many are there?' Ros asked, recognising some familiar faces, not recognising others. People came and went in the Bancroft houses, always at the nod of its master. If you did not please or measure up you were not invited back.

'Only four couples staying, but a lot of people are here for the weekend.'

'Jesus, the feeding of the five thousand at dinner, then.'

123

Johnny heard his sister draw in a sharp breath. 'Oh no, not *her*.'

'Who?'

'Penelope what'shername. Still bent and determined to snaffle another husband – especially somebody else's. I can't think why Mummy puts up with her.'

'She knows James – that's mother's P.A. They are third or fourth cousins, or something. You know how it is over here. Everybody is related to everybody else.'

'Positively incestuous.' Ros sniffed disdainfully. 'I'm going up to change then I'm going to see Rob Roy.' This was her horse; a chestnut gelding that had been Livy's last birthday present, after much pleading on Ros's part.

Her bags had already been taken up to her room and the maid who looked after her was already unpacking them.

'Hello, Smitty,' Ros said cheerfully. 'How are you?'

'Can't complain, miss, even though we've got another houseful.'

They looked at each other in silent understanding. Mary Smith had been with Livy from her early days in England and was used to life with the Bancrofts. Ros she had always liked; smuggled her tidbits when she was banished to her room, bandaged knees that had been grazed while indulging in some activity forbidden by her mother, fibbed for her when Ros had not been back after some outing and was supposed to be asleep in bed.

'I hear we have a new member of the household,' Ros said, stripping off her jeans and shirt and going into her bathroom to turn on the shower.

'Mr Luttrell-Leigh,' Smitty said approvingly. 'Ever such a nice gentleman. Taken a load off your mother's shoulders.

Knows just about everybody we've got here this weekend. And not so much as a flicker when he tells them he's not a guest but an employee. But then, he's a *real* gent.'

I'll bet Billy gets a kick out of that, Ros thought, turning her face to the powerful drive of the shower.

When she got to the stables she discovered somebody was there before her, and in Rob Roy's stall. As soon as she set eyes on him she knew who it was. He could not have been anyone else, and from the way he was handling Rob Roy, not the most placid of horses, she recognised someone who felt about them the same way she did. He was also wearing the right clothes; old but well-cut breeches, hand-made boots, a checked shirt and a tweed cap, and he had hold of Rob Roy's left foreleg in a grip that was firm yet gentle.

'Hang on old lad ... it's got itself wedged and if I don't get it out you are going to have a very sore foot. Ah ... that's better ...'

'He's not really old,' Ros said, walking forward, evoking a snicker from Rob Roy as he recognised her voice. 'Only six.'

'He's a good horse; strong clean legs and a compact body. Makes him look smaller than he really is. I'll bet he takes a fence like a feather. Do you hunt him?'

'I'm not always here for the season. I hunt in Virginia, though.'

Having extracted the triangular stone, James put down the leg and Rob Roy turned his head to nuzzle Rosalind, who kissed his velvet-soft nose.

'I suppose I had better come clean,' James said disarmingly. 'I've been riding him. Your mother said I might. And the headgroom said he needed the exercise. From the way he let loose today it was obvious she was right.'

He held out a hand, smiling down at her. 'I'm James Luttrell-Leigh and you, of course, are Rosalind Randolph.' They shook hands. 'I've given them all a try but Rob Roy is the best by far. He's from the Scots Lad strain, isn't he?'

'How did you know?' Ros asked, much impressed.

'His lines … and his colour. I've got several Highland cousins whose hair is every bit as red.' He had that mixture of languor and self-assurance which Ros, having seen more than her fair share of them since she acquired Billy Bancroft as a stepfather, recognised as belonging to the English aristocracy.

'Are you a racing man?'

'What God-fearing Englishman is not? Horses and dogs are our best friends; so much more trustworthy than people.'

Rosalind found herself liking his droll sense of humour, and responded in her own, more sardonic style. 'What are you doing in this house, then?' she asked. 'Neither my mother nor my stepfather would go anywhere near the animals here. Far too dirty and unpredictable.'

James caught the caustic-soda burn. Not so much as a chip, but a whole tree on her shoulder. A pity; she was made in her mother's image. Very young, no more than a filly, and not yet possessing the style that a few big wins would bring, but in a year or two she would dominate the winners' circle even as her mother did. She had the right bloodlines; evident in the height, the endless legs, the luminous skin and huge dark eyes, but with something added; the glow of a restless, questing intelligence that was not satisfied with the answers she'd been getting.

Sir William and Lady Bancroft returned early that evening, and they would be twenty-four sitting down for dinner that night. When he took their telephone messages up to them, James found Billy in a querulous frame of mind, while Livy's mouth had a set to it that he had learned to recognise. It meant that her made-to-measure life was pinching.

Just before they had left London Billy had said to James, casually: 'Not much point in my toting a secretary down to the country with us; we've got every bedroom in the house filled for the next six weekends. There won't be all that much to do for me, but I'd appreciate it if you could act for us both while we are at Wychwood.'

From the corner of his eye James had seen the way Livy raised a hand to examine her flawless nails, as though disassociating herself from the conversation; he had come to recognise the ploy. It meant: be careful.

'I can but try,' James had answered diplomatically.

'If you find you can't manage us both then all you have to do is say so,' Billy added, with one of his sweet smiles.

'Then I will,' James told him, in such a way as to make the smile congeal.

Livy had tactfully made it clear that her husband – who liked full value for every penny spent – would try to take him over. 'It's his way,' she had explained disarmingly, as though explaining away a trivial foible. Which was why James came down to dinner early. Something in the air around Billy – heavy as before a thunderstorm – had warned him to watch for the lightning.

Sure enough, Billy soon came down himself wearing one of his gorgeous figured-silk smoking jackets, Livy two steps behind as befitted a good wife, resplendent in yellow grosgrain taffeta and canary diamonds. He crossed the great hall with its musician's gallery and went down the three steps and through the archway to the dining room, where he stared in silence at the exquisitely laid table, an expanse of mirror-like mahogany, tall white candles, heavy lace place mats, Waterford crystal and Georgian silver, with three glorious white and yellow flower arrangements placed at intervals down its centre. The silence held its breath. Finally he turned to his wife: 'You know I loathe yellow. Why have you put yellow flowers on my dinner table? I'm not sitting down at it while they are there. Change them.'

Then he turned on his heel and went back upstairs to finish dressing.

Listening from the library next door, James entered the dining room to find Livy standing behind one of the Carolinian cane-backed, walnut carvers, her hands gripping its rails so tightly the knuckles looked like bone. Sounding his languid self, but with absolute assurance, he said: 'You go back upstairs and finish dressing. I'll see to the flowers. Go along. Everyone will be coming down soon.'

Livy swung round, her eyes wide and somehow fixed, her lower lips showing the marks where her teeth had been sunk in it. But her voice was under control when she said: 'Make them roses, why don't you? My husband likes roses.'

'Any particular colour?' James matched his tone to hers.

'Multi colours, I think. Yes; reds and pinks and creams but no yellows. Thank you, James.'

Livy smiled at him, then turned and swept from the room,

her taffeta rustling. She did not see her eldest daughter standing in the doorway of the library, having heard if not seen all, but went on up the stairs straight backed and head high, as though she had all the time in the world.

Why don't you tell him to go to hell, Mother? Ros wanted to shout after her. You are his wife, not his slave! And since when was he so down on yellow? He bought you those very costly canary diamonds, didn't he? Why do you let him talk to you like that? I'd have picked up one of those flower arrangements and brained him with it!

Ros had seen it all before. Only last Christmas she had watched as Livy came downstairs looking like a dream only to have Billy look her up and down before saying coldly: 'I trust you are not going to receive my guests looking like that!'

Without a word her mother had turned and gone back upstairs, to undo an hour's patient and skilful work by herself and her maid; redo her face – Livy's maquillage was always adapted to the colour she was wearing – her hair, likewise created to be part of a perfect whole – choose another dress and the jewellery to go with it, even her perfume would be different, and her satin slippers, then come downstairs again, serenely unperturbed. Only Ros – and Manby, who had been her maid since she married Johnny Randolph – knew about the valium capsules that were the finishing touch.

Now, Ros went quickly across the hall and into the dining room, where she found James about to remove one of the flower arrangements. He turned as he heard her step, met her eyes in a long communicative look, then Ros said: 'I'll go and cut the roses. Dump them – ' she nodded at the flowers – 'where his nibs won't see them then get another three bowls from the china room. Use the *famille rose*.' Their look held for a moment longer then James nodded, scooped up two of the bowls and took them away while Ros went to the garden room to get the secateurs.

By the time Livy came down again, this time in a drift of Balmain pure silk organza that matched the colours of the roses to perfection, pearls in her ears and around her throat, the drift of "Joy" eddying about her, the table was aglow with three bowls of beautifully arranged roses.

Livy turned to James with a look that had Ros clenching her hands. 'Thank you,' she breathed, heartfelt, holding out her hands.

James bowed over them before raising one to his lips, but shook his head. 'Not me. Your daughter. She cut and arranged the roses.'

Livy turned to Ros, who had the impression that her mother was angry. The dark eyes held a light that was not one of appreciation when her daughter shrugged and said: 'Grandma has been showing me how to do flowers. She says it is something every well-brought up girl should know.'

Just then, voices could be heard descending the stairs. 'Company coming,' Ros announced laconically.

At the dinner table, Ros was placed across from James, who sat next to Penelope Wilton, his second – or was it third? – cousin. A creamy blonde with an opulent figure and a penchant for rich men, she had been kept by a whole succession of them since her first marriage, to the grandson of a Duke, had failed. Gossip had it that she had tried to bring everyone of them to the starting gate in the Marriage Stakes but all had shied and thrown her, even though she was a superb rider and hunted with the Heythrop when she was in Oxfordshire. During dinner her high-pitched voice could be heard urging James to do likewise once the season started.

'Billy won't mind if we stay here, will you darling?' she asked him airily, in the voice of one who already knew the answer.

'My house is your house,' he told her gallantly.

'There, you see.' As far as Penelope was concerned it was all fixed.

'But I might be elsewhere,' James reminded her equably. 'I do have a job, you know.'

'Oh, but Livy won't mind giving you a few days hunting, will you darling.' Everyone was darling to Penelope.

Livy smiled but said nothing. Penelope took her silence for consent. 'There you are, Jamie, it's all fixed,' she sat back, satisfied.

'Jamie?' Billy asked.

'My friends call me that,' James explained, with a deprecatory shrug. 'Among other things.'

Penelope giggled. 'Let's not go into *that*, darling,' she said.

'Into what?' Billy asked, reminding his guests that it was their duty to keep him amused, and that he expected to be kept *au courant* with the latest *on dit*, especially the salacious kind.

'Go on, tell Billy what Queen Mary called you,' urged Penelope.

Billy sat up straighter. 'Her Late Majesty Queen Mary?' he asked.

'What did she call you?' someone else asked curiously.

'James the Less,' was the reply. 'I was only five at the time and staying with my grandmother. I was being brought downstairs because Queen Mary, who was a friend of hers, had come to tea. In the excitement I managed to wet myself. My nanny immediately sent for the nursery footman to bring me dry replacement trousers – we were expected in the sitting room on the dot of four-thirty as both my grandmother and the old Queen were sticklers for punctuality – but before the footman could come back with them I managed to escape my nanny and enter the sitting room – bare-assed, I think is the American expression. Fortunately, Queen Mary chose to be highly amused and dubbed me James-the-Less – less trousers. Whenever I met her after that she always called me by that name, to my sometimes great embarrassment.'

There was a ripple of laughter, but Ros noticed that Billy did not join in. He had his eyes on James, but with an expression that was curiously fixed.

Someone else then began to tell another story about royalty and a first night, but Ros was aware that Billy's attention was still with James. Not sure how to treat him, Ros surmised. He is an employee but one who was on familiar terms with a Queen of England. And he didn't hire him in the first place. Mummy did. Torn between treating him as the servant he is and tugging the old forelock to the gentry, knowing all the while that James does not give a damn.

Lovely! she thought gleefully. This ought to be a very interesting summer ...

After dinner there was backgammon, bridge, billiards, or, for those who wished something less demanding, the preview of a new film. Billy had a lot of contacts in the film world, having backed a couple of box office successes which had made him nice fat profits. He was now toying with the idea of investing in a musical, and that weekend the producer and his two stars, a woman who had once been known as 'the Darling of the Silver Screen' and still possessed a marvellous singing voice, and her long-time partner, also no longer young but who had in his heyday been a matinee idol, had been invited down to enable Billy to give them the once-over.

Billy devoted a lot of attention to her; she would never see fifty again but she had kept her figure, and seen from the audience neither the lines nor the wrinkles showed. She also had a tremendous following among the middle-aged, for whom she represented their youth. She flirted shamelessly, giggling girlishly and tapping him archly with her fan, an affectation of hers that had become a trademark.

Ros was only too happy to leave them to it to go and play table-tennis with Jeff, who trounced her soundly. Then she played Johnny, who had his father's reflexes but not Jeff's cunning so that Ros managed to beat him.

'A little more practice and you might make a decent player,' Jeff commented, then dodged as Ros threw her bat at him.

'Can anyone join in?' a voice asked, and they looked round to see James leaning against the door jamb.

'If you are able to stand the pace,' Jeff answered cheekily.

'One can but try.'

James took off his dinner jacket and Johnny said: 'Use my bat, if you wish.'

'Thank you,' said James, and proceeded to give Jeff the fight of his life.

'Where did you learn to play like that?' Jeff panted, as he won – just.

'Hong Kong. The Chinese are mad about it. And the very best players.'

'No wonder you play so well. Give you another game?'

'Thank you but no, thank you. You have some twenty years' advantage. Another night, perhaps.'

'I'll give you another game, Jeff,' Johnny offered.

'I must see if I am required to perform any duties,' James said to Ros, shrugging into his dinner jacket.

'Is it odd, working for my mother?' she asked in her direct way, as they left the games room. 'I mean, being an employee in a house where a great many of the guests are friends of yours?'

'No. I don't find it odd. What is odd is that other people seem to.'

Ros flushed. 'What I mean,' she continued stubbornly, 'is that you are — God, this is going to sound horribly snobbish but it is the truth — a member of a class that has it all over people like my stepfather. All he has got is the money.'

'Don't knock money,' James told her with a headshake. 'Lack of it is why I am employed by him in the first place.'

'Knock money? In this family? You must be joking.'

James stopped walking. Queryingly, Ros turned to look at him. 'Don't judge your mother too harshly,' he advised at last. 'At your age, your eyes are not experienced enough to see all the myriad shades of grey.'

'Grey is the colour of my stepfather's hair,' Ros quipped, 'except in the magazines where he is always referred to as "a distinguished, silver-haired figure".'

'He is your mother's husband,' James reminded. 'She chose him, like it or not.'

'I don't!' Ros stared into the knowing eyes defiantly. 'I

hate him! I hate what he does to my mother – and I hate her for allowing it! No man will ever humiliate me as he humiliated her tonight.'

'Have you considered that Lady Bancroft might be one of those women who take their marriage vows seriously, especially the bit about "for better or for worse"?'

'My mother is an American! We never take anything for worse! We take a plane to Reno!'

'Not women like your mother.'

Caught by his voice: 'Yet *another* admirer?' Ros asked edgily.

'I admire her enormously. She has tremendous elegance, stupendous chic and perfect taste.' He paused. 'She also has a great deal of courage. Being the wife of a man like Sir William is not the easiest of jobs, in spite of the perks.'

Ros opened her mouth to tell him that these days her mother was stupefied with valium most of the time, *that* was how she coped, then shut it again. Let him keep his illusions. And at least, she thought grudgingly, it means she has somebody looking out for her.

'I'm glad she's got you for a friend,' she said. 'You strike me as the sort of man who does a lot more than sing for his supper.' She picked up the skirts of her blue taffeta dress. 'Now I'm going to see if Rob Roy has had his. Goodnight'

James watched her walk lithely away. A handful, he thought. The wrong age at the wrong time and filled with all the misconceptions and imperfect judgements of youth. Of whom her mother is more than a little envious and afraid...

It was a lovely night; warm, the air heavy with the scent of the jasmine Livy had planted in the sunken garden just below

135

the terraces. The trees rustled softly; they reminded Ros of a sound she always associated with her mother: the rustle of her full-skirted evening dress as she came to the nursery to say goodnight. In the woods an owl hooted and some nocturnal creature screamed, probably a fox. There was a special magic about the English countryside, Ros thought dreamily. Virginia was lovely but it lacked something that abounded in England: it was not romantic. Somehow the trees and the grass and the flowers of the garden at Wych-wood had got it together in a way that was unique to this country. Helped of course by the expert attentions of her mother and a team of gardeners. Ros's feet made no sound on grass that received more intensive care than any patient in an expensive private hospital, and the canopy of the trees was lushly sibilant.

As she passed below the little garden temple which stood on its hill looking down on the house and gardens, Ros thought she heard a cry; a woman's voice. She stopped, listened. There it was again. A rising wail then a caught breath.

Being possessed of a powerful sense of curiosity, she did not think twice about going to investigate. Picking up her skirts she began to walk up the steps that shallowly circled the hill, but something, some instinct she could not name but trusted, made her, as she neared the temple, leave the steps for the grass, so that her approach was soundless. As she got closer she identified the sound as that of rhythmic moaning, which had the effect of making her stoop low so that she was concealed by the half-wall on which the columns which supported the dome of the roof were mounted. She knew what moans like that meant; she had heard them often enough when her room-mate at school had been in the throes of a passionate affair with one of the riding instructors. She had been a noisy lover: if the decibel count of her moans had been an accurate measurement on her pleasure scale, then her lover was one in a million. That same thought now occurred to Ros as she slowly and carefully raised her head above the wall to look over it, through the columns and into the circle of the temple.

A man had a woman up against the far wall, her back to one of the columns. Her dress was up around her waist, its bodice pulled down, allowing her pendulously large breasts to sprawl lasciviously. Her thighs were spread wide, and the man was thrusting into her in a rhythm that coincided with her moans, his own breathing harsh as though the exertion was too much for him. In the starlight, for there was no moon, Ros could see the woman's head was thrown back, her face glazed and slack, her mouth open, her eyes closed. It was Penelope What'shername. The man's face was hidden by the massive breast in his mouth, but there was no mistaking the silver hair. Ros could not restrain her hiss of indrawn breath but neither of them were capable of hearing her. They were approaching orgasm; and as Ros watched, curiosity firing on all cylinders, the woman began to heave and buck against her partner, her face contorting as her clenched fists started to beat against the small of his back. She began to grunt, keeping time to the beat. Like a pig, Ros thought clinically. The thrusts accelerated until the two figures were jerking up and down like marionettes; a human seesaw, Ros thought, wanting to laugh because she found it all so hilariously grotesque. Now, she pressed her two hands over her mouth and bit hard on a forefinger. Then she saw

137

her stepfather stiffen to rigidity for a moment, head thrown back, face in a grimace of a seeming pain, a strained sound that denoted immense effort coming from his taut throat until he fell forward against the woman, whose fists unclenched to become hands with fingers stiffly outspread as she heaved herself frantically against him one last time before collapsing herself, like a deflated balloon.

Ros sank down onto the grass, her back against the wall. She was out of sight of the steps they would have to descend to make their way back to the house, so she sat still, waiting and listening.

'Oh, my God, darling,' she heard Penelope gasp after a silence filled only by their laboured breathing. 'That was incredible. I honestly think you get better as you get older.'

So, not the first time, Ros thought.

'Tidy yourself up,' she heard Billy order. 'We must get back before they miss us.'

'Oh, now darling ... Livy would not miss us if we were gone a week!' Her voice lowering to a sexy murmur: 'And I can think of nothing nicer than spending a whole week doing nothing but fucking with you ...' Coaxingly: 'Can't you manage it?'

'Not in the foreseeable future,' Billy said.

Poutingly: 'Always the same answer ... Oh, well ... zip me up, darling ... and there's the tiniest hook and eye ...' Purringly: 'Then I'll do the same for you ... oh ...' disappointedly, 'you've already put him away ... I wanted to thank him for standing up for me the way he did ...'

'We haven't time,' Billy said, practically.

'Spoilsport.' Then: 'Look me over, will you darling? The

138

last impression I want to give is that of a woman who has just been gloriously and thoroughly rogered.'

Ros heard Billy chuckle. 'You are incorrigible.'

Ros heard the sound of a kiss, then the click of Penelope's high heels on the stone of the steps. Only when they had faded did she peep over the wall. They were almost at the bottom of the hill, on their way back to the house.

What would be their excuse? she wondered. An after-dinner stroll? Perhaps that Penny wanted to consult Billy's undoubted financial expertise. Yes, that would work. She was always broke.

And Mummy? Ros thought. Does she know? Does she care? Is Penelope the latest in a long line? And then: how does he *do* it? He's an old man!

She began to make her hasty way to her original destination; she would have to prove she had been to the stables since Billy would be suspicious if he knew she was out and about in the gardens at the same time as he was committing adultery with one of his wife's 'friends'.

She spent fifteen short minutes with Rob Roy, and when she heard the stable clock strike ten-thirty she said: 'Sorry, Rob, but I can't make it any longer. Double time tomorrow, okay? And I'll take you out first thing – promise!'

When she got back to the house, a bed-time drink was being served: coffee, tea, hot chocolate; whatever you thought would give you a good night's sleep. If it was a slug of good whisky that was available too.

Her stepfather was in his usual chair; the big Georgian wing by the fireplace in the drawing room, not a hair of his silvered head out of place as he chatted to the would-be producer of his show. Penelope was with a heads-together group near the window. As Ros entered the room her mother, who was being bored by the actress detailing the plot of every one of her movies, asked sharply: 'Where have you been?'

'Down to the stables.'

'You spend far too much time there.' Livy had a tense look about the mouth and her voice was snappish. She knows, Ros thought. She knows and hates it but there is nothing she can – correction – nothing she *will* do. Not if she wishes to remain Lady Bancroft.

'I haven't seen Rob Roy for ages,' Ros protested, falling into line. Her stepfather was fair game; not so her mother.

'As if he would remember you,' Livy ridiculed.

'As a matter of fact he does. He likes to be talked to; some horses do, you know.'

'Well, if their conversation is an improvement on that of some men I know, then keep it up,' the actress advised, not best pleased that her determined flirtation had gone for nothing, her plans for the evening ruined by that blonde bitch in heat. She'd had more pricks than any thousand blood donors. She glared at her host. Long-distance phone call, indeed! Not as long as that bitch's list of lovers. 'Everybody seems to have been in the garden except the fairies,' she trilled maliciously. 'Billy and Penny have only just come back too.'

Ros caught the flick of Billy's eyes and knew that the actress had just lost her musical.

Later, in bed with a forbidden cigarette – Billy did not approve of the habit so even his wife had to do it surreptitiously – Ros pondered over what she had seen, why it was

140

she had not felt anything herself. Perhaps it was because she had no time for either of the two people making such a ridiculous spectacle of themselves. If people could only watch what they did when they had sex they would never do it again, she thought.

What surprised her most was Billy – yes, Billy Goat, she thought, with a giggle, and from then on she never thought of him as anything else. He was obviously a good lover, for Penny had sounded almost smugly satisfied. Strange, she thought. She had never thought of her stepfather as a sexual being. He and her mother had never ever shared a bedroom, yet when her own father had been alive he and Mummy had always shared an enormous, specially made double bed. Sunday mornings had always been special to Ros as a child because on that day she and her brother had been allowed in their parents' bed to share tidbits from their breakfast tray and to read the funny papers.

Daddy had been fun; with a child's sense of pleasure. Ros had always been closer to him than to her mother; had basked in his undoubted love and approval. She could run into him when he was dressing and he would pick her up and swing her round; Mummy would recoil and say sharply: 'No, Rosalind, you'll crease Mummy's dress' or 'Mummy is doing her face; run and play, there's a good girl,' or 'Mind Mummy's hair, darling.'

Mummy called everybody darling. Daddy had always called her sweetheart. And he would often hug Mummy and kiss her, and she would laugh and hug and kiss him back. She had never seen Billy do that. Yet they had produced Diana and David. Ros brought to mind the image of Billy and Penny going at it hammer and tongs and tried to superimpose her mother's coolly lovely face and slender body on the opulence of her 'friend's' and found she couldn't. God, no ... all that hot and sweaty stuff is not her scene at all. She never gets hot and as for sweaty! Not *my* mother. Cool is her watchword. Well, one of them anyway. Ladylike is another. Would my ladylike mother have gone with her husband tonight up to the temple and fucked under the night sky? Never in a million years. It would ruin her dress for a start, not to mention her hair ...

She stubbed out her cigarette, got up to flush the evidence down the lavatory, opened one of her windows to get rid of the smoke. Not that she would lecture me, Ros thought wryly, but habit obviously dies hard.

God, Ros thought, as she settled herself in bed, why is everything I think of tonight connected to sex? Because, she answered herself, you had a grandstand seat at the play-offs for the National Championship. How many people get to watch other people having sex – I won't call it love because love had nothing to do with what went on tonight. Those two were in rut – and at their age! He's gone fifty and she won't see forty again – well, *she* won't but everybody else will. How many seventeen-year-old virgins get so graphic an illustration of what men and women do when they get the urge?

Which brought Ros up against the question of her mother's P.A. James Luttrell-Leigh was the perfect example of the kind of man her mother preferred; the kind who admired inordinately, but were much too respectful and in awe to do anything so gross as to touch. Did he have the hots for his employer? Ros did not think so. When he had praised her he had done so in the terms of a connoisseur praising a work of art. Which, Ros thought, nodding to herself, is exactly what my mother is. Mummy no doubt feels absolutely safe with him. No danger of him pouncing or making overtures. Mummy can sit through the whole performance and he won't even hold her hand.

6

'Darling! It's been an *age*. How are you?'

Livy turned from the jars of imported pickled herring – Billy was as finicky about them as he was about everything else – to survey the fashionably emaciated figure of a woman with whom she had been at school.

'Hello, Muffy. What are you doing in Zabar's at this time of the morning?'

'I know. *Ghastly* isn't it? But nobody else has that perfectly *divine* Swiss mountain honey and Hughes simply refuses to eat toast without it! The last time I trusted someone else to get it they brought back some *perfectly dreadful* stuff from California or somewhere so I had *no choice* but to make this trip myself.'

Muffy Hadfield's smile was feline and Livy braced herself for the sharp dig of her claws. 'Looking for some new delicacy to tempt Billy's palate?'

Not you, Livy told her with silent disdain. Nobody is more unappetising than you. Your hip bones are like flying buttresses and your neck could string a tennis racquet. But you are a Hadfield. A name Billy would just *have* to add to his trophy list. So he did.

'Just some pickled herring,' she replied. 'Billy is very particular about pickled herring.'

'He would be, wouldn't he? I mean, they are something he would have been brought up with.' Then the clincher. 'I can't say I've ever eaten them myself.'

She surveyed Livy mordantly. Even at ten in the morning, the fabled chic was evident. An understated, narrow-as-an-arrow, clerical grey flannel dress with crisp white collar and cuffs, cut by the hand of the Master; Balenciaga. It was eight years old but, like all Livy's clothes, as good as new, since it had been cared for over the years by a maid employed to do nothing else. Muffy's eyes gleamed covetously at the sight of the gleaming alligator tote-bag over Livy's shoulder, matching the plain, low-heeled pumps.

'So, tell me, how is everyone?' she asked. 'Billy? The children?'

'Very well, thank you.'

'I suppose you are going to the wedding?'

Muffy was referring to the forthcoming marriage of Livy's eldest nephew, Ward Winslow Jr., who was marrying Jane Douglas, of the political dynasty, in Washington.

'Yes. Diana is a flower girl.'

'Sweet ...' It was said without any sweetness at all. 'Is Ros a bridesmaid?'

'It's not my daughter's "scene" ,' Livy shrugged with a 'you-know-how-teenagers-are' smile.

'I heard she was in Providence.' Muffy's pencilled-in eyebrows lifted in disbelief that Rosalind Randolph should be living in such an un-chic backwater.

'You heard wrong,' Livy was able to inform her pleasurably. 'She is in California.'

'At Stanford or UCLA? After dropping out of Wellesley, I mean.'

'Rosalind is studying privately,' Livy said, overriding the dig.

'Studying what?' Disbelief became outright scepticism.

'Art.'

'Oh, yes, She does have a talent for sketching, doesn't she?' Muffy struck again. 'But I would have thought the very best place to study art was Europe? I mean, you are living there, and it is only five minutes to Italy from London. Who on earth learns anything about art in California?'

'The group Rosalind prefers to study with is based in Sauselito.'

'Oh ... *that* sort of art ...'

Satisfied that she had pencilled a moustache on Livy's portrait of Rosalind, Muffy prepared to depart. '*Lovely* to have seen you.' She turned to go then turned for one last hit. 'Oh, and my love to Billy ...'

Bitch! Livy turned her back. They had never been friends; merely moved in the same circles. Muffy had always been jealous of Livy; which was probably why she had taken up with Billy; an act of pure revenge, though by then Livy was well aware that there was no shortage of women willing and able to partake of her husband's sexual expertise. Once, whilst paying a visit to the powder room at *Lutece*, she had overheard two women discussing her husband's reputation as a lover.

'Tireless, darling,' one had said to the other, 'the kind who wears you out, which is no doubt why he goes through so many, or so I'm told.'

'*Told?*'

'So help me God, darling.'

'Which one? Yours or his …?'

But Livy was by now inured to Billy's philandering. Sex with him had been over and done with a long time ago. At first, she had found it exciting and strange. Billy did things that she had only read about, added to which she was still under the spell of his newness, his rough-hewn difference from any other man she had ever known. No man had ever looked at her as Billy did, making her feel all hot and bothered. But the attraction had not been hot enough to withstand the loss of libido which accompanied her pregnancies, and the revulsion she felt at his adultery and treatment of poor Yetta.

Johnny had never walked around naked in the privacy of their bedroom, nor had Livy. Billy did, with what she distastefully thought of as 'everything dangling'. To her, male genitalia was aesthetically distasteful. And Billy was, as they said, very well endowed. And circumcised. But then, so had Johnny been, like all males born in the thirties when it was the norm. The difference had been in size. And, Livy had to admit, performance. Billy not only knew what it was for, he had invented a few additional uses. But when she had balked at one or two of them he had not persisted. Merely gone elsewhere. His appetite for sex was commensurate with those he had for power and social prominence. Which was why so many of his conquests – those he wished to be known and talked about – were of women who were, to him, symbols of that power. Totems, Livy labelled them. The others; bit-part-players, night-club hostesses and television game-show hopefuls, he kept out of sight. Livy was well aware that when, as they did once a year, Sir William and Lady Bancroft and their entourage descended on Beverly Hills to stay at the Century Plaza for ten days or so, ostensibly to allow Billy to hold discussions with the various studios in which he had large financial stakes, it was really in the nature of a sexual safari into the Hollywood jungle.

Once she had realised he was a compulsive womaniser she had laid down new ground rules. He could, her unspoken permission said, fuck himself blind, but *sub rosa*. One glimpse, no matter how distant, of the flashfire of gossip or a finger being pointed in her direction and she would remove herself from his life, leaving him to drown in an empty social sea. Whatever he did had to leave her entirely untouched and untarnished *or else*. She became very adept at flourishing her trump card, and it always brought him to heel.

Not so her eldest daughter.

Trust Muffy Hadfield to wield the knife. It was obviously common knowledge that Livy was at odds with her eldest daughter. Once Ros had dropped out of Wellesley at the end of her Junior year and gone to live on Cape Cod, there was not much her mother could do but paint over the fresh cracks that had appeared, at the same time giving another coat to those which had opened up when Ros had told her mother she had no intention of making her début at the dance Livy had already spent months arranging.

She had long intended to present her eldest daughter to Society in the house on Long Island where as Mrs John Peyton Randolph she had spent so many happy years. It was to have been *the* début of the year.

But Rosalind had other ideas, and did not hesitate to make them known.

'I want no part of that silly, social world,' she told her mother, flatly. 'You should know by now that it is not my scene, except you don't know me at all, do you, Mother? You have never made the effort. Not surprising, since ninety per cent of your time is taken up with attending to your husband while the remaining ten per cent you spend on yourself. If you had devoted just ten minutes of your time to *me*, talking about *my* aims and ambitions, you would know that I want to study art, specialising in the Italian Renaissance; that once I have my degree I intend to spend a year in Florence and then get a job with a good museum as an Art Historian. I have no intention of wasting time on the "right" parties and dances where the "right" people will be present. I am not interested in that sort of thing. If you had ever talked to me about anything you would know that, but we don't talk, do we? Never have. Not *really* talked. As mother and daughter. About hopes and wishes, goals and dreams. Making conversation is as close as we ever come to each other: about so-and-so's dinner, and didn't X look old and isn't Y showing signs of becoming an alcoholic and have you seen Z's new collection? Life is too short to fill with such rubbish. I don't give a damn about who or what is in, out or shaken all about! I will *not* be presented to a lot of vacuous idiots who will look me over, count my assets and then discuss who will start the bidding.'

Livy, who had spent the last several months planning her daughter's début – not least the impression she herself intended to make – had never heard such a thing in her life. Nor had anybody (except Billy when in a snit) ever talked to her that way. Which was probably, she realised with a jolt, why she had always avoided *tête-à-têtes* with her eldest daughter. Rosalind had no fear of confrontation, in fact she relished it, especially when there was a principle at stake. Even when very young, she had never hesitated to wade in on those occasions when her brother Johnny was getting the worst of it in a fight with his peers. It was always Rosalind's fist which connected with a nose, Rosalind's foot which unerringly found the groin. Then she seemed to go through an endless horsey stage, but Livy's hope that by the time Ros went to Wellesley she would at long last start to show signs of femininity, was not realised. If anything, Rosalind was even more contumacious, for once there she joined the very clique her mother had hoped she would avoid: the feminists.

When this was reported to Livy by a concerned friend whose daughter was also at Wellesley, Livy laughed amusedly.

'Rosalind was always one for causes. You have no idea of the bedraggled puppies she brought home, the half-drowned kittens, squirrels with hurt paws, birds with broken wings. My daughter has a natural sympathy for the underdog. Besides,' on a knowledgeable shrug, 'one has these passions at eighteen.'

'Mine was for Gregory Peck,' her friend retorted tartly. 'I think you ought to take Rosalind a little more seriously, Livy.'

But whenever Livy was confronted by anything serious, her reaction was always the same; to call in the requisite expert and leave it to them. This time was no different. For months she had laughingly but tantalisingly fielded questions about her daughter's forthcoming début; people were asking where and when and what and how many, knowing it would be something incredibly special. How could she now tear up her detailed plans, her seating arrangements, ditto flowers, food, drink. And what, dear God, *what* would Billy say? The very thought made her feel nauseous, her desire to flee the field becoming an urge bordering on panic.

'I am not going to argue,' she said, rising from her chair at the luncheon table where Ros had made her shocking announcement, 'I will only say that I have been planning your début for months and think it both selfish and inconsiderate of you to tell me now, at almost the last minute, that you do not intend to be present. It turns all I have done into a complete waste of time.'

'All you had to do was consult me first,' Ros pointed out. 'I am not one of those cards you manipulate on that board of yours to decide the oh-so-important *placement*. But that's how you see me, isn't it? Something to be manipulated to *your* pleasure, *your* convenience.'

'How dare you speak to me like that!' Livy's voice shook even as she tried to be firm.

'Since for months at a time we don't even speak on the telephone I can't see that you have any right to quibble when I speak my mind,' Ros went on remorselessly. 'Never once has it occurred to you that this is *my* life you are arranging, *my* future, and that being so I am the one to decide what to do with them, not you, and especially not your husband.'

'Then I suggest you tell him so,' Livy said, desperately seizing the lifeline.

'Perhaps you would make the necessary appointment,' Ros flashed back, causing Livy to marvel at her daughter's spirit. The very thought of such a confrontation made her shudder. But it was a way out so she took it.

'Why can't you handle it?' Billy demanded irritably when

Livy, every edge blurred by two extra-strength valium capsules, told him his stepdaughter wanted to see him. 'This sort of thing is your department, not mine. You know very well Rosalind and I have never had anything to say to each other.'

'So I just go ahead and cancel everything?' Valium made her daring.

Billy's face darkened. '*Cancel everything?*'

'If Rosalind won't attend her own début what is the point of holding it?'

'She will do as she is damned well told!'

'Not by me, she won't.'

Billy glared. 'Then it's about time somebody made her. You've let her get away with far too much for far too long. You and her grandmother. Dolly Randolph was a bad influence on Rosalind and you should not have allowed her to spend nearly as much time with her as she did.'

Livy forebore to remind her husband that he was the one who had pursued the Randolph connection, to no avail in the end, since Dolly had never once invited Sir William Bancroft and his wife to King's Gift. As usual, that failure had been marked down on Livy's side of the ledger. His showed only successes.

'You should have asserted yourself more,' Billy thundered, conveniently, forgetting that a self-assertive wife was *not* what he had ever wanted. 'Rosalind thinks because she is clever she can run rings round the rest of us. I think it is about time I set her straight about that. And a few other things. Yes, let her come and see me. Miss Marshall will let you know when. She's got my appointment book.'

*

Livy planned to be elsewhere when that particular confrontation took place. The one thing about it which gave her any pleasure was that, in his stepdaughter, Billy was about to meet his match.

Yet Livy had to admit to a twinge of guilt where her children were concerned. Lighting another cigarette, I *should* have asserted myself more, she thought, alone in her sitting room later that night; visited Ros more, spent time with her, talked to her, discovered how she felt about things. Which is opposite from the way I feel. But I've never been any good with children; always found them impossible to relate to.

Staring at the past through a haze of cigarette smoke she saw how remote she had been with hers, but the mould had been set for too long.

She was thirty-eight years old, and legend had come to replace truth in her personal pantheon. Being necessarily emotionally void where her husband was concerned, in the last few years she had come to relate more and more to her image. It meant everything to her that the icon, Livy Bancroft, continue to be worshipped. Her marriage was a whited sepulchre, although she continued to pander to her husband's incessant demands, but she had an international reputation as Perfection Incarnate; had become an icon other women worshipped and strove to emulate.

Outwardly she was the most imitated and admired woman of her time; inwardly she was null and void. Up to smoking three packs of L&Ms a day, mostly in private – for she tried to control it in public, though even then she had made it chic by using a succession of exquisite holders, turning smoking into an art form. She also ate Valium like peanuts. But she was spoken of as Her Eminence, or The Top. Had not a new verse been added to the Cole Porter song celebrating that fact? A position she was determined to keep against all comers. Not that she had much competition. It was only when they tried that other women discovered how much hard work was involved in producing her kind of daunting perfection.

To keep it meant working at it twenty-four hours a day, but Livy was bent and determined that nobody must penetrate the façade. Nobody must know that her husband had not entered her bedroom in years. That she was remote from her children. That she was hooked on tranquilisers. She needed the public acclaim to pad the walls of her isolation cell; she needed to be admired, to be emulated, to be acclaimed. All right, so maybe I am not – normal – in the sense most people mean, but what was it Daddy used to say about people who marched to their own drum? 'Different strokes, for different folks.' Yes, that's it. That's me.

'My mother taught me how to be a perfect wife, but she never taught me how to be a *woman*,' she said to James, who had by now become her closest, indeed only confidant. Only he knew and appreciated her struggle to satisfy Billy's relentless demand for perfection; to be the inhumanly perfect wife she had been trained to be and which he had bought. Only James understood how human and therefore how imperfect Livy actually was.

He was naturally the first to know about Rosalind's refusal to make her début.

'Everybody has known for ages that I've been planning this dance. How, then, do I now tell everyone it is all off?' She shook her head helplessly, reaching for the cigarettes. 'Why does everything have to be an armed struggle where

Ros is concerned? My mother would never have stood for it.'

'She is quite adamant?' James asked.

'Absolutely. You know Rosalind; once she makes up her mind it is set in concrete.'

James smiled. 'Indeed ...'

'I don't know who she gets it from.'

'Your own mother, perhaps? From what you have told me of her, she was a very strong lady.'

Wanly: 'You mean it skipped a generation?' Then vigorously: 'But she would have wanted Rosalind to make her début as much as I did. More, in fact. She would never have understood Rosalind's attitude in a million years.' Drawing fiercely on her cigarette: 'Perhaps it is all my fault. But it never occurred to me that Rosalind would not want to be presented. And it is not as though she has not known about it for ages. I must have said it a hundred times ... "Once you have made your début" ... I cannot understand this sudden rejection.'

'I think perhaps you have never understood her,' James said.

'Like you do, you mean?' Livy asked, unable to resist the thrust.

'I like Rosalind. She is her own woman.'

'Meaning I am not!'

James looked at her. Livy turned away. 'Of course I am not,' she murmured. 'I never have been ... First I was my mother's property, then I became a Randolph and now I belong to Billy Bancroft. All my life I have been and done what people expected of me ... Rosalind is only eighteen and already refuses to do anything she does not agree

155

with …' Livy's gurgling laugh bubbled. 'She *is* like my mother, you know. Mother would argue with a steamroller.'

'Would you like me to talk to her?'

Livy's face cleared like the sky after a storm. '*Would* you? She'd listen to you because she respects you … which is why she won't listen to me.'

Ignoring the self-pity: '*Before* she talks to her stepfather, I think,' James went on. 'With any luck the one will render the other unnecessary.'

'Oh, James, if only it would!' Livy's face was heartbreaking in its hope. 'Rosalind can go her own way afterwards if only she will do this one thing for me.' With a shudder: 'I dread the thought of Rosalind and Billy having a set-to. He will be unbearable for ages and we will all suffer for it.' James laughed and Livy looked startled until she met his eyes, realised what she had said, then giggled. 'Yes, my money is on her too.' Her delicate brows drew together. 'I will never understand how I produced such a daughter; everything that I am not.'

'Ros hears a different drummer, that's all. While other girls are mooning over Robert Redford and Clint Eastwood, Rosalind's idols are Georgia O'Keefe and Mary McCarthy.'

Livy looked astonished. 'Are they?'

James smiled. Livy blushed.

'You make me feel ashamed,' she murmured. 'But it is no use pretending. I am just not child oriented. Rosalind was always a handful. Johnny was no trouble and Diana is so obedient, while David is such a sunny little soul. If you can get Ros to agree to make her début, then whatever she wants to do with her life afterwards – provided it is nothing too *outré* – she can do it. I won't interfere.'

156

'I'll do my best,' promised James. Livy held out her hands. '*What* would I do without you?'

When James at last managed to get Ros alone it was on horseback. They were at Wychwood for the weekend, a purely family one. Only Livy's sisters and their husbands were there. When Ros, who still rode regularly though her passion for horses had abated somewhat, mentioned that she would be doing so early next morning, James asked if she would mind some company.

'Not if it is yours,' she told him truthfully, for he had come to be a close friend, even if it had come as a shock to learn that he was homosexual.

Her knowledge of *them* was confined to her Aunt Toni's friend Truman Capote and certain members of her mother's coterie who always formed an adoring circle about her. James was different; he was not effeminate, he never made a play for anyone in public. He was also kind, and too much the gentleman to allow his own predilections to embarrass anyone else. He was simply James. Her friend. And ally.

So she listened to him put her mother's case as they rode through the woods at the back of Billy's estate, lush with grass and sweet with birdsong, the sun dappling the ground as it fell through the tracery of leaves, the horses – Rob Roy was still in residence – ambling placidly. In a clearing known as The Ring, because the trees formed a perfect circle, they let the horses graze and went to sit in the middle of a haze of late bluebells.

Ros had said little; gave James the courtesy of listening carefully.

157

'You have a magnanimous spirit,' he said finally. 'I don't think your mother has asked much of you, before – '

Ros laughed but he ignored it.

' – and this is frightfully important to her. What she is offering is a little *quid pro quo*; you oblige her by making your début in the way she has planned and she will allow you to go to Wellesley, take your art degree and then fund your year in Florence.'

'She won't need to,' Ros informed him with relish. 'When I am twenty-one I come into the income from the smaller of the two trusts my grandmother set up for me – I don't get the big one until I am thirty – and that will be more than enough for Italy. And as for "allowing" me to go to Wellesley; she was delighted with the results of my College Boards. I was accepted by half a dozen top class women's universities. I am and always have been a straight-A student, and if the worst was to come to the worst, I'd work my way through college. Others have done. There is no question of my mother doing anything for me. It will be a first if there is. She normally delegates to one of the servants.' Ros turned to face James. 'Do you know that when I was eleven it was my then governess who explained what had happened when I had my first period; then, when I started to develop breasts, bought me my first bra. My governess, not my mother! I was brought up by servants. Is it any wonder that I learned at a very early age to rely on myself, to keep my own counsel and work things out on my own?'

Her voice would have stripped paint.

James reached across to press one of her clenched hands. She was a smart girl, old beyond her years in many ways, but very much an eighteen-year-old in others. It was just, he thought, that she had learned not to show feelings in a so-called family in which there was no call for them.

'It's her and Billy that I don't understand, you see,' Ros went on after a moment. 'If she was in love with him, if he was important to her, then I could; but this marriage is a matter of convenience, habit and – most of all – a glittering social life. No wonder she is so thin; all she feeds on is her own legend, while the only warmth that matters is the heat from all that admiration; turn it off and she's done for.'

James's well-schooled face showed none of the surprise he felt at the shrewd insight of one so young. 'We all have our needs,' he reminded.

'But haven't you noticed that my mother has no real friends? She knows an awful lot of people she *calls* her friends, but not one of them is as close to her as you are. Other women are competition, and Billy doesn't like her having men friends.'

'Which puts me nicely in my place.'

Impatiently: 'You know what I mean, and you make no bones about what you are, but in the nicest possible way. I'm glad mother found you; it means I found a friend too.'

'But you don't need me in the way your mother does. You are not a needer, are you Rosalind? You have – perforce – become detached, but I hope not irrevocably so. It would grieve me to think that you will go on seeing life as a game of solitaire, with people as the cards to be played.'

Ros looked taken aback for a moment, but her ruthless self-honesty won out as usual. 'Yes, that's as good a description as any,' she agreed. 'And just as well, don't you think? God help me if I had been a needer. To whom could I have turned but servants?'

James saw the justice of that, but his own axe had been well honed. 'Your mother *is* a needer. She needs to be admired, needs to know her legend is intact. After all, what else has she got?' Ros frowned, and James pushed home his advantage. 'One night, that is all she is asking. One very splendid, exquisitely arranged, superbly organised dance. The kind most girls would give their eye-teeth for.'

'Just so long as she understands that I am not, repeat NOT up for auction. I have my own plans for my life and they do not include marriage. The days when that was a woman's only option are history.'

'I am sure she understands your point of view.'

'Maybe, but just in case I would appreciate it if you made it clear to her. Coming from you she will believe it, and I want no misunderstandings.'

'So you will do it?'

Ros answered: 'Only because you have asked so nicely.'

'Thank you,' James said, but in such a way as to make her swallow hard and say flippantly:

'So you can cancel my appointment to beard the lion in his den. Tell him he can, after all, present me to a garden full of WASPs, but that it means he is going to get stung for the cost. He'll love you for that!'

But once Livy – for she was only too happy to be able to impart such good news – told Billy, he took it as a climb-down on the part of his stepdaughter. And he was in such high good humour that when Livy, showing him the final plans, also showed him the cost closely followed by the guest list, he had only one complaint.

'You haven't ordered nearly enough champagne. At a Bancroft party there is never a shortage of champagne!'

7

As Livy had planned, Ros's début took place at Illyria. She had for once proved surprisingly stubborn when Billy took umbrage, since it was not one of his houses. It was a Randolph possession. But then, as Toni pointed out to him, so was Ros. Besides, Billy might have four houses but the only one he had in America was the New York town house, and that was not really suitable for what his wife had in mind.

Which was a *fête champêtre*. Livy had chosen a time when the gardens were a dream of beauty and the river of blue irises she had created all those years ago curved away into the distance to disappear into the heavy bank of trees. From the trees she hung small crystal bowls in which pink candles burned and gave off the fragrance of roses; she had a vast marquee of white hung with pink silk and hundreds of candles in glass storm-lanterns, which flattered the complexions of the women. She had piled vast, brilliantly coloured silk cushions on its carpeted floor so that her guests could lounge at their ease while they ate cold lobster, hot, spiced shrimp with creole rice, Virginia ham marinaded and honey-baked, vol-au-vent stuffed with creamed asparagus, truffled eggs and a whole baron of cold, marbled beef flown in from Scotland along with several fresh Tay salmon, all to be served with a crisp green salad and Livy's famous mayonnaise, and washed down with limitless champagne.

In another tent, this time of palest eau-de-Nil, a series of orchestras played for the guests who danced on the specially laid dance floor.

Presiding over it all was Livy, a goddess in an intricately draped masterpiece of white crêpe from Madame Gres, her swan neck wrapped in a baroque necklace of diamonds, seed pearls, pink and blue sapphires and coral. Smilingly she presented her daughter, who wore a narrow-waisted, deeply square-necked, full skirted dress made up of layers of pure silk organza, each one in a different shade of blue-grey, from slate to sapphire, so that she looked like a drift of woodsmoke. Its tight but transparent sleeves ended in a graceful frill that just reached her knuckles, and around her neck she wore the traditional string of pearls, only hers had been left to her by her grandmother and originally belonged to Serena Fairfax, who had married Henry Randolph in 1714.

Her hair, already short, since she could not be bothered with a style that had to be remembered all the time, had been shaped in order to show off her small neat head, and for once in her life she was wearing make-up. The transformation was dazzling.

Her mother had taken one look and been furious. 'That is not a suitable dress for a debutante.'

'Well, I'm not wearing that white confection you have provided. I may be only eighteen but I am not an *ingénue*. I

162

can still be virginal in shades of blue, if that's what is worrying you. I'll even carry a certificate if you wish.'

'What is wrong with the dress I chose?'

'Nothing – for some insipid blonde. White ruffles! Honestly mother!'

But Livy had wanted a foil to her own *soignée* sophistication; for them both to be in the same colour – well, almost, for whereas hers was the brilliant white of icing, the dress she had chosen for her daughter – perfect for an eighteen-year-old making her début – was softer, creamier, tenderly *jeune fille*. The subtle blues of Ros's own choice was not at all what Livy had in mind. It made her creamy skin glow, while the effect of her flesh through the organza was entrancing, as was the rustle the skirt made. And Ros wore it well. With shocking dismay, Livy saw what she had not bothered to take into account before: a rival. Her own self but twenty years younger. She had wanted Ros to emerge from her crysalis in the time-honoured way; what she had not expected was a beautiful butterfly. Ros was, she saw to her shock, a beauty. She had Livy's own hair, eyes and fabled skin, allied to her father's classical profile. With horror, Livy realised she was looking at her first really serious competition in years.

'Your make-up is wrong,' she said.

'No it's not. Under the candles it will be perfect.'

With yet another shock, Livy realised that Ros was indeed her mother's daughter. Someone else who took everything into account. When James saw them together, she immersed herself in the balm of his admiration, but knew that, this time, it was not only for her.

'Sir William is downstairs, waiting,' he reminded.

'We'll see what he says,' Livy warned her daughter, as she

163

swept out, though the tight white dress was not the kind that allowed one to sweep anywhere. It was Ros, behind her mother, her wide skirts sweeping the stairs, who had Billy staring.

'Well,' he said, in a voice filled with surprise. 'This is a turn-up for the books.'

Ros made him a sweeping curtsy. 'Will I do?'

'Do what?' His brown eyes were actually twinkling.

'Make the right impression, of course.'

'Oh, you'll do that all right,' Billy assured her emphatically. 'Now I have not only the most beautiful wife; I have the most beautiful daughter.' And with the kind of courtly gesture he had made so much his own he offered them each an arm.

James glanced at Livy. She was as cool and collected as ever, but he sensed the fissures that lay behind her mask of elegance. 'I think you'll agree, Sir William,' James said smoothly, 'that tonight Lady Bancroft has surpassed even her own impossibly high standards.'

He saw Livy's head go up, her shoulders go back, felt the white smile she threw him as she moved towards her husband like the Supreme Champion she was.

'Yes, Mummy,' Ros said, 'perfect, as usual.'

As they stood in the receiving line together, James watched the faces of the guests as they got their first look at mother and nearly grown-up daughter together; not a sight many people had seen. Most did a double-take, and he winced as he heard people congratulating Livy.

'Darling, talk about the ugly duckling! I don't know when I've seen such a beautiful swan.'

'It is incredible what Rosalind looks like when she is not on the back of a horse.'

'Like mother, incredibly look-alike daughter.'

'That dress! A stroke of absolute genius. Such a marvellous contrast – especially as one would have expected it to be the other way around!'

'You are going to find them standing in line for such a gorgeous creature…'

James saw the subtle change to Livy's limpid smile as the encomiums went on, monitored the way it sank into her face, became an etching.

The evening was a colossal success – they were still dancing at four o'clock – but not in the way Livy had intended. Livy had wanted her daughter's début to be the most talked about event of the year, enhancing her own reputation as society's perfect hostess. What she had not planned for – because it had never occurred to her – was that that same reputation would tremble in the thunder of the stampede to get to her daughter. Once this uncomfortable truth was assimilated, James knew that Livy would not press her daughter to follow the social scene; that she would relievedly see her disappear into four years of college in New England and that not only the year in Florence would be provided; there would probably be an offer of two.

But her performance was, as always, flawless, totally unconnected with what she was really feeling. She floated here and there, overseeing everything, indicating fresh champagne with a nod of the head, the removal of a flowing ashtray with a frown, tossing a smile to one, a quip to another, exchanging a word with a third.

'My God, how does she do it?' he overheard one woman

mutter to another resentfully. 'That sort of perfection is not human!'

Only James saw the little vein beating on one side of the smooth, unlined forehead and unobtrusively appeared at her side with a glass of water and a small tablet, which she took while he shielded her from the eyes that followed her everywhere. It would keep her migraine at bay for another hour or so but it meant that the next twenty-four hours at least would be spent in her big French bed, the felt-lined curtains drawn to keep out even the faintest glimmer of light.

If on the one hand her effect on her mother was unintentionally traumatic, on the other, Ros had soared in Billy's estimation. When he saw the way the young men clustered about her, registered the names they bore, he was cock-a-hoop. For the first time since he had married her mother, Billy became the doting stepfather.

He was a good dancer, light on his feet, in command of his partner, and his opening dance with Ros, who had started dancing lessons when she was seven, drew admiring murmurs and approving applause, so did the way he relinquished her to the first of the line of young men awaiting their turn.

But several hours later, having imbibed freely of the champagne that everyone was drinking like water, he sought Ros out again, and as they were both under close inspection she had no choice but to take his arm and let him lead her out on to the floor, though to her way of thinking, the obligatory first dance was all he was entitled to. The truce was with her mother, not him.

As soon as he put his arms around her she stiffened. This was not the embrace of a doting stepfather; it was that of a sexually aroused man. He held her so close that she could feel his erection pressing against her thigh. Her first instinct was to wrench violently away, but even as she thought it she knew she could not; too many people were watching.

'Seewhatyoudotome?' Billy asked in her ear, his vowels sliding together on a tidal wave of champagne.

'Unintentionally, I assure you,' Ros hissed. He was drunk, she realised, but what he was doing was still unforgivable.

'I couldn't believe my eyes when I saw you come downstairs tonight. You've been hiding your light under a bushel of oats all this time. I was beginning to think you were half horse, but not any more.'

'I'm not the horse,' Ros snapped furiously. 'You are!' What was pressing against her inner thigh reminded her of several stallions she could name.

'I'm only human.'

There was no way she could create a scene on the dancefloor, but neither could she allow this to continue. He was drunk enough to start groping her any minute. His breathing was becoming stertorous and he was beginning to tremble. So she sank her heel deliberately and heavily into his instep.

'O-o-o-w-w-w-!' Billy let out a howl of pain as he dropped his arms before half-staggering, half hopping backwards.

'Oh, how clumsy of me. I'm so sorry. I'm not normally so heavy-footed.' Taking advantage of his recoil she freed herself. 'These wretched heels... Perhaps we had better sit this one out.'

For the benefit of the watching public, Billy managed to smile over the throb of his foot, where her heel had all but penetrated the thin patent leather of his dancing pumps.

167

'It's all right,' he lied, bending over somewhat in an attempt to conceal his similarly throbbing erection and striving manfully not to swear and thus achieve some measure of relief. 'Just get me to a chair ...'

'Of course.' Leaning heavily on her shoulder Billy limped to the chair that was swiftly provided.

'I'm *so* sorry,' Ros lied. 'I should not have had that last glass of champagne, it does go to one's head, doesn't it? But I swear it's my last, no more for me, even tonight!'

In that one sentence she managed to establish that it was really all too, too much, that the party was indeed a never-to-be-forgotten one, and that she would not have had this happen for the world. The indulgent smiles she met assured her not to worry her pretty little head about it.

When, in his Jeeves-like way, James materialised from nowhere Ros turned to him to say: 'Would you be a darling and help Sir William into the house and check for damage? I'm afraid I trod rather heavily on his foot.'

'Of course,' James said at once.

'I'm all right,' Billy snapped irritably, dominating his slur. 'There is no need for all this fuss.' He did not want to get up until his erection was completely deflated. 'Just let me sit here for five minutes – but get me another glass of champagne meanwhile.'

Ros managed to stay out of her stepfather's way until just after 4. am, when things were at last beginning to wind down. All that remained was to stand by her mother and him – and she would see that her mother stood between them – and speed the departing guests on their way. After which she would sleep for at least twelve hours.

But it had been a good party; nobody got falling down

drunk, though there had been plenty of over-bright-eyed young men as eager and willing as her stepfather to paw her about. She had discouraged them too, but not quite so painfully.

She began to cross the hall to go through the east drawing room and back out on to the lawns when suddenly, out of nowhere, he stepped in front of her to seize her wrists in an unbreakable grip, saying, 'We have unfinished business, you and I.'

Now he really was drunk. Not only slurred but swaying.

'Don't be a fool!' Rosalind protested, struggling to free herself and becoming frightened when she found she couldn't.

He propelled her across the hall and into the darkness of a small room where coats and umbrellas were kept and in an instant was all over her, his tongue in her mouth, his hands on her breasts.

'Feel me ... see how I am about you?' He grabbed her hand, clamped it on his erection.

'You bastard! I don't care if you *are* stoned!'

Ros's voice rose stridently, a mixture of shock, fright and pure outrage. He lifted her skirts, fumbled between her legs, but he had inadvertently given her the freedom she needed to move.

Bringing up her knee she drove it into his groin with all her young strength behind it. Billy's breath launched itself on a great whoosh of champagne as he dropped her wrists to clutch at himself in agony. She stumbled backwards, almost falling in her haste to get away, but he was too intent on his pain to notice. She dived for the door, yanked it open and ran blindly across the tessellated marble hall. Straight into James.

169

'What on earth … ?' He caught her by the shoulders as she cannoned into him, then he felt the convulsive trembling under his fingers, noted the tear-filled glitter in eyes that were a mixture of fright and fury. 'What's happened?'

'That – that bastard, Billy Bancroft!' Ros gulped. 'That's twice tonight he's tried it on with me.'

Muffled groans were coming from the cloakroom along with the sound of retching.

'*What?*'

'He is, as you would say, pissed as a newt.'

'He must be,' James said aghast, 'to do something so stupid. Is he in there?' He jerked his head at the cloakroom door from which moans and imprecations were still issuing.

Ros nodded. 'I kneed him,' she said simply. 'Serves him right!'

'I agree, but that means he's in no shape to bid his departing guests goodnight. I was on my way to look for him at your mother's request.'

'Shit!' Ros frowned as her mind worked. 'We'll have to give him time to put in an appearance.' Then her face cleared. 'Of course … he's on the phone. That's an every day occurrence, even at a party. A vital call from England, where it is almost half past nine in the morning.'

James nodded approvingly. Billy's phone calls were legendary. People would accept that explanation with knowing shrugs. 'That will give him five minutes at least – ten would not be out of the ordinary,' he calculated. 'You go and find your mother and start telling the lie; I'll give him five minutes and then wander past asking for him in a loud voice.'

'If it weren't for the gossip I'd like nothing better than to

170

show him up for the bastard he is!' Ros said viciously. Her fright was fading, her anger still fierce. 'I hope I've crippled him!'

Ten minutes later, walking slowly and carefully – a fact he attributed to his still painful foot – Billy put in an appearance. He was pale and there was a drawn tightness to his mouth, but he managed to stand with his wife and stepdaughter as they bade their guests goodnight.

Livy did not notice that her husband and daughter never looked at each other. She was in a fog of pain and had lost half her vision. It took all her considerable self-discipline to stand there shaking hands and making pleasantries. When the last guest had gone she swayed.

'Mother!' Ros exclaimed in alarm.

'One of my wretched migraines ... help me upstairs. I need to lie down.'

'Allow me,' James said quickly, stepping forward, for it was obvious Billy was in no shape to support his wife. He was looking grey, his mouth set in a grimace at his own pain.

'I'll go and tell Manby to prepare,' Ros said quickly, seizing the excuse to get away. Manby knew all about her mistress's migraines.

'So kind ...' Livy said in a blurred voice, touched by the unexpected gesture. 'It was a lovely party, thank you, dar-ling.'

Ros reached up, kissed her mother for the first time in a very long while. 'Yes, wasn't it,' she said. 'Goodnight, Mother. Take care ...'

Hoisting her skirts she ran off in the direction of the stairs. It would be many years before she saw her mother again.

8

'She's here! The car just came round the bend in the drive!'

One of the girls keeping watch at the window turned excitedly to where Diana Bancroft was examining herself in the mirror above her chest of drawers in the room she shared with three other girls, also boarders at the exclusive school set high on the coast of the Sussex downs.

'Keep watching,' Diana requested, frowning at what looked like a burgeoning spot on her chin and applying a dab of the special cream the skin specialist had recommended. 'What is she wearing?'

'Hang on …'

The girl at the window watched eagerly as the mink-brown Bentley Continental drew up outside the front steps of the school. A uniformed chauffeur got out, opened the rear door, held it while a man got out.

'Oh.' The way it was said had Diana whirling from her mirror.

'It isn't your mother, it's your father.'

'Daddy!' Diana's voice was dismayed. 'But she *promised* …' Her large, pale blue eyes, inherited from her grandmother Gaylord, brimmed with disappointed tears. She had been so looking forward to showing off her mother; her beautiful, untouchable, unsurpassable mother, who on her rare visits to the school always caused every window to be crammed with envious girls, eager to see what Diana Bancroft's glamorous mother would be wearing this time. It gave her a brief participation in her mother's glory, and she used it to burnish her shabby self-esteem.

'Well, there's only the chauffeur beside him. He's looking up, he's smiling – he's looking for you, Diana.'

Diana flicked tears away with a forefinger, set in place the right smile and rushed to the window.

'Daddy!' she called down brightly. 'I'll be right down.'

Snatching up her blazer and straw hat – hats were mandatory while on school grounds – she ran out of her room, along the corridor, down the big staircase into the wood-panelled front hall, hung with school shields and portraits of former headmistresses, and into her father's open arms.

'How's my girl?'

Billy swung her up, with an effort, for at fifteen Diana was a big girl; big boned, heavy featured, and flaxen blonde.

'All the better for seeing you,' Diana answered promptly. She had never been in awe of her father, which was why she'd never had any trouble handling him. Daddy was Daddy, and though she knew other people went in fear and trembling around him, he had never been anything but indulgent where she was concerned. It was her mother she was not sure of, for nothing she did seemed to meet with her approval, though she had striven for it all her life. To Diana, her mother was The Incomparable.

'Where's Mummy?' Diana asked now, casually. 'I was expecting her, not you.'

'She couldn't come, sweetheart. She has a committee meeting followed by a lunch – one of her charities.'

'Oh.' Diana masked her disappointment with the ease of long practice. 'I expect it is an important one.'

'She is involved in arranging a concert at which the Queen will be present – she's the patron, and you know your mother. Everything has to be perfect.'

'Oh, yes,' said Diana. 'I do know.' She slid her arm through that of her father as they left the school for the Christmas Holidays. 'I'm glad you came, anyway.'

Billy smiled down at his daughter. 'For you, anything,' he assured her, not bothering to add that he'd just come from a private and profitable meeting with a potential business associate, whose country house was not ten miles away from Diana's school as well as being on the way back to town. Otherwise, just the car would have been sent to pick her up and bring her home.

'So what have you got planned for us this Christmas?' she asked, as they entered the waiting car. 'Are we going to Clifftops as usual?'

'I wouldn't be at all surprised,' Billy teased.

'Great!' Diana loved their house in the Carribean. Its isolation – or the nearest thing to it since the Bancrofts never went anywhere without their cushion of guests against which to bounce their total lack of anything to say to each other – meant she would have her mother practically to herself … give or take a dozen people.

'Will Johnny be there?' Diana adored her stepbrother, who did not subject her to merciless teasing as did her own brother, who had nicknamed her The Carthorse, shortened to Carty – but never used in the presence of their mother, who did not approve of teasing.

Billy, on the other hand, had pragmatically advised her to get used to it. 'You'll have a lot worse than that said of you in your life,' he'd told her. 'Once you get beyond the puppy fat stage you'll show them all, mark my words.' The trouble was, at that particular time Diana was finding it hard to get beyond anything but the food she ate – especially chocolate – for comfort.

'Johnny is spending Christmas with his new girlfriend,' Billy said now, answering her question.

'What's her name?' Diana asked on a pang of curious jealousy.

'Polly Benedict.'

'*The* Benedicts?' Diana was as knowledgeable as her father about Who was socially Who, both in England and America.

'*The* Benedicts,' Billy confirmed smugly.

'Serious?'

'I hope so. She's a lovely girl.'

She was also an heiress and a catch.

'What about David?'

'He's bringing a friend of his ... nice boy; Charlie Daventry.'

'The Earl of Wiltshire's son?'

'Yes. Do you know him?'

'No, but his sister is a year ahead of me. She's a drip.'

'Haven't you got a friend you want to invite?'

'I don't want to,' Diana shook her head. 'I don't need to. I'll have you and Mummy.' Especially Mummy, she thought. I'll make her notice me this time, I will. I've got a good report, and I've managed to lose twelve whole pounds. I do so want her to be pleased with me.

As Diana was indeed a carthorse for her height – twelve stone at five feet two inches when she began her campaign – she had a long way to go. But she'd secretly stuck to her calory counting for six weeks now, even renouncing sweets and chocolate on the excuse that they gave her spots, which excuse turned out to be true. Her skin cleared up like magic. But then, she had been eating an average of eight ounces of chocolate a day, at least one packet of biscuits and as much cake as there was. They too, were now forbidden.

It was her mother who had shown her the error of her ways. At half-term Diana had been taken to be measured for a new school uniform since her old one was giving at the seams, and for once her mother had gone with her instead of a servant. Livy had taken one look at her daughter in her bra and pants and exclaimed: 'My God! Diana! No wonder your uniform does not fit! You are as fat as a pig!'

The accusation, made on a note of shuddering revulsion, had cut Diana so deeply that she bled inwardly for days. But it also set in concrete her instant resolve to become thin. To be able to show her mother that her made-to-measure uniform hung on her, that she was no longer a size sixteen but a ten who intended to become an eight.

Like her mother.

Diana's ambition was to be everything her mother was. Beautiful, elegant, admired, imitated, written about, idolised.

Her body she now vowed to re-shape by diet and exercise (her PE instructor was both astonished and admiring of the dedication she suddenly showed after previously having to be all but threatened to take any sort of exercise) and eventually, when she was old enough, she would have her face fixed. She wanted a thin nose, like her mother (her own was a small, fat snub), cheekbones like her mother (her own were non-existent), with the same faint hollows beneath them, a clean, sculpted jaw like her mother (her own was padded with fat) and chiselled lips (her own tended to the bee-stung). Now, she could not restrain her eagerness to show her mother a Diana who had already lost twelve whole pounds and intended to lose at least four times twelve before Christmas was over.

Before the car had stopped at the foot of the steps leading to the *porte cochère* of Morpeth House, she was tumbling out of it, throwing her hat on to the footman's chair just inside the front door and running up the stairs shouting: 'Mummy, Mummy, I'm home!' proud of the fact that she was no longer panting like a grampus when she reached the top. She raced down the corridor to the double doors at the end, where her mother's suite was located, and burst through them into the sitting room like an explosion. Her mother was at her tiny secretaire, James bending over her shoulder as he pointed something out on the sheet of paper they were studying. She looked up as the door crashed open and Diana saw her wince. 'Darling, *must* you go around like a herd of elephants?'

'But I'm not –' began Diana, dying to tell about her lost pounds.

'Yes, you are. I could hear you coming up the stairs. Walk sedately, darling, don't clump. Now, come and kiss me.' Livy offered a cheek to which Diana pressed fervent lips.

'Careful, darling … I've spent ages on my face this morning. Important meeting; I shall be under inspection so

I must look my best. You have only just caught me; I must leave in two minutes.'

'You always look your best,' Diana said adoringly.

Livy was wearing a stunningly chic taupe ribbed-silk suit with a narrow skirt and a short, round necked jacket which ended at her fragile hip-bones. Her plain Roger Vivier pumps were of crocodile to match her handbag, and her hat was a small, close-fitting taupe cloche with a large, shocking pink taffeta bow by her left ear, which was matched by her lipstick and her nail varnish. In her ears she wore dime-sized pearl studs to match the double choker which sat just inside the round neck of her jacket. The fragrance of *Ma Griffe* eddied about her.

'Sweet ...' Livy's smile bathed her daughter for a moment, and Diana quivered, her eyes moist with worship, as one hand touched her cheek briefly. 'Now, run along, darling. I have to leave in five minutes and this must be right first. So much to do and not enough time in which to do it. We'll talk later.'

'But, Mummy, I want to tell you – show you –'

'Later, darling. You've got the whole holidays to show and tell me as much as you wish. Now run along, there's a good girl.'

Livy's voice was dismissive, and as she turned back to her desk she did not see the way Diana's blue eyes welled or her shoulders slumped as she did as she was told. But James did. He also noticed what Livy didn't.

'You've lost weight,' he said. 'It suits you.'

Diana whirled, face glowing again. 'Does it show?' she asked eagerly.

'Oh, yes. Most definitely.'

Livy's head lifted and she turned back to examine her daughter more closely, noting the way the new, cleverly cut uniform hung on an undoubtedly slimmer body, though one had to look really close to register the fact. Diana was still enormous, she winced. But she was trying, bless her.

'Why, yes, it does,' she complimented, sounding surprised. 'Keep up the good work, darling, because you've still got a long way to go ...'

'I've given up chocolate and biscuits and cake and –'

'Good,' Livy said, but absently, her mind once more on her speech. 'They don't do you any good anyway.'

'I eat fruit instead, and vegetables too. I'm going to be thin, Mummy, you'll see; thin just like you.'

'Yes, of course you are, darling,' Livy said warmly, if still absently.

She flashed another, finally dismissive smile, then returned to what really mattered. 'James, do you think I should say something at this point about the history of the charity?'

When she got to her own room, on the floor above, Diana threw off her school uniform and rushed into her bathroom to stand naked on the scales. Eleven stone two pounds. Her shoulders drooped as a gusty sigh escaped her. As usual, her mother was right. She still had a long way to go. In which case, she resolved, spurred on by her mother's wounding words, she would make a start by foregoing lunch. Her mother would not be present, nor would her father. He only ever ate business lunches. James would be in attendance on her mother, as usual, which meant Diana would be on her own unless her brother was back. If he was around she would have to be very circumspect. He seemed to live in some secretive world of his own but he still noticed *everything*.

She was lucky; he was not due until the next day, so the lunch that came up to her room on a tray was flushed down the loo. She spent the afternoon plucking the hairs from her legs and doing exercises.

For her tea she had an orange – vitamins were important – and as her mother and father were dining out, she asked for a chicken salad for her supper – without dressing – eating the salad but not the chicken, which followed her lunch down the loo. For her pudding she ate an apple. She was in bed before her parents returned, feeling ravenously hungry but consoling herself with the thought that her hunger was consuming her fat.

At breakfast next morning she circumspectly but very slowly ate a boiled egg, cutting her half slice of toast in two so that it seemed she had eaten a whole slice, and at lunch with her brother, who had arrived back from Harrow not long before, she kept him talking by plying him with questions about school, while she played with the small helping she took. Afterwards, she went straight to her bathroom and brought it all up.

By the time they left for the Caribbean ten days later she had lost another half a stone. It was easy to eat less – everyone knew she was dieting – then on leaving the table, go upstairs to her bathroom, stick her finger down her throat and vomit up everything she had eaten. She was obsessively eager to prove to her mother that she *could* be thin, *would* be thin. When Livy took her to buy her holiday clothes she was able, for the first time, shyly to wonder about a bikini.

'Nobody over a hundred and ten should *ever* wear a bikini,' her mother pronounced authoritatively. 'They show every pound, and you still have far too many of them to lose. Next summer I am sure you will be able to wear a bikini. For now I think the nice tailored maillot with the half skirt is the most flattering. You are still seriously overweight.'

'But I am losing it, aren't I?' Diana asked disconsolately.

'Yes, and nicely. But slowly does it. You are only fifteen, darling. I am glad to see you have started to eat sensibly and like I said, this time next year, when I am sure you will have lost all your excess poundage, I will buy you the prettiest bikini I can find.' Diana's ego swelled with pride, which her mother punctured when she went on frowningly: 'Unfortunately, you've got a big frame which takes some covering, and your thighs are far too heavy. Yes, definitely the plain navy maillot; it is very flattering and cut so as to minimise them.'

'But navy is so *dull!* Can't I have the pink one?' Diana looked at her mother beseechingly. 'Please, Mummy, *please!*'

'Oh, all right, the navy and the pink, but I want to see a few more pounds lost before you wear it.'

'I promise, Mummy. I'll swim lots and play tennis and –'

'Yes, all right,' Livy winced. There were times when her daughter reminded her of nothing more than an untrained puppy.

They finished their shopping, Diana mortified when a pair of jeans she wanted would not pull up over her large thighs. Grimly she swore to lose another seven pounds at least. Those jeans would fit her within the next week or else!

They did. She was light-headed and there were times when she would have killed to satisfy her hunger, but the jeans slid up over her hips and fastened at the waist with room to spare, justifying all her effort.

Getting on the scales one morning a week after they had arrived in the Caribbean the needle stopped at ten stone dead. She had lost twenty-eight pounds, was now eating mostly fruit and salads but still repeating her bathroom regurgitations, very carefully because her brother had eagle eyes and would undoubtedly comment if he noticed. So she took to going for walks – 'good exercise', being her excuse, up-chucking in some secluded spot where the sea would wash away the evidence. She was aiming for seven stone. Forty-two more pounds to go.

As the days went by the weight fell off her. She could actually feel her hipbones! She would lie in bed at night smoothing them with her palms, smiling happily to herself, planning how she could deny herself even more unnecessary food.

She was now past the stage where she thought of nothing else but that. Her stomach was positively concave, and her spare tires – she had had two – were long gone. As for her hefty thighs, they were anything but, nowadays. In the privacy of her room she tried on the bikini she had sneaked back to buy along with the jeans, and was thrilled with her reflection. She did not see what others would have done if they looked beyond the big shirts she had taken to wearing, thinking gleefully of the day when she would whip them off to say triumphantly: 'All the better to surprise you with!' The hollow cheeks in a face that had formerly been plump, the way her ribs and collar bones were now well delineated. She did have a big frame, her maternal grandmother's slavic peasant heritage, but where formerly she had had far too much flesh covering it, now she did not have nearly enough. But she was in the blind grip of her obsession. She wanted to be like her mother, and as yet her mirror did not tell her she was, so she continued to hide herself in her big shirts, saying she did not want to burn. Being blonde she had a very fair skin and the sun had always been her enemy, so nobody wondered why.

It was Charlie Wiltshire who inadvertently brought down her house of cards. He and David had virtually ignored Diana, in the manner of fourteen–year–old boys, until Charlie, who like David consumed food like a steam engine, observed innocently at luncheon one day, out on the terrace under the big awning that shielded them from the fierce heat of the midday sun, having watched her push poached salmon with herb mayonnaise around her plate without carrying it to her mouth: 'I say, Diana, you eat like a bird.'

'Yes, a vulture,' David said, which caused them both to fall about laughing.

'David,' warned his mother, but she frowned as she looked at her daughter. 'You do look somewhat peaky, Diana. You are not overdoing the dieting, I hope.'

'Of course I'm not,' Diana denied on a laugh, helping herself to a goodly slice of strawberry millefeuille and covering it thickly with double cream. It would all come back up anyway.

'What my sister likes she likes a lot of,' David observed to Charlie, 'because there's a lot of her.'

'Not any more there isn't,' Diana denied hotly. 'I'll have you know I've lost –' she caught her mother's eye – 'a lot of weight,' she finished lamely.

'You mean five pounds?' David asked innocently.

'No, I mean – twenty-five.' It was now forty-five, but that figure would have raised eyebrows.

Billy looked at his daughter over his glass of Montrachet and noticed the thinner face. 'You mustn't overdo it, Princess,' he warned, jocularly. 'I don't want you fading away.'

'I won't do that, Daddy,' Diana said, laughing heartily.

'Diana is losing her puppy fat, that's all,' Livy said. 'And it suits her.' She smiled. 'The Duchess of Windsor was right when she said a woman can never be too rich or too thin.'

But when Diana's Aunt Toni arrived to spend a couple of weeks in the sun, she did a double-take at her hollow-cheeked niece and in her usual straight-from-the-shoulder way and before Diana could stop her, she lifted up the all-concealing turquoise cotton shirt and exclaimed: 'My God, girl, you are wasting away!'

She turned to her sister. 'Haven't you noticed anything?' She sounded incredulous.

Bridling, sounding defensive: 'Diana needed to lose a lot of weight –'

'I agree, but not this much. For God's sake, Livy, you can see every rib, and look at those hipbones. You could positively sit on them.'

'Oh, now Toni, you are exaggerating as usual,' Livy protested, but she said to Diana: 'Take off your shirt, darling.'

'I'll burn,' protested Diana, red-faced with anger and fright. She could have killed her aunt. She had pounds to go yet and interference was something she did not need right now.

'How much have you lost?' Toni asked bluntly.

'Not all that much,' Diana evaded. 'Only about thirty pounds.'

'Times two and then some! You were size sixteen, weren't you? Let's have a look-see ...'

Before Diana could escape, her aunt had seized the shirt and was whipping it up over her niece's head.

There was a silence then 'Oh, my God!' Livy gasped. Her daughter's big frame was covered by a minimum of flesh, every rib delineated, hip bones like shelves, flesh falling away from skinny arms and thighs, young breasts shrunken.

'I am a twelve – an English twelve,' Diana lied, pleadingly.

'The hell you are. You are on the verge of malnutrition from the looks of you. How long has this been going on?'

Diana mumbled something.

'Speak up, I can't hear a word.'

'I said three months!'

Livy was shocked speechless. Never for a moment had she suspected that under the big concealing shirts, her daughter was bordering on the skeletal.

'I don't want to be fat!' Diana burst into tears. 'I want to be slender, like Mummy. She's five feet eight and she only weighs a hundred and ten!'

'Your mother has bones like a bird, that's why. You have the bones of a dinosaur, like me.' Toni slapped her own ample rear. 'We are not meant and never will be model thin like your mother. We are not designed that way. I got down to a hundred and fifteen once and everybody thought I was dying! One hundred and twenty-two is as low as I can go without everybody asking me what is wrong with me. You, my poor deluded infant, are cut from the same cloth. You need another fifteen pounds on that king-size cladding of yours.'

'No!' Diana's voice soared until it went off the scale. 'I won't be fat, I won't! I want to be like Mummy. I *will* be like Mummy and nobody is going to stop me!'

Seizing her shirt she rushed off the terrace, sobbing hysterically.

Toni turned to her stunned sister. 'So?' she asked sardonically. 'What else is new?'

'I had no idea she was – well – that she had been dieting so drastically,' Livy defended. 'I'd better go to her,' Livy rose from her lounger, but with enough reluctance to make Toni command exasperatedly: 'Stay where you are. I'm better at these things than you.'

Livy subsided gratefully, justifying her relief by saying: 'I know, and I only wish I found it as easy but I don't and that's all there is to it. I don't know how to be your kind of mother, Toni! And it is not as though I haven't tried.'

Self-pitying tears brimmed but, as always in the manner of Livy's weeping – never actually spilled. That would mar her make-up.

'It is supposed to come naturally,' Toni snapped acidly. 'If anyone should have been the lousy mother it's me. I'm supposed to be the good-time girl, you always played Snow White. All you have to do is spare them a little time, give them a little attention. They are your flesh and blood, you know.'

'I do know, but I just can't seem to get close to them – besides,' Livy hesitated. 'You don't have a husband like mine.'

'So leave the bastard! Divorce him!'

Livy's smile made her sister flinch. 'Where would I go? What would I do?'

'Make a new life for yourself.'

Livy shook her head. 'I was taught how to make a life for my husband. Mother never taught me how to make one for

186

myself. I'm Livy Bancroft, my whole existence is based on being Livy Bancroft. I don't know anything else. As mother would say, I made my bed, now I must lie on it.'

'She never meant that to include a bed of nails!' Urgently: 'You have to do something, Livy, and soon. You are already estranged from Ros, who I hear is living the *vie bohème* in California – and I'd dearly like to know what made her pack her bags the very morning after one of the most successful débuts ever – and unless you do something about Diana you are going to lose her too.'

'Ros and I made a bargain,' Livy said colourlessly. 'She would make her début as I wanted after which I would let her live her life as she wanted.'

'Including dropping out of Wellesley after her Freshman year?'

'We did not discuss details. She said she wanted to become an art historian, and once she had her degree to go and study in Florence for a year. I didn't know she would drop that idea and choose California instead.'

'Was there a man involved? There usually is in such cases.'

Livy's smile was faint but derisive. 'Where Ros is concerned?'

'Okay, so she tends to intimidate, she is still a beautiful girl, and to a lot of men, women like Ros are a challenge.'

'Ros loves conquering challenges.'

Toni laughed, if ruefully. 'That she does. Ros is tough, she can handle herself. Not so Diana. She worships the ground you walk on, you know that –'

'Poor Diana,' Livy said, but distastefully, and Toni knew that to Livy, the tragedy was not that Diana hated what she was but that she *was* what she was. Toni was very fond of

187

her sister, but there were times when she wanted to shake her till her teeth rattled. Right now was one of them.

'Ah, shit!' she swore violently, and stamped off to look for Diana.

Left alone, Livy reached for her large straw hat, which she tilted to protect her face – she *never* sunbathed since too much sun was bad for the skin and terribly ageing – and lay back on her padded lounger, reaching for her iced tea. She *had* thought of leaving Billy; had even sat down with pad and pen and calculated how much a year she would need to maintain her present life-style. Her Randolph money would have given her scope to do so, but it would also have meant being on her own, and always, the spectre of poor Sally Remington rose up before her when she thought of life without Billy. Even now it still had the power to stay her hand. She could never, *ever* go back to being a lone woman again, especially now that she was forty-seven, though daily care and attention to her face and body denied that fact.

There was also the position she held as Lady Bancroft. She and Billy no longer had anything to say to each other but he still dominated her life. Everything she was stemmed from him; he had urged her on to the heights because her reflected glory lit him in the most flattering glow; she was a household name because that was what he had wanted. The trouble was that she was now as hooked as he was; she needed to go on being what she had become, and the thought of not being Lady Bancroft and all that entailed, of being a divorcee (and the thought of taking Billy on in a messy – and vindictive where he was concerned – divorce) was not to be borne.

Yet she had found herself, of late, thinking a lot about the choices she had made in life, wondering what would have happened if she had not married Billy. The trouble was that Billy had chosen *her*; even if she had taken another road she would still have come across him standing at one of its corners.

Perhaps we should not have had any children. I did not particularly want them. I had Johnny and Rosalind, and Billy had his twins. God help them.

Billy bullied them mercilessly. Both moved like shadows in their father's orbit, stunted by its size and power, and deliberately starved of anything that might have enabled them to grow. She could not accuse him of doing that to Diana or David.

No; I am the failure, she thought. Although if I were to go to Billy right now and tell him that his daughter was on the road to anorexia he would merely interrupt one of his endless telephone calls to make another one; to a doctor specialising in its treatment; Diana would be off the island in an hour or so *en route* to a private hospital where she would remain until the problem was solved. That was Billy's way. Call in the professionals.

No! thought Livy, sitting up abruptly. Why should it always be his way? Why not mine for once? He is not here to countermand my orders. This is my chance to do something on my own. It's about time I did. Toni is right: its always 'Billy says' around here. Before her normal cowardice could sap her strength she got up from the lounger and made her way purposefully into the house.

Toni was sitting on Diana's bed, her arm around what were now very bony shoulders. Diana was red-eyed and heaving dry sobs, but no longer weeping.

Both looked up as Livy entered.

'I think,' Livy said, 'it's time Diana and I had a little heart to heart.'

'Livy –' warned Toni, who had already wasted ten minutes trying to talk a hysterical Diana out of her fixed resolve to become her mother's clone.

Livy said firmly, 'I am her mother, Toni, and this is something between Diana and me.'

'You won't make me change my mind either!' Diana cried wildly. 'I *am* going to be thin, *I am*. You have made it quite clear that you don't like me fat, so I'm going to be thin and maybe you'll like me then!'

'Diana … darling, that's not true … I love you no matter what you are.'

'No you don't! You couldn't even come to school to pick me up because you had something more interesting to do. You hardly ever come to Speech Days or Open Days and you were revolted when you saw how fat I was when we went for my new uniform.'

'I was shocked,' admitted Livy lamely. 'I hadn't seen how fat you were getting.'

'Why should you? You never really see me anyway!' Diana was sobbing again. 'You like being thin: You are always saying that you can never be too thin, so that's what I'm going to be. I want to be like you; I want people to stare at me and envy me and say how beautiful I am. But I'm fat and ugly and nobody cares … even Daddy said I was a great big lump.' The crying was escalating into hysteria once more. Diana's grip on her emotions had always been a loose one.

Livy cowered; as always, she was unable to handle

190

unbridled emotions. Her good intentions were falling apart and she had no idea how to stop the disintegration.

'Diana …' she faltered. 'Please don't do this to yourself, you can't afford to lose any more weight. You will make yourself ill.'

'If I do *then* maybe you will take notice of me!' Diana was now well into hysteria, her voice wild and high, her now much depleted chest heaving, her face contorted. 'Nobody has ever taken any notice of me when you are around, so if I have to look like you to get noticed then I will – and if that means being thin then I will be thin, do you hear me!' Bending forward to scream the words at her mother Diana repeated her vow. 'I WILL BE THIN!'

Then she turned and ran in the direction of her bathroom door. Before they could gather their scattered wits she had slammed it behind her and turned the key in the lock.

Livy fell onto the bed, shaking badly. Even her voice shook when she said: 'Well, I made a mess of that, didn't I?'

'She was upset before you came in. I was having a hard time convincing her myself.' Toni paused. 'She's in the grip of an obsession, Livy, which means she needs the kind of help we can't give her. Professional help.' She stared hard into her sister's shocked eyes. 'What Diana needs is a psychiatrist.'

Livy moaned and put her head in her hands. 'Oh, dear God … Billy will be furious …'

'What the hell is going on here?' were Billy's first words, when his sister-in-law collected him from the plane which had brought him from Miami. 'What's all this about Diana locking herself in her bathroom and refusing to come out?'

'We discovered she has been starving herself,' Toni said

briefly, starting up the car. 'She got this idea into her head that she was hideously overweight so she went to the other extreme. Now she is nothing but skin and bone.'

'She looked all right to me a week ago.'

'Have you seen her out from under those loose shirts she's been wearing?'

Billy scowled. That meant no.

'You'll see what I mean when you see her,' Toni said.

'She's out of the bathroom, then?'

'After they managed to break the door down. Which was when we discovered she'd taken a couple of handfuls of Tylenol. So we had to get a doctor to her. Fortunately, the Howards have one staying with them on Paradise Island – it's all right; he is not the kind to blab to the press about it. Livy soon had him eating out of her hand anyway ... She told him Diana was on a slimming-kick and that she had taken the tablets in mistake for laxatives – I know, I know, I wouldn't have believed it either, but once Livy fixes you with those big brown eyes you'll believe anything. He gave Diana an emetic and she was very, very sick, but she got rid of the Tylenol. Right now she is asleep, has been for hours. The doctor will be back to see her tomorrow.'

Billy grunted, but Toni recognised his expression. Heads would roll.

Livy was sitting by their daughter's bed when he went in to see her.

'She's all right,' she said quickly, forestalling his question. 'Sleeping peacefully, and will do for quite a while yet. The doctor says she should come through this with no ill effects.'

Billy said nothing. He went to the head of the bed, bent

over Diana for a moment then seizing hold of the bed clothes, swept them back. Diana was wearing a thin cotton nightshirt, sleeveless and thigh-length. Her stick-thin arms and legs were plainly visible, as were her prominent collar bones. Billy re-covered his sleeping daughter then he jerked his head at his wife before stalking out of the room. Without a word she followed him, closing the bedroom door sound-lessly behind her. He went into his study, passing Toni and James, standing in the hall, without a word. Livy followed him. That door shut them in.

Toni turned to James, drew her finger across her throat then asked: 'Do you want to eavesdrop or shall I?'

'If we go out on to the terrace we can both hear,' James said. 'I think it as well to be close-by, just in case. I don't think Sir William is very pleased.'

They went out onto the flagstone terrace, which ran right round the house, and sat on the wide, flat top of the wall which edged it, outside but not directly in front of the windows of Billy's study, which were open but screened by Venetian blinds.

At first they could hear nothing. Whatever Billy was saying he was not raising his voice to do so.

'How did he take it?' James asked eventually.

'He was not best pleased. It will all be our fault, of course. The fact that he saw Diana every day for weeks will be conveniently forgotten; we will be the ones who should have noticed, said something, done something … the usual list of errors and/or omissions.'

They listened in silence for a while. 'I don't like it,' James said. 'Normally, when Sir William takes someone to task he raises his voice.'

'Not when he is giving them fifty tongue-lashes,' Toni said. 'Billy can flay skin with a whisper.'

James frowned, stared out to sea.

'I can just about – knowing her all too well – understand my sister not noticing,' Toni said after a moment, 'but I thought you were fond of Diana.'

'I am – of all the Bancroft children, and I *had* noticed she was losing weight.' James was deadly serious when he said: 'But I never forget that in this house, I am first and foremost a paid employee. Anything else is a bonus.'

'You mean Livy?'

James's eyes gleamed, but: 'I know my place …' he murmured.

Toni's head went back as she gave vent to her whooping laugh.

'Yes, at the top of the list. We may have the money, my dear James, but you have got what we Americans call class.'

'Which lies, I think, at the bottom of all this. Why Diana is, unlike Rosalind, nothing like her mother.'

'Because she is like her grandmother,' Toni informed him. 'Our mother, Livy's and mine. She was – I discovered after her death because during her lifetime she kept it well hidden – from a remote part of Eastern Europe, a place called Ruthenia, once Hungarian now part of Czechoslovakia; of peasant stock; broad of face, big of body, flaxen blonde. Livy and Cordelia have our father's looks. I got the Ruthenian genes, like Diana; but whereas I have made the best of what I have – '

'Indeed,' murmured James.

'Poor Diana thinks she has had a raw deal. She does not

want to be a peasant; she wants to be an aristocrat, like her mother.'

James said compassionately: 'Poor Diana. And what about David? I can see nothing of his mother in him except maybe her charm, but from what Sir William has said occasionally, I get the impression that David is himself when young.'

'Which accounts for the fact that he is his father's favourite.' Ruefully: 'Mind you, he is a charmer. God help the female population once he starts testing it out.' Then Toni frowned. 'I can never quite figure out what is going on behind that smiling countenance. That blinding charm conceals unexplored depths.'

James's glance was an acknowledgement. 'You've noticed too?'

'So does he – which is why I wonder what made him miss this.' Probably because it suited him to, Toni thought. She had seen David sitting, ostensibly looking at a magazine or constructing one of his model cars, but she knew he was taking in every word said. He never drew attention to himself; was capable of appearing to be absorbed for long stretches of time, but Toni had the sense of a huge radio dish turning ceaselessly, picking up every signal and sorting them out in the computer of his mind, before storing them in his memory. He was also effortlessly clever. Not for David the laborious plodding of his sister, who had been last in line when brains were handed out. His reports from Harrow were uniformly excellent, and it was taken for granted that he would go on to Cambridge, where a First was a matter of course.

What disturbed Toni about David was that unlike Diana, who was ruled by her emotions, David did not seem to have any. As a child he had been a small, self-contained, secret-holding buddha. Now a teenager, he seemed older and wiser than many of his peers, and already possessed a body – as Toni had noticed when he sauntered on to the terrace in a bathing slip that left nothing to the imagination – that promised perfection in a year or two: broad of shoulder, deep of chest, narrow of hip, long of leg. Not for David the torment of spots or puppy fat; he was a beautiful adolescent; he would be a stunningly handsome man.

'Poor Diana,' Toni echoed, then flinched as a sound plummeted through the Venetian blinds. The sound of a hard hand slapping wood. Toni could visualise it: Billy behind the big partner's desk; bent forward, face red with anger, mouth pouring forth vitriol; Livy facing it, still and silent, white-faced and terrified.

For God's sake, Livy! she seethed inwardly. Pick up the lamp and brain him with it! *Why* do you allow him to treat you like this? Raise your own voice! Get a word – a hell of a lot of words in edgewise! Her expressive face was a thought monitor and James read them all.

'She won't, you know,' he said quietly. 'Whatever the cost in personal terms – and Diana's is not the only tragedy in this family – she has not the will to escape her role as public icon, private victim.'

Toni said nothing. What James was saying was all too true.

In Billy's study, Livy stood in front of his big desk like a pupil called before a headmaster prior to being expelled. Her eyes were glazed, her gaze fixed on a point above her husband's head. The moment Toni had left for the airport – Livy had begged her to collect Billy because she knew that her sister could soften him up – she had swallowed a couple of valium, and the moment she heard the car return she took two more, so she was distanced from the immediate impact of Billy's anger. She could hear his voice, cutting, saying virulently horrible things, telling her she was a bad mother, a selfish bitch who thought of nothing and nobody but herself, but its power was muted. The valium acted as a buffer between him and the nausea such tirades caused if she did not take it. She had learned long ago that the way to handle his rages was to keep silence. Arguing — not that she was capable of rebuttal — only made him worse; weeping produced his contempt. Silence he took for guilt.

'… you are expected to handle things in my absence!' Billy was almost shouting now. 'I'm sick and tired of coming home to crisis after crisis. What the hell do you do all day?'

His voice was the barking staccato which, without the blur of valium, used to hit her ears like sledgehammers. 'Jesus Christ!' he snarled, 'I am sick and tired of you and the careless messes you make, always expecting me to clear them up!'

That was unjust so she opened her mouth to tell him so. She never made messes. They had been forbidden by her mother.

'I'm talking about your children, for God's sake! Your elder daughter took to her heels years ago, now here is your younger trying to starve herself into your image!'

'I became what you wanted me to be,' Livy told him blurredly. 'I've always done what you wanted … don't you want me to any more?'

'That's right, blame me … it's always my fault.' His voice curled round her like a whiplash.

'What do you want me to do then?' she asked, stupefied by the valium.

197

'You've already done it!' he accused viciously. 'By doing nothing, as usual. By doping yourself with those damned pills! By ignoring your daughter; allowing her to starve herself. Now I've got to put things right. Diana will have to go away, of course. She needs professional help. I'll make arrangements for her to leave as soon as possible. We'll say that she's gone down with some unknown virus which needs specialist attention. That's your job. You know who to call and what to say, how to start the right story on its rounds, so do it, and do it right.' The staccato bark was back. 'We must both go with her of course, show a united family front. I want no pointed fingers about this, not a word of conjecture or gossip – do I make myself clear?'

Livy nodded obediently. She had the sense of looking through the wrong end of a telescope; Billy seemed a long way off. Yet his presence smothered her like thick black smoke. 'See that we are packed and ready to leave as soon as the air ambulance gets here. I'll call Miami and have the Gulfstream readied. You know the part you have to play. A distressed mother; concerned, worried. I'll write the script; all you have to do is look the part and say the lines. Do I make myself clear?'

Livy nodded again, obedient to her master's bark.

'Then get out of my sight before I say something I'll regret!' And with that he turned his back on her.

9

David took a deep drag of the joint, drawing the best Colombian Red deep into his lungs, before allowing the residue to trickle away through his nose, after which he let out a deep sigh of contentment. 'Mmmmmmm ...'

His companion abstracted the joint from his lax fingers and drew on it herself, but less deeply, since she was not nearly so accomplished in the art of enjoying marijuana. She coughed a little, spluttered some more, handed the joint back again with tears in her eyes.

'It's no good,' she husked, 'I shall never get used to this stuff. It's not as though I even smoke cigarettes. Why do you need it? I would have thought that after all the exercise we've taken this past hour you would be exhausted, never mind relaxed.'

'The joint puts the finishing touches, that's all.'

'Well, you nearly finished me. I don't know how you keep it up – ' she touched him lightly, 'in more ways than one.'

'Long practice,' David assured her with mock solemnity. 'I had my first sexual experience with one of the girl grooms

at Wychwood. I was fourteen, she was twenty-one. Jilly ...
that was her name. Blonde, athletic, tireless ... We used to
meet in the hayloft ... Incredible thighs ... she could get you
in a grip that was impossible to escape. All that riding ... Ah,
me ... happy days ...'

'I haven't noticed you being particularly unhappy lately,'
the girl flared aggrievedly.

'I'm not. I'm one of those people who is never unhappy.
What goes up must come down and vice versa.'

'And I've noticed you always seem to land right side up.'

'Just my luck', David assured her. He stubbed out the
remains of his joint. 'I must go, I've got a supervision in
fifteen minutes.'

'What about tonight?'

'Can't. I've got an ADC dress rehearsal.'

'How did you get into *that*?' Envy and awe vied for
supremacy.

'They asked me.'

Yes, thought the girl, also in the last term of her first year
at Cambridge; you'll always be asked. Not for you standing
with your nose pressed against the window. Apart from *who*
you are – Sir William Bancroft for a father and Olivia Gaylord
Bancroft for a mother – Harrow behind you and Trinity
College, Cambridge in front of you, what you are will always
ensure that you will never be excluded from anything. They
are probably already preparing the vellum for your First ...

She climbed out of David's bed, pushing her long blonde
hair back in the gesture of the times. Perhaps it was just as
well. Mocks were coming up and, unlike him, she would
have to work hard to get a good grade. Besides, David did
not like his girls to become possessive. If they did he became

200

unobtainable. She would just have to concentrate, try not to think about him and the identity of the girl who would tonight take the spot she had vacated this afternoon; try to accept that where he was concerned she was just one of many.

'An incredibly apt pupil,' David's housemaster had told his proud parents, and Billy was especially proud since, at last, he had a son he *could* be proud of: a real Bancroft, through and through. To look at and in his capabilities. The twins would never fail to remind him of their mother, which was why he had written them off long ago. They were useful; they did competent jobs provided he kept an eye on them, but they were Yetta's sons, not his. David, on the other hand, was almost pure Bancroft. All he showed of his mother was her charm.

David was very clever. As his housemaster had also said: 'A first-class brain in a remarkably handsome head. It does not surprise me that David got a Major Scholarship. He has it in him to achieve whatever he wants.'

Billy intended to see that David achieved it all.

The scholarship was a start because Billy bought him the new car he wanted, though Livy had been appalled when David had gone out with his father in the Bentley and come back driving his own Porsche. But David had soothed her fears. 'I have had the very best of driving instructors; a man who for years drove an area car for the Metropolitan Police. I intend to live a long life, my dear Mama, so don't fuss. Tell you what, come out with me and I'll show you how good I am.'

His father had chuckled. 'Go on,' he had urged his wife.

'Find out for yourself. I'd let him drive me anywhere and you know how particular I am.'

Livy was of the opinion that her husband spoiled his youngest son in a way his eldest two would never have understood. But then, Livy had to admit, David was so *good* at everything. He had played cricket *and* run for his school; he was reading at four and chattering in flawless French at six. He was obedient, never gave any trouble, and his manners were enchanting. Livy's friends, whenever they came to the house for lunch, always clamoured to have him brought down from the nursery so that they could exclaim over the way he bowed over their hands, as he had been taught by his French Mademoiselle. His charm was legendary, and as he grew older, no matter what havoc it left in its wake, none of it was ever attributed to him. David Bancroft, they said, led a charmed life.

Even when he encountered tragedy whilst punting on the Cam during his second term up at Trinity, he emerged from it whiter than white. Afterwards, nobody was quite clear exactly what had happened; only that there was a lot of good-natured bantering between David and another scholarship boy from Birmingham named Robert Dixon, which ended up as a not so good-natured challenge and David and Robert jumping in the river to see who could swim to Queen's Mathematical Bridge first. Nobody realised that Robert – not, like David, a strong swimmer – had somehow or other been hit on the head by one of the poles which were being moved around in an effort to stop the punts from drifting, for though he went down he did not come up. Those who thought he was swimming under water became concerned when David reached the bridge and there was still no sign of his rival. David and two other undergraduates dived and dived again until the drowned nineteen-year-old's body was brought to the surface.

David went to visit Robert's parents. An only son, they were devastated by his death, pathetically grateful for David's visit, assuring him they did not blame him in the least. It was a tragic accident and one they would give anything to be able to reverse, but he must not blame himself.

David said they were very kind. Privately he thought in surprise he had never had any intention of accepting blame for something that was not even remotely his fault. Yes, there had been a dare, yes – foolish now, in retrospect, since he was such a poor swimmer – Robert had accepted it. All he need have done was admit that he was not up to it and nothing more would have been said. David thought it was incredibly stupid of Robert to have accepted a challenge that on his part had been nothing more than an attempt to lighten the boredom of an afternoon he was already regretting. He himself never took risks, and this unnecessary death served to confirm the rightness of that decision.

The truth of the matter, he thought with his normal clinical dispassion, was that it was all Robert's own fault. But he consulted his mother's perfect taste as to the kind of flowers he should send to the funeral.

He was sixteen when he was accused of impregnating the fourteen-year-old daughter of one of his mother's friends, and when confronted by both mothers readily and honestly admitted that yes, he had had sex with Patty; adding, with some surprise that he should have been singled out: hadn't everybody?

203

That Patty's mother had no idea her daughter had for some time been sleeping with any male who showed the remotest interest or offered a kind word was evidenced by her subsequent hysterics, and when Patty subsequently admitted that she had no idea who the father was but that as David was the last man to have sex with her she had decided on him, David was not only exonerated he was apologised to.

Patty was despatched to a clinic in Switzerland where her pregnancy was terminated, after which she was incarcerated in a convent run by an enclosed order of nuns who permitted no males but their Confessor on the premises.

His father told him he was proud of him for owning up, but David knew the real reason because he knew his father. His mother said he ought to have been more careful – and how did he come to know about all the others? Because, David answered truthfully, on his very first time there had been four others ahead of him in the queue.

It was different with the dancer he met when his father took him to see a television spectacular – produced by his company – being made at Pinewood. She was no fourteen-year-old; she was twenty-five and she was a tall, lithe, spectacular blonde. David saw the way she looked at him and knew all he had to do was wait for her to make the first move. It lasted six weeks, by which time his interest – always short lived – had flagged. He was back at Cambridge when he had a letter from her telling him she was pregnant and what was he going to do about it, suggesting that unless he did something – such as forwarding her the £500 she needed for an abortion – she would inform his father. David beat her to it, having pondered over the problem whilst beating his room-mate at backgammon. If he paid her off himself – and it was not a question of being unable to afford it since he had a more than adequate allowance which he rarely touched, being of the opinion that it was so much more sensible to let other people spend their money on him – it might well be only the first of a whole series of blackmailing touches. After all, he was who he was, and the world was full of people willing to take advantage of that fact. Her story could be nothing more than a farrago of lies. If, on the other hand, he went to his father and told him honestly that he was in a spot of bother and only the vastly experienced, knowledgeable, and, last but not least, powerful Billy Bancroft would know how to get him out of it, he was sure his father would do just that, since while he would approve of his son's womanising – a real chip off the old block – he would not stand for some cheap slut of a dancer daring to presume, etc. etc.

It was like pressing the right button of his father's programme, he thought later. Billy's reaction was exactly as David had expected. The matter was taken in hand and dealt with. David never enquired how. It was enough that it was no longer worth worrying about. A few months later he watched the TV spectacular along with his mother – viewing of anything in which his father was involved was mandatory – and there she was, kicking her endless legs and smiling her capped smile. Which, David reflected, helping himself to another stuffed olive, she was no doubt not smiling any more. Stupid bitch. If she did not have the commonsense to take precautions, then serve her jolly well right. If, on the other hand it was a try on, she'd picked the wrong fellow. But it made him realise that it was a mistake to get involved with the hired help.

Which had the effect of making him realise how lucky his mother was where James was concerned. He was the perfect employee. Related to half *Debrett's* and flat broke. His mother's confidant and one of the group of homosexual *Cavalière Servante* who formed Livy Bancroft's coterie, all of them fulfilling to the letter the strict criteria she demanded from all her admirers: well connected, amusing, single-mindedly devoted to her, and never likely to do anything so vulgar as make a pass. It was from this group that David learned his other sexual interests, and, by the time he was eighteen he was bisexual.

Of all the Bancroft children, David was the only one James did not particularly like or trust. There was too much prompt and smiling deference about him, too much sunny charm. His smile was shellacked. And to quote Toni von Anhalt (she had just married for the third time) on another doubtful character, as fake as a three dollar bill.

Rosalind had been feisty and salty of tongue but intrinsically honest and straight as a die. Her brother Johnny was so good-natured as to be thought stupid by some people, but James knew that his kindness was as true as he was. It would never occur to him to lie or cheat. James was sure that David did both, cold-bloodedly and without compunction. He had more than once caught him mercilessly teasing his sister Diana, who was too conscious of her own shortcomings to fight back, and could only weep as David ran verbal rings around her. He had apologised both times, even looked shamefaced, but James's keenly sensitive inner ear had caught the ring of false coinage.

He also knew that while David seemed to adore his

mother, in reality he held her in contempt. James had watched him watching her, though as soon as she smiled in his direction he was all deeply attentive deference, and he was always eager and willing to escort her anywhere, seemingly proud to have her on his arm. It was his father who really mattered to David, which as far as James was concerned was a flashing indicator as to the true character of the youngest Bancroft.

So he was at once aware of what David was up to when, one hot and sultry afternoon on the island, after snorkelling in a secluded cove on the far side, just the two of them, they came out of the water after leaving their catch in a keepnet, to sunbathe for a while. James was a dedicated swimmer with a sensuous appreciation of water on skin; which was why, whenever he could, he swam naked, which was possible only when he was on his own.

When David stripped off his brief bathing slip – nothing more than a *cache-sexe* – to say, 'No ladies to put to the blush and I do so like sunbathing naked, don't you? I hate a deadly white strip,' before spreading himself out supine on the rocks to soak up the hard hot sun, James did not remove his own trunks. He merely lay back and awaited events.

After a while: 'What's it like, being a homosexual?' David asked. When James did not reply at once he went on anxiously: 'I don't mean to pry, but – well, a fellow made a pass at me the other day and to tell you the truth, I felt quite tempted … I hoped – well, if you wouldn't mind – you might put me straight about one or two things.'

'I thought you were straight,' James said.

'So did I, up till now. Have you ever had a heterosexual affair?'

'Yes.'

'Before or after – you came down on your particular side, I mean?'

'Before.'

'What decided you to go the other way?'

'I fell in love.'

'With a man?'

'Yes.'

'Was it – reciprocated?'

'No.'

'So what did you do?'

'Got over it.'

'But – you had an affair?'

'Yes.'

'And it was better than with a woman?'

'Yes.'

'Have you had many affairs?'

'What is many to one person is a few to someone else. How many have you had?'

David shrugged. 'About a dozen – not including one-night stands.' Then, tactfully, but inexorably he led the conversation back to homosexuality, wanting to know how and what and who and when and why. James answered him honestly and factually, careful never to reveal anything of importance in his own sexual background which, he sensed, was what David wanted to know, all the time acutely aware of the absorbed brown eyes in the handsome face, even more aware of the beautiful brown body, wide at the shoulders, narrow and lean at the hips, glistening with a mixture of sweat and sun-tan oil and leaning indolently back on its elbows, its thick, brown, mouth-watering sex lying half tumescent on one firm thigh.

James knew that all he had to do was lean down, kiss that tempting mouth and he was done for. Knowledge and experience painfully acquired ensured that he did not. Circumspection had been a necessary part of his life for so long that it was now deeply engrained in his psyche. He had lost a promising career once because he had allowed his desire to overrule his commonsense. He was not about to do so again. Temptation was something he had trained himself to combat; the onset of AIDS had strengthened his resolve not to throw away a lifetime for the moment. He took his opportunities where and when they occurred, providing he was sure there was no risk. David Bancroft was a risk of the kind that could destroy the cushiest berth James had ever had in a storm-tossed life.

He enjoyed his job; he lived in the lap of luxury and was well paid for it; he liked and admired his employer. To maintain this long-coveted position in luxury's lap James was prepared to do whatever it took. If being nice to his employer's children was part of his duties then so be it. But what David was after would take that niceness into territory James was much too commonsensical to enter, yet still found a matter for regret. Sex with David Bancroft would be, he was sure, of the kind that remained in the memory for ever.

He also knew that David was testing out his own sexuality, which was, at going on nineteen, already remarkable. Women found him irresistible. In fact, such had been his success with women that James was surprised he should need to explore the other side, and yet, on reflection, not surprised. Along with a great deal else, David had inherited his father's compulsive sexuality and that had a drive like a three litre engine, even now, at the age when most men would be slowing down.

As his body, in spite of his brain, began to respond to what was being offered, James realised that he would have to be very, very careful. Should he allow himself to be seduced he knew that if and when it came out – and it would, David would see to that; it was all part of what he considered 'fun' – he too would be out. On his ear. With David's sunny smile seared into his memory.

Oh, no, he thought. Very definitely no, thank you. As aware as he was of the pleasure to be obtained, of what that mouth would feel like, the silk of that firm, muscled body in his arms, he was even more aware of the danger he would be courting and no five-minute fling was worth jeopardising the rest of his life for. So he stood up, said: 'Time to cool off, I think,' and dived into the vivid turquoise water, before his arousal betrayed him.

Six months later, David lay in a canopied bed, above which was a mirror which had reflected the night's doings, arms behind his head, ankles crossed, smiling up at his reflection.

Sitting on the side of the bed, head in hands, the middle-aged man with whom he had just indulged in a bout of pure sensuality, said in a muffled voice: 'Dear God, how did I ever allow this to happen? Your mother is one of my oldest friends ... how can I ever look her in the eye again? She will know, I know she will. Livy has a sixth sense for these things. She will know something is wrong between us and never for one minute suspect what it is. – Not my pure and perfect Livy ... unsoiled and unsullied; so exquisite in every

way … To have seduced her son! Her very own son …'
Something like a sob escaped him.

David laid a hand on the freckled back, feeling the slack of
the skin, the aged roughness of it, but his voice was pure
concern when he said: 'Luddy, don't take on so, please. If my
mother says anything I shall be honest with her – tell her – '

'No!' It was hoarse and violent. The man swung round,
revealing a distraught, lined face under thinning grey hair,
pale blue eyes teary and desperate with a mixture of fear and
panic. 'You must not say anything! You don't understand
… so young …, so innocent …'

'But mother knows you are homosexual; she has always
known and it never made any difference; she has always
regarded you as one of her oldest and closest friends. Why
should this change anything?'

'Because of *you*! She would at once think I had corrupted
you – and God knows, I suppose I have. How could I have
got so drunk?'

'We were both the worse for wear,' David assured him
helpfully.

'That is even worse! Drunk *and* dishonourable … There
is no excuse for what I have done!'

'Luddy, I am nineteen years old …'

'And I am more than twice that! I know your mother;
her standards are of the very highest; she has accepted what
I am and never condemned me, but you are her adored son!
What I have done is so terrible she can do no other than
condemn it. Hitherto she has been the soul of tact and
discretion; my private life has been my own affair; bringing
you into it is something she is not likely to forgive – ever. I
shall be cast out …'

211

'Then go away for a while. If you feel so guilt-ridden that you are unable to face her then don't. Invent some vital reason but go away until you think you can.' David allowed his voice to falter. 'Of course ... I shall miss you terribly ... This has been so wonderful ... I had no idea it could be so wonderful ...' He laid a hand on Laurence Ludbrooke's thigh, felt it quiver, continued on nobly: 'but since you feel so strongly ... I know how much my mother means to you – '

'Everything! *Everything*!' Laurence 'Luddy' Ludbrooke had been part of Livy Bancroft's 'Court' for the past twelve years, one of the stable of 'walkers' who escorted her when Billy was unavailable. Livy confided in him – not the 'Ears Only' intimacies she shared with James – but small things which she made seem more significant, since she knew how vital their friendship was to him.

In a drab, for the most part unsatisfactory life, dominated until he was well into his thirties by his mother, that very *grande dame* Constance Ludbrooke, Livy Bancroft had set alight a flame that lit and warmed it; no longer just 'an extra man' her friendship gave him an importance he had long wanted but never managed to achieve. He received invitations purely because he was a member of her Inner Circle; he arranged his life around hers, spending part of every year in England simply to be with her, following her back to New York when she returned home to visit family and friends and see to her affairs there.

Livy had no idea of the young men he bought, of the things he did to them or they did to him: it was part of his other life, which he had so far carefully concealed from her. She had no idea he frequented clubs where sex was openly

212

offered for sale along with drugs; where any and every perversion was available, where groups of men discussed why this fister was better than that one, and others either suffered or inflicted pain of a kind that no one could imagine unless it was experienced.

Which was how he had come to have David Bancroft in his bed. He had seen the beautiful body first, like all the others, naked and unashamed, standing by the bare brick wall of Hades, the club he frequented most, in that part of it known as the Meat Rack, where the boys who were for hire plied their trade. The boy had his back to him.

Luddy gazed greedily at the beautiful buttocks, firm and tight and unbelievably luscious, like a ripe peach. He began to push his way towards them, but when he was only about three paces away the boy turned and he saw the face that belonged to the body. David saw him at the same time and his lack of expression – a mask in which not even the eyes had life – dissolved into one of delighted, even relieved, recognition.

'Luddy!'

Luddy put a finger to David's eager lips. 'We don't use real names here,' he hissed, pulling him away from the Meat Rack and over to a secluded corner, ignoring the two men already there, kissing and fondling one another.

'What are you doing here?' he demanded, his eyes darting everywhere in case there should be someone present who knew them both.

'I came with Pa, he is tutoring me in the Long Vac. I'm learning the business, so to speak, and I also came along for the ride in his new plane – have you seen it? It's a Grumman Gulfstream 2 and flies –'

'I don't mean New York I mean here, in this club.'

'Oh, I was brought by a fellow I know but he seems to have vanished ... can't think where he can have got to ...'

'What's his name? Do I know him?'

'I doubt it. He's a New Yorker but not a social one. He works in Pa's office. He's showing me the sights non–New Yorkers never see.'

'That I can believe! Your mother would be horrified if she knew you were in a place like this.'

'You are,' David pointed out.

'That,' Luddy said with dignity, 'is different. Now, come along. This is no place for the likes of you.'

'But I haven't seen anything yet! I was told to wait here like a good boy and that's what I've been doing. Mind you, it is absolutely fascinating to watch ...'

'Yes, yes ...' Luddy said hastily. 'Now come along. The sooner I get you back to the right part of town the better ...'

'At least let's have a drink,' David protested. Wheedlingly: 'Please, Luddy. This is a real eye-opener for me. I've never seen anything like it in my life. To tell you the truth I didn't know such places existed.'

'He had no business bringing you here. If your father knew ...'

'You won't tell him!' David laid a hand on Luddy's naked shoulder. It was warm and tactile and caused Luddy's lower belly to flutter uncontrollably.

'Of course I won't!' he said sharply. 'You must not even be seen here. Now come along ...'

'Even if I wear a mask? Some people are, I notice. Where do I get one?'

214

'I don't think —' began Luddy, his resolve weakening rapidly as David took him by the hand, said: 'If I get one of those masks no one will have any idea who I am. Oh, come on, Luddy. I shall be quite safe if I am with you.'

'But your father —'

'Is dining with some of his business cronies. He told me not to expect him back before the small hours.' David grinned. 'Which means he will be going on to his own kind of club …'

Meeting the beautiful, melted chocolate eyes, Luddy read there a knowledge that for a moment chilled him, then he thought pragmatically: How can he not know? It is an open secret. Everyone knows but nobody mentions it in Livy's presence.

His chill changed to warmth as he once again became conscious of the hand holding his, felt it squeeze gently.

'Well, just one drink, then,' he agreed helplessly. '*After* we get you a mask …'

But one drink became two, then three, all doubles, after which things were hazy. He remembered dancing, holding a warm, naked body in his arms, nuzzling a neck and an incredibly soft cheek … He remembered a mouth, a tongue. Then his own tongue lapping, lingering, laving, sucking. Oh, Christ! He curled up and died inside. Livy would never forgive him; never. How could he ever face her again after what he'd done?

No matter that they had both drunk too much, that he had not intended … So many of his intentions already paved the road to his particular hell. After tonight he had no doubt that his name was on Satan's own computer.

'I can't ever face her,' he moaned. 'I shall never be able

to look her in the eyes knowing what I've done, knowing she will despise me. Oh, God, I wish I was dead ...'

'She is not in New York with Pa and me,' comforted David. 'She is in Paris buying clothes. But you'll be in London for her birthday next month, won't you?'

Oh, the *innocence*, mourned Luddy. The sweet boy had no idea. Just like his sainted mother; no dirt could possibly ever cling to her either.

David was frowning, as though pondering pros and cons. 'If you really feel you cannot face her, why not go to Gloria's first? Time spent with her will make you *long* to get back to mother.'

'Well, I suppose I could, except that your mother and Gloria are still at outs, even now. I don't think it would be politic.'

'Oh, mother's cold-shoulders always thaw eventually. She and Gloria are such close friends they could never be split permanently and while Gloria may bear grudges in her Latin way, mother never does. Only recently I heard her say something about letting bygones be bygones ...'

'You think the feud is ending, then?' Hope sprang eternal.

'I'm sure so. Go and spend a few weeks with Gloria – that house of hers in Baja California is the most incredible place. I'd like to see it myself. Perhaps you'd put in a good word for me ...'

'If you are sure the split really is being mended ...'

'Would you like me to call my mother and find out?'

'No! No.' Consternation overflowed. 'We must do nothing to arouse her suspicions. She must *never* know of this. I want your promise that she never will from you. I need not add that she never will from me.'

'I absolutely promise,' David swore solemnly. 'This is something I too would rather was kept strictly *entre nous*.' He laid a hand over Luddy's. 'Even if it is something I shall never, ever forget ...'

A few weeks later, David sauntered into his mother's sitting room in Morpeth House and perched on the arm of her chair, glancing at the chart spread out in front of her. 'And what are you doing, my pretty thing?' he enquired.

'Planning the guest list for the Island ... trying to fit everybody into the right weeks; making sure I don't put enemies down for the same week or separate inseparable lovers or put an ex with a current ...' Livy raised a laughing countenance. 'You have no idea how difficult it all is.'

'But you love it, don't you? Arranging things is your forte, my dear Mama. Nobody does it better.' David bent over the list, read the names in the various squares, each corresponding to a date. 'I don't see Luddy anywhere ...'

His mother's face closed. 'He won't be coming this year – or any other for that matter.'

'Luddy! What on earth has he done to be banished from Paradise?'

'Stabbed me in the back by taking up with Gloria Guanarius. He has been at her house in California for the past three weeks.' Livy's eyes brooded and her mouth thinned. 'After all I did for him, this is how he repays me. He knows that "La Gloria" is Out as far as I am concerned yet he goes to stay with her! How does that make me look? Like a fool, that's what!'

'Surely not,' David protested.

'I know ... I couldn't believe it either. I hate believing

the worst of people but when a particularly loathesome gossip columnist rings up to ask if it is true that Luddy has switched alliegance – well … that *is* the worst, and from a person of whom I had never expected anything but the best.' Livy raised a hurt face. 'The worst of it is I don't know what I have done that he should desert me. The last time we met he was as affectionate and sweet as ever. I would have sworn that Laurence Ludbrooke had not a spiteful bone in his body, but now …' Livy shook her head. 'Of all people – Gloria Guanarius!'

'What was it you fought about?' David asked. 'Nobody seems to know the truth of why two such close friends should turn into deadly enemies. It must have been something hideous.'

Livy looked back down at her chart. 'It was.' Something I would never have believed my best friend, even if she was my closest rival, would ever do, she told him silently. She became my husband's mistress. Livy felt her hands clench on her pen. Even now the betrayal still bled. But she had wreaked her revenge. Unable to punish her husband, she punished her erstwhile friend. She dropped her.

Society was riven by The Great Divide; you were on one side or the other because there was nothing in the middle. It became a *cause célèbre*, especially since half a dozen reasons were being touted as the cause of the schism. When it was first noticed that they no longer lunched together; that their table at Le Cirque was now occupied by only one of the duo at lunchtime, speculation spread like a flash fire. Some said that Livy was piqued because her position as The Incomparable had been unsurped by Gloria, whom people were now calling 'La Gloria'. Others said Livy had accused Gloria of offering inducements to those people who had the power to choose who would be *the* fashion icon of the decade. Yet another faction claimed Gloria was piqued because she had not been invited to a private dinner Livy had given for the Queen of England and her husband at Morpeth House, and that when asked why, Livy had replied that she could not possibly seat Her Majesty at the same table as a woman who had started her career as a blackjack dealer in a gambling hall in Reno.

In no time you could entertain one or the other but never both. If Gloria was invited to dine by a certain hostess Livy sent regrets, and vice versa. Neither, of course, set foot in any of the other's houses. Livy's edict had gone forth: Gloria Guanarius was pronounced anathema, and if any one of Livy's friends associated with her in future, such friendship would cease.

No one pronounced the obvious reason why, since nobody dreamed Gloria would be so obvious. She went to great lengths not to be. She and Billy were also friends; it was he who had christened her Glorious Gloria. He was also very tight with Basil Guanarius, possessor of one of the world's greatest fortunes and a business partner of Sir William Bancroft in many ventures. Born in Uruguay, but now a naturalised Swiss, he was an international figure. Gloria was from Nicaragua, and her Indian ancestry gave her her hand-carved beauty, free-flowing carriage and mind-boggling chic. It also got her Basil Guanarius, who was a very jealous man.

So when Livy, as was her style, 'never complained, never explained' but merely acted, Gloria perforce had to do the same. Truth to tell she had regretted the lapse more than she had enjoyed it. Billy was good but she had had better, and if she had not been feeling jealously pissed off with Livy over that Fashion Hall of Fame award she would not have needed to lift her spirits with a snort of coke which, when taken with liquor, had the effect of giving a jump start to her libido. She had been feeling randy and Billy had been handy. End of story. And the beginning of the end of a beautiful friendship.

The one good thing about it was that nobody – but nobody – had any idea. She had gone alone to the safe house she had bought under another name (Billy had arranged it all for her; he owned a lot of prime real estate in all five boroughs) in a quiet, tree-lined street overlooking the East River in a place where nobody would expect her to go: Brooklyn Heights. She went there when she wanted to be alone; to be with a lover, when she needed to think or to sulk and plan revenge. Gloria had a lot of Indian blood.

Which was how she had thought of Billy.

A phone call was all it took. He, of course, took it all in his stride. All he said was: 'I wondered how long it would take …' He was rough, the way she liked it, talked dirty, stood no nonsense, had her screaming her head off knowing nobody could hear because it was an end of terrace house and he had advised her to buy the one next door too; that way she could be sure of no nosy neighbours.

It was not until afterwards, head pounding, mouth thick, that she had looked at the stained and rumpled bed and thought dully: '!Aiee … !Por Dios, Gloria! !Stupida! !Tonta!' But it was done. All she could hope was that Livy did not find out.

Livy knew within hours. As luck would have it, she and Billy arrived back home within minutes of each other, Livy having been to a concert at the Lincoln Centre followed by a late supper which had been so enjoyable it had gone on and on and on ... She saw the light in Billy's study and put her head round the door. She had not seen him for days; their schedules were so arranged that they often did not see each other for weeks at a time unless they had joint engagements.

Billy was sitting at his desk, a half-filled glass in his hand. He looked up as she entered.

'How was the concert?' he asked.

'Divine ... I adore Placido Domingo. You?'

Billy shrugged. 'The usual ...'

'Do you know,' said Livy, 'I think I would like just an inch of scotch ...'

Since she never touched spirits, Billy looked surprised but reached for the bottle and another glass.

'I have just the tiniest touch of indigestion,' Livy explained, putting one fabulously jewelled hand to her breastbone. 'It must have been the devilled shrimp. Spices are fatal where I am concerned. A little undiluted scotch works wonders for some inexplicable reason.'

She floated round the desk to take the glass he held out. She was glorious in stiffly rustling black and white – colours he always associated with her since she had been wearing them the first time they really met – and filigree diamonds. She was her flawless, immaculately cool and soignée self, not a hair out of place, not a crease, not a crumple. And therefore quite unreal. Inhumanly perfect. Billy thought of Gloria; warm, naked, rumpled, smelling of sex and her own musky perfume. Not a remote and untouchable goddess. A woman. He moved his shoulders slightly; did not move a muscle of

221

his face as his shirt brushed the deep scratches she had gouged in his back.

As Livy bent to take the glass from him, the antennae that were her nostrils flared as she inhaled a scent which flashed up a name on the screen of her mind.

Gloria Guanarius.

Her very own perfume.

Created for her.

Worn only by her.

It was all over Billy.

Livy took the glass, drifted with absolute control to the other side of the desk again.

Billy had been with Gloria.

Gloria had been with Billy.

He had her perfume on him. Which meant he had to have been close enough for it to have impregnated his skin. Sweat did that; mingled hot and sweaty bodies.

Billy had had sex with Gloria. He had only just now left her bed and body.

Livy wanted to turn on him; rend and claw and scream.

What she did was sip her scotch, slowly and deliberately.

Her best friend.

How *could* he?

How *could* she?

How *could* they?

She gripped her glass, forced herself to sip slowly, when what she wanted to do was hurl the glass at him.

She gathered her three-feet wide satin stole − black one side white the other − about her shoulders, then with her glass in one hand, her small, flat *minaudaire* − zebra stripes of diamonds and black pearls − in the other, she said on a

222

yawn: 'I'm for bed, it has been a long, long day. Goodnight ...'

Billy flipped a hand before burying his nose in his glass
again.

'Night ...'

Livy went upstairs to her bedroom and locked the door
behind her. Her maid had gone to bed; she saw no point in
keeping someone waiting around for hours just to hang
away clothes she could perfectly well handle herself. Her
dress went on its specially padded hanger, the stole on its
rack; the satin pumps were left to breathe; they would be
treed and put away next day. Her wisps of satin and lace
were dropped into their special basket from which they
would be removed to be laundered by hand; her all but
invisible tights followed. Her jewellery was put away in the
carved and padded satinwood box in which it was kept.
Finally, she wrapped herself in a Japanese silk kimono,
slipped her feet into velvet mules and went into the walk-in
closet next to her draped and canopied bed. From it she
took a big leather cushion, thick and squabbed; once part
of a massive sofa. She laid it square in the middle of her bed.
Then from a drawer which she unlocked with a key she
carried on the charm bracelet which never left her wrist, she
took a thin Malacca-cane. She rolled back the wide sleeves
of her kimono, picked up the cane, swished it a time or two
and then, approaching the cushion, began to beat it, using
all her strength, first panting then sobbing with a mixture
of exertion, despair and rage, repeating, over and over again
in time with each whipstroke: 'Bitch! Bastard! Bitch!
Bastard!' She thrashed the cushion until the leather, already

deeply scarred, parted like skin to reveal the stuffing within.

Panting, arm aching, she dropped the cane, pushed the cushion from the bed then collapsed on to it herself, lying back, arms outflung, small breasts rising and falling rapidly, eyes closed. She lay there until her breathing had quietened, then she got up, replaced the cushion at the back of the closet, locked away the cane, and went into her bathroom where she stood under a pounding shower for ten minutes. Afterwards, she performed her nightly ritual. First she washed her face with the special rinse she used, before creaming it and her throat with long, upward-sweeping strokes. Then she delicately patted a second, specially formulated cream around her eyes, firmly massaged a third into her hands and arms. Finally she brushed her teeth, wielding the electric toothbrush for exactly three minutes, after which she rinsed her mouth, switched off the light and went back into her bedroom, which she also darkened before drawing back the heavy brocade, felt-lined curtains. Her last act was to curl herself up in the big deep chair by the windows opening on to the terrace forty floors above East 85th Street, where she spent the rest of the night staring out at the already lightening sky, thinking, thinking ... It was dawn before she went to her bed, where she fell instantly into deep, exhausted sleep.

Several days after Livy's conversation with David, James was woken at four o'clock in the morning by the warbling of his bedside telephone. His caller was an incoherent, intermittently inaudible, now *persona non grata* Laurence Ludbrooke.

'Tell me the worst, James,' he pleaded. 'Am I done for?'

'She is very angry, Mr Ludbrooke. And very hurt.'

'Oh, God ... I never thought – I didn't mean ... I only wanted ... but he told me it was for the best, and I couldn't face her – not after –' Here the voice faded and James, straining his ears, thought he heard the sound of heart-broken sobbing. But Luddy sounded firm when he came back. 'Tell her I never meant to hurt her. I thought it was only a minor spat and he said it was just one of those female things ... that she would come round in time ... Livy never holds grudges, he said, and he should know ... just as I should have known about him because he knew about me ... all about me ... but I didn't know him at all ... that he was so cruel, so vicious ... he knew how ashamed I was ... how I couldn't face her, but I should have. I should have looked her in the eye and lied ... that's what he did to me ... so two-faced ... I never knew he had two faces; one so seductively innocent, the other so viciously evil. Be warned, James, he has no love in him ...' There was a definite sob. 'My poor Livy, she has no idea what she has hatched ...' The voice faded; James heard the clink of glass on glass. He's pissed, he thought, and drinking more, trying to drown an unsinkable conscience.

'Mr Ludbrooke, why don't you write to Lady Bancroft. Tell her what you have told me. She will always listen to reason, you know.'

'... trouble ...' James heard, as the voice ebbed and receded. 'No reason to it ... just spite ... I would never have gone to Gloria if he had not suggested it ... he swore it was all a storm in a tea-cup. That was a another lie. It was a terrible thing Gloria did ... no wonder Livy thinks I have betrayed her ...'

'Did Mrs Guanarius tell you what was the cause of the rift

225

between them?' James probed. Livy had confided in him, weeping bitterly as she did so. That Gloria Guanarius should confess how she betrayed her best friend he found doubtful. Though she was known as an arch gossip it was because she loved relaying other people's peccadilloes; her own she was careful to keep in solitary confinement. Even in a society as cut-throat callous and self-serving as what passed for it in New York, to betray The Incomparable by having sex with her husband was tacky in the extreme. There were certain things One Just Did Not Do.

He marshalled his wandering thoughts as Luddy came back on the line again.

'Gloria was high,' he hiccoughed sadly, 'we both were. But as soon as she told me, I understood what he'd done; what I still don't understand is *why*? I only know it was all – every bit of it – deliberate. He knew where I would be ... He planned the whole thing ...'

'Who did?' asked James, sickeningly all too aware but needing to have it confirmed.

'He knows ... and I know ... but Livy must never know. Do you hear me. Livy must *never, ever,* know. It would destroy her, and I know how that feels. I'm done for, James. All that meant anything to me is gone. Nothing else left. Tell her I'm sorry. You understand, James ... you are one of us. Really one of us. But never – promise me you will never tell My beauty ... promise ... '

'I promise.' It was one James would have no trouble keeping. Luddy's drunken, despairing plea had painted a monster, but it was one James recognised from his own nightmares.

'Tell her I love her ... that she is still, will always be my

226

guiding star, My beauty ... and tell her I'm sorry ... so very, very sorry.'

There was a click and then the sound of the dialling tone. James replaced his receiver, his hand groping for the cradle because his mind was still staring at Luddy's version of *The Picture of Dorian Gray*. Surely not, was his first appalled thought, followed instantly by: but surely yes. There, but for the grace of God and prior experience ...

But why Laurence Ludbrooke? What possible reason could there be for destroying someone so harmless and inoffensive? No reason, no reason at all. That's what makes him so deadly. If I had done what he wanted I would be the one drowning my sorrows. I didn't, so he went looking for another toy to break.

James flung the covers back. Sleep was out of the question. He needed a drink and a cigarette. He had started smoking to keep Livy company, but he consciously tried to keep to a maximum of ten a day, less if he could manage it, and unless he was under stress – which was rare – he usually managed to make it no more than five. Now he reached for his cigarettes and lighter and dragged smoke deep into his lungs as if its acrid strength could clear away the even more deadly smog in his mind.

Unease lingered. There had been something about the tone of Luddy's conversation. It had sounded like someone going away for a long time ... Christ! He lunged for the telephone, but Luddy was not at his duplex apartment in New York, not at his beautiful Meeting Street mansion in his home-town, Charleston, South Carolina, nor at the six-bedroom, four-bathroom house three hundred yards from the beach in Southampton.

He wondered if he could trace the call. The international operator said she would try. James chain-smoked while he waited. God, what a mess, he thought, checking his watch for the umpteenth time. When the operator came back and said the call had been made from a payphone in a bar in San Fransisco. Did he want to call them back? Yes, said James, he did. Urgently.

He eventually spoke to a bartender. Yes, a man had made an overseas call – some drunk. No, he wasn't here. He'd made his call, tossed some bills on the counter – a twenty dollar tip had made him memorable – and departed about fifteen minutes before. No, he had no idea where.

San Francisco, James thought. Whom do we know in San Francisco? He went for his duplicate of Livy's thick, morocco bound address book. Not many names. Livy knew more people in Los Angeles, thanks to Billy's movie connections, than she did in San Francisco. But there were three names worth trying. Except what could he say? Laurence Ludbrooke is in your city and I think he is going to kill himself. No, I don't know where and no I have no proof, just what he said and the way he said it when he called me a few moments ago ... But then they would want to know just exactly what he had said.

And *nobody* must know that. James lit a fresh cigarette from his stub. There must be no scandal, and this had the hallmark of a sensation. I can say and do nothing, he thought. I could be leaping to wrong conclusions. How do I know that Luddy is not just on a bender, already on his way to another bar, determined to drown his guilty sorrows? I cannot sacrifice the good of the many for the benefit of the one just on my uneasy feelings. Livy has more than enough to bear as it is what with Ros and Diana. If I tell her about this I'll be loading yet more guilt and grief on to her shoulders. After all, he did not actually *say* he was going to kill himself. And he was pissed. One tends to say all sorts of things when one is half-seas over, and Luddy Ludbrooke was in the process of turning turtle.

There is nothing you can do, he told himself firmly, without revealing secrets best left untold. He has probably gone to a hotel to sleep it off. Tomorrow, if you still feel the same, ring round them all and find out.

He got back into his now-cooled bed but found himself going over the conversation, trying to remember Luddy's final words. What was it he had said again? Something about, 'tell her I love her ... that she is still, will always be my guiding star' ... yes, that was it. Not *was* always my guiding star but *will* always be, which means he will feel the same in the future. And he finished off by saying ... 'tell her I'm sorry, so very, very sorry ...'

James exhaled with an audible sigh of relief. Idiot! he berated himself. Leaping at all those over-ripe conclusions. He blew a whistling breath of relief and turned out his light. He'll probably ring again tomorrow to apologise, he thought on a grin.

But it was not Luddy who called next day; it was the San Francisco press. Would Lady Bancroft care to make a statement about her friend Laurence Ludbrooke, whose body had been found in a motel south of Market Street, along with an empty bottle of vodka and a similarly empty vial of Seconal.

10

When Rosalind Randolph drove away from Illyria the morning after her début the only person who saw her go was James.

'What shall I tell your mother?' he wanted to know.

'She won't ask. I have made it plain to her where I stand, and it is not to be photographed for *Town and Country*. As for Billy-boy, his only reaction will be of relief.'

'Where are you going?'

'To my old governess. I'll stay with her until I go to Wellesley.'

'Will you keep in touch? I'd like to know how you do. Not just for your mother's sake; for my own. I don't have that many friends that I can afford to lose one. Just a postcard now and then, perhaps the occasional phone call.'

Ros reached up to hug him. 'It shall be done.'

She got into the dark-green MGB that had been her eighteenth birthday present, and James watched until she had turned the bend in the drive. Then he sighed and went inside. He would miss her. She was not easy but she had a distinct and memorable personality, a very independent spirit and a decided sense of humour. She also had a great deal of courage. Of course, he told himself cynically, as he went up the great curving staircase, it is easy to be courageous when one is also inordinately rich, but what this particular eighteen-year-old is doing takes courage nevertheless. Nobody brushes off Sir William Bancroft lightly …

Ros reached Provincetown, Massachusetts by noon. Helen Wickersham, her former governess, had been born there, and in her forties had returned to the house where she had spent the first eighteen years of her life, to paint seascapes which, with their compelling depiction of the sea in all its moods, had a haunting, mysterious quality. People would stand for hours in front of them and see all sorts of things, which meant they took the public's fancy and attracted the interest of a local gallery owner who now handled all her sales. Every canvas was now sold before her brush made the first stroke, although she was unknown to the high-profile, Madison Avenue, six-figure-sales art world; had never had a *vernissage* and would have laughed at the suggestion, regarding that incestuous and pretentious world as one full of fakes, pseuds and poseurs, every one of them a naked emperor.

Ros had been only four when Helen Wickersham became her governess, and she had at once taken to the forthright, incisive woman who after teaching at an exclusive girls' school for eight years was sick and tired of spoiled brats *en masse*. Livy's sister Cordelia had recommended her.

'She stands no nonsense but she is a very warm person. And clever! She was a double major in Art and Literature at Vassar. She also has a way with children. I think she would be just perfect for Rosalind, who needs a firm hand from someone she can respect and who can also satisfy her voracious thirst for knowledge.'

Ros had not only come to respect she had stayed to love. Wicky, as she had soon been re-named, had become Ros's mentor, guide and friend. Through Wicky her thirst for knowledge was quenched and her undisciplined mind formed and shaped to question everything, accept nothing on *anyone's* say so, especially those with academic or intellectual credentials, and most of all to bring commonsense to bear on all things.

You took me over, Ros thought with an affectionate smile as she reached Cape Cod and took Route 6A, the old King's Highway, with its roadside orchards and cranberry bogs, its pretty churches and villages full of second-hand bookstores, antique shops and good restaurants. Like the song says, 'You Made Me What I Am Today ...' She felt her eagerness quicken. Just as she had left Southampton without a qualm, so she approached Provincetown with pleasurable anticipation, in spite of the fact that Labour Day was still some way off and the Cape therefore still in the throes of its summer season. She preferred it in the fall and winter, when all the 'Closed for Season' signs went up and the wind blew, the Atlantic turned grey and you could walk for miles along the dunes and not see a soul. But just to be here was enough. She stopped in Orleans to call Wicky and say she was only minutes away.

When finally she stopped the car on the sand-strewn road above the dunes, there was the familiar figure on the veranda of the grey-shingle house, surrounded by her many pots of green herbs and bright flowers.

Ros waved and started down the dunes at a run. Wicky

came down the steps and they met half way, hugged each other hard, put each other away to exchange a long, examining look, then hugged each other again.

'I've got scallop chowder for lunch,' Wicky announced, 'followed by broiled lobster with salad, and a sourdough loaf I took out of the oven only a couple of hours ago.' Strong white teeth gleamed in her wide, mobile mouth.

'If ever you get bored with seascapes you could make a fortune as a cook. I repeat my offer: any time you want to set up as a restaurateur, I am ready and willing to invest,' Ros assured her.

'No sale, but I've got some new seascapes if you still have any blank spaces on your walls.' Wicky pushed open the screen door and the familiar smell of the house had Ros closing her eyes and inhaling deeply of paint, linseed oil, herbs, spices and good food.

'Oh ... it's so *good* to be back,' she sighed.

'Go put your bag away, then come down and tell me all about whatever it is that has brought you here so precipitously'.

Ros's room was at the front of the house overlooking the sea; which was the last thing she heard at night, the first thing she heard in the morning, and it was filled with the luminous light of the Cape. The bed was brass, covered in a mountain-snow white quilt worked in concentric circles; the curtains at the open French windows were likewise white but it was their sheerness which filtered the bright sunlight into something glowingly radiant, like the halo of a saint. The sanded wooden floor had been polished to a satin gleam, the rugs were of rag and brightly coloured, another of Wicky's accomplishments, and there was a thick cluster of poppies, cornflowers and daisies in a Sandwich glass jug on the washstand, a pile of paperbacks on the table by the bed.

Ros washed her face and hands, brushed her hair then went downstairs to find Wicky ladling the chowder into big earthenware cups. 'I'm *starved*,' she complained happily. 'I stopped for a cup of coffee and a muffin at about eight o'clock but my stomach thinks my throat is cut.'

'What time did you leave?'

'Daybreak.'

'Why the rush?'

'Let me eat my chowder then I'll tell you.' Ros rapidly demolished one bowl of the thick, creamy, scallop-filled chowder in concentrated silence, relishing every spoonful. With her second, she gave her old governess a laconic account of her stepfather's assault. 'It was the last straw. I mean, I know he is a compulsive womaniser, but why me? There has never been any love lost.'

'You know him better than I do.' Livy had been Lady Bancroft only a few months when it was decided that Ros should go to school.

'That's because you never got the chance. He took one look at you and knew you were not the pushover my mother was – and is. If you'd been somewhat more – malleable – you might have been able to stay and me with you, but malleable, my dear old Wicky, you have never been.'

'Listen who's talking,' her old governess commented drily.

Ros wiped her lips with her napkin. 'Superb, as always. Now bring on the lobster.' This in turn was demolished, leaving every bit of shell squeaky clean, the sourdough, also

234

dipped in sweet butter, along with it. For desert they had last year's cranberries baked in a pie under a blanket of ice-cream.

'Oh, boy …' Ros said on a groan. 'You don't mind if I belch like the pig I am?'

They took their coffee out on the veranda, Wicky in her rocker, Ros in the canopied swinging lounger.

'So, are your plans unchanged?' Wicky asked.

'Oh, yes. I'm still for Wellesley – not so far that I can't visit as often as you'll let me – and some serious study. Then, Florence here I come.'

Wicky sipped her coffee, and stared out to sea. A black sloop with scarlet sails was meandering along in the half-hearted breeze.

She was a tall, angular woman, with a face that in repose looked stern, since its bones were strong and its lines uncom-promising, under hair the colour of the sand at the foot of the steps; a thick lion's mane skewered atop her head with wicked looking pins. Her eyes were a clear, brilliant, sage-green, which she could use to unnerving effect. She had never been pretty, but she was now, at forty-eight, handsome in an intimidating, Amazonian way. She had never married because, she said, she had never met a man she could not do without. Her powerful personality and original mind had struck Ros like ten thousand megawatts, setting off a flare which lit her her mind so powerfully she was still, fourteen years later, dazzled by the brilliance.

Helen Wickersham knew this and it troubled her. It was not that Ros was still impressionable, as she had been when Wicky took her over, which meant that there were in Ros a great many of Wicky's own, strongly opinionated ideas and beliefs, not in the least concerning the position of women in society.

It did not surprise Wicky that Billy Bancroft should make a pass at his own stepdaughter; he was a man first and stepfather second and a highly-sexed man at that, bound to notice that Ros's bud was now in glorious flower. Unlike some girls, who were fully-fledged Marilyn Monroes by the time they were fifteen, she had been slow to mature, until quite recently she had been all legs and mouth; flat chested and tomboyish.

Now, she was a young woman. The flat chest had become a 36B-cup, swelling above a narrow waist, while the bony hips curved enticingly with firm young flesh. But her face was still her mother's. It was in the mind behind it that the difference lay, and Ros was not yet aware that a lot of the things she did were in direct rebellion against the very fact of Olivia Gaylord Bancroft. Which, Wicky was sure, had a lot to do with her decision to become an art historian. It was something so very far removed from anything connected to Livy Bancroft as to be the cause of amusedly raised eyebrows. On the other hand, it was closely connected to her beloved governess who had, in Ros's eyes, been dismissed by a philistine stepfather, thus allowing him to achieve his real objective, which was to get rid of an unwanted stepdaughter by sending her away to school. That, in Wicky's opinion, had been Billy's first mistake. From then on, in his stepdaughter's eyes, nothing he had ever done had been right. Her mother's mistake had been in not preventing him.

And now this. It was as well that Ros's character was a strong one, not needing any lessons in self-reliance. Like

Wicky, she was a loner, which was perhaps why they had recognised each other all those years ago and spent seven very happy years together. What disturbed Wicky now was the uneasy feeling that Ros was starting out down the wrong road; that her choice of career, having been made for the wrong reasons, would not give her what she either wanted or needed, which was a sense of belonging; of being securely attached to something important and unchanging. Art was something which was very slow to evolve. It had taken several thousand years to get to Picasso.

Ros had not had anyone to belong to since her father died. She had adored him unreservedly and his death had left her bleak with misery for a long time. She and her brother had turned to each other, but first he then she were sent away to school and that was another bond broken. Once Wicky too went away, Rosalind had no one but herself.

Well, Wicky thought, as she got up to clear away the dishes, she will just have to find her own way. Thank God I taught her how to do it.

It took only Ros's freshman year at Wellesley to confirm Wicky's forebodings. She found she had no enthusiasm for her studies, or the people who formed the nucleus of the 'arty' crowd of her discipline, who were the kind, she described vividly to Wicky, who studied trends rather than talent and argued for hours over the merits of Andy Warhol's *Campbell's Soup Can* versus Lichtenstein's *Marilyn Monroe*; not over the undoubted fact of their both being works of great genius, but fiercely disputing who truly deserved the supreme accolade. Ros had made her first black mark by gushing, wide-eyed 'that it just had to be Andy Warhol with

237

the prices he was getting'. From then on she was regarded with great suspicion.

'I don't like it,' Ros told Wicky, with whom she spent Christmas of that year, 'I don't like them. I don't like the pretentious crap they talk. I am tempted to record them sometime and play it back … the utter *fatuousness* of it all!'

But being who she was she stuck it out that first year. She just did not go back for her second. 'I'm no quitter,' she told Wicky, 'but I've been warned that if I don't keep my subversive opinions to myself they will have to "reconsider" their position and mine. I told them that I was not prepared to reconsider mine and treat Pop Art as though it was – and I quote – "Serious Art". For God's sake, Wicky, who in God's name could ever take that charlatan Andy Warhol seriously? He is not what I had in mind when I decided to become an "art" historian. Any Warhol is a footnote, not a whole damned chapter! No wonder he painted money!'

'Art encompasses the sublime as well as the ridiculous, as I showed you a long time ago. Not only the artists but those who profess to know what the artists are trying to express. Nowhere is there more bullshit talked than in the art world. What you have to do is sort out the gold from the dross; utilise what your mind is fed in the same way as your body utilises the food it eats. What you don't need, get rid of.'

'But I have absolutely no interest in the ridiculous, only the sublime – '

'Then you must bear in mind that the ridiculous has a purpose to serve, which is to make you realise just how superb the sublime really is.'

'Well, I'm not going to realise it in my present course. The professor is a trendy liberal who sees all the – and I am quoting him – "so-called" Great Masters in political terms. I do not. He should teach me the history of Art, not the politics of its artists. He is a pretentious nerd and I don't see why I should waste my time on him or his wrong-for-me course, so I am not going to.'

'What will you do, then?' Wicky asked mildly.

'Spend the summer with you, if you'll have me, and think about where I go from here.'

'Of course you can stay. Just so long as your mother knows where and what and why ...'

'Don't worry. I keep in touch with James and he passes it on to her.'

'You don't ever talk to her?'

One of Ros's shoulders lifted. 'What's the point? We have nothing to say to each other ...'

She spent the last weeks of the summer swimming, sailing, sunbathing, spending the occasional rainy day browsing in the antique shops in Provincetown, taking the boat to Martha's Vineyard, where she rented a bike and cycled to Edgartown, always assiduously avoiding the 'smart' New York crowd, who reminded her of the very people she had avoided at Wellesley; getting up early to go and pick blueberries in West Barnstable, tending to Wicky's sand-strewn garden.

As the summer ended she bird-watched through Wicky's binoculars, studying the arrival of the plovers, the turnstones, the yellowlegs and the egrets, all exploring the mudflats, while Wicky painted them.

The foliage began to thin and the first signs of autumn blush appeared, the marsh grass grew high and back-to-school sales started in local stores. Summer was almost over.

239

One night, indoors because now there was a nip in the air after supper, they sat listening to Brahms on Wicky's state-of-the-art hi-fi, which Ros had bought for her last birthday.

Suddenly: 'What do you think of California?' Wicky asked.

'I never think of California. Why?'

'An old and good friend of mine gives the Literature course at Berkeley, and she tells me there is a new man in charge of the Art History Department who is causing quite a stir. Quite the iconoclast, but his students achieve remarkable results and his classes are over-subscribed. Add to that the fact that his book on Gericault is reckoned to be the best ever written and I think you have every reason to hope you have found someone whose views and teaching you can respect. A little sleight of hand will be necessary to get you transferred, but you are a straight A student, and if we add a glowing encomium (which I will write) from my friend, I think we might manage to get you into a course that will get your interest in an armlock ...'

Two years later, Toni Standish drove slowly along a narrow, winding street that wound upwards through a terraced hillside to which pretty little houses clung like blossoms, all but buried in leafy foliage, and thought how much Sauselito reminded her of the Mediterranean; very Capri. She was searching for the number Ros had given her over the telephone, finally spotted it on a little pink house that sat alone, its window boxes full of an assortment of bright flowers.

'Aunt Toni!' As Ros flung open the scarlet front door her face lit with delight and her hug was fervent. 'The prodigal returns,' sparkled her aunt, fresh from six weeks at The Golden Door, ten pounds lighter and looking ten years younger as a result.

'Not to fatted calf, I'm afraid. You've got fish ... this is California, you know, and we get the biggest, freshest ...'

'Fish will do nicely provided it is salmon.'

'It is. I remembered, you see. Poached and served with my own mayonnaise.'

'Get you!' marvelled Toni. 'Cook *and* art historian?'

'Well, I can cook now – Wicky gave me personal tuition as well as being to hand on the telephone when things got rough, and the art historian bit is a shoo-in.'

'You'll get your degree?'

'All being well.'

Toni surveyed her favourite niece critically. 'Well, I have to say that is exactly how you look. You seem at last to have managed to get life to agree with you.'

There was a glow about her. She was as slender as ever, and in a pair of denim shorts and a sleeveless, champagne-coloured silk jersey tee-shirt she was also elegant. A natural, Toni thought. Like her mother. But so much more ... open. Hitherto Ros had always been shut tight, with a 'show me' attitude. Looking at her now Toni perceived that at long last, Ros had indeed been shown. And by someone who knew what it was all about. Her smile rivalled the sun outside, and while she had always been confident, now she was relaxed with it. No more the uptight, argumentative girl of old. Somebody had softened her up.

Ros's responsive laugh was full-throated and not in the least put out. 'We are nowadays the best of friends. Come on, I've got a pitcher of margaritas on ice.'

'Angel!' Toni followed Ros into a sitting room brilliant with sun from picture-windows overlooking a terrace which in turn over-looked the bay. The poppy-strewn chintz-covered sofa and chairs were comfortable rather than elegant, two of the walls were lined with crammed bookshelves and there were more books and papers lying on the big coffee table in front of the sofa. A marmalade cat lay in the pool of sunlight which bathed one of them. There were several vases filled with flowers that had not been arranged, and the one wall without bookcases was hung with paintings.

'Whose?' Toni asked.

'The seascapes are Wicky's, the rest are Peter's.'

'I knew he lectured; I didn't know he painted too.'

'Only for his own pleasure. He has the most amazing insight into other people's paintings but he has no talent himself – of the kind that *he* would admit worthy of the name. His standards are stratospheric.'

'I've seen worse hanging in Madison Avenue galleries with hundred-thousand dollar price-tags on them.'

'He would agree with you, since he believes that real talent is beyond price, and monetary worth no way to judge any work of art.' Ros grinned. 'Frightfully unfashionable.'

'You sound like your mother,' Toni commented.

'How is she?' Ros asked, filling two large glasses with pale green liquid.

'Same as ever. But smoking three packs a day.' Toni met Ros's eyes. 'He hasn't changed either. But enough of them, it is you I have come to see.' Toni picked up her margarita, said: 'Here's looking at you, kid,' sipped and savoured. 'Now *that's* a margarita.'

'A bartender in San Diego gave me his recipe after I told

him that the painting he had hanging behind his bar – which he'd taken in lieu of a large bar-bill – was an early Rothko.'

Toni did for half her margarita. 'Well, I never got beyond Norman Rockwell so what do I know?'

Ros leaned forward to top up her glass. 'What do you know?' she asked directly.

'I told you – nothing has changed since you left. Everything is trapped in amber. Your mother is still on the same tracks – or should I say in the same groove; your stepfather is making even more millions. Diana is his spoiled darling, David is a cherub and James is still guarding Livy's temple.' Toni paused. 'But I thought he wrote to you and kept you *au fait*.'

'There are things you know that he doesn't.'

'How about putting me in the picture about something I still don't know … Like what it was that had you abandoning the field after your triumphant début?'

'Billy made a pass.'

'Aaahhh … I knew there was *something* but not that. He must have been drunk.'

'He was plastered, but that still does not excuse him trying to grope me. So I kneed him – hard. If I had stayed on there would have been an atmosphere – '

'You mean there already wasn't?'

'An even worse one. He would have been furious at his own stupidity and I would have been furious at his nerve. Sooner or later, Mummy's carefully maintained façade would have done a Solomon's Temple. I wouldn't have had any objection to it burying him but I didn't see why she should get hurt by the debris. Besides, I was leaving anyway. It was conditional on me making my début. I just made it

243

sooner rather than later. It was fortunate in a way, since I don't think she expected much of me afterwards.'

'She didn't know you'd done a bunk for three days. She had the mother and father of all migraines – which are getting worse, by the way, and she is now absolutely hooked on tranquilisers.' Toni leaned back against her cushions. 'But now that you have a relationship of your own, perhaps you see your mother in the light of your own experience.'

'If Peter treated me as Billy treats Mummy I'd have thrown him into the bay long since.'

'Things are good between you, then?'

'I had no idea how good they could be.'

'Ah … That tells me a lot,' Toni smiled. 'I am dying to meet him.'

'You wouldn't look at him once, never mind twice, but he has got the most marvellous mind.'

Toni shook her head on a rueful smile. 'Only you would fall in love with a man's mind. What about his physical attributes?'

A small smile which Toni's experienced eye at once accurately deciphered flickered over Ros's mouth. 'I have no complaints.'

'Does he live here with you?'

'Not permanently. That sort of thing could affect his tenure, even at Berkeley. But he spends as much time here as he can.'

'Will you marry?'

'No'.

'Why not?'

'Why should we?'

'Children …'

'Not planned for – yet, anyway.'

'It does not matter that he is twice your age?'

'Only chronologically.'

'And what about Florence?'

'Eventually …'

'My, you are in love,' Toni marvelled.

'Yes,' Ros admitted simply. 'I am.'

She had not meant to be. She had taken one comprehensive glance at the too-thin-for-his-height, untidily rumpled man said to be the Aimee Semple McPherson of art and thought: *I hope you sound better than you look*, for as always, the microscope of her eyes magnified every fault. His kitchen-mop of grey hair needed cutting, he wore heavy horn-rims with one ear-piece held on by a band-aid and his clothes said 'thrift shop'. He had a hawk's profile and a cleft chin, but when he began to speak she looked in dumb amazement at her arms and the gooseflesh which pricked, the hairs standing straight. He had the voice of a spellbinder; deep, resonant, his European accent reminding her of someone … who was it … . Paul Henried! Yes, that was it. Paul Henried in *Now Voyager*, with whom she had fallen in love the first time she saw it on television. This man sounded even more like him as his voice became impassioned and he got into his stride, and what he said converted Ros there and then.

He made her see paintings she thought she knew in a way that made it clear she knew nothing. He would take the central point of a masterpiece, tug gently and unravel the whole thing, laying it out so that its complex construction was made clear. When he talked of Rembrandt, of Goya, of Caravaggio, of de la Tour and Delacroix, Poussin and Pisarro, it was as if he had known each and every one of them and just what it was that had made them create a particular work. He was in love with great paintings and his gift was to be able to communicate this love to others; inspiring them to a love of their own. Since Ros already had a passionate attachment to art, she fell in love with him instead. For months she was just another face in the crowd which occupied every chair and stood round the walls to listen to him, watch him point to a figure here, a use of paint there in the blow-up of the particular painting he was illuminating that day.

It was her written work which made him seek her out.

Her name meant nothing to him. He took no interest in the kind of world she came from; had no idea that she was rich. Peter Dzundas – his mother was Viennese, his father from Budapest – had come to America in 1949, the family having fled before the Communists could arrest his father, a political journalist and activist. They had settled in Pennsylvania, where there had for generations been a sizeable Central European community, mostly working in the steel mills of Scranton. His father already spoke, read and wrote English as well as German, Hungarian and Magyar, and so got a job as a translator of captured German documents. His mother, who had been a teacher, got a job in the technical library of Bethlehem Steel. Peter, then aged fourteen and multi-lingual like his parents, went to the local High School, where he got unbelievable grades before graduating top of his class. From the many scholarships he was offered he chose the old and distinguished University of Pennsylvania, which awarded him his B.A. Magna Cum Laude, likewise his M.A., and eventually his Ph.D in Art, for which he wrote a brilliant dissertation on the mysterious genius Gericault.

246

Hung with qualifications he then took his pick of various jobs with prestigious museums, finally accepting one with the Kuntzhistorisches Museum in Vienna where he worked in the Old Masters Department, learning to restore paintings stolen by the Germans during the war. He stayed for five years. When he came back he taught first at his Alma Mater and then applied for and got an Assistant Professorship at Berkeley, where, at the age of forty-two, he was making a name for himself in academic circles. He already had one in art circles. For being out of step with current thinking.

Ros had named him the Nutty Professor, and once she became more to him than the name on some brilliant essays he christened her Rosie. Rosalind was a name from her world; Rosie was a name from his.

Art was the major force in his life, but politics – his father's influence – occupied what space was left. That was why he had come to Berkeley, even though the radical sixties generation were now sober citizens. Watergate had come and gone, taking Richard Nixon with it and Patty Hearst had been sent to jail not long before. Listening to Peter excoriate that particular débâcle, Ros was glad he had no idea she too was a Poor Little Rich Girl.

She for her part had become involved in the women's movement, even more so when congress failed to get the necessary votes to ratify the ERA amendment, and Peter Dzundas was the only man she had ever met who was entirely in agreement with women's quest for true liberation. He did not see women as his inferiors either physically or intellectually, though once he and Ros started their relationship they had some fierce arguments as to the lack of great female painters and why this was. It also made up for what Ros considered to be his blind prejudice against the rich.

Apart from that, he was the most open-minded man she had ever met, except on one particular subject. Money. He totally disapproved of rich men paying fortunes for great paintings which then disappeared into bank vaults in case some thief stole them. These wealthy buyers were not art lovers, they were art collectors. To them a great painting was not an expression of human genius, illuminating some part of human experience and thus enabling the people who saw it to enrich their own, it was an investment, something to be held on to until it could be resold at a vast profit. He railed against the fantasy prices paid that were, he said, an insult to the artist, especially someone like Van Gogh, who had never in his life time managed to sell a painting. It was a very sore point with him and Ros was careful never even to remotely touch on the name Sir William Bancroft, for he was such a collector. If his accountants said buy, he bought. If they said sell, he sold. It was a possession, no more. That sort of thing was a red rag to a bull where Peter Dzundas was concerned. He was bitter in his hatred of such philistines.

He felt passionately about most things, but where art was concerned his feelings were incandescent. The only other area in which he expressed comparable passion was sex, and here again, to Ros he was a revelation. But he was not in the least surprised to find she was a virgin. When Ros told him that men did not take to her he only said: 'I am not surprised. You can be very intimidating. I do not think you realise just how intimidating. Something that is anything but conducive to attracting young men, who are usually unsure of the opposite sex to start with. I, on the other hand, am no longer young and women have never terrified me anyway.'

'I can believe that,' Ros retorted. 'You can be awfully humble in the face of great art but you are equally arrogant when it comes to women.'

'Not arrogant,' he disagreed, being as particular in his use of words as he was about brushstrokes, 'just confident.'

'How is that?' marvelled Ros. 'I mean, you look as if some wind had just blown you in the front door.'

'Which is what appeals to a great many women. They want to take me in hand, tidy me up, mother me.'

'That is not what I have in mind!'

'Which is why I am here now. I have had a mother, thank you, and a very good one.'

'What about a wife?'

'I am married to my work. One would perforce be neglected in favour of the other and that would lead to trouble.'

His toffee-brown eyes poured themselves over her. 'I do not wish for trouble even though I am courting it. Members of the faculty, even assistant professors like me, are not supposed to have affairs with their students, even their best and brightest.'

'Which is why I took this house all the way across the bay in Sauselito. Nobody I know at the University comes here.'

'How easily you cope with life's vicissitudes.'

'I told you; my grandmother left me some money – '

'More than "some", I think.'

'All right, more than some. I have a small trust fund; it pays for my tuition and this house and whatever else I need. Would you rather I still lived on campus?'

249

Ros was telling the truth with minor variations. Her 'small' trust fund gave her a net income of one hundred thousand dollars a year, paid quarterly. The Randolph lawyers had solemnly explained the details of the small trust to her when she became old enough to receive it at eighteen; the large trust, which would give her a net quarter-of-a-million dollars a year, would become payable when she was twenty-five. When she reached thirty that sum would be increased to half a million. At that time, should she have conducted her life to the satisfaction of the other trustees, which meant without so much as a hint of scandal, she herself would become one of them, dealing with the multi-millions which comprised the Randolph Trust, and possessing the right, as a Randolph, to reside at King's Gift at certain times of the year.

Of all this, Peter knew nothing. He was a radical, after all.

'Another margarita?' she asked her aunt.

'Not if we've got wine with lunch.'

'We have.'

'Then better not. I've got the Golden Gate Bridge to navigate when I go back to San Fransisco.'

Over lunch – 'My God, this salmon! You could give my chef lessons!' was Toni's verdict – 'Does your boyfriend know just who and what you are?' she asked.

'No, so act accordingly. He knows I have a trust fund, but not how much it is. He has no time for the rich, purely because of their attitude to art. Peter sees everything and everybody in the light of their attitude to art.'

'Oh, dear, and me without one.'

'That's all right, he'll at once feel sorry for you and show you what you have been missing.'

'Is that why you don't want him to know — because it might lead to you missing him?'

'I don't think for a minute that he would up and leave in high dudgeon,' Ros answered truthfully. 'But he would be — disappointed. And I wouldn't want that.'

'And you used to look scathingly at your mother and the lengths she went to to keep the peace.'

'Oh, I don't do it to keep the peace. We have some humdinger rows. I do it to keep Peter.'

'You are not sure of him, then?'

'Not as sure as he is of me.'

'Ah, one of them,' Toni said, fitting the missing piece into place.

'Explain "one of them".'

'The kind of man who does not know what it is to fail with a woman; who is catnip to them and therefore sits back and lets them do all the work. And they don't have to look like Paul Newman, either.'

'He doesn't,' Ros said on a laugh, 'but you've got him right in every other respect.'

'Yet he chose you.'

Toni saw her niece go pink with pleasure. Got it bad, she thought. She had meant the comment to include the unsaid: 'I wonder why?' The old Ros would have pounced on it at once to challenge the assumption. The new one took it at face value, as a compliment. Love will do it every time, Toni thought, even to a girl like Ros …

'How was she — and what is he?' Livy asked her sister later, in the latter's suite at the Stanford Court. She sounded concerned, as indeed she was. She had not seen her eldest daughter for three years and apart from James' reports, the only way she could find out exactly what was going on was to use her sister as her surrogate. She needed to reassure herself that Ros was safe and well, even happy, in order to redeem her guilt, for though she found it difficult to express, she did love her children and worried about them when she did not get regular and comprehensive reports on their progress from the people she paid to look after them.

When she knew her sister was going to San Fransisco she had begged her to go and see Ros, as though Toni had not already intended to do so.

'For God's sake, Livy, she is my niece – my favourite one too. Of course I'm going to see her. Why not come with me?'

At once Livy retreated. 'Oh, no, Ros made it plain that she wants nothing to do with me or my world. I would not want to intrude where I am not wanted.'

'Doesn't it ever occur to you that your going to see Ros is the very thing she might want?'

'I doubt it. She could not wait to get away from me.' And having now seen Ros, Toni was not about to enlighten Livy as to why she left so suddenly. Let sleeping dogs lie when there is risk of rabies … But she was happy to tell her sister about the man who had captured Rosalind's mind and heart.

'Charm is his middle name … there is something about the Viennese. He is clever, and he talks a blue streak in an accent that pours itself over you like heavy cream, but from the first word he has you spellbound. Very opinionated, holds strong views on just about everything and has no hesitation in expressing them.'

'Is he handsome?'

'No. He looks what he is; an intellectual and a European intellectual at that. He was born in Vienna.'

'Is he a fortune hunter, do you think? He is, after all, no longer young ...'

'He has no idea Rosalind is a Virginia Randolph.'

Livy nodded, reassured. 'She is happy, then?' She sounded wistful.

'Undoubtedly. Not nearly so stroppy, as James would say. Much more ... light-hearted.'

'Did she ask about me?'

'Yes.'

Livy nodded, but her wide mouth turned down in a grimace that said: I can imagine how. Like someone enquiring about a mutual acquaintance. 'Well,' she sighed, with a brave little smile, 'as long as she is happy ...'

One morning about nine months later, Ros opened the bedroom curtains to see only the towers of the Golden Gate Bridge looming out of the fog.

'You've got a fine day for it,' she informed her lover, who was drinking his first cup of the day's sinfully black coffee, made the Viennese way.

'I shall be indoors all day, so the weather is unimportant,' Peter dismissed.

'You'll let me know how it all goes?' Ros asked.

'Of course I will, but it will go well. I have a feeling that they will snap up the book before anyone else can get their greedy hands on it.'

'Oh, I hope so, darling, I do hope so ...'

Peter had written a book on Austrian painters, including his favourite, Klimt, and was dickering with a New York publisher who, on a visit to his San Francisco office, had invited Peter to discuss possible publication within the next year. It would require many colour plates, which would make it expensive to produce, and since Peter was fiendishly particular about things like artwork, Ros had the feeling that today's meeting would be a fraught one.

'You won't lose your temper, will you?' she cautioned. 'Remember, he holds the cards. You want him to buy your book and produce it as you wish to see it produced. So go easy on him.'

'If he will pay me what I ask I will be putty in his hands.'

'That will be the day!'

'Today *is* the day, but to make quite, quite sure, let us start it off the right way ...' He held out his arms.

'Have we time?' Ros asked practically.

'I do not have to be there until noon. First we will argue, then we will lunch, then we will argue some more. If you wish me to be all sweetness and light then you must put me in the right frame of mind ...'

'Not to mention body ...' But Ros was already out of her robe and sliding into bed.

He was ready for her. He could come to erection with incredible speed, and what he could do with it had enslaved Ros in a way that had not only surprised but shocked her, uncovering as it did a passion of her own she had not realised existed. Now, as his long fingers sought out that place where he himself would shortly be, she felt the by now familiar dissolving sensation as her insides liquified, melting in the heat he ignited in her. His foreplay was leisurely, deliberately prolonged, until she was damp and delirious with desire, then, when he knew she was about to go under, in one deft movement he had reversed their positions, he on his back, she on top, riding him like a horse, penetrating her so deeply she could feel him pressing on her cervix.

His hands on her hips guided her; now straightforward thrusts, now a sideways tease, now a circular grind, now deliciously slow, now frenziedly fast. As she bent over him, he hot and stone-hard inside her, his mouth and tongue tugged at the hard pink nubs of her exquisitely sensitive nipples, so that she was utterly consumed by two ecstacies. Her increasingly deep and uneven breathing indicated how far along she was as she fell through one shattering orgasm after another, eyes shut, mouth open, her total responsiveness spurring him on to greater efforts until, after a particular frenzy of passion she arched her body before stiffening in a bow. The cords in her throat stood out as a sound somewhere between a scream and a shout strained from her throat, which was when he allowed himself his own release.

Exhausted, they lay entwined until breathing had returned to normal and Peter's energy – phenomenal for a man his age – had him leaping from the bed proclaiming dramatically: 'Bring on the dragons! Nothing shall stand in my way this day!'

'You won't forget to call me?' Ros persisted over her laughter. She was as eager as he was to sell his book. This was the fourth publisher; it might well be his last. If he would just bridle his tongue, not talk to them as though they were fools, temper his arrogance with a modicum of allowances. But that, alas, was the root of the trouble. He was never prepared to make any of them when it came to art.

'I will call you as soon as I have something to tell you. No, I do not know what time that will be. It might be early, it might be late. I am booked for lunch, it could be that it will go on through dinner. But you will be the first to know.'

So she was not unduly worried when she got back from Berkeley to find there were no messages on her answering machine. It was only four o'clock.

She waited until seven before starting dinner for herself. The arguments must have been humdingers, she thought ruefully. Just as well it was Saturday tomorrow; no classes and a lazy day. If he came back the worse for wear – which was highly probable if he had sold the book – she would pour black coffee down him then put him to bed. If he came back morose and sullen, she would hold his hand, smooth his fevered brow and gentle him back from despair.

She went to sleep in the chair, waking stiff and with a crick in her neck where the cushion had slipped. Rubbing it and straightening her cramped shoulders she saw that it was eight a.m. In case she had slept through his call she checked the answering machine. Nothing.

He's sold it! was her exultant reaction. He's sold it, got roaring drunk and had no choice but to sleep it off. She toyed with the idea of ringing the Mark Hopkins, which was where the New York publisher was staying, but put the idea away again. Peter had a thing about being checked up on. 'Either you trust me or you don't,' he had told her early on in their relationship.

They had to be extremely circumspect because of his job; there was a certain faculty faction to whom he and his opinions were anathema. It was for this reason that on campus he and Ros were never more than professor and student, even if he proclaimed her publicly as his 'star'.

Nobody even now, after almost three years, had any idea

of the nights he spent in Rosalind's bed. Since she was regarded as stand-offish – she did not join any of the clubs or mix with any particular group of students – and he lived across the bay in San Francisco leading a private life in which Berkeley played no part, nobody had any idea of the true state of the affair. Peter was paranoid about discretion. He had not felt safe until he knew who her neighbours were, if they had any connection with Berkeley or any interest in either Ros or him. A negative answer on all counts had reassured him, even though Ros had been to some pains to find a house hidden away in the hills with few people to remark on comings and goings. She would just have to possess her soul in patience, as her English nanny had been wont to say.

She ate breakfast, did her usual Saturday stint on the house, changed the beds and put the dirty linen in the washing machine. At eleven she made a cup of coffee and stood by the phone sipping it; the temptation to call the Mark Hopkins was strong, but his strictures were stronger.

At eleven thirty the phone rang. She leapt for it, almost cried: 'Peter, thank God! Where on earth are you?' but did not. Instead she said sedately: 'Hello ...'

'Ros?'

'Mercer?' Ros was surprised. Mercer Andrews was a girl with whom she shared classes but nothing else. Miss Co-ed personified, like Ros she was a Grade A student and from the start a rival for Dr Dzundas's favour. 'To what do I owe the pleasure?' Ros asked suspiciously.

'You haven't heard, then?'

'Heard what? That you've been elected Homecoming Queen?'

'About Dr Dzundas.'

Ros's blood congealed. Even her lips were frozen when she managed to ask: 'What about Dr Dzundas?'

'He's dead.'

A bubble descended, absorbing Ros into its centre. Everything receded to a vague blur; the only reality was the deadness inside the bubble.

'Ros? Did you hear what I said? Dr Dzundas is dead … shot some time last night in San Francisco … they found him in his car in the parking lot of a bar in the Mission District. He'd been robbed, of course, but they found a letter from a New York publishing house on the floor of the car … it seems he'd just sold them his book on Klimt …'

'How do you know all this?' Ros heard herself asking, though from a great distance.

'Becky Steen – she's a girl in my Phys.Ed. class – has a brother with the San Francisco Police Department and his was the car which answered the 911 call. Once they identified the body as that of a Berkeley professor, naturally he called his sister. She has a mouth that flaps in the wind; the whole campus knew by the time she'd finished calling every number in her address book.' There was a pause. 'I thought you should be told since you were so "special" to the good doctor …'

'When did all this happen?' Ros asked, amazed at the calm clarity of her voice.

'Around two a.m. this morning was when they found him – and that was from Becky herself … As soon as she told me I just had to tell you …'

'Yes,' Ros said, 'of course you did.' With the forefinger of her left hand she pressed the cut-off bar of her phone, got the dialling tone and then as she began to dial, realised she did not know the number.

She dialled the operator and requested it. Then she dialled again.

Becky Steen must have been sitting by the phone because it was picked up instantly. Rosalind identified herself, mentioned Mercer Andrews and then asked if what she had been told was true. It was. All too horribly true. Peter Dzundas had been shot, seemingly in the course of a robbery, late last night. There had been so much noise in the bar where he'd just been drinking that apparently the shot had not been heard. The body had only been discovered when another customer, going out to his own car, found he was unable to get it past one which was slewed across the lot and blocking the exit. On going to remonstrate, he had found what he at first thought to be a drunk slumped sideways over the wheel – with a bullet hole in his head.

Full of her unexpected importance Becky related how she had informed the Dean – who was going to have to identify the body since Dr Dzundas had no family in San Francisco – who had in turn informed the faculty and ...

'Yes, thank you for telling me ...'

There must have been something in her voice because Becky said subduedly: 'I know, I couldn't believe it either, not Dr Dzundas, he was so alive, so vital, so – '

'Yes,' Ros said again, imprisoned in her bubble, seeing but not feeling. Understanding but not believing.

'Mercer says you were his star student so I suppose you'll miss him more than the rest of us. I wonder who they'll put in his place? Mercer says it will probably be that old bore Professor Gardner, in which case Mercer says she'll probably

259

transfer because no way is she going to sit through his dreary dronings, not after Dr Dzundas and his –'

'Yes,' Ros said again. 'I have to go now. Thank you for explaining it all to me. I just wanted to know for absolute certain ...'

'I know exactly how you feel. I told my brother, I said now look here, Steve, are you quite sure – ' Ros hung up a second time.

She had no memory of the days that followed, which she spent sitting in Peter's big chair by the window cradling Rusty, her marmalade cat, staring at nothing, not eating, not sleeping, not even feeling. Just numb.

There was nothing she could do, not for him, not about him. The only thing she could do now was keep silence. Let their secret remain so for ever. Somehow, she knew that was what he would have wanted.

The ever helpful Mercer, curious as to why Ros had not been to classes, called to keep her informed as the unfolding of events. The Dean had identified the body, after which it had been taken back east to Pennsylvania for internment – 'By guess who?' Mercer asked silkily.

'He had parents, I believe.'

'Yes, but they didn't come. It was his wife.'

Ros felt the bubble enclose her in its thick silence again, but through it she could hear the loud ticking of a clock.

'Ros? You still there?'

'Yes, I'm here.' How calm, she sounded, how in control, though those two words had blasted her numbness to flaming fragments. And she began to hurt.

'I thought that would throw you. Wasn't he the sly dog? Nobody had any idea he had a wife back east – a wife

260

anywhere – and not only a wife, but a twelve-year-old son! How about that?'

Ros said nothing.

'This particular death has opened up quite a few cans of worms. Such as the Senior he had an affair with when he first came to Berkeley. Some rich kid from Pasadena with whom he had a mad, passionate fling before she graduated and went off to take her Masters at the Sorbonne. She had this little house down the coast near Carmel – some small town or other; like you and Sauselito really … isn't that a coincidence? Wifey was nowhere in the picture then, either. And it seems he was under suspicion when he left Pennsylvania because of a girl in one of his classes. Who would have thought that our Nutty Professor, as you so aptly named him – except his nuts were anything but the crazy kind – would have been such a ladies' man? Talk about appearances deceiving! I mean, Robert Redford he was not!' Mercer sighed. 'It was all that charm, I suppose … and that voice. It gave me goose pimples the first time I heard it …'

All things to all women, Ros thought, then realised she must have said it aloud when Mercer laughed and said: 'And then some!' Ros heard her sigh. 'Ah, well … the widow has taken him back to Scranton, or wherever. In a week's time it will be as though he never existed. You'll be back in class by then, won't you?'

Which was when Ros realised that Mercer, never slow in completing puzzles, had found the missing pieces to this one. 'Like the show, life must go on,' she said.

Sounding disappointed at Ros's reaction, Mercer said spitefully: 'Well, mine does … I don't know about yours …'

'Bitch!' Ros went to replace the receiver, but she could

261

not get it to fit into its cradle. She fumbled with it, her fingers thick, useless and without feeling, finally dropping the whole thing on the floor. Her face contorted and a sound like a growl rose from the depths of her, finally exploding from her lips in an animal-like howl of pain and despair. She bent down, picked up the telephone and still screaming, hurled the whole thing against the wall.

She was back in classes a week later, emotionally scoured to a hollow emptiness. She had worked through the whole range of her feelings, beginning with grief and ending with anger. Not being able to stand the silence of the house, she had spent hours driving aimlessly, roaming far up the coast then down. Deliberately she sought out places that had been 'special' to them, or so she had thought, biting on the tooth until the pain no longer had any meaning, wondering about her predecessor(s), if he had brought them to the same places. He had been, after all, a man who believed in an ordered life. Like a wife and son in Pennsylvania and a mistress in California, three thousand well ordered miles between them.

I was taken, she thought. To the cleaners, for a sucker, for granted. So she took up all reminders of him and dumped them in the garbage. His special Viennese coffee; the mug he had used, the books he had handled – hers, since he had been oh-so-scrupulous in the care and attention he had given to leaving no trace of himself in a house he had shared for almost three years. She had no gifts of his – 'the only gift I can give you is myself'. He had been a taker, she saw now, with hideously clear, twenty-twenty hindsight, unfogged by the steam of passion. She had bought the gifts; clothes, books, the Rolex oyster his murderer had stolen – ('no inscription' he had reminded), likewise the calf-skin wallet and the Louewe briefcase. When she was finished there was nothing to say he had ever set foot in her little house. Which she then had a cleaning service go through from top to bottom, scrubbing away even his smell. That done, she got maudlin drunk on a pitcher of margaritas, was very sick, awoke feeling limp but cleansed. Enough to go back to school, anyway. One day at a time she told herself. Take what he did give you, which was considerable, and use it as he used you. Get your degree. Don't let him spoil your future the way he has spoiled your past.

He may have been a liar – oh, God, the hypocrisy; married to his work indeed, but no, be honest. He had not actually lied. He *had* been married to his work. Which was probably why his wife lived in Pennsylvania. And his son. Don't forget his son. How could *he* forget his son? In three years you never heard him mention children except with disapproval as 'distractions'. Thank God he insisted on the Pill. She disposed of hers down the toilet. Once bitten … she thought. In future I'm going to be very, very shy. She graduated Magna Cum Laude. Twenty-four hours later she was in Florence.

11

'What on earth is this?' Diana asked, holding up a silver object she had just lifted from its bed of tissue paper.

Her mother lifted her head from the lists she was poring over, ticking off names as she went through the thick pile of invitation acceptances. She frowned at the object, something like an old-fashioned car headlight but made out of solid silver. 'I haven't the faintest idea. Who is it from?'

Diana studied the card. 'Somebody called Holman–Prentiss.' Her eyebrows expressed total mystification.

'Probably people your father knows, but possibly from Brooks' list. Put it to one side and I'll ask James to find out.'

'If I don't know them, why are they coming to my wedding?' Diana wanted to know.

Still bent over her lists Livy said answered: 'Darling, if Daddy wants them there is no more to be said. His word is law, besides which, he is paying for all this, and a very pretty penny it is costing him.'

'He can afford it,' Diana pointed out, 'and I am his daughter, am I not? His *only* daughter?'

This was a dig at the half-sister whose absence from the

family was now ten years long. Diana did not really remember her stepsister very well, but at Johnny's Newport wedding to Polly Benedict, which Ros had attended, it had been like a knife to the heart to see how like their mother she was. After Diana's hysterical collapse, and the family row that followed it, that fateful winter three years ago, Diana had been diagnosed anorexic and admitted to a clinic in Switzerland. The doctor there, herself a former anorexic, had possessed the necessary sympathy and understanding plus the shrewdness to show Diana the difference between being slim and being skeletal.

After long, patient counselling and daily hour-long sessions with a therapist, Diana had been made to see that her mother's elegance depended upon being able to wear clothes, rather than have them hang on her. And to wear clothes you had to have flesh on your bones; not too much, as had been Diana's trouble, but most certainly the right amount, which meant the clothes hung properly. The demonstration had gone a long way to convincing her that her obsession to become her mother had made her dangerously thin.

Slowly, with much coaxing and enormous encouragement, the doctor had brought her back to a weight that allowed her to copy her mother's style *the right way*. In return, against Livy's better judgement – which was as usual overruled by Billy who saw nothing wrong in Diana's wish to be like her mother: 'I would have thought you'd be enormously flattered' was his brutal retort to his wife when she demurred at such slavish imitation – Diana was allowed to have her face fixed by a world-famous plastic surgeon who gave her a new nose, superb cheekbones, and a delicately pointed chin. Once the bandages were off and the scars healed to invisibility, she then had her hair darkened. The flaxen became burnished gold, cut short and styled like Livy's to show off her remodelled face. Her new figure, in the couture clothes Billy lavished on her, weighed one hundred and ten pounds, while her five feet two had become five feet six because of the high heels she wore at all times.

'You will ruin your feet!' Livy had warned, to no avail. Nothing her infuriated mother, who was appalled by the very thought of a clone dogging her every footstep, could say had any effect on Diana's obsessive determination to remake herself in her mother's image. She could now wear Livy's clothes, and when she looked in her mirror wearing them plus her heels, she saw the woman she had all her life wanted to be.

There was only one last thing to do. She had to find a Billy Bancroft clone to marry. Only then would she regard her battle as won.

She found him in Brooks Hamilton – or rather, he fell over her, for Billy placed her square in his path. Diana took one look and said: 'Daddy, buy me that ...'

Brooks was tall, dark and handsome, just like the best romances said. Like her, he was half-English, half American, though in his case the order was reversed. His mother was English, one of the two daughters of Sir Reginald Brooks, the merchant banker; his father American, a descendant of Alexander Hamilton. Brooks had dual nationality, but he had been brought up and educated in America – Groton and Harvard. He was rich, social on both sides of the Atlantic, and he was thirty to her eighteen. Billy approved wholeheartedly. Brooks was everything he had planned for in a son-in-law. For his part, Brooks was both flattered and shrewd enough to perceive the advantages of being Diana Bancroft's husband. The Hamiltons were classed as rich, but compared to Billy they were no more than well-to-do. Billy was Croesus. Billy could have bought and sold the Rockefellers *and* the Astors.

That appealed to Brooks no end. Diana would make a perfect partner. She was slim, pretty, always exquisitely dressed, not bright enough to be a threat and not dumb enough to be an embarrassment. She was the product of a life Brooks wanted for his own. If he had to marry Diana to get it so be it.

The wedding was to be held at Wychwood in two weeks' time, when the garden – it would be late-June – would be in glorious flower. Livy had taken her garden into consideration when planning the colour of the wedding; the dresses of the six bridesmaids, the bride's bouquet, the marquee into which the guests would walk straight from the terrace of the house, her own dress, even the food to be eaten. Everything was planned down to the minutest detail with her usual obsessive perfection.

Her son Johnny's wedding had been handled by his bride's parents, and though the Benedicts were both social and undoubtedly well-connected, the wedding – held at Beau-Soleil, the Benedict's Newport 'cottage' – though very pretty, had, for Livy, lacked the prime ingredient of such occasions; style. No one would be able to say that about this wedding.

Which was why she had been very selective about her invitations, only to have that plan ruined by Billy who had slapped down two pages of names before ordering: 'Invite them.'

'But I am trying to restrict numbers ... You know how small the church is ...'

'So get rid of some others. These people come. All right?'

'As you wish.'

'Exactly,' Billy reminded.

But he had given her a blank cheque. 'Whatever it takes,' he ordered expansively. 'This is my one and only daughter getting married.'

Livy ignored the dig at Rosalind. Billy was always taking swipes at his stepdaughter. And the last time any of them had seen her, at his stepson's wedding, at which Diana had been a flower girl and Rosalind a guest, he had behaved as if she was a stranger, neither speaking nor going anywhere near her.

Later that night, over dinner at San Lorenzo, Diana said to her fiancé:

'Who are the Holman-Prentiss's?'

'Haven't the faintest idea. Why?'

'They sent the weirdest present... neither Mummy nor I have any idea what it is supposed to be, except it is solid silver.'

'Then they are rich, whoever they are. Probably connected to your father in some way.'

Brooks sounded respectful. Like his prospective father-in-law, money was his *raison d'être*. Enough was never enough. But marrying Diana Bancroft would undoubtedly bring him nearer the 'Full' sign. And being Livy Bancroft's daughter, she would undoubtedly provide for her husband the dead-ringer of the feather-bedded life her mother had always provided for her father. Billy had as much as told him so.

'Diana is her mother's daughter — as no doubt you will have noticed. You've won a First Prize, Brooks. I hope you realise that.'

The warning was implicit. Keep it in perfect condition and on display at all times, never let it get tarnished and above all don't let anybody else handle it. As if I would, Brooks had thought.

Livy, on the other hand, had told Diana nothing. She had summoned her engaged daughter to her sitting room, after working her way through a pack of Dunhill's, and attempted to start a conversation about married life. Diana had smiled indulgently.

'Mummy, I know all about that, we took Human Biology at school, you know, as well as sex education. I know what to expect.'

'I was thinking more along the lines of what is expected of you.'

Diana had frowned. 'What do you mean?'

'Like your father,' Livy began, 'Brooks is very demanding ...'

'Oh, I know all about that,' Diana interrupted. 'Daddy told me that I had to be as perfect a wife to Brooks as you had been to him.'

Livy asked: 'In what way, exactly?'

'Why, always to be stunningly well dressed, always to be the perfect hostess, always to show my husband in a good light, never to forget a name, even if the face is no longer familiar, always to run the house perfectly without having to ask for help or advice, because he will have his own job to do and the house is my responsibility, not his; to supervise the upbringing of the children, never to be the cause of gossip

269

or scandal, but always to be a source of admiration, even imitation. Just like you, in fact.'

'And did he also tell you what Brooks had to do to be a good husband?'

Taken aback by the acid coating her mother's voice Diana said placatingly: 'No, but he did say that I only had to follow your example.' With simple truth: 'I told him I had never wanted to do anything else ... '

'I see,' Livy said at last. Shading her eyes with her hand she looked down at her engagement diary, fiddled with the gold pencil kept with it. 'It's a lot harder than it looks, you know,' she said at last. 'I wonder if you realise just how much harder ... '

'It never seemed hard for you.'

'That's because I have always been careful never to show it.' Understating the obvious: 'Your father is a very demanding man; if Brooks is – another, then you will have to be on your toes at all times; anticipate, intuit, pre-suppose, check and double check ... '

'But that's what servants are for.'

'You are the one who will have to control them, see that they do what not only you want but what Brooks expects. You are the one who will have to learn what his tastes are.'

'I already know.' Diana was enjoying this; it was not often she could show her mother that she had it all under control. 'He prefers savoury to sweet, Evian to Perrier, hates all green vegetables, loathes anything curried, likes his eggs boiled for four minutes, his coffee strong and black, his red wine at room temperature and his white wine chilled for one hour, no more. He likes three pillows and a window open no matter what the weather – oh, and he hates me wearing

270

green; he says it is unlucky. Since it's not a colour I wear much anyway I don't mind.'

'Are they his only expectations?'

'Well, he says there are bound to be lots more but that I can learn as I go along. I've made a list of my own likes and dislikes so we can both keep each other happy.'

'How considerate of him.'

'Oh, he didn't ask. But marriage is no longer a one way street, is it? At least, that's what Aunt Toni says, and she should know seeing that she is now on her third husband – who just happens to be fifteen years younger than she is!'

Livy looked at her daughter's limpidly innocent eyes and thought: it is a one-way street where your father is concerned, and I suspect you are going to find yourself married to a man who thinks the same way. Billy would not be so enamoured of Brooks Hamilton otherwise. But how can I destroy your illusions? Not that you would believe me if I told you. Billy is your adored Daddy, while you have taken your emulation of me to lengths I find both alarming and which, to be honest, I resent. You have no idea of the truth of the matter and would not thank me for making it known. Come to that, I don't want it known either. If I were to show you around the ornate tomb that is the reality of my marriage it would destroy your admiration for your father, your absolute faith in me and, worst of all, the focus of your own life, because you would then see you have based it on a lie.

I am a bad mother, she admitted, staring dispassionately at her own weaknesses. I *know* it, but I can't change it at this too-late stage. Besides, *I* chose this life; it was what *I* wanted and if I suspected the price would be high I also expected someone else to pay it. The ultimate responsibility is mine.

Livy stared at the entries in her engagement diary; every hour filled. Wasn't that what Sally Remington had complained of so despairingly all those years ago.? All the blank pages in her own. 'When I was half of a couple there weren't enough hours in the day. Now there seem to be forty-eight in every one.'

Is this what you meant by a rich, full life? Livy thought bitterly. I cannot deny that mine is rich, but what fills it is nothing. Lots and lots of nothing … This is not what you meant or what I wanted, but it is what I've got and if I give it up what do I get in exchange? Even more nothing. But it is too late to change now. I couldn't, anyway. I have been living the lie for so long it has become the only truth I know.

She felt Diana's hand on her arm, looked up to see her daughter smiling at her tenderly, as usual reading her mother completely wrong. 'You don't have to worry about me, darling Mummy. It will be all right. I love Brooks and he loves me. Daddy is for him one hundred per cent and I chose him because I want what you and Daddy have had … '

Livy reached for her cigarettes.

'Everybody says you are the perfect couple … those that don't – well, they are just jealous, that's all. Brooks says there are always those whose own imperfections make them resent perfection when they see it, and that's what you and Daddy have. A perfect marriage. That's what I'm going to have, you'll see. I'll make you proud of me, Mummy, you see if I don't … '

She was a beautiful bride. As she came down the red carpet on her father's arm through the bower of multi-coloured flowers Livy had created in the small village church at Upper Wychwood, crammed with the two hundred guests which were all the church would hold, Livy had drawn in a deep breath of satisfaction that she had persuaded Diana not to chose pure silk tissue for her dress but clouds of crisp white organza, treated so that it would not crease. Livy had winced when she saw the state of Lady Diana Spencer's wedding dress as she got out of her carriage at St. Paul's Cathedral; as creased and crumpled as a dishrag, besides which the dress had been far too fussy to start with. Not so this Diana. Her dress was simple, uncluttered, relying on line and the sumptuousness of its layers of spreading, dazzlingly white organza and the wide sweep of its train for effect. Her head-dress was a wreath of white roses, freesia and orange blossom to match her bouquet – picked and swiftly made up by a team of specialist florists not thirty minutes before she had taken her father's arm – and her only jewellery was the single string of pearls with which her father had presented her that morning: eighteen of them, each perfectly matched and the size of ripe blueberries.

To contrast Diana's blinding whiteness, Livy had chosen coral; a Givenchy sheath of pure silk under a sheer organza coat, twisted ropes of coral, pearls and sapphires at her throat and in her ears, her hat a wide cartwheel of stiffened silk chiffon to match her coat, worn dead straight and impossible to get away with unless you had the right face. Livy did. She looked fabulous, since the vivid colour enhanced her clotted-cream skin, her dark eyes and the mouth which was a match to her ensemble.

'My God, that outfit is to die for,' groaned one guest to another.

'How in God's name does she do it? I mean – she is fifty-one years old! What hope is there for the rest of us when she sets such an impossibly high standard?'

The mother of the groom, who was the same age as Livy but looked at least ten years older, had taken as her model Her Majesty the Queen and chosen powder blue crêpe topped by a hat that looked like a hydrangea.

Livy totally eclipsed her.

The reception was held in a vast circus-tent-sized marquee lined in soft pink, which flattered the skins of the women guests and was big enough to hold not only the two hundred guests who had attended the service, but also the three hundred who had been invited to the reception. They ate halves of tiny cantaloupe melons filled with raspberries, redcurrants and peaches; creamed chantarelles, smoked salmon and asparagus mousse, terrine of duck and quail with truffles, crisp lettuce and watercress salad with orange dressing, and a classic English sherry trifle which, one guest commented, had more kick than the Krug.

'As usual, perfect, just perfect,' someone commented tipsily.

'Too bloody perfect', her companion snarled. 'I'm up to here with perfect Livy Bancroft. Right now I find my strongest emotion is not admiration but a sincere desire to see that inhuman pattern of perfection daubed with only too human graffiti!'

Watching the newlyweds – Diana in a pretty Dior dress and jacket the exact colour of her eyes – being pelted with rose petals as they ran for the car that would drive them to Heathrow and the plane – Billy's Grumman Gulfstream 2 – waiting to fly them to the Seychelles for their honeymoon, James commented to Ros: 'Two down and two to go.'

'I've been, thank you,' Ros's tone was dusty. 'Besides, if the attention David has been receiving from women young and old is anything to go by, he is going to be next one.'

'I would not count on it,' James demurred. 'David thrives on mass admiration and would not dream of depriving his fans of their pleasure.'

Something in his voice, amused though it was, had Ros flicking him a glance before asking: 'Do I detect a touch of acid in the wine?'

'Of all your mother's children he comes last on my list.' Pause. 'You still come first.' He eyed her with pleasure. 'How nice you look.'

Rosalind was wearing a dress she had gone to Rome to buy specially. By Valentino, it was of soft, butter–cream yellow chiffon with a floating skirt and ruffled neckline, and her silk–straw hat was crowned in yellow roses, flattering to her skin.

'Thank you.'

'You have inherited your mother's taste.'

'I don't always look like this! I paid more for this dress than all the clothes I have bought in the last five years.'

'It was worth it.' James examined his old friend before enquiring: 'And are you happy?'

'I am — content. I like my work, I live in a city which is a living museum, I have made friends — '

'What about lovers?'

'I don't love easily.'

A nicely evasive answer in James's opinion, and one which had him saying: 'You are of independent mind as well as means, but I don't think you are one of those women meant to live life alone. You are still young … Rest assured, someone will come along eventually. You are fortunate in that like your mother, you will never look your age. Something in the genes.'

Ros turned to survey her mother, as always the centre of a group of admirers. 'She is incredible, isn't she?'

'The more so when one considers the enormous stress she is under.'

'Something she could walk away from if she wished.'

'In which direction? And towards what? Or who? Your mother knows she made a Faustian pact but she will keep it until death.'

Ros caught the inference at once. 'Why do you mention death?'

'Because she has not been well for some time. Not – ill, exactly, but not one hundred per cent. She won't listen, of course, when I suggest she has a check-up. Tells me not to fuss and she feels perfectly all right. But I am worried.'

'Mention it to His Nibs. He's a hypochondriac; tell him you think its infectious and he'll have her in isolation before you can say Sir William Bancroft!'

'Not for much longer,' James said, *sotto voce*. At Ros's raised eyebrows: 'He is to be the first Baron Bancroft in the New Year Honours List. Nothing official yet, of course, but he has been approached through channels … all that remains to be decided is his title.'

'That's easy … Baron Bancroft of Bermondsey.'

'Wrong side of the river. He was born in Whitechapel.'

'Baron Bancroft of Whitechapel, then.'

'I doubt it. One's antecedents recede further into the

distance with every passing year. When one becomes Lord Bancroft, I doubt if we shall hear of them again.'

'What about Tweedledum and Tweedledee? They are not here today.'

'They are relics of a previous life,' James murmured, 'not wanted in this one.'

'They always were an odd, self-effacing pair. I never did get to know them.'

'Nobody does. I don't think Sir William wishes them to be known. His latest entry in *Who's Who* makes no mention of a first marriage or the issue from it; only the second, and only Diana and David are named.'

Ros laughed. 'Of course ... ' Then she sighed, frowned slightly. 'I never really got to know Diana either. She was only a child when I cut myself loose ... ' And hardly more now, had been her first reaction when, on her arrival at Wychwood shortly before the bride was due to leave for the church (she had timed it perfectly), she had gone to greet her half-sister and been received with a handshake but no sisterly kiss.

Diana's greeting had also been coolly distant,

'It has been so long I hardly remember you.' As Ros met her eyes, there had for a moment been a flare in the china-blues that told of long-held resentments. Her own reaction had been astonishment at the difference between the plump teenager and the fashionably thin young woman. This Diana was no longer a flaxen-haired Dutch doll but a sophisticated Barbie. She had the assured best Finishing School manner and the clipped vowels of her class, but Ros had noticed that even her mother sounded English rather than American these days. Somehow it intensified the gulf between them. Ros was one hundred per cent American, but after twenty years of living among them Livy had become very English while Diana was wholly English. Unlike her husband.

'Who and what is Brooks Hamilton?' Ros asked James now, curious about the personality behind the male-model exterior.

'Ambitious. Your stepfather looks on him as an heir-apparent, until David is old enough, of course. David is to inherit the earth – the universe if his father can take it over.'

'I think he knows it,' Ros hazarded thoughtfully, gazing at her half-brother, whose every word was being hung on by a group of eager women. 'I hope Brooks has his wits about him.'

That Brooks also had a temper Diana discovered on the very first night of their honeymoon, spent in Paris, at the Crillon, where Billy's name and money had paved their way. Brooks was well satisfied with their suite, the marble bathroom especially, until he went to the refrigerator to discover that it was stocked with Perrier and not Evian. As Diana wept to her mother over the telephone when, after four hours, Brooks had still not returned after storming out in a rage, 'He threw a wob, Mummy ... he said he could have understood it had I not been Livy Bancroft's daughter; the fact that I was made it inexcusable.' Diana's sounded incredulous. 'For heaven's sakes, Mummy ... it is only water!'

From then on, Livy charted the decline and fall of her daughter's marriage by the frequency and tone of the complaints. Unlike her mother, Diana had not been brought up to regard her husband as an object of worship; *she* had expected to be the deity. That shock, coupled with the

278

constant unremitting effort necessary to maintain not only her own standing but that of a demanding and, to her way of thinking, hyper-critical husband, soon brought home to her the fact that she had not known the half; never even begun to appreciate or understand the enormous effort her mother had been making all these years to maintain her father's life in perfect order. It was all Diana could do to keep the cracks from showing, and the deepest, most serious one was her disappointment over sex.

On their wedding night, she had come to Brooks in a cloud of diaphanous chiffon which she felt gave tantalising glimpses of a body she had bathed and anointed with sensuous oils, but instead of admiring her as she had expected, he said only: 'You won't need that,' and had almost torn the chiffon from her. There had been no slow and tender build up. He had not worshipped her, reverently told her the things she had expected to hear, gentled her along slowly — for she had absolutely refused to sleep with him before he had the legal right; what had been good enough for her mother was an eleventh commandment to her — while her father warned her: 'You are *my* daughter, and I have only the highest of expectations where you are concerned.'

Nothing had been said about Diana's expectations and she had felt cruelly let down when her impatient husband had forced her legs apart, fingered her in a way that hurt, taken her hand and put it on him, so large and hard that she had let out a yelp of fright which had made him angry at what he called her girlish 'act'. When Diana protested that it was not an act, he did not believe her. 'I'm not your Daddy, I know what goes on and so does he — boy, does he not — so you don't have to act the virgin with me, nobody's a virgin these days ... '

'I am, and I am *not* acting!'

And when Brooks discovered that she had stated the truth; that the proof was all over the sheet after he had lost patience with her tears and cries, pinioned her wrists with one hand, spread her legs with the other, penetrated her fully with some difficulty so strong was her hymen, and then come almost before he got started because he had got stuck in the gate, he was furious with her. 'Christ, you know nothing! There is a hell of a lot more involved than just lying back, you know! Haven't you ever been in a back seat, for Christ's sake?'

'No, I have not!' Diana was appalled that he should think she would do such a common thing.

'I suppose that Swiss school of yours had you guarded like Holy Grails.' Since the story was that Diana had been at school in Switzerland rather than a clinic for anorexics, she could only mumble: 'They were very strict,' which was the truth anyway.

'Oh, well, I'll just have to teach you, then.' He had yawned, patted her shoulder. 'The first time is always a let-down. Like most things in life, practice makes perfect ... '

But Diana had not liked his practices. She loathed taking him in her mouth, always gagged and rushed for the bathroom afterwards; she squeezed her eyes tight shut and squirmed with embarrassment when he used his mouth and tongue on her. Pleasure did not come into it. When finally he entered her she tried to do what he wanted, to lock her legs about his waist or put them over his shoulders, but she had always loathed gym, her favourite exercise being reclining on a cushioned sofa with a box of chocolates and a pile of magazines.

She let her hands lie limply on his shoulders and suffered his thrusts and grunts in silence, at first urging him silently to get it over and done with, later learning to close off her mind and dwell instead on what to wear next day when she went to lunch at the Dudleys; whether Armani had it over Versace and if that Donna Karan body suit really was her, and should she have her hair darkened *just* a smidgeon more and she really must have her nails done again because that new varnish did not last five minutes ...

She had inherited her mother's lack of libido; and therefore could not understand what all the fuss was about. When Brooks soon lost interest, Diana was relieved, but when a girl friend told her he was catting around her *amour propre* had her confronting him in a hissing tirade, informing him that while she did not mind who he screwed as long as it was not her, he had better be more discreet or else, because married or not she was still her daddy's girl ...

Brooks heeded the warning. His wife wished bitterly that someone had taken the time and trouble to warn her. It was not scales so much as shutters that had been removed from her eyes; married life involved things that had not even crossed her mind before. Too late she scrutinised her parents marriage and understood it for the first time; saw what a lifeless, loveless, formal arrangement it was. Too late she watched her father when there was a pretty woman around; too late she understood where he was and what he was doing the nights when he was not at home. Like father like son-in-law, she thought acidly. But, far more important, like mother like daughter. More than ever she had reason to emulate her mother. Anger drove her on; at her mother, at her father, at her husband, at herself. I was robbed! she wanted to howl. Nobody told me a thing that *really* mattered! Well, if this is all there is then, by God, just like Mummy I will make the best of it. Her apartment in New York was a replica of Morpeth House, and she even found a house ten minutes away from Illyria and started to redecorate it in her mother's style.

When her father began hinting about becoming a grandfather, Diana dispassionately timed her ovulation with great exactitude, got herself just drunk enough to be able to stand it, and coldly seduced her husband. Duly impregnated she gave birth to a fine seven-pound girl she named Olivia Bancroft Hamilton. Brooks and Billy were very pleased with her, and everyone said that marriage was the making of Diana Bancroft. 'Her mother's daughter,' they said. 'And *she* had better watch out … '

But Toni, as usual, saw different. As she observed to Ros, taking her aside after the christening of Diana's daughter: 'I know they are saying that marriage has been the making of Diana but speaking for myself I can't say I care for what it has made her in to.'

'Which is?'

'A one hundred per cent pure, triple distilled bitch.'

'I know what you mean.' Ros agreed. 'These days she looks as though she has just been resprayed.' Ros paused then went on: 'Mother, on the other hand, is not looking her usual self either, but with her it is because the glow has gone.' She looked directly at her aunt. 'Is she still refusing to see a doctor?'

'She had to when she had pneumonia.'

'When!' Ros looked taken aback. She still lived in Florence, but was on a visit to London which coincided with this family occasion. She had no idea about her mother's recent bad health – except for the hints dropped by James at Diana's wedding. Which, she thought, feeling surprisingly guilty, she had not heeded.

'Last year. She and Billy were cruising on the Niarchos yacht when she went down with a fever – her temperature went up to a hundred and four and she had trouble breathing. The helicopter took her to hospital in Sardinia and they diagnosed pneumonia. Billy flew in doctors from all sides but they all said the same thing so he brought her back to London and another army of doctors gave her a thorough going over – X-rays, blood-tests, the lot. They confirmed the pneumonia and said she should give up smoking. As you can see, she has not.' Toni paused. 'She has got a persistent and troublesome cough. The X-rays reveal nothing but the cough gets no better. I want her to see my own doctor – no bedside manner but I'd trust him with my life. She won't. She says she has seen enough of them for the foreseeable future.' Toni's second pause was longer. 'What worries me is that she might be putting the wrong estimate on that.'

She met Ros's shocked eyes. 'She's losing weight. More than she can afford. Oh, she's clever enough to camouflage it – nobody knows more about clothes than she does – but my guess is she has dropped about ten pounds, and for one whose weight has not deviated by so much as a pound for the past thirty years I find that worrying.'

'So do I,' Ros said.

'Then why don't you try and talk to her?'

Ros shook her head. 'I am the last person she would listen to. Our lives have hardly touched for too long now.'

'She still takes more than an interest – lately not so much

283

an interest as a devoted concern. She was enormously thrilled and proud when you published your book. She must have bought something like a hundred copies to give to friends.'

Ros was bemused. 'I had no idea mother had any interest in art.'

'Always,' Toni said. 'Years ago she used to paint.'

Now Ros was astounded. '*Mother*!'

'There are a lot of things you don't know about your mother,' her aunt told her tartly. 'I think it's about time the two of you got together properly to talk about them.'

'We've never really talked at all; the first time was when I spoke my mind about my début.'

'Then why not try and bridge the gap. I think she'd like nothing better. She has got Diana breathing down her neck at all times and David – well, let's just say I think she would be deeply touched if you were to make the first gesture. You are able to. Your mother's ability to make emotional gestures of any kind atrophied a long time ago.' Toni levelled a look at her niece. 'She has come to realise what a mink-lined prison she has been living in all these years, but she is not the type to go around doing a Cassandra; we were brought up to solve our own problems. Your mother has been seeing a shrink twice a week for a couple of years but she still can't get past her own introversion.'

'A psychiatrist!' Ros was aghast. Things were indeed critical if her coolly rational mother was seeing a shrink.

'She had to talk to *somebody*, or go crazy, and being what she is who better than someone paid to listen? Your mother has never had any trouble dealing with the hired help; it's her own flesh and blood she can't handle. So why don't you make the first move in her direction? Hasn't this ridiculous estrangement been going on far too long?'

'It seemed better than arguing all the time.'

'She won't argue, believe me. She hasn't got the strength.' Toni's still bright-blue eyes met Rosalind's dark ones in a long, deep look which told much. Then Ros nodded.

'Yes,' she said. 'Perhaps, at last, the time is right … '

Seemingly drifting aimlessly, she began to make her way through the throng, stopping now and then to chat; to her Aunt Cordelia and her husband; to various cousins and their husbands, to people she had not seen for years, always keeping her mother in her sights until, as she got closer, she saw that as usual, her Aunt Toni had her sister taped. Ros had never seen her mother's inner light so dim before. It rendered her skin papery, and there was a hectic flush on her cheekbones that was neither excitement nor skilfully applied blusher. The cheekbones themselves were now rocky prominences. She was wielding her long ivory cigarette holder, and as usual she was unbelievably chic in an ivory silk tussore suit with a cropped jacket, its wide revers made of champagne-coloured mink; the skirt trim and straight, a small, matching mink beret set aslant over one ear.

But the clever cut of the suit was not enough to disguise from Ros's now keen eyes the fact that her mother was no longer fashionably slender; she was painfully thin. Yet the smile was bright, the chat sparkling, if the laughter which greeted her sallies was anything to go by, and she was availing herself freely of the plentiful champagne, but Ros knew of old her mother's way of lowering the curtains on her emotions and sending on the stand-up comic to keep the audience amused.

So she deliberately positioned herself where her mother's roving eyes could not fail to see her, and when they did, fixed her own to them with an intensity that had them widening in nervous surprise before shying away. Ros waited, and as she knew it would, her mother's gaze came back to her. This time, as she read the question in it, written on what she was sure was hope, she flashed a silent but urgent message which her mother read instantly, and between them flowed a surge of direct understanding such as had not happened between them before.

'I think we should talk,' Ros's message read. 'Isn't it about time?'

Ros saw the brown velour eyes flare, as if a light had been lit in their depths, saw the slight nod of the head, the way the champagne glass was laid down. Only then did she move forward to penetrate the group, saying easily: 'I've come to carry my mother off. We haven't had a moment together all day ...'

'Of course,' chorused the courtiers, backing away from the Queen and bowing to the Princess. 'Of course ...'

When they were alone: 'Could we sit down? My feet are killing me,' Ros lied.

'That would be nice,' Livy agreed gratefully.

'Somewhere quiet.'

'That would be even nicer.'

'I know just the place ...' Ros led the way across the lawns to the large conservatory at the side of the house. The glass room, its roof panels shaded by white holland blinds, was cool and white, set about with ferns and ornamental shrubs, the white wicker furniture bright with multi-coloured cushions.

'Oh, how nice ...' Livy sighed as she sank into a deep chair. 'One seems to stand around for so long at these affairs.' She leaned back, closed her eyes. Ros was aghast at the drawn-tight suffering in her mother's face.

'I seem to tire so easily these days,' Livy apologised lightly, on opening her eyes unexpectedly and thus catching Ros's expressive face. 'Age creeping on, I suppose.' Her throat seemed to clog and she coughed; her breath caught and she sat up straighter, struggling for breath as the cough racked her.

'Here ... take a drink.' Ros poured a glass of ice-water from the jug on the wicker table, but Livy could not drink; her whole body was shuddering under the violence of her cough.

'This is not right!' Ros exclaimed, jumping up.

Livy put out a hand as if to prevent her from leaving, shaking her head, for she was unable to speak.

'Mother, you need help.'

'No.' Livy managed, eyes streaming. 'Better soon ...' And sure enough the cough began to fade away into rasping breaths and occasional sputterings, but when she fell back against the cushions she was grey-faced and exhausted.

Ros picked up her clutch-purse and extracting a tissue, tenderly blotted her mother's cheeks, careful not to smudge the carefully made-up eyes.

'Thank you.' Livy murmured shyly, emboldened by the gesture to make one of her own by reaching out to take her daughter's hand and squeeze it. 'Just let me rest here a little longer ...'

'Take as long as you like.'

Finally, when the deep straining inhalations had quietened

to normal breathing, Livy said: 'I know … I smoke too much …'

'Far too much,' Ros said curtly, knowing that what had happened to her mother was no smoker's cough.

Livy's eyes opened to look at her daughter. 'Don't scold …' she pleaded. Then on another note: 'Not now …'

But Ros was not to be moved so easily. What she had seen and heard had disturbed her. 'I won't scold if you will see a doctor.'

'I've lost count of the doctors I've seen … it is a hangover from a bout of pneumonia I had some time ago. It left my lungs somewhat the worse for wear.'

'Why don't you go and see Aunt Toni's doctor? She swears by him.'

'Toni always has something she swears by – a cream or a diet or a doctor.'

'Better to swear by than be sworn at.'

Another smile, reminiscent this time. 'Not by you … your father put you across his knee the first time he heard you use a forbidden word; it shocked you so much that he could do such a thing you never did it again …' Livy's eyes met those of her daughter. 'You always had a mind of your own. Unlike me. I found it easier to go along with someone who did. So I was always ruled by someone else – my mother, my first husband – though Johnny was never despotic, and then by Billy, who was, is and always will be …'

'Why have you stayed with him?'

Livy's eyes met Ros's more openly and honestly than they ever had: woman to woman. 'Because I had nowhere else to go.'

'Oh, now mother –'

Livy held up a silencing hand. 'Let me explain something you have never fully understood. The way things were thirty years ago; the kind of life we lived then. It was all very different from the way we live now. Being a wife was the only career open to women in the fifties. If you wanted to devote your life to something – medicine, architecture, writing, designing, then you usually did it at the expense of marriage or gave it up when you did marry. Oh, some professional women did both; there are always the exceptions. But for the majority, marriage was their only destiny. The unthinkable alternative was to be an old maid.' Livy paused to sip at the glass of water Ros had poured. 'The women's movement was no more than an idea, back then. Women were wives, period. Their duty was to care for their men, provide a comfortable home and bring up the children those men made with them. They were not supposed to want more; if they did, there was something wrong with them. Something – unfeminine.'

Livy paused again before continuing. 'I was brought up to be the perfect wife. My mother expected all three of her daughters to make what she called "good marriages", and we more than fulfilled her expectations. When your father was killed and I was left on my own I did not expect it to be for long; after all, what else could I do? But I thought – well, in a year or two. There is no hurry. Then, one night, I met a woman who had divorced her husband for one too many an infidelity and come to regret it bitterly. She painted me a picture of life as a single – she called it "extra" – woman which terrified me. I'm no good at being alone; I'm not independent, like you. I need to know there is someone I can turn to, someone who will handle things when I can't.'

Another pause. 'I thought I had found the perfect solution when I met Billy.' A faint, but bitter smile twisted Livy's mouth. 'I knew he was interested at once, but I also knew he was married. I thought I had played him so cleverly when he came and told me he was now free and wanted me to become Lady Bancroft. I actually thought *I* had played *him*.' A short laugh turned into a cough which she controlled. 'What I was too naive or egotistical to realise was that *I* was exactly what he wanted. Each married the other for purely selfish reasons. I wanted the security of marriage to a rich, powerful man because I'd been badly frightened by Sally Remington. Billy wanted a wife with impeccable social connections and right of entry into a world he wished to make his own; someone who would know how to create for him a perfect lifestyle that would be the envy of the world. If I also created the perfect Lady Bancroft along the way so much the better.'

Livy drew a careful breath in case she coughed again. 'We each got what we wanted but in my case, over the years the image I created took me over; our relationship became – what is the word – symbotic ... ?'

'Symbiotic,' Ros said. 'An association of dis-similar organisms for mutual advantage.'

'Yes, that's right. We fed off each other, each taking what we needed to survive.'

'Human beings are basically selfish,' Ros pointed out, 'most especially when it comes to survival.'

'But it is not a pretty story, is it? Not one I ever wished to become known.' Her voice, tiring rapidly, gained strength as she held her daughter's eyes: 'But I wanted *you* to know.' Ros saw her mother's eyes fill with tears. 'If only I had told you years ago, but I did not know it then, you see ... It took me a long time to come to understand not only what I had done but why I had done it.'

For once in her life Livy allowed tears to spill unchecked, running down her skilfully rouged cheeks. That one thing, more than anything, brought home to her daughter just how ill she was.

'I wish I had possessed the courage to tell you back then. You would have understood the situation at once and put me right.' Livy raised a trembling hand to touch her daughter's face. 'You have the brains I lack,' she said simply. 'Delia was the intelligent one, while Toni was always bright as a button … at my christening I got handed good looks and style and had to make do with them.'

'Some make-do,' Ros teased lightly, steering her mother away from the rocks of remorse. 'I know a lot of clever women who would give every one of their degrees for one tenth of your style and grace.'

As always, the compliment acted like a shot of adrenalin. Livy laughed as she brushed away tears, looked about for her glacé-calf handbag.

Ros handed it to her and she took from it her small, gold-framed mirror, examined her face. 'God … talk about the Wreck of the Hesperus!'

'Never!' swore Ros on a headshake.

'Oh, but I am, especially recently.' Livy searched for her matching gold case containing lip-gloss and brush. 'It is taking more and more effort just to keep the ruins in a decent state of repair.'

That this was no understatement became clear to Ros when she saw how even the effort of holding up the mirror made her mother's hand tremble.

'Here, let me ...' She took the mirror, held it while her mother managed, by dint of holding her right hand steady with her left, to repair the tear-damage.

Restoring her equipment to her handbag: 'Now, all I need to complete the restoration is a glass of champagne ...' Livy announced brightly, obviously bent and determined that her new face should be a bravely defiant one.

'I'll go and get you one.'

'Thank you darling ...' As Ros rose to go Livy caught her wrist. 'For everything,' she said, managing to encompass her own confession, Ros's compassion and their new, unexpected understanding, in those two words. For a long moment their eyes held and for once, Livy's did not slide away. Then Ros smiled.

'My pleasure,' she said. She spied a waiter not a dozen steps beyond the conservatory and taking two glasses from his tray retraced her steps. 'Here we are,' she announced, 'as sparkling as your eyes and as cold as – Mummy!' Livy was no longer in her chair. Somehow she had fallen out of it and was lying on the ground. Slamming the glasses down on the nearest table Ros ran to her, knelt by her. 'Oh, God, Mummy ...' But Livy did not hear her. She was unconscious.

'There is a small tumour on her left lung,' the doctor said gravely, 'which is malignant. Its removal will necessitate removing part of that lung. It is the only way to prevent a recurrence.'

Billy rose to his feet in towering wrath. 'Are you telling me that after all but monthly X-rays over the past year or more you have *now* discovered my wife has cancer? What kind of doctors are you, for God's sake! You've had her under supposedly close surveillance so why was this not discovered before?'

'Because it did not show up before. Now that it has we must remove it with all possible speed.'

'Barring the stable door with the horse a hundred yards down the road?' Billy was red in the face, a sure sign of increasing temper. He was also, Ros thought contemptuously, terrified. Ill-health had always been anathema to him. He had been careful always to distance himself from anyone suffering from it. Cancer was the ultimate terror.

Beside him, Diana was white-faced, her hands showing shiny knuckles. Her husband, sitting next to her, laid a hand over them. She shook it off as she would a fly. David sat bent forward, hands between his knees, staring at the carpet. Only Johnny was missing, because he was somewhere in the Pacific testing his new catamaran.

'I warn you,' Billy wielded his whip, 'my wife had better come out of this cured, or there will be questions asked where they will do you the most harm! Do I make myself clear?' He turned on his heel and swept out, leaving his children to follow on behind, like always.

Two days later surgeons at the Royal Marsden removed the tumour, and with it a third of Livy's left lung. She withstood the surgery well but her convalescence was slow. She spent the first part of it – some six weeks – at Wychwood. James, as always, went with her, leaving Billy free to go on the first of what were to become many peregrinations looking for a way to beat his wife's cancer.

Diana was in London, where Brooks was running Bancroft Holdings in the absence of his father-in-law. David had returned to Cambridge. His mother had insisted he not abandon his studies. 'I am under orders to do nothing but rest; there is no need for you to sit around watching me do so. Go back and work hard, darling; get your law degree; make me twice as proud of you when I come to see you receive it.'

He needed no urging; he was in the middle of a most lubricious three-way affair, dividing his time between one of his male professors and a female fellow student. He always enjoyed the affairs he ran in tandem; they were a challenge to his ingenuity and he liked the danger of balancing on a knife edge, since neither knew about the other and both believed they held sole rights.

Rosalind returned to Italy. Again Livy had insisted. 'I shall have James. Go back to your work, but don't let's lose touch now that we have found each other at last.'

Regretfully: 'What a lot of time we wasted ...' Ros sighed.

'Would you have understood then as you have done now?'

Ros's innate honesty had her considering then answering: 'I doubt it. Too young and too intolerant. But I'm older now and no longer see things in black and white. Life is more of a Van Gogh than a charcoal drawing.'

'I rather think mine is a Hieronymus Bosch,' Livy giggled, dimples showing, surprising her daughter yet again. 'But I'm so glad I did confess my sins. It closed the gap between us, didn't it?' Anxiety haunted the sunken eyes, old insecurities still refusing to quit.

'Tight as a drum,' Ros assured, bending to kiss the papery cheek: 'I think we understand each other at last.'

Livy nodded relievedly. 'That's how I feel too.'

'That being so, if you need me, you'll send for me, won't you?' Ros asked. 'Promise?'

'I promise,' Livy agreed gladly.

Billy had arranged for his private helicopter to take her down to Oxfordshire, for it was the end of January and bitterly cold in the damp, bone-piercing English way she had never managed to get used to.

When she got down to Wychwood she found huge log fires blazing in every room; a brand new central heating system operated by a press-button console, the latest state-of-the-art twenty-six-inch screen television set in her bedroom, and a newly installed lift behind the linenfold panelling in the Great Hall, which took her up to her bedroom. Billy had presented her with a new Russian sable coat, long enough to brush the floor and with a great shawl collar into which she could huddle when she sat out on the terrace to watch the birds come to the table he had had erected just beyond the balustrade. He knew she loved to watch the cheeky little robins in their bright scarlet waistcoats, the bright-eyed blackbirds, the tiny blue and green tits, the occasional goldfinch and the ever present sparrows. He ordered a ten pound bag of wild bird food just so she could scatter it for them. He had become fiercely, even ferociously, protective.

'Of himself as much as me,' was Livy's pithy verdict to her sister Toni, when she came for a long weekend preparatory to leaving for St Moritz and the ski slopes. 'He wants to beat the rap because if he doesn't get me off, he'll have his own sentence to serve; solitary confinement to a lonely old age. And you know how Billy *hates* being on his own.'

295

It was true, Toni saw with amazement. Billy was a man possessed. He spent hours on the telephone, calling anyone and everyone who could be of even the remotest help in his fight to prevent his wife being taken from him. As his perceptive stepdaughter had surmised, he was terrified. His carefully structured life was showing signs of cracks in the foundations, dry rot, wet rot – everything that would lead to an eventual collapse. He kept having nightmares about being buried in the ruins. Used to controlling every aspect of his flawlessly maintained life, he treated his wife's illness as he would a threatened hostile takeover of one of his companies. Not one had succeeded. Nor would this.

When, in the late spring, Livy appeared in public for the first time since her illness, the occasion was reported in the *Tatler, Harper's & Queen*, Nigel Dempster and Londoner's Diary.

'A fashion-icon returns to bedazzle us once more,' one fashion scribe gushed, 'making a grand entrance at Le Gavroche, shiveringly chic in narrow-legged black velvet pants and a sheer white chiffon shirt over a white satin camisole, huge diamond solitaires in her ears and on her slender fingers. If you have been wondering, in her absence, how to do it, this, and only this, is how it is done.'

But after a seemingly full recovery, Livy's fragile health went into a sudden decline. She began to have trouble breathing; it was back to using the lift again, after she had been so proud of once more being able to climb the stairs. Billy went into overdrive. Leaving Livy in the care of James, Diana and Cordelia – Toni was in Brazil having her eyes and throat done – he combed the world for advice and/or anything which would help him, as Livy had said, beat the rap. But in the summer another tumour was diagnosed and the rest of her left lung was removed.

Utterly devastated and terrified as he had never been, Billy became obsessed with finding a cure, travelling thousands of miles in some cases to see anyone who claimed miraculous recoveries, to have discovered a wonder drug, or be able to charm disease away. He consulted every cancer specialist in the business, grilling them as to the odds on a complete eradication of the disease.

One evening, Ros answered the telephone in her flat in what had once been a grand house on the Piazzale Michelangelo. It was James. He had bad news to impart but concerning himself, rather than her mother, who was as well as could be expected. He had just heard that his brother and his wife and their two children had been killed in a multiple pile-up on the M4. They had been travelling back to Chelm after collecting the heir, Charles, from Eton and his sister from St. Mary's, Wantage, when a forty-tonner had crossed the central reservation and jack-knifed, swiping one car head-on and tossing it straight into another with a domino effect which resulted in some thirty cars smashing into each other, causing eleven deaths and forty-two serious injuries.

Apart from anything else, it meant that he was now the seventeenth Viscount, which in turn meant that he could no longer remain with Livy as her trusted right arm.

Ros, who had subconsciously been prepared for such a call, though for different reasons, said: 'I'll come at once. I laid the ground work when I returned last time for a projected – and probably protracted – leave of absence.'

'Always so well organised,' complimented James relievedly.

'Let me know your arrival time and I'll lay on a car at Heathrow.'

'Is my stepfather at home?'

'No, in China, investigating their herbal medicines. He has given a new meaning to the phrase "leaving no stone unturned".'

'Is anyone else with my mother right now?'

'Mrs Winslow flew back to New York the day before yesterday; the Princess von Anhalt is in Bavaria redecorating the family castle; your sister is in London acting as her father's surrogate hostess while her husband runs things in Lord Bancroft's absence; your brother John was here for a month and has only just returned to San Diego with his wife – who is newly pregnant, by the way; they came to tell your mother the good news – and David is still pursuing his law degree. All would come at a moment's notice, but your mother did not ask for them. She asked for you.'

Ros did not hesitate. 'Tell her I am on my way,' she said.

12

'You're late,' Colly Prentiss reprimanded the woman who came through the doors of New York's currently most fashionable restaurant at the trot and made for the table to the left of the door.

'So would you be if you'd seen the traffic! Some protest parade or other has got it backed up to East 88th! Pour me a glass of that lovely Perrier please ...'

Muffy Hadfield collapsed into the fourth chair, loosened the sable collar of her jacket and said: 'If I'm late, where's Cissy?'

'In hiding,' Colly said with relish. 'While you were in Mexico there was an almighty hoohah over an interview she gave to *Vanity Fair*, complete with pictures, all about her new triplex on Park – on which she has just spent God knows how many million dollars, while at the same time, in the *Times Sunday Magazine* there was an article on Izzy and how he is one of the biggest slum landlords in New York. He went positively ape! Banished her to the boondocks – well, that estate of his up in patroon country. She'll be lucky to see New York again this side of Christmas.'

'Never mind Cissy,' one of the other women, a hard-faced redhead named Harriet Stotes interrupted. 'Come on, Colly, what we want to know about is Livy Bancroft. Did you or did you not see her while you were in Europe?'

'Of course I did! I was one of the permitted few.' His smirk was, like his manner, superior. 'She sees very few people nowadays – and no wonder.' He paused for effect. 'It is the end of an era, my dears. Livy Bancroft is not long for this world …' His poached-egg eyes, the result of a slight thyroid condition, popped even more. 'Which will leave a vacancy – not to say a gap.'

'Tell that to Gloria Guanarius,' Muffy Hadfield suggested snidely.

'The hell with Gloria Guanarius,' Harriet brushed her aside impatiently. 'Tell us about Livy.'

Colly frowned slightly. Harriet Stotes always had been, always would be, a vulgarian. She might be married to one of America's richest men but it was New (made yesterday) Money. And didn't it *tell*? He shuddered distastefully. But Willard Stotes was very powerful because he was so very rich, so it did not do to cross his wife.

'Yes, Colly,' drawled Muffy on one of her feline smiles, 'do tell us about the almost late Lady Bancroft …'

Colly moistened his mouth with a sip from his glass, dabbed his rather full lips with his six-hundred-threads-to-the-inch double damask napkin, then began: 'Well, she'd only just come back to town after being in the country – that magnificent Elizabethan manor house of theirs in the Cotswolds, so I dropped a line to her at Morpeth House to say I had shoals of messages from friends in New York which I would be only too happy to deliver. Livy never was one for unexpected visitors, you know.'

'Was Billy at home?' Harriet interrupted again.

'No; these days he spends his time hobnobbing with seers and fakirs, seeing as orthodox medicine can do no more than wring its hands.' He paused dramatically. 'But you will never guess who was?'

'Rosalind Randolph,' Muffy answered.

Deprived of his dramatic announcement: 'Who told you?' Colly demanded peevishly. He had never liked the Queen Bitch Hadfield. How right he had been!

Her smile curled at the edges. 'My dear Colly, I have known Livy since we were both in diapers.'

'But I thought Rosalind and Livy had been at outs for years?' Harriet interrupted. Dishing the dirt on the supposedly ultra clean was her favourite food.

'Not any more,' Muffy said. 'It seems that Diana is out and Rosalind is in.'

'Why?' Harriet asked avidly.

'Oh, come on. Would you like looking at a clone of your younger, healthier self day after day? Everyone knows Diana Bancroft has spent her whole life making herself over into her mother's image – and apropos of that, it seems she has made a better job of it than she knew, since her husband is likewise doing *his* best to emulate his father-in-law.'

Sensing he had lost his usually rapt audience, Colly sulkily threw himself back in his chair, making plain his annoyance, but his greed for gossip – his *raison-d'être* – had him asking in spite of himself; 'In what way?'

Muffy regarded him blandly. 'Why, screwing everything in sight.'

301

'My brother was at Groton with Brooks Hamilton's father,' Bunny van der Gelt said. A Randolph by birth, and thus a cousin of Livy's first husband, she was now sadly impoverished since her husband lost everything in the Black Wednesday disaster. But she was very well-connected, so she was still invited everywhere. 'He wasn't very nice either.'

'What's nice?' Harriet Stotes asked nasally. 'Brooks Hamilton is as gorgeous a piece as ever I've seen – '

'Of which I am sure you have seen more than your fair share,' Muffy murmured.

Harriet glared but left it at that. Mrs Hughes Hadfield was the one woman whose tongue she feared, added to which she was married to a man who could do Willard a power of good where it mattered, which was why Harriet was under orders to be "nice" to her, such as paying for her and Bunny's lunch in this hideously expensive restaurant where nobody came to eat anyway; only to see and be seen and remark on who was with who as they sifted the constantly shifting sands of the clientele; their social, financial and marital standing and whether they were still of a calibre to be given one of the choice tables – by the windows or near the door, or relegated to the Siberia of the second room.

Having made it, thanks to Muffy, from the back to the front, Harriet was resolved to be a best-table person from now on, and if sucking up to this supercilious bitch was part of the price then so be it.

'Ah … I see Lally Somerset over there.' Piqued by the lack of both interest and respect he was being shown – after all, he had a reputation as the town's best gossip to protect – Colly made to push back his chair but Muffy was having none of that. She had known him when he was plain Colin

Prentice, newly arrived from England without a penny to his name but bearing several letters of introduction, including one to Muffy from an old school friend who had married a Foreign Office Mandarin. 'He's an odd little man,' her letter had said, 'but a positive genius at a acquiring the choicest titbits; listen to all he has to say but tell him *nothing.*'

'Sit down, Colly. You don't table-hop when you lunch with me,' she said, jerking on the bit.

Harriet watched with calculating eyes as Colly subsided back into his chair. Colly Prentiss was a social power in New York; a word from him could put you in or boot you out, while a mention in his syndicated column 'Colly's Comments' had the authority of Holy Writ. Harriet read him every day. Yet Muffy Hadfield had spoken to him like a servant – and he had taken it!

Is there *anyone* in this town who doesn't have something to hide? Harriet wondered, but she only said: 'Yes, Colly. Do tell us about Livy. That's why we are here, isn't it?'

'Lady Bancroft to you.' Colly took out his humiliation on someone who could not hit back. Upstart! he thought. Just because your husband is one of the new billionaires … and I'll bet the way he made his first million would not bear investigation! He addressed himself to Muffy and Bunny. They, at least, were of the same social category and closely acquainted with the almost deceased, something he envied to his soul. He had always, without exception, written about Livy in the most sycophantic terms; to him she was, as he invariably named her: 'Perfection's Self', and though she had always been unfailingly and charmingly polite to him at the social events at which they had both been present, he had never managed to get her to address him as 'Colly' instead

303

of Mr Prentiss. Nor – and not for want of trying – had he ever managed to penetrate the Inner Circle, the way Luddy Ludbrooke had for instance.

Now, full of his own self-importance, Colly launched into his story. 'My dears ... the magnificence! Morpeth House always was one of the most splendid private residences in London, but it had been neglected for years and was threatened with demolition or conversion into a block of flats when Sir William, as he was then, bought it from Freddie Morpeth. And thank God for that, say I, because it has to be seen to be believed.' That it was the first time he had seen it he kept to himself.

Pausing to make sure he had their rapt attention: 'Her daughter Rosalind took me up to her. It seems she has replaced James Luttrell-Leigh, now Viscount Chelm, as her mother's personal assistant. I was the only visitor. Everyone else had been and gone; she kept the last half hour just for me.'

'How was Rosalind?' Muffy was bored with Colly's self-importance and brought things back to where she wanted them.

'How should she be?' Colly asked with asperity. He did not know Rosalind Randolph; had not set eyes on her until she came to greet him and take him upstairs to her mother.

Bunny nodded to the waiter to refill her glass. Might as well enjoy a decent lunch. She picked up the menu and began to study it as Colly droned on.

'Rosalind took me upstairs – such a staircase, my dears; one could drive a coach and four up to the first floor – and along to where Livy was enthroned – I do not use the word lightly – in the most stupendous bed, once the property of

Pauline Bonaparte; all gilt and silk and sumptuousness. And there was Livy.' His voice dropped to a hush. 'She was wearing the most magnificent caftan; multi-coloured silk as supple as skin, a matching turban around her head' – in a voice just above a whisper – 'the poor darling has lost all her hair, you know. Chemotherapy. Indoors she wears the turban; when she goes out she has a whole range of the most marvellous wigs.'

'I thought she never went anywhere,' Harriet Stotes said.

'She accepts very few invitations and entertains hardly at all, but I have it on the very best authority that when she does she wears a wig. And even so,' he pronounced with unshakable certainty, 'she is still the most elegant creature in the world. *Terribly* thin, of course. Where once she was as slender as a wand now she is – '

'Skeletal,' Muffy said with relish, smiling into his affronted face. 'I told you. I have my own sources.'

'Well …' Harriet said, affrontedly. 'I mean … cancer!'

'Her own fault.' Muffy was nothing if not callous. 'She has smoked three packs a day as long as I've known her.'

'How long is that now?' Harriet Stotes asked innocently. 'Forty years?' Her laugh tinkled like an icicle. 'Heavens, I wasn't even born.'

'Hardly,' Muffy drawled, unmoved. 'Since you were born only – when was it you married Mr Stotes?'

'Now look here – '

'Ladies, please …' Colly's voice was pained. 'Remember where you are?'

'And how you got here,' Muffy reminded nastily.

'Ladies!' Colly said again, but crossly this time. 'Will you mind your tongues.'

305

Muffy threw him a look. 'Be careful, Colin,' she said. His mouth shut like a trap but his glare was borrowed from the Medusa.

'So go on,' Harriet urged. 'Tell us about how she was and what she said.'

'She was, as always, a great lady,' Colly intoned, in the reverent tones of one speaking about a deity. 'Not a single word of complaint; such dignity, such innate taste and elegance…'

'Who has the good fortune to be married to Billy Bancroft,' Muffy said sarcastically.

Harriet caught the hint of viciousness in Muffy's voice. 'What's wrong with that?' she asked innocently. 'He was a great catch, wasn't he?'

'I wouldn't have Billy Bancroft if he was gift wrapped,' Muffy snapped.

'Well, what would be the point?' Bunny asked woozily from her corner, where she had been sitting sipping away at the Perrier – (Jouet), 'You've already had him, haven't you?' She hiccupped daintily. 'Several times …'

Thus it was that the rest of the Ladies Who Lunch had the unexpected pleasure of seeing Super-Bitch Muffy Hadfield storm out of Le Poule de Luxe leaving a table of two women and one well-known columnist in hysterics.

When Rosalind went downstairs James smiled and went to meet her saying: 'How nice to see you again, old friend.'

'James …'

They embraced, kissed and hugged each other.

'So how are you finding it, being the seventeenth Viscount?' Ros asked.

'Damned hard work. I was never trained for it, you see. Bertie was, from birth. But I'm learning.'

'I'm rooting for you, we both are, though Mummy misses you terribly. I'm trying to fill your shoes, but my feet are smaller than yours and I had no idea you worked so hard. Mummy is panting to see you. She's been primping all morning. You'll stay to lunch?'

'I should be delighted.'

'Good.'

As they went upstairs together: 'How is she, really,' James asked.

'Not too good. She tires very quickly which means she sleeps a lot, and she eats like a bird no matter what delicacies Jean-Jacques prepares for her. The one thing she likes at all times is well-chilled champagne which her doctors say can do her no harm so there is always a bottle by her bed.'

'I have brought her some quails' eggs … from our own birds at Chelm. I'm hoping to market them in quantity quite soon. She always adored them with tarragon mayonnaise so perhaps they will tempt her. Just the thing with a glass of chilled champagne.' He showed Ros the small basket lined with moss on which reposed several dozen quails' eggs.

'Show them to her and then I'll despatch them to the kitchen.' James's upbringing stood him in good stead when, on entering Livy's bedroom, he got his first sight of his former employer in many weeks. She was sitting up against a pile of lace-trimmed pillows, vibrant in vivid pink, green and gold, a matching turban twisted round her hairless head. Her face was as exquisitely made up as ever, and as he bent to embrace and kiss her, gently because she was so frail, he caught her fragrance: the one he identified with her: Ma

Griffe. But he was shocked at the greyness under the skilfully applied blusher; the marvellous eyes were sunken and deeply shadowed, while her cheekbones were now promontories. As he put his arms around her it was like enfolding a skeleton.

'James ...' She breathed with difficulty, spoke in a breathy, top-of-her-one lung voice, but her warmth was a glow. 'How good it is to see you again ... I still miss you, you know.'

'And I you.'

'We had a lot of good years, didn't we?'

'That we did.'

Ros had put a chair nearby but Livy patted her vast bed. 'Sit here where I can touch you.'

Since Livy had never been a toucher – James could not remember her ever hugging and kissing her children – he took this as further evidence of the great change brought about by her finite outlook.

'I'll leave you to it, then,' Ros said. 'I have letters to write ...'

'Thank you, darling,' Livy said, and the tender gratitude with which she spoke was also new. Knowing that now he could, James said when Ros had gone: 'I am so glad to see that you have healed the breach.'

'She has been marvellous,' Livy said simply. 'When I asked her to come to me she did so without hesitation. So many years wasted, James, and all my own fault. I just could never relate to my children. I always found it so difficult. Yet now that she is grown up – and so well, James, so very well – we are close friends, talk together for hours at a time yet can also sit in companionable silence.' With simple truth: 'I do not know what I would do without her.' Then on a sigh: 'Of course, Diana took umbrage. She is terribly jealous of Rosalind; accused me of putting her where she, Diana, should stand. But having Diana around only reminds me of what I was … and quite honestly, I find I don't like either myself or her.' Livy leaned back on her pillows. 'How wilfully one blinds oneself to the truth of things; sees only what one wishes to see. I knew I had made a Faustian pact but I chose not to admit it until I had no choice. I thought it would be easy to be Billy's creature as long as I had the creature comforts he provided, and I have to admit, he gave me the very best of them. But in the last analysis they were never enough, even though I kept telling myself they were more than most people had. I know now, of course, that life is not possessions, reputations, retouched photographs and pages of adoring comment in the magazines. Hold them up to the light and they are all transparent; apply the slightest pressure and they fall apart. They won't *sustain*.'

She seemed to need to talk, but obviously found it tiring, for she fell back against her pillows, eyes closed, struggling for breath.

Then he felt her squeeze his hand; her grip was as feeble as a child's but her murmur was heartfelt when she said: 'You have always been the best of friends. Fate was kind when it brought us together that morning.' One of her teasing smiles appeared. 'I have never used anything but Leigh's Fine Leaf Teas ever since …'

She seemed to fall into a light doze, but James sat on, holding her hand. Odd, he thought, it not only comforts her, it comforts me …

When the butler entered Livy's sitting room, which Ros

309

used as her office, to say that a Mr Ross had called — by appointment — to see Lord Bancroft, Ros asked, 'Are you sure? I thought all appointments had been cancelled by Miss Marshall?'

Damn! she thought irritably. There was no way of checking because the ever-faithful Gladys Marshall was travelling with Billy as always; she did the donkey work.

'I informed Mr Ross that His Lordship was abroad,' Baines told her, 'but he insists his appointment was not cancelled.'

'Very well, I'll have a word with him. Thank you, Baines.'

When Ros went into the library, the man was standing in front of the fireplace, his back to her, staring up at the Annigoni portrait of the then Sir William Bancroft he did not hear her enter, so absorbed was he in studying the painting and she had the distinct impression — he was not standing to attention for a start but had his hands casually in his pants pockets — that he was convinced he was looking at a fake.

'Not considered to be one of Annigoni's best,' she said. 'He was getting old by then.'

The man turned. He was very dark; hair and eyes both black, and saturnine. Cassius! Ros thought instantly, before saying: 'I am sorry, but your appointment ought to have been cancelled by my stepfather's secretary. He is abroad right now. You are sure no one from his office contacted you?'

'I've just come back from South Africa to find a whole heap of messages but none from him. He was the one who wanted to meet me in the first place. About an article I'd written … '

'Ah!' Light dawned. 'You are Jack Ross.'

'I had no idea my fame had spread so far.'

310

'Infamy, more like. In this house, anyway. I'm Rosalind Randolph.'

'I know.'

'Have we met?'

'No. But you have your own reputation – as an art historian, I mean.'

Ros eyed him narrowly, convinced he meant something else. Her status as a women's libber, for instance. He met her eyes blandly but there was a glint in them. Something about him put her on her mettle. 'Do sit down,' she invited, changing her mind about seeing him out – and off. 'Would you like a drink?'

'No, thank you. And if Lord Bancroft is not here to see me then I had better go and talk to people who are.'

'Are they also in your book?'

Now he eyed her. 'How do you know about that?'

'My stepfather is not very happy about being – he says – pilloried by you and/or classed as a twentieth-century buccaneer – I use your own phrase.'

'I thought "pirate" sounded too libellous.'

'And Lord Bancroft has fought many a successful libel battle in his time.'

'Don't worry; subtle pressure has already been brought to bear. Fortunately, my publisher is not without his own power.'

'Can I ask who it is?'

When he told her she laughed. 'No wonder you have been summoned. Your publisher is much too rich and powerful to be frightened off.' Her smile faded. 'But why are you publishing here anyway? You're not British, are you.'

311

'No, I'm from over there – like you.'

'Whereabouts?'

'Philadelphia.'

'So is my mother.'

'I know.' Jack Ross said again.

They locked eyes. 'What made you include an English tycoon in your book?' Ros asked to break it.

'I include two. The other one is Jimmy Goldsmith.'

Ros raised an eyebrow. 'So are you no longer an investigative reporter?'

'This book is the result of my investigations and the articles that came out of them, expanded and brought up to date.'

'Like the one you did on Vietnam?'

'You read it?'

'Yes. That was based on your own experience, wasn't it?' Ros considered him. 'You are not doing an "Answered Prayers" with this one, are you?'

'I write non-fiction.'

'So did Truman Capote in that particular book!'

Jack Ross shook his head. 'My book is a study of power and how it is used; not scabrous gossip about the socially rich, in which I have absolutely no interest.'

'How rare.'

'That's how I like my steak.'

Ros rose to her feet. 'I am sorry you have had a wasted journey.'

He also stood. 'I wouldn't say that.'

Ros thought how unusual it was to have a man tower over her; so few ever did. Peter had been slightly shorter.

'I shall tell my stepfather you called,' she said, turning to lead him out. 'No doubt he will be in touch again.'

'No doubt.'

They shook hands. His grip was firm but not macho. And his smile, when it came, was high voltage.

As she went back upstairs Ros thought that what Billy had obviously intended was an exercise in damage control. In his eyes, Jack Ross was a dangerous man. Ros had been impressed by his outspoken and controversial book on Vietnam, which had been published while she was at Berkeley. He had actually come to speak there, but she had not gone to hear him; at that time the only voice she had been listening to belonged to Peter Dzundas.

After lunch, which Livy insisted on eating at the table laid in her sitting room and which she managed to make by leaning on James's supporting arm, she went back to bed and almost before Ros had drawn the covers over her, was asleep.

'She has run out of strength,' James observed sadly.

'She has run out of a lot of things,' Ros told him as they went out, 'or to be more accurate – discarded them. Things she would once have accepted without comment she now remarks upon, ascerbically, in a way that is new. It's as though she has arrived at the point where "what the hell, I've got nothing to lose" is the only attitude to take.' Ros paused. 'Which, of course, is only too true ...'

'Circumstances alter cases?' James paused. 'As they have altered mine.'

Something in his voice had Ros asking: 'For better or worse?'

'As a matter of fact, I would like to talk to you about it.'

'Let's take a walk,' she suggested, sensing he had something

313

on his mind. 'We have access to one of the few remaining private gardens left in London.'

Wrapped up against the inclement weather they went out through the morning room windows and into the gardens, which Livy had brought back from a wilderness to its original eighteenth century elegance.

'I hope you will not take what I am going to say as the last desperate grab of a drowning man or, how shall I put it, a makeshift solution,' James said after a while, sounding, to Ros's acute ears, both anxious and uneasy. 'I assure you, it is not', he went on. 'I have thought long and hard about the matter and come to the conclusion that my proposed course of action makes sense.'

'I'm all for that. My old governess was great on common-sense.' Ros realised that for the first time ever in her experience James's hitherto perfect aplomb was not steady on its feet. His upbringing had trained him to cope with all situations in a manner unlikely to leave a nasty taste in the mouth; as P.A. to Lady Bancroft he had handled innumerable awkwardnesses pregnant with unfortunate possibilities and delivered every one without complications. What was exercising him now was whether or not to use forceps.

'As you know,' he continued stiltedly, 'I have been, as they say, "translated" to a position I never expected to occupy. My brother was the heir who in turn produced his heir; that both would be killed at the same time was something I never envisaged, but they have been and I am the seventeenth Viscount. It is therefore incumbent upon me to see that there will be an Eighteenth. To do this I must marry.' He stopped dead, feet scraping on the gravel walk. 'I would like, if you would have me, to marry you.'

Ros had also stopped, and for a moment she was so taken aback she could only stare in wide-eyed, open-mouthed astonishment.

'We get on so well,' James continued, holding her astonished eyes doggedly, 'always have done. I regard you as a person of integrity and honour and I consider you would make the perfect Viscountess Chelm. I am deeply fond of you, and I think I am right in saying that you are fond of me; many good marriages have been built on less firm a foundation.' In the face of Ros's continued silence he hastened on. 'I am not pretending it will be anything but a marriage of convenience – mostly mine, but if I must do my duty – and I have no choice if the line is to continue – then I can at least choose someone with the intelligence and understanding to appreciate what must be done, and help me do it well.'

'But you prefer men,' Ros pointed out, her robust commonsense bobbing to the surface.

'I was heterosexual before I was homosexual and can be again for the right reasons. I am not pretending it would be a marriage of mutual passion; it would not. But it would be companionable, you would not lack for material comfort, you would have a position in society – though I am aware that you do not hold such things in high regard – and I would do all I could to ensure your happiness. There is no one in your life who matters, is there? No man, I mean.'

Ros shook her head.

'You do not love easily. Neither do I. But we *like* each other enormously, do we not? Have long been the best of friends? We feel no strain in each other's company; we share many similar tastes. I have watched you grow up from a rebellious, somewhat contumacious girl into a balanced, independent, fair-minded woman and I regard what you have done for your mother after such a long and deep schism as typical of the kind of woman you are. Eminently fitted to be my wife, and, I hope, the mother of the next Viscount.' James winced as he added: 'God, that sounds insufferably snobbish, but you know what I mean. It makes *sense*. I must marry and have a son; ergo, I can at least marry someone who knows what I am and is under no illusions as to why I am. You are such a person. The only one I could truly – and humbly – ask to be my wife.' He ran out of breath, stood looking at her hopefully, trying not to look as anxious as he felt.

Ros contemplated him for so long he began to fidget.

'The idea does not appeal,' he said finally, and dead flat. Tread carefully, Ros told herself. This is a sensitive man, yet like all the English aristocracy, when it comes to duty and the continuance of the line, pragmatism rules, okay? She was at once touched by his sincerity and turned off by his cold-bloodedness even while another part of her recognised, as it always had done, that he was still a very attractive man. She had thought, long ago when she had first found out he was unattainable, 'what a waste' but now, the thought that she would be wasting herself was uppermost in her mind.

With unexpected astonishment she realised that she had not after all accepted that she was passed the stage where there was no hope of Prince Charming boarding the coach. I don't want a marriage of convenience, she thought, no matter how convenient it would be. I am not old enough to be reduced to a 'sensible' marriage.

I am only thirty-three! she thought aggrievedly. Surely Peter is not the only try I get! There must be some other man somewhere with whom I could have a relationship where convenience has nothing to do with it! For no good reason she thought of Jack Ross.

She owed it to James to make her refusal as gentle as she could. 'This has thrown me, James,' she said. 'It is not something to which I can give an immediate answer. There is a lot to consider.'

'Of course, of course.' He sounded only too relieved that she had not said: Pull the other one, it's got Big Ben on it!

'I was worried that you might think the proposal too cold-blooded,' he admitted. 'Americans are much more sentimental than we English about marriage. But I promise you, Rosalind, that this would be a true marriage, and I should do my very best to be a good husband.'

Like Billy promised my mother? Ros found herself thinking. All these years I have condemned my mother for her obsession with keeping up appearances yet here is James, of all people, riven by the same desire, even to denying his sexuality.

But even as she pitied him she knew beyond doubt that she had had no intention of giving up her own ghost for somebody else's salvation. To tell the truth, she thought, I am tired of the shade of Peter Dzundas. It is time he was exorcised. High time ... Once again the dark, saturnine face of Jack Ross materialised in her mind's eye.

'How long do you need to think about it?' she came back to hear James asking.

'Right now, my mother comes first; you obviously thought long and hard about asking me; I promise to do the same with regard to my answer.'

'Fair enough.' He was not wholly satisfied but it would have to do.

Rosalind was the most fair-minded of women. If she said that she would give serious consideration to his proposal then that is what she would do. He would just have to wait. And hope for the best, for Rosalind was the best of the bunch. There were other women who would jump at the chance, marriage of convenience or not. In English Society they were as common as adultery. But he did not want them. He wanted Rosalind. And the fact that she had a great deal of money was not exactly unimportant either. He could do so much for Chelm …

Yes, he told himself. Wait, and hope. Just so long as my cause is not hopeless …

Which was how Billy felt when he arrived back from yet another fruitless trip. He was slumped in the big chesterfield in front of the fire, and had not even taken his coat off when his stepdaughter knocked and came into his study.

'Mother is sleeping,' she informed him. 'She had a bad bout of pain this afternoon. I called Dr Jacoby and he said to increase her medication.'

Billy nodded, staring into the bright flames of the fire.

'Any luck?' Ros asked.

His shoulders rose and fell under the black vicuña of his topcoat.

'While you were away, a man named Jack Ross came to see you – by appointment. The ever-efficient Miss Marshall omitted to tell him you would be going abroad.'

Billy shrugged again, then: 'Jack Ross!' His voice was stronger and he turned from staring into the fire. 'That son-of-a-bitch has been writing scurrilous stories about me. I wanted to put the record straight. By God, I *will* put the record straight. I'm not having some tuppenny muck-raker printing lies about me.'

'I told him you would no doubt be in touch again.' Rosalind produced the card he had given her. 'He left this. Shall I give it to Miss Marshall or do you want him to stew a while longer?'

Billy held out a hand. 'I'll see to it,' he said.

'I think you'll have a hard time,' Ros told him. 'He told me he stands by everything he wrote.'

Billy jeered. 'He's let his Pulitzer Prize go to his head! He's just another reporter who fancies he is writing The Book of Samuel.' But to Ros, his bark lacked its usual sound and fury. He looked tired; worse, he looked old. His hair was now completely silver, and his well-barbered features were not only lined but deeply creased. But his menace returned when he said malevolently: 'I've got my own ways of dealing with shits like him.'

'May I have a ring-side seat?' Ros asked.

Billy levelled a look. 'This is no time to be trading insults. My wife, your mother, is dying. I've seen every goddamned quack in the business. None of them can do anything.' He turned back to the fire. 'I've had to fight for what I wanted all my life. Marrying your mother was one thing; being blackballed from all the right clubs was another, so I formed my own and I made your mother the secretary and by God, I was even more damned particular about who I allowed in! I've fought and won most of the battles I've had with life but I can't seem to win this one!' His clenched fist beat angrily on the leather arm of the big chesterfield. He sounded baffled, impotent. Always before he had managed, as he would put it, to "suss out" his opponent, anticipate his moves because he had already had him investigated in depth. Billy had never gone into any deal blind. This opponent had the very latest in radar; was always one step ahead; every time Billy thought he had him cornered he would find the corner empty.

Ros asked: 'How long will you be staying this time?'

'As long as it takes. I won't be going away again. There's no point.'

Billy's perfect life was unravelling and no matter how frantically he re-wound, he seemed to have yards and yards of it in his hands. What or where had he gone wrong? Of course, if Livy had heeded his warning, stopped smoking those goddamned cigarettes, none of this would be happening. She'd still have her health, he'd still have his peace of mind. But she just could not stop. A good Monte Christo with a glass of brandy after a memorable dinner, that was all right. But sixty cigarettes a day! And for why? What did she have to worry about? He had given her everything, hadn't he? Whatever she had wanted she had got. All she'd ever had to do was keep him happy. All right, so he'd asked – well, demanded – certain things as standard, but they'd reached a *modus operandi*, hadn't they? So why had it turned into a nightmare?

Because of a habit she bloody-well would not quit! he answered himself resentfully.

When he thought of the millions he'd either given or helped raise for cancer research he wanted to shout at the useless doctors: 'So why the hell are you still no nearer finding out what causes it? You've been looking all *my* life and now

320

that of my wife is going to end because of this accursed disease and you tell me there's not a goddamned thing you can do to stop it! Well, you had better stop it or else you don't get so much as a penny piece from me ever again! Do I make myself clear?'

Such denunciations had always worked in the past. Billy Bancroft never made idle threats. But cancer could not be threatened. It knew it had the upper hand, and Billy was finding himself in a position he had not occupied for very many years. Dragging himself to his feet he shed his coat, letting it lie where it fell, before plodding wearily up the stairs and along to his wife's room. Her nurse was in a chair under a pool of lamplight reading a copy of *Cosmopolitan*. She put it down and rose to her feet.

'Lady Bancroft is sleeping.'

'So I see. Leave us for a while, will you?'

'As you wish.'

Billy pulled a fragile French chair to the bedside, sat down heavily. Livy was breathing shallowly; under the covers her body hardly showed, she was so skeletal, yet as her body had wasted so had her hostility to him grown. She had never spoken to him then the way she did now; derisively, contemptuously. She had taken to calling him 'Billy-Boy' which was, he knew, how her daughter Rosalind had always referred to him.

The last time he had come back from a trip, empty-handed yet again, she had looked him up and down before asking derisively: 'And where have you been all the day, Billy-Boy, Billy-Boy?'

And when he tried to explain that he was searching for something to cure her, to keep her with him, he needed her so, she said cruelly: 'I know you can't bear the thought of losing me. After all, what are you without me? Who are you without me? You married me for my social position; my job was to plug you in to the right connections, to get you past the doorman and into society. You'll never find another woman to do for you what I did. To suffer in silence, to look the other way, to be humiliated in private and talked about in public!' Her voice had risen, causing her to cough and pant, but she was running on hatred, and it was high octane.

The wheel had turned full circle; Livy now had the upper hand, but so desperate was he that he took all she could throw at him. It was at times like these, late at night at his wife's bedside, that Billy Bancroft, the rich and mighty Lord Bancroft, examined his Grand Design, searching for the fatal flaw. He had plotted it all out so carefully many years before, when he was young; a nothing and a nobody who desperately wanted, and fully intended, to be something and somebody.

And he had, hadn't he? Billy Banciewicz had achieved the pinnacle so why, *why* was it all being taken away from him now? She was only fifty-four years old! Surely she was entitled to the full three score and ten? He himself was only sixty-nine and he intended to make eighty at least. They had years to go yet, lots more to do, even more money to make.

There had to be a way round this, there *had* to be! He was always at his best when cornered; that was when his mind worked fastest and he saw everything most clearly. But at this most important juncture his mind seemed to have turned sluggish, he was tired, no longer able to read the small print without a magnifying glass; he who had always scrutinised even the microprinting, holding it up to the light to check for traces of sno-pake, particularly between the lines.

322

Nobody had ever put anything over Billy Bancroft. He was known to be the greatest living practitioner of the art of the deal, the more complicated the better. Why, then, was he losing the most important deal of his life?

As time went on and every trip ended in failure he had reverted to type. At dinner one night in the house of his daughter Diana he met an old school friend of hers; young and fresh and quickly bedazzled. Just what an old man needed. At first, they were very discreet; he always visited her at her flat; they never went out together, but then he was seen leaving early one morning and the affair became the talk of the town. Except that for once, for the first time actually, it was not an affair; it was a friendship. What he wanted was someone to talk to. Rosalind knew him far too well and disliked him too much, Diana did not know him at all while David was never at home. Rose Daventry was kind, patient, a wailing wall Billy used to relieve his feelings. But once Livy took to her bed permanently Billy became more and more frantic until finally Rose told him she could not continue the friendship because she could not cope with his demands on her.

She was no Livy.

Then Billy located a doctor in Brussels who had, he said, discovered a revolutionary experimental new kind of treatment. Billy sent his plane to Brussels to bring back glass vials of liquid with which Livy was injected four times a day; it was supposed to boost her body's ability to absorb nutrition. After a month's treatment it was obvious that it was a failure. Now, the cancer had invaded her nervous system. It was only a matter of time. Billy reached out to touch his wife's hand, lying lax on top of the silk bordered sheet. It felt very hot though it was nothing but bones, but the nails (false because the chemotherapy had ruined her own) were exquisitely manicured and painted bright pink. Even now, she would not let herself be seen as the physical wreck she was.

Billy put his head down on his wife's hand. 'You were everything I ever wanted, Livy,' he said despairingly, 'ever since I first laid eyes on you at a party where you didn't even notice me. Why are you punishing me like this? Is it your way of paying me back? I know I haven't been a perfect husband but this is the most terrible revenge you could have exacted. Don't leave me, Livy, please, please ... don't leave me ...'

When the nurse, worried by the length of time she had left her patient, re-entered Livy's bedroom, she found husband and wife fast asleep, his hands tightly grasping hers, his head resting on both.

13

'I want you to arrange a lunch,' Billy said.

Ros looked at him.

'Please,' then glossing it with a final: 'As a favour to me.'

'What kind of lunch?' Ros asked. 'To impress, coerce, flatter, frighten or bribe.'

Billy gave her one of his 'looks', but did not follow it up, which indicated to Ros that he really did need her help. 'Just a friendly lunch,' he said casually. 'Nothing elaborate, but up to your mother's standard. You know what I mean.'

'Perfectly,' Ros answered, but Billy had only ever seen jokes by appointment. 'Where, when and how many?' she asked.

'Next Thursday, here and just one guest. Jack Ross.'

'Won't be told?' Ros commented waspishly. 'Or his publisher either? What a pity it is not one of those you already own.' He did not answer, but Ros had not studied him for years for nothing. 'I told you this one would not lie down and roll over. You'll have to do a Robert Maxwell and use the law to gag Jack Ross.'

'Unlike Robert Maxwell I have nothing to hide and therefore no reason to hide it,' Billy rapped.

'Then why are you so worried about this particular book? Is it a case of not so much what he says as how he says it? What are you going to offer him? A job? Such as writing your "authorised" biography?'

Billy remained impassive. When he stonewalled it was ten feet high.

'All right,' Ros relented, as it was for Jack Ross. 'One damage limitation lunch. Do you have any preference as to food. I do know he likes his steak rare ...'

Billy flashed her an interrogatory look but answered: 'My information is that he likes good food but nothing too fancy. Make it a steak; one of your mother's perfect fillets, with some Béarnaise sauce, those tiny potatoes roasted whole in olive oil and garlic, and a green salad; do it like your mother does; young celery hearts, a mixture of various kinds of lettuce: feuille de chêne, frisée and radicchio, leavened with a few of those tiny scallions. Use her own dressing. No sweet; my information is that he doesn't eat them. Cheese, I think. Some of the mature Stilton with Bath Olivers and the special digestive. Plenty of good coffee.'

'What about wine?'

'I'll see to that.'

'What time?'

'Twelve forty-five for one. Don't use the dining room; set it up in the morning room.'

Ros made a mock salaam. 'It shall be done, O Master.' At the door, hand on knob, Billy turned. 'No wonder you're not married,' he said.

*

326

'Why the hell do you need that stuff?' David's lover demanded angrily, as David bent over the line of coke and inhaled deeply.

'Because it helps me cope with things,' David answered, falling back against the high back of the couch, eyes closed, feeling the charge lift him, physically and mentally.

'What have you got to cope with, for God's sake?' his lover asked derisively. 'You have a hell of a lot more than enough money, your grades are high, you have no trouble attracting men or women, and your father thinks the sun shines out your ass! I should have such difficulty coping.'

'Don't take the holier than thou route, please. I'm not up to it.'

'You were a little while ago.'

'These days sex seems to take it out of me, and I haven't been feeling too well lately.'

'Is it any wonder? You burn your candle not only at both ends but in the middle!' The boy, as beautiful as an angel and built like an athlete, shook his head admiringly. 'Only David Bancroft ...' But he paused in his dressing to frown and say: 'I've noticed you haven't been your usual self lately. Maybe you should go and see your doctor.'

'I'm never ill,' David dismissed. 'I've been overdoing it, that's all, and I'm worried about my mother.'

'How is she?'

'Not good.'

'I'm sorry.'

'So am I.'

Dressed now, the boy lingered. 'Will I see you later?'

'I'm not sure. Depends how I feel.'

'Should I call you?'

David opened his eyes to meet the concerned gaze of his lover. 'I'll be okay,' he said easily. 'You were right; I have been overdosing on the sex, drugs and booze bit lately. Maybe I should give one of them up for Lent. Which one would you suggest?'

'The dope *and* the booze.' A grin. 'You don't want to overdo it the other way either.'

David smiled again but his eyelids fluttered closed as if too heavy to support. 'I've never been one to do things by halves... As Wilde said, "nothing succeeds like excess" ...' He yawned once, hugely, and was suddenly fast asleep.

'Why didn't you ask me to arrange your lunch?' Diana sounded hurt. 'You know I am only too willing to do whatever I can to help. I thought you and Rosalind were at daggers drawn? Or have you arranged a temporary truce.'

'You have enough to do, what with Brooks and the baby,' Billy pointed out.

'I hardly ever see Brooks and I have a nanny, remember? Is it any wonder I feel pushed to one side? Ever since Rosalind Randolph came back I've been supernumerary. It's the Prodigal Son all over again – re-written by a feminist of course!'

'Your mother wanted Rosalind,' Billy said wearily, for the thousandth time. He loved Diana as much as he disliked Rosalind, but he had to admit she could be bloody tiresome. Winge, winge, winge. Rosalind was a contumacious bitch but she never complained and, he had to admit it, she was her mother's daughter in a way Diana could never be, no matter how slavish the imitation. 'She knows how your mother likes things; she has eleven years on you.'

'Do you think I need reminding? The first-born is always the favourite.'

'Your mother has never played favourites,' Billy said sternly. Soothingly: 'I was the one who did that. Haven't you always been mine?'

'And David,' Diana reminded jealously. 'He's the heir, isn't he? And from what I hear he is flying on all cylinders these days.'

'Who told you that?' Billy barked.

'Some people who know the crowd he runs around with at Cambridge. By all accounts a very weird one.'

'What do you mean – weird?'

'Exactly what everybody else means. Strange, odd, abnormal ... queer.' Normally she would have quailed before the look Billy threw at her; the kind that pinned you to the wall, but she was burning high-octane jealousy and could not see for smoke. His voice, though, would have penetrated solid rock.

'Don't you *ever* repeat such things about your brother, do you hear? Either in private or in public. I am sick and tired of your petty little temper tantrums every time you think your standing is threatened. You are twenty-two years old and it does not become you to play the spoiled brat.' That he was responsible for spoiling her never crossed his mind. 'This is precisely why I asked your half-sister to arrange what I consider an important lunch; she does not take every suggestion as a threat to her security and she can carry out orders. Nor does she constantly carp or criticise her brothers and sister as you do! Is it any wonder your mother does not want you around when all you do is winge and whine?'

Diana burst into loud wails and rushed from the room.

He heard her running up the stairs followed by the slam of a door, but his mind was not on her. It was on his son. Going to his desk he reached for the telephone and from memory, dialled David's number.

Ros was making a final inspection of the table – the Royal Doulton China (Carlyle pattern), the Georgian silver (Bead pattern) the Waterford crystal. Baines had decanted the wine, a Pomerol 1947. 'Watch out, Mr. Ross,' she murmured, 'you are a marked man.' She tweaked the arrangement of red poppies, blue cornflowers and yellow tulips in the small silver bowl set as a centrepiece. 'All quite informal,' she murmured. 'And wait till you take a bite of your steak …'

Billy entered as she turned away from the table. He walked round it, examining carefully, straightening a knife, re-aligning a palest green pure linen napkin exquisitely embroidered with drawn threadwork. Then he nodded. 'Perfect,' he said. 'What about the food?'

'I've done a Duchess of Windsor. The fillets are identical twins; the potatoes all the same size and shape, the lettuce is being picked this very moment, and the dressing I shall make myself. The Stilton has to be tasted to be believed, and the Bath Olivers are as crisp as the nice new notes brought for your wallet every morning. The coffee will not be made until you ring the bell.' Helpfully: 'I have even put Mummy's little gold-plated notebook by your plate so that you can note down anything that does not come up to standard. I know how high they are.' Pause. 'Mummy has told me so many times …'

Unexpectedly, Billy threw back his handsome, leonine head and laughed. 'It has never ceased to amaze me where you get that spirit from. Not from your mother, and not from your father if what I have heard of him is true. Probably your two grandmothers; both of them tough as old boots. They didn't have feminism in those days –'

'Oh yes, they did,' Rosalind interrupted. 'It was underground, that's all.'

'Where they both are ... but they bequeathed their spirit to you.'

'Thank you for the compliment,' Ros said, surprised that he should make it. It was a first.

'Your Gaylord grandmother couldn't stand me because I wasn't Social enough and worst of all, I was a Jew.'

'One would never know it,' Ros assured helpfully. She saw his eyes flare but his tone had not changed when he went on:

'Your Randolph grandmother did not so much as acknowledge my existence. People like me didn't, exist I mean, for people like her. But I admired her; she was a great lady.'

'I know,' Ros said.

Then he went and blew it. 'You should have been a man.'

Now it was her turn and she took it. 'What a pity I can't return the compliment.'

Their eyes met and held. Irresistible force met immoveable object, then into the silence the deferential tones of Baines said: 'A telephone call for you, My Lord. Mr David.'

Ros saw Billy's face change as he turned at once. 'I'll be right there.'

Jack Ross's taxi drew up under the enormous *porte cochère* of Morpeth House just as Billy picked up the telephone receiver in his study.

Baines apologised for his non-appearance, and asked if Mr Ross would care to wait in the library, but Jack had caught sight, through the door Billy had left open in his haste, of Rosalind Randolph's tall, elegant figure bending over what was obviously a luncheon table, so he said: 'I'd rather talk to Miss Randolph,' and began to walk across the hall in her direction.

She did not hear him coming; and he stopped in the doorway to admire her as she bent over the table, settling its already perfect flower arrangement. A beautiful woman, he thought, again, if something of a skyscraper, but size apart, still formidable. The first time he had set eyes on her he had thought she had her mother's famous looks, but glossed over with the incisive intelligence her mother lacked. Twenty-odd years ago, as a cub reporter fresh from Columbia's School of Journalism and a legman for a famous columnist, he had covered a charity event at which all three of the Gorgeous Gaylords had been present, and been bowled over by the sheer perfection of Olivia Gaylord Randolph. Her daughter was not so perfect, but it made her more human, even if in the unmistakeable Upper-East-Side, Gold Coast, old money and long pedigree, perfectly-formed-vowels of the right finishing school kind of way, which knew to a nicety the effect it had on people. Such self-assurance in a woman was invariably a goad to a man.

Ros was breathing fire and smoke. She should have been a man indeed! What can any man do that I can't do just as well and probably a damned sight better! Come to that, what can any man do for me that I can't do for myself?

She stared furiously at the beautifully laid table, where she had no doubt Billy would do his best either to suborn, stifle or otherwise prevent Jack Ross from publishing what he considered to be dangerously damaging material. You'll be lucky, she thought. Jack Ross is not the type to be pushed around either. Still, he would get a damned good lunch out of it. That thought struck a chord and she laughed, her good humour suddenly restored.

'The condemned man ate a hearty meal,' she chuckled.

'Just as well I brought my appetite then.'

She whirled from the table to see Jack Ross regarding her from the doorway. Her whole body blushed. This is ridiculous! she thought. 'I didn't hear you arrive,' she said coldly 'Nor did Baines inform me that you had.'

'I told him not to bother. I don't stand on ceremony. Condemned men rarely do.'

'That was not meant for your ears.'

'But it is always the overheard I find most interesting.'

Furious at being caught out by this man, flustered not only by his obvious amusement but her own uncontrollable reaction to him, Ros said: 'I don't care for smart-alecs.'

'My name is Jack – not short for John, by the way. I was christened Jack.'

Pure sorbo rubber, Ros thought, as she said with cool politeness: 'Let me get you a drink, Mr Ross.'

'Make it a straight tonic and you've got a deal.'

'You don't drink while you are working?'

He shook his head. Oh, shrewd man, Ros thought happily. You've done this before. So much for the Pomerol. Bad luck, Billy-boy.

Jack Ross was matter of fact, quite without embarrassment, but she had the feeling that embarrassing him would not be easy. He was not in the least intimidated by who she was, what she was, the house, the overpowering evidence of huge wealth, or the reputation of the man with whom he would shortly be lunching. She liked that. Peter had been the same, though he had never really known just how rich she was or how powerful her family. Or had he? He had been such an expert at concealment ...

'Tonic it shall be,' she said, as she went past him and out of the door.

Following her into the small drawing room – only sixty by fifty as against the large drawing room's ninety by eighty, he whistled and asked: 'Is all this original?'

'As near as dammit. My mother had the fabrics specially re-woven from scraps of the originals that had to be carefully peeled from the walls, but the carpet is the one that Robert Adam designed to go with the ceiling, the mouldings are his and the fireplace as he installed it. The furniture is of the period, but only the chairs by the window and that sofa table are part of the furniture he designed. Are you interested in antiques?'

'I like good design. This is a lovely room. But then, your mother is famous for her taste.' Watching Ros's face he asked, in an entirely different voice: 'How is she?'

'Not good,' Ros found herself admitting as she handed him his well-iced tonic, replete with slice of lime. She added gin to her own before taking it to one of the twin, elegant Madame Recamier couches on either side of the fireplace. Watch yourself, she warned. This man is an investigative reporter: he knows what sort of questions to ask – and how to ask them.

'Do sit down, Mr Ross.'

'Thank you, Miss Randolph.'

Their eyes met and held. His were the darkest she had ever seen. As black as his hair. His brows were also strongly marked. But he had the most beautiful mouth she had ever seen on any man.

'Did you interview my stepfather before you wrote your article about him?' Ros asked, to break free.

'Yes.'

'Then why is he so – put out – at what you wrote?'

'Because I wrote about what he did not say rather than what he did. Rags to riches is part of the American Dream, and my editor wanted to reverse a circulation dip. The articles were very well received so my agent suggested I expand them into a book. I found the research became even more fascinating the deeper I dug.'

'Do tell,' Ros encouraged.

He considered her. 'But he is your stepfather. You should be in a position to tell me, surely.'

'I know absolutely nothing about my stepfather's business affairs; only that he is a financial genius who has, over the past forty years, made himself into one of the richest men in the world. Just how rich I could not begin to say.'

'How does two billion strike you – pounds that is; three and a half billion dollars American.'

Ros's jaw dropped.

'That is a conservative estimate,' Jack Ross said helpfully.

'But how does anyone make two billion pounds in only forty years?'

'By split-second timing; by getting into a particular financial speculation so early that nobody has any idea he is sitting there, waiting. Your stepfather has made insider trading into

335

an art, and the beauty of it is there is absolutely no proof. He has to get his information from somewhere but nobody as yet has been able to put a finger on anybody or anything. He has a God-given nose for a deal – something no money can buy, and a sixth sense for danger that is likewise priceless, but he also has to have had information from somebody somewhere to have accomplished what he has.'

'And is this what you have written about.'

'Among other things.'

Ros shook her head. 'No wonder he is buttering you up. Watch out; he has a very large bite.'

'I know his reputation.' Jack Ross paused. 'As I know yours.'

With drop-dead coolness: 'I didn't know I had one,' Ros said.

'As a maverick art historian, I mean. The one who does not hesitate to call it as she sees it; like what you said about art students not being taught to draw or the use of perspective. Is that true?'

'Unfortunately, yes.'

'But not in Italy, where you live?'

'Italy is a living museum of its past; there is far too much work of towering genius around for today's half-baked imitations to be taken seriously.'

'You must have made a lot of enemies in the art world.'

'I admit to being an unrepentant classicist, and I know that there are those who consider me more trouble than I am worth, with shockingly reactionary views.'

'Like those you hold on abstract impressionism?'

Ros looked at him. He looked back. 'You've been researching me,' she accused. 'Why?'

'I like to know as much as I can about anything that interests me.' Their eyes held as if by velcro. Ros swallowed. Her throat was dry. 'Would you have dinner some time?' he asked into the silence.

'When?'

'You say. I know your time is taken up with your mother. Here …' he reached into his inside pocket, took out a small leather notecase, flipped it open and scribbled a number. 'Call me whenever you have a free night.' Then he added, in a way that had Ros's toes curling: 'Please.'

She nodded; for the life of her she could not have got her voice to work. As he held out the piece of paper and she reached to take it their fingers brushed and Ros felt a frisson so violent she jumped.

'Electricity,' he smiled, his high-voltage smile sending out its own charge.

Then the door opened and Billy came in.

Ros went upstairs to her mother in a daze. She had not felt this way since – no, there was no since about it: she had never felt this particular way before. Peter had grown on her slowly, as she had come to appreciate the breadth and depth of his mind, for he had been no Adonis. Jack Ross had struck her like a blunt instrument, with all the physical force of a stunningly attractive, sexually potent male.

She had never been one for casual sex; those affairs she had had after Peter Dzundas – with Fulco di Buonanova that summer in Bologna, and Harrison de Witt from the American embassy in Rome – had been quite long in duration and years apart, entered into only after thoughtful consideration on her part. Had Jack Ross asked her to go upstairs and have sex rather than dinner she would have gone, without thought to consequence. I must be mad, she thought, but her head was buzzing and her feet were light. As she put her hand on the handle of her mother's sitting-room door she knew that there was no way she could ever marry James and become Viscountess Chelm.

'Darling...' Livy held out her arms to her youngest son, her smile radiant. 'What a lovely surprise ... nobody told me you were coming.'

'Nobody knew,' David lied, bending down to embrace his mother's fragile body with great care. 'I just wanted to see you, that's all.'

Livy put a hand to his face then she frowned. 'What's that on your chin,' she asked, fingering what felt like a scab.

David withdrew, to stand straight again. 'My damn fool barber used a new aftershave; it brought me out in a rash.'

'Like me, you have a sensitive skin,' Livy sympathised. 'I always had to be *so* careful what I used ...' She patted the chaise-longue on which she was lying, covered by a light vicuña throw. 'Sit down and tell me what you have been doing.'

'Working.'

'Playing too, I hope. "All work and no play", and "you are only young once" and all that sort of thing ... Don't forget to lift your nose from the grindstone now and again, will you?'

'I don't, believe me, I don't.'

'Good, now tell me where you have been and who you have seen and what is going on these days ...' Then she frowned: 'You are awfully thin. Are you eating properly?'

'Now I am. I put on a lot of weight over the summer; so much I decided it had to come off again.'

'Not too much, darling. You won't do a Diana, will you?'

'God forbid. How is she?'

Livy winced and flapped her hands.

'Yes, isn't she?' grinned David. 'No wonder you sent for Ros.'

'Have you seen her?'

'No, she's out.' David got up to wander over to the windows, where he peered out over Green Park. 'So is Pop. How is he, by the way?'

Livy's face, all bones now, sharpened maliciously. 'Furious because for once in his life he can't win.' Her laugh was gleeful. 'That fact alone almost makes all this worthwhile.'

The force of her hatred exhausted what little strength she had and she sank back on her pillows.

'But I thought – that you had stabilised,' David said concernedly.

'If you mean am I being eaten away at a slower rate then yes, I suppose you could say that,' Livy said, eyes closed. 'There is no way to stop this, David. I know it, my doctors know it, Billy knows it. Why else is he so mad? It's because he just can't stand not to win at anything.'

David turned back to the window. 'Yes,' he said. 'I do know.'

'How long can you stay?' Livy roused herself to ask.

'Just for the weekend.'

'How are things up at Cambridge?'

' "Up at Cambridge?" Mama,' he mocked. 'After twenty-odd years you have become more English than the English. You don't even sound All-American any more.'

'But I am. I was born there and I intend to be buried there.'

David whistled soundlessly. 'Have you told Dad?'

'Yes. And put it in my will.' Livy took hold of his hand. Hers felt like a claw. 'See that my wishes are carried out, won't you, David? I want to be buried beside my Johnny. Rosalind is a Randolph Trustee; she has the power to authorise it and I've told her the same thing. Put me beside Johnny. He was the good part of my life, before ... don't let your father prevent it whatever you do ... promise me you'll carry out my wishes – promise!' Her insistence was almost demonic.

'I promise,' David soothed.

Livy released a sigh. 'That's my good boy,' she said. Her face smoothed out and there was a smile on her face when she drifted off to sleep.

David was going downstairs when the front door opened. 'Hello!' Ros said in surprise. 'What are you doing here?'

'Paying a flying visit. I felt uneasy about Mummy.'

'You've seen her?'

'Yes. There's hardly anything of her. How is she – really, I mean?'

'Dying,' Ros told him harshly. 'Slowly but surely.'

David said: 'She made me promise to see her buried beside your father.'

'And did you?'

'Of course! But you must know *my* father won't allow it! It would be the most frightful insult.'

'Do you think she doesn't know that?'

As always, Ros was challenging, but David was saving

himself for his father so he sighed and said: 'It is her illness, of course. People say all sorts of weird things when they are dying. She knows very well that Pa had the Bancroft mausoleum built years ago; she even had a hand in its design.'

'She is still bent and determined not to be the first to occupy it.'

'Oh, well, you've never got on with him have you?' David said, as if that explained everything. 'So you know you will have a fight on your hands.'

'Only if you break your promise.'

His eyes widened as if hurt. 'I could do no less than say what she wanted me to; she was so insistent. But sick-bed promises are like death-bed promises. – '

'One and the same in this instance.'

' – I don't see that one can strictly be held to them.'

'Spoken like a true Bancroft.'

Sunnily: 'Thank you,' David said. Then: 'What's this about you being a Randolph Trustee?'

'The truth. I am.'

'I learned about the Randolph Foundation when I was in the States. I had no idea it was so rich or so powerful.' His smile stung. 'But not quite as rich or as powerful as Pa.' He regarded his half-sister pityingly. 'When it comes to the crunch, we both know whose teeth will be doing the chewing ... ' But his smile, when he went into the library, vanished as he shut the door behind him and leaned against it. He made for the tantalus standing on the table by the window, poured himself a hefty slug of scotch and swallowed it at a gulp. He checked his watch. Ten minutes to one. His father's note had said to present himself here, in the library, at one o'clock. Ten minutes to go. He checked himself in

341

the mirror that had once hung in Napoleon's bedroom. That damned lesion. The only good thing was that his father was not likely to recognise its source. He would just have to bluff it out, and in future be more careful. Just because he had nothing to lose he had gone a little wild; nothing mattered any more, had been his attitude, so what the hell. Naturally, there had been talk and Old Big Ears himself had picked it up. Trust him. Except, of course, that David knew better than to do such a stupid thing. He was not his father's son for nothing. Which was why he had his story ready. He had memorised and rehearsed it while driving down the M11 towards this confrontation.

And now he had another tidbit to add to it. His father should be warned about the insult his wife was planning. Really, David thought on a laugh, of *all* people; my mother developing fangs. But he had more regard for his father's bite than his mother's lately developed bark. He needed his father's goodwill, and to retain it he would use any and every piece of leverage that came his way. As long as Billy heard what he wanted to hear everything was always all right. And after years of telling him just that, David was confident he could do it again. All he had to do was divert his wrath, along with the questions that would follow, which David had no intention of answering. This little tidbit should send him thundering down a lengthy side road. By the time he got back on the main road his son's latest transgressions would have dwindled to minor violations. They absolutely and positively had to. Apart from all the rest, he was overdrawn at the bank again.

When Ros went in to say goodnight, Diana and Brooks were

sitting with Livy, who was not yet in bed but ensconced on her chaise-longue.

'Darling, how lovely you look …' Livy greeted her elder daughter with pleasurable relief. Even now, when she knew Diana's earnest intentions were her over-eager best, ten minutes with her younger daughter still rasped her nerves to ribbons. Ros never grated; she soothed even while she stimulated, sensing instinctively what her mother wanted or needed at any particular time; floating delicately where Diana trod heavily.

Though Ros had made light of the fact that the investigative journalist who was preparing to blow Billy out of the water had asked her out to dinner, Livy had detected undercurrents but said only: 'Of course you must go, darling. You have no quarrel with Mr Ross, who is only doing his job, after all.'

'Well, I don't think he wants to interview *me*,' Ros had answered demurely.

'Of course he doesn't! For heaven's sake don't look on it as I am sure Billy will: giving aid and comfort to the enemy. What is he like anyway?'

'Tall, dark, not exactly handsome but – devilishly attractive. He could play Mephistopheles any time.'

'Then wear red. It is the devil's colour, after all.'

Now, as her eyes met those of her daughter she said approvingly: 'That dark red suits you as it used to suit me. We have the right kind of creamy skin to set it off.'

Ros was wearing raspberry red satin suit from Valentino – her favourite designer – its short jacket nipped at the waist and worn over a black silk camisole with shoestring straps. Her straight skirt was the new, shorter length which did not go to the extreme of stopping just short of the buttocks but nonetheless revealed the long length of her admirable legs in sheer black stockings and plain black pumps. She had jet clusters in her ears to match the buttons of her jacket, and a small diamond pin in her lapel. She carried a small black-satin-trimmed-with-jet evening purse from Ferragamo, which she had borrowed from her mother.

'*Tres, tres chic*,' Livy approved. 'Are you going anywhere nice?'

'I shan't know until I get there.'

'Who is the lucky man?' Diana enquired sardonically, adding spitefully: 'It is a man, I trust?'

'It is. Named Jack Ross.'

With superior blankness: 'Who?'

'Is he calling for you?' Livy interrupted, well aware of Diana's paranoid jealousy.

'Yes.' Ros checked the small Fabergé wrist-watch, of diamonds set in rock crystal, left to her by her grandmother Randolph. 'In about five minutes time.'

'I should like to meet him,' Livy said. 'May I?'

'Of course, if you are sure you are up to it?'

'Don't I look it?' Livy was wrapped in one of her caftans, a barbaric combination of turquoise, silver, and hot, singing pink. A matching turban swathed her head. Her face was marvellously made up to give the illusion of glowing health while her nails were flawlessly enamelled the same hot pink as her lipstick, which matched exactly the pink in her caftan.

'You put the rest of us to shame,' Ros said truthfully, and was rewarded by the light in her mother's sunken eyes.

'Jack Ross,' Brooks said suddenly. 'He's the one Billy is having trouble with over the book he's writing.' Turning to his mother-in-law: 'He's one of these so-called "investigative" reporters who spend their time grubbing through garbage looking for so-called "truths" about great men.' Turning back to Ros he asked disapprovingly: 'Does Billy know?'

'It is none of his business,' Ros answered pleasantly, but in a voice that had Brook's handsome face tightening on its beautifully modelled cheek-bones.

'You realise he is probably only using you to get even more scurrilous information.'

'What a pity I don't have any, then. All I can tell him – should he ask – and I am not expecting him to – is the truth as I know it.'

'I can tell him *that*,' Livy put in.

'Mummy! You wouldn't – you couldn't!' Diana was shocked.

'Try me,' Livy challenged.

'Oh, no you don't,' Ros protested in mock-alarm, diverting a collision. 'I'm not having his attention distracted. Once you start on him that's my evening out of the window.' Once again she saw the wasted face glow. 'I'll bring him up so that you can meet him, but if you want to take the acquaintance further then he can come back another time.'

'Coward,' Livy giggled happily.

The buzzer on the internal phone by Livy's bed sounded. Brooks answered. 'The gentleman in question has arrived,' he announced, in tones that left Ros in no doubt that she would be reported as having defected. As she went downstairs to where Jack Ross was waiting, his eyes watched her every step of the way. Pitch, she thought bemusedly. Or is it obsidian? Whichever is the blackest anyway.

'Hello,' she said, shyly, for her.

'Hello.'

His voice made her feel that he had laid his hands on her. Steadying her voice: 'Have you five minutes to spare? My mother would like to meet you.'

'I should like to meet her. Genuine living legends are few and far between, especially in my business.'

'She is – literally – a shadow of her former self,' Ros explained as they went upstairs. 'My sister Diana, however, is not, nor is her husband. They are sitting with Mummy tonight. Unless she says otherwise there is always one or other of us with her, apart from her nurses. She never was one for being alone. She would have a dozen people at a time if we let her, but I'm afraid she is just not up to that any more.'

'Then we won't stay long.'

Once again Ros was struck by his lack of intimidation, and when she led him up to her mother, he took the wasted hand she offered, and in a gesture that was one of homage and respect, bought it to his lips.

'Lady Bancroft.'

'Mr Ross ... I understand we are both from the City of Brotherly Love. Which part?'

'South, but I was only born there. We moved to New York when I was two.'

'Italian?' Livy hazarded.

'No. Jewish.'

'So is my husband.'

'I know.'

Ros watched her sister, who had moved from surprise – God knows what she had expected, Ros thought amusedly – through envy to something like chagrin. The glance

346

Ros intercepted and which slid away the moment she did, was positively rancorous. Yes, isn't he? she thought luxuriously.

When Livy moved as if her pile of pillows were causing trouble, it was he who rearranged them for her, earning a brilliant smile and a warm 'Thank you.' True to his word, within five minutes they were on their way downstairs again.

'Thank you,' Ros also said as Baines opened the front door for them.

'My pleasure,' he answered, and the way he said it left her in no doubt that he was making the understatement of this or any year.

'Well!' Diana sneered, 'and well again! Ros with an attractive man? I thought she had given them up for this or any Lent, like the rest of the Sisterhood.'

'Ros has already given up a great deal for me,' her mother said in a way that had Diana's face flushing unbecomingly.

'She didn't have to,' she flared, defensive as ever. 'You knew I was here. There was no need to bring her back from Italy!'

Livy closed her eyes. Christ, Diana! Brooks Hamilton thought tiredly. Do you have to shove both feet in it every time?

'I don't think Billy is going to be very happy about Ros socialising with a man who is about to publish a book that does him no favours,' he said, bringing the subject round to a different angle.

'Rosalind is in no way concerned with her stepfather's reputation as a businessman,' Livy reminded sharply. 'And since when was Billy Bancroft unable to look after himself?

Now, would you ring for Nurse please, Diana? I am feeling rather tired … '

Jack Ross drove to a restaurant Ros did not know, in Battersea, of all places, overlooking the river; unpretentious from the outside, small but comfortably furnished and decorated inside, with a small menu which turned out to be ambrosial. He was warmly greeted by name before they were shown to their table, which was by the wall of windows at the back, with a view of Chelsea Reach.

'This is nice,' Ros exclaimed.

'Don't sound so surprised.'

'But how come you, an American, know about such a delightful place? I've lived in London on and off since I was twelve and I've never even heard of it.'

'I spent a couple of years here as a London correspondent. There is no better way to get to know a city.'

Later: 'What are you smiling at?' he asked, as they perused the menu.

'This … the table, I mean. In New York a table this far back would mean you were either dead or from Milwaukee.'

'I come to eat, not to be looked at. I like good food. Don't you?'

'Good food, yes. Pretentious food, no.'

'You don't have to worry. They don't serve it here.'

His smile had the effect of making Ros step out of character.

'Then since you know what to expect I place myself in your hands.'

'I was hoping you would say that.'

348

God, she thought, but he is *so* attractive! How come he is not already spoken for? Past experience shoved its oar in. How do you know that he is not? Determinedly she bundled the past into a deep closet far at the back of her mind before locking the door. She was not going to let suspicions ruin *this* one.

But once their food was served, her qualms could do no more than watch in silence, since she was rendered speechless by its perfection. First a small cup of a hot, curried soup which she, who normally loathed all forms of curry, found delicious. It was called, he informed her, *Crème Senegale*, and he had first eaten it in Mogadishu. This was followed by a classic *truite au bleu* with a perfect hollandaise, after which came a mouth-watering casserole of plump breasted pheasant, darkly rich with wine and smooth with sour cream, accompanied by small crusty, potato dumplings. With it they drank a magnificent twenty-year-old St. Julien, big, full and earthy, the perfect companion to the highly flavoured birds.

Ros declined a sweet, but ate several pieces of nut-stuffed turkish delight with her coffee.

'That,' she complimented seriously, 'was ambrosia.'

'But you must be used to food like this on a daily basis. Your mother's dinners are famous for the food as well as the company.'

'I didn't attend them very often as a child and I left home at eighteen.'

'So did I.'

'Where did you go?'

'College.'

'So did I! Which one?'

'Columbia.'

'I went to Wellesley then changed to Berkeley.'

'Was art your major?'

'Yes. Was yours journalism?'

'No; I was originally going to be a lawyer.'

Over the coffee they reconnoitered each other's pasts; she had been at Berkeley when he was in Vietnam; while he was in Angola she had been a newly arrived student at the Volpe in Florence; she spoke excellent French, Florentine Italian, could get by in Spanish. He spoke French – a year in Paris as a stringer for a Hearst paper; German, he was stationed in Bonn for some time; Arabic from his time in West Beirut, and Spanish from his coverage of the Contras/Sandinistas affair. He liked modern jazz; loathed Country & Western, was not, as she might have expected, a sports fan; he had an older sister and a younger brother; his mother had been dead ten years and his eighty-year-old father absolutely refused to leave the now far-too-big-for-him house in Brooklyn Heights to which they had moved from Philadelphia back in 1952 when his father's company – he had been an industrial chemist – relocated.

'I've never been to Brooklyn,' Ros confessed.

'I've never been to Florence. Is it like they say, a living museum?'

'Yes. That's why I love it. I am an unrepentant classicist.'

'I read the article you wrote in *Art Today* about abstract Expressionism. It was, to put it mildly, sulphurous.'

'Which is exactly how I feel about that so-called kind of art. I'll take a Renaissance primitive any day. But why go to the trouble of reading about my opinions?'

'I told you. I always do my own research … '

Once again Ros felt that treacherous wave of heat, so took the opportunity to excuse herself.

'The door to the left of the bar,' he said, then: 'Shall I order more coffee? We've drunk this pot dry.'

He didn't want to end it yet either.

'Yes, Yes, please... '

Ros relieved her bursting bladder, checked her watch – ten-thirty, then, seeing the telephone on the wall, took it as an omen and called Morpeth House. Her mother was asleep. Her night nurse was on duty. All was well.

Staring at her face in the mirror after wiping off her old lipstick and applying fresh, she thought: Well, your time is your own. Now it all depends on whether or not he wants to use it for purposes of *his* own. What she knew beyond doubt, reasonable or otherwise, was what she hoped they were.

The consummation Ros devoutly desired was incredibly swift and powerful. When he asked her back for a drink she had agreed, for once in her life totally without qualms for consequences, though she was nervous as a virgin when she crossed the threshold of the flat in Cornwall Gardens where he always stayed when he was in London. It belonged to a foreign correspondent friend of long standing who was at present covering the Colombian drug wars.

'What would you like to drink?' Jack asked, taking off his coat then throwing it over the back of the big couch.

'Nothing, thank you.' She met the dark eyes and held them steadily.

'A drink wasn't what I had in mind, or you, for that matter? Am I right?'

'Absolutely and in every way.'

They came together like a magnet and iron filings. Nothing in Ros's experience had prepared her for what Jack did to her, brought her to, that night. Of her three lovers, Peter had been the most earthy, the most uninhibited. The other two had been the products of their upbringings; too well-bred to let themselves go. Not so Jack Ross. He did everything, and it triggered off an explosion of sensuality the like of which she never known, blasting loose the paralysing grip Peter Dzundas had had on her sexual memory, prompting her to respond in a way that had them both lost to everything but each other. The first time was pure carnal frenzy. The moment their mouths and tongues found each other they went wild. Clothes were all but torn off and they had each other on the floor, half on the rug in front of the fire, half on the wood-block floor, which they left marked with their sweat.

Still entangled, Ros said, on a half-laugh, half-gasp, 'You've done this before?'

'Many times.'

'I haven't – I mean on what *Cosmopolitan* would call a first date.'

'There's a first time for everything.'

'And as first times go that was pretty wild.'

'The second will be better.'

'Promises, promises ...' murmured Ros.

But it was. Incredibly, heart-stoppingly, it was. Afterwards he got up, quite unconscious of his nakedness, giving her time to admire his body, surprisingly powerful for a man of his height and leanness, and went into the kitchen, bringing back two glasses of beautifully chilly orange juice. Ros drank hers off; she felt parched. Not surprising, she thought. The heat we just generated would dry the Thames. He took her glass, put it to one side then bent down and drew her to her feet.

'You are a tall one, aren't you? Even in your bare feet.'

Challengingly: 'Do people say that of you? You are even taller.'

'Six-two and yes, they do.'

'And I'll bet every one a woman.'

'You'd win. But don't get me wrong. I like my women long and lean, and all of you is very nicely distributed, or as Spencer Tracy would say "Cherce".'

'I beg your pardon?'

'You never saw *Pat and Mike*? One of the movies he made with Katharine Hepburn? She played a natural athlete. He was a sportswriter who described her to his sidekick as "Choice" but in his native Brooklyn accent it came out as "cherce".' Pursuing his lips teasingly: 'You, never having been to Brooklyn, would not recognise this, of course.'

'Next time I'm in New York I swear I will make it my business to cross the Brooklyn Bridge.'

'Let's cross another one first … it's much nearer.'

The third time, in the big bed, it was leisurely, long-drawn out. He spent a lot of time exploring every inch of her body, pleasuring her, letting the feeling between them build until she could wait no longer and moaned: 'I want you inside me – now!' thrusting her hips at him, wrapping her legs around his waist as he sank into her, deeper and deeper until he gasped at the heat of her, fucking her with long slow thrusts, until her whimpers became moans and gasps as she peaked then came, again and again and again, at which point he let go and allowed his own orgasm to transport him to a shared state of bliss.

After which they fell asleep.

It was the telephone which woke them. Ros, a lark, was fully awake at the first ring only to find he was already reaching out for the instrument by the side of the bed. Her first thought was that it was her mother until she realised nobody knew where she was. Unless Billy was on the job; his network could find anybody anywhere at any time.

But Jack Ross, after sitting up against the padded headboard, was listening rather than speaking, asking the occasional question. The conversation was brief, and when he put the receiver back in its cradle he said explosively: 'Shit!'

'Bad news?'

'Undoubtedly. For me and a lot of other people. Iraq has invaded Kuwait. That was my editor in New York; he's just had the news. I'm to get myself and my lap portable to Heathrow by noon today, where a specially chartered plane will arrive loaded with a whole lot of other correspondents, journalists, TV crews and God knows who and what else to pick up even more before flying us to the Gulf.' He was unmistakeably regretful when he added: 'I'm afraid I am going to have to put you on hold. Time and Saddam Hussein wait for no man – or woman, come to that.' He paused then said something which had Ros reeling. 'And I've waited a long time for you.'

'Yes,' she found herself responding. 'And I for you.'

'Shit!' he said again, even more furiously. His big hands cradled her face. 'I'd only just got rid of those tension lines around your eyes,' he said with regretful tenderness. 'I had planned to work on your mouth next ... '

'Please ...' Ros murmured. 'Feel free ... '

354

After a long, deep, achingly sweet kiss: 'Was I so uptight?' she asked.

'You were the first time we met – or should I say collided. I wasn't sure whether it was my head ringing or somebody's car alarm.'

Ros, sounding amazed: 'It's a long, long, time since that happened to me.'

'And me.'

'Shit!' Now it was Ros's turn. Jack laughed again. 'You even swear like a lady.'

'I am what I am ... do you mind?'

'There is nothing I mind about you, except my lost chance to smooth out those edges roughened by your mother's illness. You are much more loose than you were a couple of hours ago but – '

'Loose! If you loosen me any more I'll fall apart!' Then: 'Was it so noticeable?'

'How long have you been caring for a mother for whom there is nothing you or anybody else can do?'

'Five months now.'

Jack nodded. 'It showed.'

'I suppose it is the strain of not letting her see ... though she knows her own condition.' Ros leaned her face against the wall of his chest. 'It's the waste I mind more than anything; the sheer waste of a life that was never fulfilled. I used to wonder where I got my deep love of art from since my father neither knew nor cared and mother was her own work of art, until she told me – quite recently – that when she was young she had wanted to go to art school; that she had been told by a distinguished painter she had talent. But she got married instead; it was expected of her. By the time

355

she was twenty she had me, and my brother a year later. She put her paints away with her dreams and set to work instead to create Olivia Gaylord Randolph who became Lady Bancroft ... dead at the early age of fifty-four.'

Jack rested his cheek on the rumpled black hair. 'I wish I'd met you earlier and for once in my life I wish I didn't have to catch a plane.'

'Likewise, I'm sure,' Ros mocked, disturbed by the depth of her own feelings. Too fast, too much, too soon, a little voice warned. But she silenced it.

She checked the bedside digital. It was almost eight a.m. 'You must go, and so should I.' Her smile was wry. 'I haven't stayed out all night since I was a teenager, and that was only a show of defiance.' She sighed. 'And that was a long time ago.'

'I can give you ten years.'

'No, thank you. I have more than enough as it is.' She put her arms around him, felt the steady reassuring thump of his heart under her cheek. 'But right now I feel as if I can never have enough of you.' She withdrew slightly to grin up at him. 'I can't complain though. I mean, I've already had you three times ...' Her hand slid down his chest and under the sheets to grasp the silky length of him. In glad surprise: 'Not to mention a fourth ... '

His taxi dropped her off at Morpeth House.

'I'll be in touch,' he said, holding her hand tightly. 'If I can call I will, otherwise – '

'Send me a postcard,' she quipped. 'Never mind about the wish you were here bit.' She stepped back on to the pavement. 'Good luck,' she said.

356

Ros stood there and he looked out of the back window until the taxi turned the corner into St. James. Then she went into the house.

Her mother was still sleeping. The nurses were changing shifts; she could hear their soft-voiced conversation in the room that had been given to them for their private use. Closing the bedroom door quietly she went along to her own suite where she took off the red suit – badly crumpled now – dumped her underwear in the basket for laundering, then put on a robe and went downstairs into the hotel-sized kitchen to make some coffee. She and Jack had showered together and had a quick cup of instant but Ros wanted to sit down over a cup of strong, milky coffee and *think*. She certainly needed to.

Something had happened that she had not bargained for. She had never for a moment suspected she had hit him as hard as he had hit her. Their mutual attraction had kindled at their first meeting; what she found so incredible was the sexual heat it had generated. It was only afterwards, when the fire had dimmed, that she wanted to ask him questions; the who and the what and the why of him. They had told each other some, but by no means all of their respective histories. Truth to tell he was still, after all they had had done together, a stranger. A very intimate stranger, but nonetheless still a largely unknown quantity.

Who had come and gone in the same night. There was no telling how long he would be away or what would happen to him while he was. He had gone to cover an invasion, which meant fighting. Best not think of that. He was a correspondent, after all, not a soldier. But hadn't he told her he had been wounded in Beirut by a sniper? She

357

had been able to put her finger in the shallow-depression the wound had left in his shoulder.

No point in thinking about that, she told herself forcefully. Think instead about what it will be like when he does come back. And if he feels the same, of course. Remember the old Italian adage: *'L'amore fa passare il tempo; il tempo fa passare l'amore.'* Love makes the time pass; time makes love pass. Except nobody has so much as mentioned love so we will leave that alone for the time being. She got up from the kitchen table and shoved her chair back violently. You are doing it again! Analysing everything. Take what the gods have given you, my girl and be thankful. How long is it since you felt like this? Do you recognise the feeling? It's called happiness. How often has it come your way? Only once in your lifetime. For God's sake don't look this gift-horse in the mouth; all you will see are its bad teeth. Possess your soul in patience and wait for him to come back. He might only be gone a week or two. Well, maybe a month, perhaps two. It all depends on how real and how bad this invasion is. The memory of his lovemaking made her stomach clench. The thought of her unbridled wantonness caused a weakness to spread through her loins like liquid flame. Not even Peter had made her feel like this. But her response to him had, she realised now, not been nearly so physical. With Jack Ross it had been fiercely so. Had he been a brainless idiot she would still have wanted him as much. Well, not totally brainless. She was not capable of being attracted by anyone with nothing upstairs. Jack's top floor was crammed with all sorts of information and ideas she longed to explore as she had the middle. She pulled her mind sharply to attention before taking a tray with the coffee pot upstairs, along with a couple of warm croissants and butter. Then she made herself comfortable on her bed and over her coffee and croissants began to read *Loser's Weepers* by Jack Ross: his personal experience of the conflict in Beirut. She had seen it in the flat and asked to borrow it. It meant she had something belonging to him.

Along the corridor, in her mother's bedroom, the day nurse was checking the patient, and at once noted that there had been a change. One she recognised and noted on the chart, which she did not leave lying around. She would not be on this job for much longer. It had always been only a matter of time, but that time was now very short. The family would have to be told. Fortunately, they were all nearby except for the eldest son, and he would have to make it quick if he wanted to see his mother before she died.

14

Livy Bancroft died as she had lived, gracefully, elegant to the last, her face a work of the visagiste's art since she herself was no longer able to lift so much as a lipstick. Semi-conscious for the last twenty-four hours, she was still able to thrust away the oxygen mask when she began to have difficulties with her breathing.

'Do as she wishes,' Ros ordered, not caring that Billy was there, anxious only that her mother's suffering should not be prolonged. But Billy made no objection. He seemed paralysed by grief as he sat silently by the bed, his son and daughter flanking him, each holding one of his hands. Diana's husband stood close behind. Diana was weeping, not her usual noisy lamentations, but silently, endlessly.

On the other side of the big, wide bed Rosalind Randolph sat alone. She had long since shed her own tears. Now, all she wanted was for her mother's long struggle to be at an end. Added to which she knew she must be strong to fight the battle which would begin the moment death was confirmed. Livy had warned her. 'Get in the first blow otherwise he will, after which he'll kick you while you are down. Catch him off guard, then hit him a second time while he is floundering. I have done all I can to give you the power you will need because he is going to muster every bit of his own, and you know how enormous that is. But you are strong. Of all my children you are the strong one. Billy knows your strength. That's why he does not like you.'

'He said I should have been a man.'

'He would. He does not have any use for women except for sex and children so he would never accept that you are his equal, but you are. I have seen it these past months. It makes me realise how much I threw away when I let you leave me all those years ago. If I had been a better mother to you ...' An angry sigh. 'So much time wasted ...' Then, fervently: 'But I would not have missed these past months for anything. We have really come to know each other, haven't we? Become the mother and daughter we did not know how to be all those years ago?'

Rosalind had nodded, unable to speak through her clogged throat. Livy's long fingers had brushed away the tears which clung to her daughter's long lashes. 'Don't mourn me, darling. *Fight* for me. Get justice for me. I let him run my life; don't let him take over my death as well.'

Now, holding her mother's lax hand, Rosalind silently reaffirmed the promise she had made. Checking the little rock crystal clock by the bed she saw that Johnny ought to be here any minute. She had called him as soon as the doctor warned her that the end was near, and as if she knew her favourite son was on his way, Livy was holding on tenaciously. Even as Ros was thinking about him the door opened and he came in, breathing hard as if he had been running. Ros rose to her feet and brother and sister clung together for

361

a moment then Ros moved away so that Johnny could bend over his mother.

'Ma? It's Johnny …' He took her hand, held it against his cheek. As if its warmth gave her strength, Livy's lids fluttered before lifting slowly. When she saw who it was her sunken eyes glowed and she smiled, a smile brimming with love and tenderness. Her lips moved but no sound issued. Johnny put his ear to them, listened then said something in reply which had her smiling again and trying to nod even as her eyelids closed for the last time.

He was still holding her hand when she silently made the transition from life to death about thirty minutes later. It was only when he realised the difference in the feel of the bird–claw hand that he said: 'She's gone.'

Billy looked for the nurse, who came forward from the back of the room to take the hand Johnny was holding and feel for the pulse. She nodded. 'Lady Bancroft is dead,' she confirmed.

Diana slid from her chair. Moving forward, Brooks picked her up then carried her from the room. Johnny lifted his mother's hand, kissed it and then both cheeks. Rosalind and David did the same. Then they left Billy alone with her.

Downstairs, Ros led the way into the library. She had ordered a fire lit; it was not cold but it gave a cheerful glow, for it was a miserably wet September day.

David stood in the middle of the room as though lost and unsure of his direction, sounding bereft when he said: 'I can't believe she is gone. I mean, I've been expecting it for months now – we all have, yet I still can't accept that she won't ever be with us again.' Abruptly: 'I could use a drink.' He turned to his half-brother. 'Johnny?'

'No, thank you.'

'Ros?'

She shook her head. David poured himself two fingers of whisky and tossed them back. Staring into the glass he sighed. 'Poor Pa,' he said. 'Now what is he going to do?'

He looked at his half-sister as he spoke but she was staring into the flames. They were still keeping their silent vigil when Billy came in, supported by Diana and Brooks who each had an arm through one of his. Ros wondered if it was for allegiance or support.

He moved slowly and heavily, like the old man he really was. His face looked stretched on its bones and it was only then that Ros realised that he too had lost weight. Like his son, he was having trouble accepting that it had finally happened. David went to him, and father and son embraced tightly. When Billy spoke it was to echo his son: 'I can't believe she's gone.' Both were acting in character in refusing to accept what they chose not to recognise; the fact that death, unlike everything and everybody else, had not been intimidated by the Bancroft name.

'Do you want us to make all the necessary arrangements?' Brooks asked, ever helpful. 'Take the strain off you?'

'What? Oh ... yes ... arrangements.' Before their eyes Billy pulled the pieces together and snapped the fastenings on the persona they knew. Lord Bancroft, Billionaire Tycoon. There were things to do, a funeral to organise, orders to give, people to manipulate. He had a show to run. His voice was calmer, firmer when he stepped away from his son to answer courteously: 'Thank you, Brooks. That was a kind offer and I appreciate your consideration and concern, but I know how I want things done. I planned my dear wife's funeral some time ago. I only have to set the arrangements in motion.'

Now! Ros thought, then said in a light, easy voice: 'There is no need to do anything. It is already arranged. Mummy meticulously planned her own funeral.'

Everyone turned to look at her. Ros stood her ground, feeling it begin to tremble. 'There is no need for you to do anything. She left detailed plans. You know Mummy; ever the perfectionist.'

Everyone was still staring at her. The tremble had become a threatening rumble.

'What plans?' Billy demanded finally, menacingly. 'Livy was in no shape to make plans ...'

'Not recently, no. But she was last year, and she acted the moment she knew her cancer was incurable. She knew exactly the kind of funeral she wanted.' Rosalind paused. 'And where.'

'What do you mean – where?' Diana sounded hostile. 'Mummy is to be buried in the Bancroft Mausoleum – '

'No.' Rosalind was trying to keep the fires low, but there was no way to avoid a conflagration. 'Her instructions are that she is to be buried in Virginia. At King's Gift. With my father.'

There was a stunned silence. Then: 'W–h–a–a–t!' Diana's voice rose, thinning as it disappeared. 'I don't believe it! Mummy would never do such a foul thing!'

Ros ignored her. To Billy she held out the long, buff, legal envelope she had taken from the safe behind the Fantin-Latour flower-piece in her mother's sitting room. 'It is all in here. This is the copy she had made for you.'

Billy made no move to take it so Brooks, ever the equerry, took it for him.

'What do you mean, *my* copy,' Billy asked,

'The arrangements for her funeral, plus a copy of her will. Her London solicitor has the original – he wrote it according to her instructions; another copy is with her American lawyer; I have the fourth. All three of us are named as executors.'

Billy waved that aside as he would a fly. 'I already have the original will that my wife made at the onset of her illness. Arthur Sterling made it after she and I discussed what should be done with her property at her death.'

'This will supersedes it. It was made once she knew death was something that would arrive sooner rather than later. This will contains *her* wishes, and her wishes only. I made a solemn promise to her that I would faithfully see them carried out.'

Billy had never taken his eyes from Ros. Watching his father's expression David moved unobtrusively backwards, out of his line of vision.

Diana's vindictive shrill broke broke the silence. 'I told you she was a bad influence, Daddy. Obviously she has been working on Mummy all this time ...' Scornfully, to Ros: 'How do you know about any so-called new will? You were with Mummy for only the last five months of her life. For the previous twelve years you had not so much as sent her a fare-thee-well!'

'She told me what she had done,' Ros answered, 'and asked for my promise.'

'She made me promise too,' Johnny said, turning from the window.

'When?' Diana asked suspiciously.

'Tonight was the last time, when I had to bend down to

hear her voice. But she'd already spoken to me several times – it was on her mind all the time. She even called me specially in San Diego. I told her that whatever she wanted was fine with me, but tonight she asked me again to promise her that I would see her wishes carried out. So I did.' His voice was calm, matter of fact, but firm and respectful when he told his stepfather: 'And I will.'

'It's a conspiracy,' accused Diana, taking centre stage. 'You Randolphs have always thought yourself superior to us Bancrofts.'

'Oh, for God's sake, Diana,' David sounded disgusted. But to his father he was regretful, 'I did warn you.'

'You took advantage of Daddy's being away trying to find a cure for Mummy to conspire behind his back and persuade her to do something you knew would hurt him!' Diana accused Ros, playing yet another game of sibling rivalry with her brother; this time the version called Who Loves Daddy Best? 'You are the one behind this! You came back here and wormed you way into Mummy's good-graces so you could hurt a man you've always hated just because he had the nerve to marry your mother! Well she was my mother too – though sometimes she seemed to forget that fact – and if you think I am going to let you humiliate Daddy in this way then you are mistaken!'

Then she ruined her Joan of Arc pose by adding: 'Remember who he is and what he is! He could crush you between his fingers.'

Billy took the envelope from Brook's grasp and ripped it open, drawing out several closely typed foolscap sheets which he leafed through before beginning to read.

Johnny left the window to go over to his sister, so that

the room contained two opposing camps. Billy, his children and his son-in-law made up one; Rosalind and Johnny Randolph comprised the other.

'Battle-lines drawn,' David's eyebrows matched his voice.

'So now we all know where we stand,' Diana added unnecessarily, anything but amused.

'Where we two stand, she means,' Johnny murmured to his sister. 'In the doghouse. I can see her trying to remember where she put the chain.' His glance was both proud and affectionate. 'You always did love a fight but this one is going to be a doozie.'

'I know,' Ros affirmed, sweet-sherry eyes glittering with the light of battle. She had been brooding too much of late, either about her mother or Jack Ross, and felt the need to *do* something, to shake off the miasma of grief and loss which she knew, if she gave in to it, would render her useless. She was aware of a bracing relief now that war had been declared and it was a case of 'Action this day!'

To Johnny, she said: 'All our mother wanted was justice; a chance to even the score, revenge all *his* betrayals. She spent half her life with Billy Bancroft; she had no desire to spend her death.'

Billy heard her. Not bothering to refold the pages he had read, he stuffed them back into their envelope which he then tossed contemptuously at his stepdaughter. War had been declared.

Without so much as a glance he strode out of the room, Diana hurrying after him, cutting her half-brother and sister dead. They were now the enemy. Brooks did not look in their direction either as he obeyed His Master's Choice, but David stopped by Ros, cocking his head consideringly. 'You never did lack for courage,' he complimented, 'but who was it who said: "How stupid are the brave?"'

Ros began as she meant to go on. First off she sent the obituary her mother had composed to the papers she had specified: the London *Times*, the New York *Times* and the Randolph *Courier*. The first two were brief, the third lengthy, but all made prominent mention of her first husband and the two children she had borne him. It also said that the funeral was private; attendance would be by invitation only. There would be two separate memorial services later; one in London and one in New York.

The very first visit of condolence was from the Viscount Chelm. During Livy's long illness he had been a regular visitor until only a few weeks ago, when he was thrown by a fractious gelding, badly fracturing one leg, which had put him out of action. He was now only just back on his feet, and was on crutches when he entered Morpeth House.

Billy was not available; he was in his study, consulting his lawyers. Diana was at her dressmaker, being fitted for her blacks. Johnny was on the phone to his anxious wife. Where David was nobody knew. So it was Ros whom James embraced, and his emotions were obvious.

'Would you like to see her?' Ros asked gently. 'You, she would not mind, though our American custom of viewing the body is one she always loathed and it will not be observed in her case.'

'No.' James shook his head. 'I want to remember her as I knew her. Vivid, vital, so very much alive.'

Ros took him into the sitting room where he used to work

with Livy. Looking round he sighed. 'So many memories ... Most of them happy ones.'

'How are you, James? You've lost weight.'

'This wretched leg ... It is not setting as it should ... I am disobeying my doctors by coming here, but I could not let such a sad occasion pass without marking it. She was a one-off. I counted her as one of my dearest friends.' Sadly reminiscent: 'Once I saw her every single day; lately I have not seen her at all and I have missed her. I shall always miss her.' He fell silent and Ros did not break it. Finally he continued: 'And I wanted to see you ... I wondered if you had yet come to a decision about the proposal I made you.'

'Yes, I have,' Ros answered, with a lack of hesitation James recognised as fatal, though her voice was kind. 'I can't marry you, James. I would not make the kind of Viscountess you want. Added to which I find I want more from marriage – if indeed I ever do marry – than a *marriage blanc*.'

'But I told you –'

'Yes, you need an heir. But I don't want to be married for breeding purposes either.' She saw James wince at her bluntness, but the memory of Jack Ross was too strong in her to allow anything less. 'I would rather we remain the friends we have always been.'

James was obviously disappointed but he said at once: 'Of course. Let us not lose everything. Friends it is.'

As though she had not just handed him a severe disappointment he then turned to the funeral. Ros gave him a brief rundown of the situation, after which he said: 'If your mother decided on such a course then, knowing her, she must have wanted it very much. She was not given to sudden whims.' Appreciative understanding glimmered in his eyes:

'I can also well understand how upset Lord Bancroft is. I should like to see him if I may.'

'And he you, but right now he's conferring with his legal battalions. Once they are gone I'll have Baines take you to him. He and I keep out of each other's way as much as possible. In the meantime, how about a glass of your favourite amontillado?'

As Livy had known he would, Billy pulled out all the stops. His own lawyers, including the mighty Lord Sterling himself, were summoned. There were meetings, conferences, eminent authorities consulted, much poring over precedent. The two camps took up positions, and the Randolphs found that theirs was in Coventry, but since Ros was busy carrying out those of her mother's wishes for which the Randolph lawyers gave the go-ahead, she did not really notice. Pending the outcome of negotiations, Johnny flew back to Boston, for his wife had returned to her family in her husband's absence and would remain there until their twins were born. He would return to London should his presence be needed by the lawyers, but before he left he made a sworn statement describing his mother's disclosure of her intentions to him and her request for his solemn promise to see them fulfilled. When they were he would fly to Virginia for the funeral.

Ros therefore went ahead with Livy's detailed instructions, such as her body being dressed in the sumptuous Dior she had worn for her wedding to Johnny Randolph. Afterwards, it had been carefully wrapped in layers of lavender-strewn tissue and laid in a box in the storerooms of Illyria, where it had remained ever since. Her face was made up by the visagiste who had tended to her in the final weeks of her illness, and her hairdresser styled the wig of real hair in the way Livy had always worn her own; short and crisp and brushed away from the face. Only her family saw her in her coffin once she had been prepared for burial, and it remained in her bedroom, its internment held back until such time as the dispute over where that would be was resolved.

When Cordelia and Toni arrived, Ros took them up to see their sister. Cordelia, normally so queenly, with the calm composure of the absolutely certain, was shattered, and had to be handed over to her maid to be put to bed with a tisane and a fragrant compress over her forehead.

Toni stood a long time looking at her sister. 'Beautiful to the end,' she said at last. 'Only Livy could do that. Her face didn't really change, did it? It only got thinner ...' Her voice cracked as she turned away. 'As the poet said, we shall not see her like again ...'

She bit her lip and Ros thought she saw the glitter of tears but then Toni said in her usual brittle way: 'God, I need a drink – and an explanation. I know you couldn't say a lot on the phone, but what you did say has had me palpitating ever since for the full story.'

They went downstairs again, Toni obviously upset, for once inside the door of Livy's sitting room she began to weep. 'I am going to miss her so much. We were so close, she and I, with only three years between us.' Ros knew what her aunt needed so went to make a pitcher of potent margaritas.

'Oh, bless you ...' Toni sniffed, wiping her eyes and blowing her nose before accepting the salt-rimmed glass Ros held out to her. She took a long swallow. 'Ah ...' She closed her eyes in blissful gratitude. 'I needed that. Now, come and sit down and tell me what the hell is going on here. I saw Diana when I arrived and she gave me the frozen mitt. Am I *persona non grata* or something?'

'No, but you were a Gaylord. Around here Bancroft is the only name they recognise.'

'Do tell!'

Ros did so.

'Why, the sly puss! She never said a word the last time I was here, or the time before that.' Toni's giggle was gleeful. 'Talk about revenge is sweet ... Billy must be having forty fits!'

'And then some.'

'But what made her do it? Though now that I think of it, she talked an awful lot about the old days during my last visits; it was all she did want to talk about. Things I hadn't thought about in years ... about our mother and father and Dolly Randolph, and your father. Such a lot about your father ...'

'I think she spent a lot of time reviewing her life; seeing where she went wrong and understanding why. We talked about it; I mean really talked. She explained a lot of things I had not fully understood before; like the kind of world it was when she was young; the limited choices women had, the expectations they were loaded with, the assumptions that were made. What she has done was not done lightly, you know.' Ros's gaze was frank. 'And if she didn't tell you, then you have only yourself to blame. She said you never could keep a secret.'

Toni looked indignant for a moment then giggled. 'How well she knew me. The only ones I have ever kept are my own.'

'And she said Aunt Cordelia would have been shocked and disapproving and done her utmost to change her mind, so she did not tell her either.'

'So what's the score right now?'

'I think Johnny and I are ahead. Nobody has stopped me from putting things in motion; everything is now ready for the funeral. The sticking point is where that will be.'

'I am sure you appreciate,' Lord Sterling said, his mountainous bulk regarding Ros with judicial understanding from behind his big desk, 'just how deeply this action on your mother's part has hurt and distressed your stepfather. It is, to say the least, a very public humiliation.'

'And one area in which my mother became an expert during her marriage is humiliation.' She met the seemingly kind but penetrating blue eyes with a cool gaze of her own. 'She did not take this action out of pique, Lord Sterling. And since my lawyers tell me her will is valid, there is no reason why probate should be withheld, so why can't her funeral go ahead exactly as she planned?'

Lord Sterling shook his big head, making his heavy jowls quiver, and pursed his rubbery-looking lips. 'This is not purely a matter of legality, Miss Randolph, as you well know. It is to do with a twenty-five-year marriage, a deeply offended husband, a family divided. It is, to put it bluntly, a snook cocked in the face of a man who was never anything else than a good husband.'

'Define good,' Ros countered. 'Do you mean good to be unfaithful within weeks of the honeymoon? Good to have an affair with your wife's best friend? Good to be so obsessively pernickety that your wife is reduced to smoking sixty

373

cigarettes a day plus swallowing a handful of valium and seeing a psychiatrist twice a week? Is it good to come downstairs to check a dinner table on which your wife has spent *days* organising every last tiny detail, only to take a look and say: "I don't like it. Do it again?" That definition of the word "good" does not exist in any dictionary *I* have ever read. If my stepfather had been a good husband to my mother do you think she would have arranged to be buried with the one who really was?' Ros stood up. 'You are wasting your time, I am afraid. I will not be pressurised into denying my mother's right to be buried where *she* chose to be. She spent her life doing things his way. She will have her death *her* way if I have to go to the House of Lords.' She regarded the prominent member of that august chamber with uncompromising resolve. 'And if I do, you may tell your client that I will produce as evidence the names, the dates, the places, of the hundreds of times her "betrayed" husband betrayed my mother with another woman. Oh, yes ... she kept a record. As neat and perfectly ordered as everything else she did. And there are diaries in which all her anguish is written in blood. It is not something I would wish to do, but I will if I have to. Make no mistake, Lord Sterling, I *will* do it! Then we'll see what the gossip columnists make of that juicy tidbit! They have already gnawed the current one to the bone!'

Lord Sterling knew when he had lost a case but he was a famous arbitrator so tried once more. 'I appeal to your sense of the fitness of things. People will talk of revenge, of spite and malice aforethought. Think of the scandal already caused, the slur on a man whose reputation is of the highest – '

'Only to midgets! I don't give a damn about his reputation;

374

it was his insistence that my mother's was kept in a state of sterile perfection which ruined her life! As for the scandal; he knows as well as you and I do that people have been talking and writing about him for years. He and my mother were endlessly discussed, both in the columns and over dozens of dinner tables. Haven't you yet appreciated that it takes very deep feelings to do what my mother did? She knew the consequences and did not care. She had but one thought. To be buried beside my father. And she will be, Lord Sterling, Make no mistake. She will be. Or else. Good afternoon.'

As the door closed behind Ros, the one behind Lord Sterling's desk opened and Billy came through it.

'I told you she was a contumacious bitch,' he growled.

'But a clever one. This has been very carefully orchestrated and is being beautifully played. Someone knows how well you yourself play, my dear Billy, and has not only cut your strings but broken your bow!'

'Every bit of it is that bitch's handiwork. Livy would never in a million years have thought up something like this. It wasn't in her nature. But it's typical of that bra-burning harpy. She took against me the first time we set eyes on each other. I should never have allowed her back in the house.'

'But I understand your wife asked her to return?'

'Something else I should never have allowed.'

'And something you will not, I trust, say in the witness box, should it become necessary to enter one.'

Billy's eyes evaded the knowing ones of his eminent lawyer. 'You know I can't go that far.'

'She could have been bluffing.'

Billy shook his head. 'If she says she has names, dates and places then she has — in triplicate!'

There was a pause before the eminent lawyer asked: 'Am I to take it, then, that we cease to oppose Miss Randolph and allow her to take her mother's body back to Virginia for burial?'

'I don't like it, but tell me what else I can do?' Billy challenged.

'Nothing, dear boy, nothing.' Lord Sterling sighed regretfully, but his headshake was admiring. 'I never thought to see the day,' he said, 'when someone would get the better of Billy Bancroft.'

'You haven't!' said Billy, and there was a menace in his voice, 'and you never will, either! I'm not through with that bitch yet. Nobody crosses me and gets away with it!'

That night, David Bancroft became involved in a fight in a Soho club. A man who thought he was muscling in on his girlfriend broke a beer bottle and carved David's cheek with it. It hurt like hell and he passed out. He came to in an ambulance, and the first person he saw when he opened his eyes was his father, bending over him.

'Pa? Outch!' David winced as he moved and splinters of pain jabbed him. 'God, my face hurts and my head aches ... what happened?'

'Some yob attacked you with a broken bottle. Your face was cut rather badly. I'm having you moved to a private hospital. I'm not leaving you to the mercies of some National Health student, especially since you will probably need plastic surgery. The cuts are pretty deep'.

Someone jabbed a needle in David's arm and he passed out again. When he came to, he was in a private room, quiet

376

with the hush which only money could buy. His face was swathed in bandages and it hurt to move his head.

'Don't,' a voice said. 'You are bandaged. I had them redo all the National Health cobbling and stitch you up properly. You lost quite a lot of blood.'

It was his father's tone of voice rather than the words which told David the worst, and his stomach clenched.

'They had to give you a transfusion, which meant they had to discover your blood type.'

David kept his eyes closed.

'It is Type A. It is also HIV Positive.'

Billy's voice had David babbling: 'I was going to tell you, honestly I was, I was waiting for the right time, it couldn't be now, not with Mummy dying and you with more than enough to cope with. I thought it best that I handled this on my own ...'

For once David's soft soap did not lather.

'Her death did not stop you from going to a bisexual haunt in Soho!'

David knew terror because he also knew that voice, what it meant. Oh, God, he thought. Oh God, oh God, oh God. He tried to think; his mind, usually so supple, was sluggish. All he could think to do was let tears trickle from his eyes. 'I was going to tell you, honestly,' he pleaded, sounding the right note of stricken shame. 'It was preying on my mind ... that's why I went out ... to take my mind off things ... everything came together at once ... first this about being Positive and then Mummy ... it was all – I just felt I had to get away for a while.'

'Then you shall. Right away. As far away as I can send you. But not until after your mother's funeral – '

David opened his eyes. 'You won?'

' – which is to take place at King's Gift on Friday. I want you there. If you have to be supported I want you there along with the rest of the family, as though everything was perfectly normal. Do I make myself clear? After that you will enter a private clinic. You have taken your mother's death hard, and coming on top of intensive study, the stress has taken its toll. You need rest and seclusion for a while. You will remain there until I decide what is to be done. Until then, and from now on, you will do nothing, repeat nothing, unless I tell you to do it.'

'Pa – '

But his father had turned on his heel and gone.

David let out a long shaky breath He felt weak from a combination of fear and relief. Well, it was done. He would have chosen a different way, but his father now knew the worst. So what was a few months' banishment? He could handle that, no sweat. Truth to tell it was what he needed. A nice bout of R&R. And it was not as though he actually had AIDS. He didn't. He only had the AIDS virus. You could have that for ten years or more before the disease itself hit you. And by then they would have a cure. His father would see to that, no matter how much it cost. By God, yes. That he would. Nothing and nobody ever beat Billy Bancroft.

Except his wife. It dropped into David's mind like an ice-cube, chilling his relieved euphoria as it dawned on him what had happened. His gentle mother, meek and mild, had turned rabid, (infected, of course, by her militant feminist daughter) and bitten Billy Bancroft. No way Ma did this on her own. Pa had her too well trained. No, this was Ros.

Nobody else would have the nerve – or the guts. Which Pa would now have for garters. All the same, he thought admiringly, I would never have said my mother would be the one. She was always far too careful never to do anything that would put so much as a hair out of place. Now she's turned into Medusa! Who'd have thought it? Pa is so used to having everything *his* way. In spite of the pain, David began to laugh. Poor Pa, he thought gleefully, none of this is going his way ...

Then he frowned and uneasily began to think about his own...

Ros accompanied her mother's body to King's Gift. It was as though Billy was now standing back and saying: 'All right. You want it your way? Have it. But you are on your own.'

Except she wasn't. Livy's two sisters went with her, in a specially chartered plane since Billy made no move to offer the use of his own Grumman Gulfstream. Patronage had been withdrawn since the Randolphs had been banished beyond the pale.

Delia and Toni nodded with admiring recognition as Ros carried out her mother's meticulous instructions to the letter, in no way surprised when everything went off faultlessly, even to the deft expulsion of one of Billy's claimants to the vacant throne, but not until it was all over with everything done in accordance with Livy's wishes did her daughter relax.

Toni found her on the terrace, watching the sun go down in a glory of rose red haloed by gold.

'Going to be a fine day tomorrow,' Toni said. 'Here, I've

brought you a small libation.' She handed her niece a tall, frosted glass.

Ros took it, drank deep. 'Mmmm ... it took me a long time to acquire the taste for mint juleps but now that I have ... thank you.'

'Thank *you*. Livy would have been proud of you today. Not a hitch.'

'Yes ... It went well.'

'I liked the way you saw off the blonde.'

'I don't give a damn how many women he has elsewhere; but not here. Not on this day and in this place.'

'It is lovely. And always special to your mother, even when Dolly Randolph lived here, because this is where all the Randolphs are born and buried.'

'I think that's why mother wanted to come back. Things have been the same here for centuries; timeless, certain, a continuing thread that has yet to be broken. The kind of permanence she never had as a Bancroft. Everything about Billy is raw and new. Here, everything is old and familiar; traditional. I've felt it so strongly today. I had forgotten that I belong here too. I think it is time I came home. I've been away a long time.'

'What will you do?'

'The National Gallery is looking for an Assistant Curator. I might apply, but I haven't yet made up my mind.'

'More museums!' Toni protested. 'Why don't you come to me in New York instead? Live a little! Have some fun, meet some men ...'

'I've met one.'

Toni's eyes sparkled. 'Do tell!'

Rosalind did.

'Sounds gorgeous.'

Ros shook her head. 'Not gorgeous. Just – exactly to my taste.'

'You mean he grabs you like the Professor did?'

'No ... that was first love; the kind of intense insanity that comes only once. With Jack Ross it is different, yet equally as intense. Somehow we – recognised each other.'

To Toni's experienced ear her niece still sounded dazed, and she was right. Even now, talking about him, remembering his touch and the sensations those long fingers had created throughout her body, Ros felt a warm wave of desire.

'Have you heard from him?'

'No.'

'But it's a month since he left for the Gulf and nothing has happened there since. The United Nations only wrings its hands. If you ask me the whole thing is a stalemate, so why does he stay?'

'Something has to happen sooner or later.'

'I wouldn't count on it. It takes George Bush hours to decide whether to get out of bed or not. Hasn't he even telephoned? They do have telephones in Saudi Arabia, you know.'

At the look on Ros's face: 'Do I detect signs of seriousness?' Toni asked hollowly.

'It is serious,' Ros told her, 'in one respect anyway. I'm pregnant.'

Toni's drink missed her mouth.

'I have always had a monotonously regular, twenty-eight day cycle,' Ros explained, 'but I am two whole weeks overdue. So I did one of those home predictor tests. It was positive.'

'I don't believe it! You had sex right in the middle of your cycle without protection?' Toni was aghast.

'Neither of us was thinking straight at the time.'

Ros smiled in such a way as to give Toni a pang of remembrance. 'I've been there once or twice myself – but not since AIDS.' Severely: 'And you, my girl, ought to have known better.' Then, practically: 'So? What are you going to do?'

'Have it.'

'On your own?'

'If necessary.'

'But you'll tell him?'

'Only to his face.'

'And if you never see him again?'

'Then I do it on my own. It is not as though I was some penniless eighteen-year-old. I have a home, I have family – ' Ros cocked an eye. 'Haven't I?'

'Don't be stupid!'

'Well, then. I think I would make a good mother.' The smile that appeared was dusty. 'At least I know what *not* to do. And the responsibility is mine own.'

'Not all of it. Don't be *too* independent.'

'I'd rather go it alone than with a reluctant partner.'

'Do you think you will see him again?'

'He left me with the impression that he wanted to see me.'

Toni pursed her lips. 'Yes … well … men are adept at leaving impressions that last longer than their promises.' She eyed her niece. 'I never would have thought it of you. You always seemed so – butter wouldn't melt. My own Camilla, yes. She went through men like a hog through swill, but at twenty-one she was married and at thirty-six she has four

382

lovely children and a doting husband. Mind you, I was two months' pregnant when I married her father ...'

Ros looked at her aunt's creamily bland face and burst out laughing.

'You must stop brooding, Daddy,' Diana chided tenderly. He looked so grave; had done since that *awful* day. Thank heavens they were leaving. She had hated it all. The avidly curious stares, the whispers behind hands, the surmise in the glances. Billy had seemed not to notice, but then he was used to being stared at and talked about, no matter what he did. Diana had emulated her mother: with the company yet not of it; looking but not seeing. And never saying a word unless she had to. Now she said: 'All this has been the most awful strain and you have been absolutely marvellous in the face of it. Now you must come and stay with us for a while until things are back to normal. It will be no more than a nine-days wonder, you'll see.'

'I don't want to stay here either,' Billy assured her. Nor would he ever return. The name Randolph and all it stood for was part of a past he was done with. As he was done with *her*. She had betrayed him humiliatingly; a humiliation far worse than his own, trifling indiscretions. What had she expected when she was so indifferent to sex? That he amputate his cock? Sex was necessary to him; varied, different, many-sided sex, and he needed it often. Something Livy had never understood, even while he had given her everything necessary to her. The clothes, the jewels, the houses, the title, and the reputation. How the hell had she thought to achieve that without his money to bankroll her? She'd gone through millions over the years and he had never begrudged a penny. Well, he was finished with all that now.

What was important was David and what to do with him. All his plans in that direction were now useless. David was no longer his heir. How could he be? He was tainted. He also had a doubtful life expectancy. Billy had been grooming and training him to engrave the name Bancroft on his generation, incising it so deep it would last for a thousand years. Now, he probably did not have even ten years of his own.

One thing was paramount: there must be not even the slightest hint of AIDS in the Bancroft family. As it was, the cover story he'd invented; that David had developed an abscessed tooth which had had to be got at from the outside, had explained the pad and sticking plaster on his cheek from eye to jaw, added to which he had looked pale enough to convince people that he really was not well enough to be at his mother's funeral but that nobody had been able to persuade him to stay away. He had received every bit as much sympathy as his father, especially from the women, his presence going a long way to counteract the bush-fire of gossip.

At the end of this horrible day, Billy was in no doubt that he would survive Livy and her spiteful will. He had already begun to manipulate the situation, instigating the rumour that his wife had not been quite right in the head when she'd made it. All that chemotherapy … All those drugs … 'Is it any wonder she went weird?' he'd heard one woman whisper to another. That had gone a long way to soothing his lacerated pride. He'd also planted various stories that would put Rosalind Randolph in her place. Rumours about undue

384

influence, unreasoning hatred and jealousy, poisoning her mother's already sick mind.

Make mischief, would she? Billy smiled inwardly. He'd been making it before she was born. He'd invented deviousness, for God's sake! Been moulding opinion and making and breaking men all his life. Human weakness was his stock-in-trade.

But his son's weakness was a disaster. David had been The Heir and as such had to be perfect. As Livy had been perfect. Except for that bloody first marriage. It had been a mistake to marry a widow with two children. But she had been so absolutely *perfect* for his purpose. And willing to marry him. How was he to know her daughter would be the worm in the flawless bud? He had also relegated Livy as David's mother, taking him over completely as Billy Bancroft's son. Another mistake, for David had inherited his mother's weakness of character. Which was why his father had not hesitated to invent the rumours. The hideous reality of this thing in his son's blood must also now be buried, and buried deep. After which Billy Bancroft had the money and the power to keep that lid screwed on so tightly no wrist would ever be able to take it off. He knew there was no way he could survive the world knowing his son had AIDS. Or how he got it.

So he thought dispassionately, what had to be done must be done with the greatest of care. Fortunately, it was mostly his money which had built the hospital in St. John's Wood, which ensured that silence would prevail as to the result of his son's blood test. Likewise the clinic in Switzerland where David would shortly be sent to serve his life sentence. It made its money from rich people with secrets to hide. As David would be hidden, until such time as the perfect cover story was prepared; watertight and impenetrable. Now it was time to prepare his daughter.

Drawing her to him he said sadly but with finality: 'I loved Mummy very much, but after this awful thing she has done, I find I can't forgive her. She swept us aside; you and David and me, for a man who had been dead twenty-five years. That was most cruel. She could not have found a more painful way to show me the truth of her feelings.'

Diana's eyes brimmed.

'She was not what I thought she was and it hurts me, puss. It hurts me very much.'

Diana put her arms around him. 'I know, Daddy, I know,' she wept. 'I've decided I don't want to be like her any more. It isn't good to make yourself over in somebody's image, especially when that image is a false one. From now on I intend to be myself. I really did think she was the perfect woman, you know, but it was all outward show. Inside she was shallow and spiteful and she never really loved me; I don't think she ever loved anyone but herself ...'

'I will always love you.' Billy comforted. 'Whatever you do, you will always be my girl.' Tenderly but ruthlessly he tightened the emotional bonds that tied her to him.

Diana's face shone as her allegiance was transferred smoothly and easily on the oiled wheels of Billy's assurance. 'I'll take care of you, Daddy. I know how you like things. I'll make sure they go on as they always have done. I learned those lessons too. If you like, Brooks and I will move in with you; you need Brooks at your side, don't you, while I can run the house, act as your hostess, entertain for you. Would you like that? We will be a family, one for David to come home to.'

Billy took the opportunity offered. 'I am worried about your brother,' he said deliberately. 'His mother's death has hit him much harder than I had realised.'

Diana looked surprised. 'I had not realised either. It is so hard to tell anything with David …'

'Haven't you noticed how thin he is?'

'Now that you mention it, I suppose he is, but I thought it was because he'd been burning the candle at both ends. He's probably run down and that's why he's got this awful abscess.'

'Burning the midnight oil more like,' Billy corrected. 'He knows I expect a great deal of him … perhaps I have been expecting too much.'

'But David is clever!' Spitefully: 'Too clever for his own good, if you ask me.'

Yet still not clever enough, Billy thought, before saying: 'Company Law is very complex nowadays. He has been studying hard and I think he needs a break so I am going to see he has one before he has a nervous breakdown!'

'David!'

Billy's look was a rebuke. 'You are able to express your feelings; David keeps his under too strict a control. That sort of things eats away at you inside.'

'If you say so,' Diana agreed obediently, doubting very much if anything ever ate away at her brother's inside except not getting what he wanted. 'All the more reason to make a home for him to come back to, then.'

'Yes,' agreed Billy, 'I think you have the right of it, puss.'

His use of her childhood name was deliberate and as he knew she would, Diana took it as a dose of pure self-esteem.

'We'll do just fine, Daddy, now that we don't have to

have anything more to do with those awful Randolphs. It's "Bancroft for ever" from now on.'

'Right!' approved Billy, adding: 'And I hope to see more of them. When am I going to be able to hold my grandson? I'm not getting any younger, you know. And I want to talk to you and Brooks about making a slight addition to your name. You are my only daughter and I want people to know that. What do you think about Hamilton-Bancroft? Brooks must be consulted, of course ...'

Consulted by way of a rubber stamp. Brooks would have changed his name to Mudd if Billy told him to. From Diana's expression the idea appealed to her too, and not just because it meant she would have a double-barrelled name.

Putting an affectionate, My-Best-Girl arm around her shoulder: 'Why don't we three discuss it on the plane going home? I would hate to do anything that might seem to suggest I am consigning Brooks to an inferior role ... '

Lovingly: 'As if you would ...' Diana said.

EPILOGUE

That evening, when everyone had left and the house was empty of all but the servants, Ros went for a walk.

She felt unsettled, unable to achieve that sense of finality which would allow her to close the door on a chapter of her life; filled with a restless unease she could not pinpoint except for the conviction that she had reached a turning point. Being of a rational turn of mind, she dealt with it as she tended to deal with everything: by analysing it. Lost in thought, she eventually found herself back at the burial ground.

Set behind the small church, it was in the style of an English country churchyard, for it had been built by transplanted Englishmen. It reminded her of Upper Wychwood, where, by dint of a very generous donation towards the restoration of the twelfth century church, Billy had managed to get permission from the Bishop to build a mausoleum-type tomb with the name BANCROFT engraved above its door. Even in death he would not be buried as a Jew. His intensive efforts had been rewarded; to all intents and purposes, Billy Bancroft had become what he had always wanted to be: a WASP.

When Ros had asked the Randolph Trustees for permission to bury her mother beside her father they had enquired delicately if Lady Bancroft's religion was what it had been when she was Mrs John Peyton Randolph VI: Episcopalian. Ros had been able to assure them that although her mother had married a Jew, she had not become one herself. It remained unsaid that it was Billy who had done the converting, though in his case it was more of a rejection. And now, Ros thought, strolling slowly down the gravel paths between the neat headstones, her mother had rejected him, because the names presently being carved on the new piece of black marble that would cover the grave when it was complete, would read:

JOHN PEYTON RANDOLPH VI 1932–1966
and his Wife
OLIVIA GAYLORD RANDOLPH 1936–1990
In their death they were not Divided

Billy had not asked her about the stone. Nor had he inspected the grave, which Ros had discovered to her surprise was big enough to contain two coffins side by side. Obviously her mother had made her decision a long time ago and her second marriage had given her no reason to change it.

The site was near that of Nicholas and Alice (though she had never been known as anything else but Dolly) Randolph and there was room for another couple of graves. Once they were occupied the Randolphs would either have to extend beyond present boundaries or make other arrangements. After all, they had been burying the family here for more than three hundred years.

Room for Johnny and Polly, Ros decided, stooping to move one of the many baskets of flowers – Livy had specified 'no wreaths' – to a more secure position. And perhaps their children, for her brother had called not long before to inform his sister with drunken delight that he was at last the proud father of twins; one of each. John Junior and Alice. Mother and babies were fine. So the Randolph line would continue. Out of death had come life, as always.

And my child? I wonder what mine will be? Ros thought, moving towards the carved wooden seat by the wall, placed there in memory of Charles Lee Randolph, who died in 1826. I wish I had been able to tell you, Mother. You would have been pleased, I know, because we finally came to understand and appreciate our differences, didn't we? Finally managed to cross the generation gap. And it was a hell of a gap. Unbridgeable for so long. Perhaps because we were so different. You naturally submissive; me the rebel against anything (and anybody) that said Thou Shalt Not. Whereas you would obey, my reaction was always: Why not and who says so? What women were in your generation is so very different to what they are in mine. We know more, we want – no, demand – more, *expect* more. And get it. Still not as a matter of course but it will come. There are still attitudes to change, opinions to alter, entrenched male prejudices to uproot.

But not those of Jack Ross, she thought. He never showed a single one, standard or otherwise, and God knows he showed me so much ... For a moment she wanted so fiercely to be shown even more that she burned with longing.

That is one thing that hasn't changed since your days, she told her mother wryly. A woman hung up on a man she is

391

not sure of. All the independence in the world can't control those male/female situations. Only deprivation can do that because what you don't have you can't miss.

And I didn't have it for a long time. The real thing, I mean. The reality of *felt* life. I'd become detached. I see that now. Jack Ross reconnected me to life. And how! she thought with a reminiscent tingle. All that was dead is now vibrantly alive; *I* am alive and so is the embryo in my womb. As if to confirm it, Ros placed her hand on her still flat-as-a-board stomach. Had not her overdue period and the colour of the paper in her pregnancy test made it abundantly clear, she would never have believed she was pregnant. She had no morning sickness – poor Polly had heaved up her guts from conception – no signs at all, except perhaps slightly tender breasts. The result of one – well, four, actually – passionate couplings with a man who was still, even now, an unknown quantity. Whom I want to know. All there is to know. I want him to know about me. I want – Ros laughed wryly. I just want, she admitted.

Gazing at the glowing profusion of flowers around her mother's grave – Livy had arranged even for that to be done professionally after the funeral – that was your trouble, wasn't it? Ros said aloud. You had nobody. Only an image and a reputation. And in the last analysis they were not enough.

I treasure my independence. I'm not looking to attach myself to anybody but I would like what was begun to continue to its natural conclusion – whatever that is. I am not drawing up any blueprints, but I feel very strongly that Jack Ross and I are incomplete. We did not get much beyond the starting point, and I want the rest of it. A proper, physically and emotionally fulfilling affair with a beginning, a middle and, if that's the way it must be, an end. Perhaps if you had been able to have one or two, with men who wanted *you*, the woman you were; not the fashion icon or the mistress of chic, but Livy Bancroft, woman, you might have been happier. But you couldn't. You didn't much go for the pleasures of the flesh, did you? And you were uneasy around emotion. It was just not your nature. But it is mine. I have your looks, but I don't have your character. Wicky – you remember Wicky, my old governess? She was not on your list but she called and we had a long talk and when I leave tomorrow I'm going to stay with her for a while – well, she always used to say that there were two kinds of women: those who did as they were told and those who did what they wanted. You were one of the former, I am one of the latter. You were always the loyal wife, dignity intact. I could never allow myself to be used as a stage prop; to fix a smile and stand by my man. If I did he would sure as hell have to do the same for me. Still, you wrecked the stage in the last act, didn't you? Left Billy not knowing his lines and unable to hear the prompter.

Rosalind tilted her face back to the early evening sun, still warm, even in September.

I'm not *consciously* going to try and be a good mother, she resolved, but I'll do my damndest to avoid the mistakes you and I made. If you had been a little more outward in your emotions, been able to talk to us, explain your feelings, hug and kiss and demonstrate that we were important to you instead of all the time looking obediently in only the one direction, it might have gone differently. If I had not been so hurt by the fact that you could put someone in my father's place, or if that someone had been other than Billy

Bancroft ... Ros sighed. How clearly one sees with hind-sight. How myopic I was at the time; how arrogantly young and stubbornly prejudiced. God, I must have been an awful pain in the neck. You were probably glad to get rid of me.

Well, this time around I'm not going to plan anything, how about that for a lark? Me, who likes everything cut and dried to a crisp. I am going to take the future one day at a time. I don't know what is going to happen with Jack Ross, or even if I shall ever see him again. I'd like to. Oh, please God, yes. I don't think he is entirely immune to me either. I believe I got to him as he got to me. But only time will tell. And I've plenty of that. And it's not as though I have not always been on my own, which now I am not, unless I wish to be. There's Aunt Toni, best of aunts, Aunt Delia, the kindest, Johnny and Polly and my new niece and nephew. Lose one, find two ... My kind of arithmetic.

As to the others, I doubt if I shall ever see Billy again unless I have to, which I don't.

Diana has no desire to see me.

I don't know about David. But then, nobody ever knows about David. Truth to tell, the Randolphs and the Bancrofts were never One Big Happy Family. I was away too long and your second family was that much younger than your first. It was a case of the Montagues and Capulets sans Romeo and Juliet ...

Ros stood up, gazed her last fill of the flowered grave. She would come back when the stone was to be fitted; see it was done properly. If she came back to live here, have her baby here, she would be able to visit her mother whenever she felt like it.

Ros would have laughed at the suggestion she was

psychic, but in this place she was filled with a strong sense of her mother's presence, and that sense was of deep, tranquil peace. Beyond doubt, she was certain that whatever the consequences – and she knew Billy well enough to know that eventually there would be a bill to pay – she had done the right thing. Her mother's spirit had ceased to chafe. She had come home. Better, still, her own sense of unease no longer had her so uptight ...

She turned to walk back to the house, but it was into the setting sun and she had to put up her hand to shade her eyes. Only when they became accustomed to the glare did she see the figure in the distance, coming towards her down the gravel path. Squinting against the sun's molten glow she saw it was a very tall, very dark man. Her heart leapt, then began to knock against her ribs in a frenzy of excitement. I *must* be psychic, she thought dazedly, no wonder I could not settle ... As her pace quickened the radiance on her face matched that of the sun. The man coming towards her saw it and quickened his own stride.

She ran to meet him.

A Selection of Fiction Available from Mandarin

While every effort is made to keep prices low, it is sometimes necessary to increase prices at short notice. Mandarin Paperbacks reserves the right to show new retail prices on covers which may differ from those previously advertised in the text or elsewhere.

The prices shown below were correct at the time of going to press.

☐ 7493 1447 8	**Hard News**	Tess Stimson	£4.99
☐ 7493 1470 2	**Georgia**	Lesley Pearse	£4.99
☐ 7493 1251 3	**The First Wives Club**	Olivia Goldsmith	£4.99
☐ 7493 1105 3	**A Double Life**	Vera Cowie	£4.99
☐ 7493 1098 7	**Too Rich Too Thin**	Rose Shepherd	£4.99
☐ 7493 0980 6	**Best Kept Secrets**	Sandra Brown	£4.99
☐ 7493 0919 9	**Mirror Image**	Sandra Brown	£4.99
☐ 7493 1312 9	**Breath of Scandal**	Sandra Brown	£4.99
☐ 7493 1320 X	**Obsession**	Susan Lewis	£4.99
☐ 7493 1180 0	**Darkest Longings**	Susan Lewis	£4.99
☐ 7493 0380 8	**Stolen Beginnings**	Susan Lewis	£4.99
☐ 7493 0166 X	**Dance While You Can**	Susan Lewis	£4.99
☐ 7493 0977 6	**Facets**	Barbara Delinsky	£4.99
☐ 7493 1169 X	**A Woman Betrayed**	Barbara Delinsky	£4.99
☐ 7493 1435 4	**The Passions of Chelsea Kane**	Barbara Delinsky	£4.99

All these books are available at your bookshop or newsagent, or can be ordered direct from the address below. Just tick the titles you want and fill in the form below.

Cash Sales Department, PO Box 5, Rushden, Northants NN10 6YX.
Fax: 0933 410321 : Phone 0933 410511.

Please send cheque, payable to 'Reed Book Services Ltd.', or postal order for purchase price quoted and allow the following for postage and packing:

£1.00 for the first book, 50p for the second; **FREE POSTAGE AND PACKING FOR THREE BOOKS OR MORE PER ORDER.**

NAME (Block letters) ....

ADDRESS ....

....

☐ I enclose my remittance for ....

☐ I wish to pay by Access/Visa Card Number ⬜⬜⬜⬜⬜⬜⬜⬜⬜⬜⬜⬜⬜⬜⬜⬜

Expiry Date ⬜⬜⬜⬜

Signature ....

Please quote our reference: MAND